BOUNCING

By the Author

Agnes

The Common Thread

Bouncing

BOUNCING

by
Jaime Maddox

2015

BOUNCING

© 2015 By Jaime Maddox. All Rights Reserved.

ISBN 13: 978-1-62639-344-8

This Trade Paperback Original Is Published By
Bold Strokes Books, Inc.
P.O. Box 249
Valley Falls, NY 12185

First Edition: May 2015

CREDITS
EDITOR: SHELLEY THRASHER
PRODUCTION DESIGN: STACIA SEAMAN
COVER DESIGN BY SHERI (GRAPHICARTIST2020@HOTMAIL.COM)

Acknowledgments

The people at BSB do a wonderful job in creating their books, from helping with concepts to making sure my name is spelled correctly on the cover. Thanks to Rad, Sandy Lowe, Cindy Cresap, Stacia Seaman, Ruth Sternglantz, and everyone else who made this book possible. Thanks to Sheri and Rad for the cool cover. Shelley Thrasher, my editor, is always encouraging and wise and helpful, and if this book is any good, it's because of her help.

I took some liberties with the Pennsylvania high school basketball calendar. They were necessary to help this story flow, and I ask forgiveness from the coaches, players, and purists who took note.

I'm a huge basketball fan, but not such a great player, and never a coach. I owe much gratitude to my friends and family who are players and coaches, for sharing their insight with me—Bob Bessoir, Billy Bessoir, J, Carolyn, and Jamison. Likewise, thanks to my teacher friends who helped me out, Elizabeth Abdalla, Maria Hubbler, and Karlee McConnell.

Thanks to my niece, Tiffany Maakestad, for sharing her adventures in Brazil with me, and to Billy B once again, this time for perfecting Anke's accent.

The thing I liked most about writing this book was transporting myself to Rehoboth Beach, Delaware, my favorite place on earth. I've had great times there, thanks to so many great people who've shared my adventures—my former roommates, J, Wallstreet, and Chris; my landlords Sandy and Patty; my golfing buddies Lisa, Kimmer, Al, Nina, and Jag; and my dear friends, Clara, Kelly, Jan, and Sue.

My alpha readers Margaret and Nancy are wise and wonderful women and they helped with major issues in this book. As always, the lunch conversation was a hoot.

Finally, but most importantly, thank you to Carolyn, Jamison, and Max. There's a line in this book somewhere that sums it all up: It doesn't matter what we're doing, if I'm with you, I'm happy.

To Yankee—my playmate in golf, and basketball, and life—
thanks for letting me win sometimes

Chapter One

Cheaters Never Win

The sun was shining in her eyes and the wind blew through her hair as Alex Dalton pulled her Jeep into the parking lot of the golf course just north of Rehoboth Beach, Delaware. It was the Thursday before Memorial Day, a glorious, warm afternoon, and Alex hummed to the tune on the radio. She'd spent her morning at the beach, reading. She had nine holes of golf on the agenda for the afternoon and hundreds more in the coming months. She would enjoy cold beer afterward with a good friend. Life was easy and relaxing and fun, exactly how she wanted it, and for the seventh consecutive summer, that pleasure would be hers.

She'd begun coming to Rehoboth after her first year at the University of Delaware, when a friend had invited her. She'd been awed back then, and the magic hadn't faded. The beaches were still pristine, the restaurants fabulous, and the bars hopping. Even better, it was the most gay-friendly beach within driving distance of her home in the Poconos. Same-sex couples walked hand in hand on the boardwalk beside vacationing families—some of them sporting two moms or dads. The majority of businesses flew rainbow flags beside their front doors.

She felt free here, like she did in the Jeep. She'd bought it at a military-surplus store and it was older than she was, bare bones with a quarter-million miles. The ride was awful on her back, but the complete freedom of driving without sides and a roof made it a good trade.

Alex pulled on her golf sandals and plucked her bag from the seat beside her, then headed toward the driving range. The cars in the lot were much different from hers—expensive, foreign, new. Alex didn't care. She'd quit thinking about material possessions like houses

and cars years ago. She focused on living, on the fun she could have each day and the joy she could take in coaching a basketball game or shooting a round of golf under par. Those were the things that mattered.

It was a short walk to the range, and one stall opened just as she approached. After stretching, she began to hit practice shots.

She'd grown up at the country club, playing golf as a child just as other kids rode bikes and played baseball. Her swing was textbook, her shots perfect. After a dozen balls landed close to the target flag, she switched clubs, with the same results. Near perfection. Finally, she picked up her driver and placed the ball on the tee. Her back swing was slow, the turn of her hips quick, and as she rotated her wrists her arms followed into a smooth finish. She made solid contact, and as she looked at the flag positioned farthest away from the tees, she saw her ball land near it, some 250 yards away. After a dozen more similar shots, she put her clubs back in the bag. No point wasting such beautiful shots on the range. She needed to save a few for her golf round.

A stop at the practice green was next, and Alex chipped and putted until she knew the speed of the green. Alex felt loose, and relaxed, and she had the feeling she was going to shoot a great round of golf.

Walking back toward the clubhouse, she searched for her playing partner.

"There you are!" Sally Conklin greeted her when Alex finally found her, hidden in a convoy of thirty golf carts.

Alex set down her bag and was quickly pulled into Sal's arms for a ferocious, playful hug. At six feet tall, Alex didn't look up to many women, but Sal was one of the few.

"It's good to see you," her mentor said, and Alex returned the sentiment.

Sal wasn't just her mentor but her confidante as well, and one of the few people in the world she trusted. Sal was the only one except her parents who knew Alex's secret.

"It's great to see you, too. How are you?" After they caught up for a moment, Sal nodded to the clubs standing beside Alex. "Let's get those loaded on my cart—we'll be starting soon."

"Riding a cart these days?" Alex asked.

"It just makes it easier. They're all paranoid about the pace of play in the league, so they encourage us to ride."

"Fair enough."

"Hey, nice sandals." Sal looked down at Alex's feet. "Does this mean your toe's better?"

A rash on the second toe of her left foot had been the start of it all, back when Alex played on the high-school girls' basketball team that had won Sal a state championship. The doctors had treated her for athlete's foot, and then eczema, and then staph before finally admitting they had no idea what was causing the painful blisters that itched constantly. Through the years the rash had come and gone, sometimes forcing her into sneakers on the beach to protect it from the sun. Since she'd started her newest medication, though, it came less often.

"Yeah," Alex said, wiggling them in proof. "They're perfect."

"Will I be seeing some nail polish this summer?"

Alex stopped and faced Sal, glaring at her. "If you ever see nail polish on my toes, you better start CPR."

Sal didn't crack a smile, but her eyes twinkled. "Chest compressions, maybe. But no mouth to mouth."

They found their cart and Alex secured her clubs on the passenger side, then took a seat beside Sal. A scorecard was pinned to the steering wheel. "Who are we playing? Anyone I know?" Although Alex hadn't played in the league before, over the years she'd made quite a few friends in Rehoboth, and many of them were golfers.

"I don't think so."

Alex glanced at the scorecard, noted their opponents' high handicaps, and chuckled. "It looks like an easy victory tonight. How about a wager? Just to keep it interesting. Loser buys the first round."

Sally shook her head. "Don't be so cocky, Alex. The match will be challenging. Ann Marie Abbott tends to play a little better than her thirty handicap."

"Sal, c'mon. A thirty? Does she use a driver on the par threes?" Alex couldn't keep the smirk from her face.

Sal chuckled. "I don't want to color your judgment, but I'll say this—she's never lost a round in the league. Her team has won the championship five years running."

"With a thirty?"

Sal shrugged. "Like I said, she tends to play better than her handicap."

"Hmm," Alex said, and turned to look at Sal, hoping for more information. Before she could ask, the starter took his bullhorn and made

the customary announcements about pace of play and sportsmanship. Then they were off. Because of the shotgun format, Alex and Sal headed to the eighth hole, a hundred-and-fifty-yard par three, nestled into a copse of trees and landscaped with a half dozen sand traps.

"This plays true, but the green breaks right," Sal advised her as they exited their cart. Although Alex had played the course before, she wasn't as familiar with the subtleties as Sal was. She appreciated the advice.

The twosome they were playing was already there, impeccably dressed in golf skirts and matching shirts, chatting as they took their practice swings. Alex suppressed a smile as she looked at her own rather plain black shorts and blue shirt, and Sal's outfit, which was similar.

After introductions, Sal offered them the tee first. Alex looked to the blue sky and the late afternoon sun filtering through the stand of trees along the fairway and closed her eyes. She breathed in the fresh air, and felt her body relax. Then she opened her eyes and watched as Pearl Lennox hit a five wood left of the green into a trap and tried hard to keep a straight face as she listened to the series of expletives that followed. And then, to her surprise, Ann Marie Abbott, who tended to shoot lower than her handicap, approached the tee with an iron in her hand. Alex knew the average golfer with a high handicap would need a wood to reach that distance. Amazed, she watched the smooth swing and clean contact Ann Marie's club made with the ball, sending it high into the air. It landed on the green, a few yards short and to the right of the flag.

"Nice ball," Alex said. I bet that's the best shot she's ever hit, Alex mused.

A half smile appeared briefly on Ann Marie's face as she headed back to her cart. Sal and Alex both used irons to put their balls on the green as well, and as they drove along the cart path, they assessed their next shots. Both had short birdie putts. Ann Marie's putt was longer, but uphill, while Alex and Sal had to go down to the cup. After Pearl chipped on, Ann Marie lined up her ball and nailed the putt.

"Very nice," Alex said with a nod.

The compliment was barely acknowledged as she pulled the ball from the cup and deposited it in her pocket, then stood back to watch as Sal and Alex finished the hole. Sal's ball lipped the cup and fell out

for a par. Alex's putt ran true, and she pumped her fist as it fell in the hole for a birdie. She'd needed that putt to tie the hole, and it felt good to make it.

"Nice one," Sal said, patting her back as they walked off the green toward their cart. "But Ann Marie gets a stroke. We lost the hole."

"Ah, shit. I forgot about giving her strokes."

Alex carried the lowest handicap in the group—one. It meant she scored the best but also that she had to give everyone else strokes to level the playing field. Because Ann Marie had a handicap of thirty, Alex had to give Ann Marie a stroke on every hole and, on the hardest holes, two strokes. That didn't worry her, though. She'd never lost to someone with a thirty handicap, and she wasn't planning to make this night the first.

"Lucky hole, Sal. No worries. We have eight more to make that up."

The number-nine hole was a long par five, and all four of them approached the tee box with drivers in hand. Since their opponents had won the previous hole, they took the first shots, and Alex's jaw dropped when Ann Marie whacked the ball two hundred yards down the middle of the fairway. She and Sal did the same, and as they climbed back into the cart, Alex squinted at her. "I smell a rat," she said.

Sal's expression was neutral as she looked into Alex's sunglasses. "Much worse than a rat. A sandbagger."

Alex sat up and took off her glasses, then slammed her hand onto the dashboard of the golf cart. "Well, we *cannot* have this! The integrity of the game is resting on our shoulders, Coach. Let's kick some butt."

Sal chuckled. "If anyone can bury her, it's you."

Ann Marie's next shot was short of the green, and Alex's was right. They both chipped on and two-putted for par, but Alex had to give Ann Marie two shots on that hole. Her team was two down through two holes.

Their third hole played out the same. "Fuck!" Alex said as she turned to Sal on their way to the number-two hole, a short par four. "We need to start playing as a team, Sal. You play conservatively for pars, and I'll let loose and go for birdies. We need birdies to win." Sal nodded, and after Pearl and Ann Marie both hit their drives in the first cut of rough, Sal put hers on the fairway. Alex put a little extra

effort into her drive and found herself just short of the green. Their opponents' shots missed the green, and everyone except Alex scored a bogie. She made a birdie, and they found themselves only two down.

Alex and Sal won the next hole and then split a few before winning again. As they stood on the tee box on the final hole, the score was tied. Before them, a short par four curved to the right around a tall stand of oaks. Sal hit a perfect iron shot into the landing zone but was still left with a hundred yards into the pin. "I'm going to try to slice this around the corner," Alex told Sal.

Sal winked and Alex pulled her driver from the bag. She teed the ball higher than she normally would and pushed her hips through the ball a little faster, too. The resulting shot not only curved around the trees, but it flew over them as well, and although they couldn't tell where the ball had finally come to rest, both of them knew it was a magnificent effort. "Wow," Sal said as Alex sat down in the cart beside her.

Alex turned to her and grinned. "I couldn't do that again in a million years!"

"Since this is the last hole, you won't have to. Ties are final."

"Well, then. Let's see what Miss High Handicap can do with those trees," Alex said, nodding in the direction of the formidable wall of timber blocking the path to the green.

Pearl put her drive in the fairway, close to Sal's. Apparently thirty-handicappers could make four pars and a birdie in eight holes but couldn't slice the ball over trees at will. Ann Marie's effort to match Alex's shot fell short, landing deep in the woods. Alex's par was good enough to win the hole, and the match.

Later, on the patio where the members of the ladies' league were enjoying sandwiches and drinks, several people approached their table to congratulate them on their win and invite them to play again.

A woman with short dark hair approached their table, and although they'd never met, Alex recognized her face, probably from the beach. Sal introduced her as Bree, and after they spent a few minutes rehashing their victory, Bree asked if Alex could play the following week. Coincidentally, Bree was scheduled to play Pearl and Ann Marie.

Normally, Alex wouldn't have considered the invitation. She still had another week of classes, and to play she'd have to miss school.

Besides, confrontation wasn't normally on her agenda. She'd won, and she had every right to be happy and walk away. She was sure Sal and Bree and everyone else in the league would think well of her for simply putting the sandbagger in her place. But Alex hated cheaters, and clearly that label fit Ann Marie.

She'd purposely blown three holes when she realized she couldn't beat Sal and Alex, hitting eights on every one, and Alex knew that was how she kept her handicap so high. It wasn't right, and it wasn't fair, and after Ann Marie had walked off the green in a huff after losing the final hole, Alex wanted nothing more than to drive to Rehoboth the next week and beat her. Again.

"Okay," Alex said as she looked up from her beer. "I'll play."

As the day faded so did the crowd, and as the stars began twinkling, Alex and Sal were still sitting in the same place. Other members of the league had said good-bye and left, but they stayed and talked until the workers began cleaning up around them, subtly hinting that they wanted to close the bar and go home.

They took the hint and walked toward their cars, but not before making dinner plans for the next night. Alex looked forward to their date as she drove back to her condo. Sal had been a part of her life for more than a decade, the first one Alex came out to, the one who'd taught her about basketball and winning and courage and commitment. Alex's parents were amazing and wonderful people with whom she had pathetically little in common. Their love was unconditional and constant, but they lived in a world so far removed from hers that their ability to understand or appreciate her life was severely limited. Sal, though—she was Alex's soul mate, and if she hadn't been thirty years older and married to the most wonderful woman in the world, Alex might have been tempted to settle down.

Back in her room at the condo, Alex slept soundly and awoke to a bright sun shining through dented blinds. Stretching out the kinks in her back, she stared at the ceiling, wondering how many women she'd brought to this room over the years. Many. She was like the balls she loved so much—bouncing around from girl to girl, never content with one. There was nothing wrong with that, was there? She was just a normal girl—an athlete, a coach, a teacher, and a friend. A daughter and a sister. Never a girlfriend, though, and never a partner. As more of

her friends settled down, the curve was shifting, and she found that her single status placed her squarely in the middle of abnormal. She didn't like it one bit.

Climbing out of bed, she stretched yet again, then made her way to the bathroom. She removed a syringe hidden in her travel kit, loaded the drug into the chamber, and then leaned against the sink as she slowly delivered the poison into her body. Her eyes were closed and she could immediately feel the burn, followed by the inevitable calm and then a tremendous sense of relief. Carefully wrapping the syringe in tissue to conceal it, she placed it back into the bag and got ready for her day.

"Honey, I'm home!" Alex shouted twelve hours later as she walked through the door. She'd spent the day cleaning the house, readying it for the summer, then enjoyed another wonderful evening with Sal and her partner Sue. Her roommates had been vague about arrival times; beach traffic was always unpredictable. Alex had been delighted to see a car in the drive when she pulled in, eager to see her friends.

Like a dog set free of its leash, Tam came bounding from the living room, leaping into Alex's arms and wrapping her arms and legs around her. She didn't appear to notice Alex cringe. It was the great irony of her illness, Alex knew: inside, a deadly war was raging, but on the outside everything seemed perfectly calm. Alex was tall and in great shape and shouldn't have given a second thought to the petite woman who tackled her, but she feared the jolt of Tam's tackle would haunt her in the morning. Alex gingerly set her friend down and led her to the living room.

"I see you were expecting me," Alex said, nodding to the ice chest full of beer sitting on the coffee table.

"Yep. Kim will be here shortly, too."

Alex pulled one out and twisted off the cap. "So, tell me a story."

Tam smiled at their ongoing joke. Alex, the English teacher, had the opportunity to read the classics, and Tam, the kindergarten teacher, was reading Dr. Seuss. Alex knew her friend loved her job as much as she did, though, and the teasing was all friendly.

"It's almost a shame to even go back to work. I have school Tuesday and Wednesday and then I'm done. I should just stay here and have fun."

"I'm coming back Wednesday. We can hang out."

"To stay?"

"No, just for one night." Alex explained the situation with the sandbagger as they put their feet up on the hassock and sipped their beers. Alex sipped, anyway. She'd had two beers with Sal and Sue and had already, in two nights, equaled her alcohol consumption for the prior month. It was time to slow down. Drugs and alcohol didn't mix, and she needed her drugs much more than she needed the alcohol. Tam was unwinding, though, ready to open her second bottle.

She turned to Alex with a look of eager anticipation on her lovely face. "Oooh! This sounds so wonderfully butch, you taking on the bootlegger. Can I watch?"

"It'll actually be rather boring. Have you ever watched golf? Or any sport?"

Tam cocked her head, looking offended. "I went to every home game when you played basketball. No one cheered louder than me!"

Alex smiled at the memory of her friend, dressed in a skirt and heels, sitting in the student section next to Kim and the rest of the student body, who were clad in T-shirts and sweats and jeans. Some students wore only paint to the games, but Kim was right next to them as they celebrated their common love of the women's basketball team. Tam was a fish out of water, but she was Alex's fish—her always loyal and loving best friend, since their first semester of college when they were paired for a project in their public-speaking class.

"Yes, my apologies. You were always there. Golf isn't quite so exciting, and there's no scoreboard, so you'll have no idea what's going on."

"I can be your caddyshack."

Alex inhaled her beer and began choking, sitting forward as she gasped for air, fighting to rid her lungs of the liquid she'd aspirated. When she could finally speak, she started laughing all over again. "It's a caddy. *Caddyshack* was a movie."

"Oh," Tam said, looking terribly disappointed in herself.

"I met someone you might like, though. Her name's Bree and she's kind of cute."

Tam's eyes lit up. "Yeah? Tell me more!"

"I don't know anything else. Just her name. And she looks a little like Tom Cruise. Just your type."

"You don't have a last name, an address, or a phone number? What am I going to do with you, Alex?" Tam frowned.

"I know where she'll be next Thursday night!" Alex turned her head and winked.

"Maybe I will come to the golf match, then."

The grinding noise from the garage indicated that the last of their party had arrived. Alex kept her seat, but Tam ran toward the kitchen and into the garage to greet Kim. The sound of their laughter wafted in from the garage, and Alex couldn't keep from smiling at the sound. As much as she loved Tam, Kim loved her more. And the feeling was mutual. Their attraction and chemistry were obvious to everyone except the two of them. Alex kept hoping they'd figure it all out. Maybe this would be the summer.

Kim abandoned her suitcase in the hall before she joined them on the couch for a beer. "I wanna go to the Frogg Pond," she said when Tam suggested refilling their bucket.

Alex looked at Tam for a response. Her day had been easy and she was always agreeable, open to ideas and suggestions and adventure. Whatever they decided was fine by her. When Tam smiled at the idea the plan was sealed, but she of course had to change clothes and refresh her makeup. Alex and Kim were comfortable in shorts and T-shirts and caught up while they waited.

Thirty minutes later they sat at a table in the corner of the bar, where they joined a group of friends who they knew from years of summers at the shore. It was after ten, and the bar was crowded. Alex occupied the corner, where her view of the ladies was unobstructed. It didn't take long to notice one in particular.

Blond hair fell straight down the stranger's back, and as she stood at the bar, she occasionally tossed her head to keep it in place. Alex was too far away to tell the color of her eyes, but they were light, just like her complexion. She obviously needed copious amounts of sunscreen to protect that fair skin from burning, and Alex could imagine her own hands applying it. Everywhere. The blonde didn't smile but seemed rather serious as she talked to the woman beside her. Friend? Lover? Alex watched, hoping to learn more. The last thing she needed on the first weekend of summer was a fight with a jealous girlfriend.

After a few minutes, the woman turned her back on her companion, effectively ending their conversation, and Alex watched as the other woman shrugged and began talking to the woman on her other side. It was time to make her move.

"Excuse me," Alex said to her friends.

Pushing through the crowd, she made her way to the bar and stood beside the blonde. They were nearly the same height, but Alex thought she was a fraction of an inch taller. Curious, she looked down and saw that the woman wore flats. Impressive.

Alex turned slightly and found her eyes. They were blue, a pale, icy shade that sent a tantalizing chill through Alex. Not a word had been spoken, but Alex could tell this woman would be a challenge. And worth it. "I had to come see if you're really as tall as you look. Or if you were cheating."

"Chee-tink?" she asked with a distinct German accent and a look of curiosity.

"High heels," Alex explained.

"Ah, no need zoo cheat. Already I am 1.83 meters."

Alex laughed, both at her choice of words and the serious manner in which she shared them.

"Really?" she said. "So how many meters do you think I am?"

The woman looked at Alex from head to toe. "Stand straight," she commanded, and when Alex did as she was told, the woman surveyed her again. "You are perfec for me."

Alex looked her in the eye again. "I'm Alex."

A slight tilt of the head served as acknowledgment. "Anke. Do you have house, Alex, or should ve go zoo mine?"

Anke's expression never changed, but Alex noticed a glimmer in her eyes as she offered the invitation. "Oh, I'd love a trip to Germany," Alex whispered, moving close enough to feel the softness of Anke's hair brushing her neck.

"Follow me," Anke commanded.

After bidding her friends good night, Alex followed her instructions and minutes later found herself in a tiny apartment above a garage a few blocks from the beach. A double bed was the only significant piece of furniture in the room, but it was all they needed. They didn't get out of it until noon the next day, when Alex was politely asked to leave. Anke's job demanded her attention, but she expressed a desire to see Alex again that night. And in the interest of international relations, Alex agreed. She continued her diplomatic efforts the following night as well, and for the first time since college, she was planning to see the same girl for the fourth time.

They set ground rules on that first morning, though. Anke was only in town for one summer, and while she'd like to see Alex again, she wanted to reserve the option of seeing other women, if someone interesting materialized. They would have no contact after the summer—they would simply go their separate ways.

It was a new situation for Alex. She didn't date, she had sex. But how could she argue with this proposal? Anke had been dynamite in bed. She was beautiful, intelligent, and how could you beat that sexy accent? She could have her whenever she wanted, and if someone else turned up, she could have them, too. She could have it all! Alex was willing to play the game, and if she tired of it, she could always quit—after all, that rule had been established. It might be sticky to see Anke at the bars if it didn't work out, but she'd take that chance. After the night they'd shared, she'd be a fool not to. It was exactly what she'd always done, but with a new twist. Instead of a one-nighter, she'd have a full season.

And so a few days later, she found herself sitting back on the patio at the golf course, staring out at a beautiful afternoon, wearing a golf shirt and shorts and a fresh-fucked look. Anke had finished work at ten the night before, and by eleven they were busy in her bed. They didn't slow down until the sun was coming up the next morning. She'd left Anke's and headed directly to the golf course. The back nine was on the agenda for the league that night, and Alex had decided to play in the morning to familiarize herself with the pin positions. Playing against the sandbagger, she needed every advantage she could get. The par threes were both birdie opportunities for her, and she hit several shots from the tee on both of them, deciding which club and approach would give her the best chance for an easy putt. After she finished her nine holes, she went back to the condo and crashed. Sleeping half the day recharged her batteries, and she came back and met Bree on the driving range. They headed to the patio for water before the round started.

"Ready?" Bree asked upon returning from the restroom.

"Oh, yeah," Alex answered. The strategy was the same as it had been the week before, only this time, Alex knew her opponent and the pin placement as well.

"Hello, again." Ann Marie greeted them on the starting tee box, a polite smile briefly raising the corners of her mouth. It was the last smile Alex saw that afternoon. Alex and Bree needed only seven holes

to win the match, and instead of finishing nine holes—customary but not mandatory in this format—they thanked their opponents and headed back in. Alex was glad to have made short work of the match. Her SUV was packed and she was heading straight home from the golf course. Four more days of school, though, and she'd be back to stay.

After depositing their clubs in their respective cars, they met up on the way back to the bar. Alex hadn't had a chance to chat with Sal and Sue before teeing off, and she hoped they'd finish their round early, too, so she'd be able to spend a little time with them. Before they could even place their drink orders, an older woman approached. She was meticulously dressed and wearing golf-club-shaped earrings that appeared to be made of real diamonds. Her makeup was expertly applied, and even her hair, half-covered by a visor, looked as if it had been professionally styled for the golf round. The woman's manner matched her sophisticated appearance.

"Pardon me, ladies. Are you Alex Dalton?" she asked, raising a tweezed eyebrow at Alex.

Alex smiled cautiously. *Beware of strange women who know your name.*

"Yes, that's me."

The woman's manicured hand appeared before her, and Alex was quite tempted to kiss it. Her regal bearing seemed to warrant such an address, but instead she simply took it in her own and shook it firmly.

"I'm Evvy Whitford. Sal Conklin gave me your name. Are you available to substitute with me next week? Something unexpectedly came up, and my usual playing partner won't be available." Evvy looked around to confirm no one was eavesdropping before continuing. Wearing a sweet smile but with fire in her eyes she said softly, "We're playing Ann Marie and Pearl."

Alex met her fierce gaze and then overtly studied Evvy. In spite of the large diamond on her left hand and the fact that thirty years separated them, the woman was flirting with her. Alex felt the unusual sensation of heat in her face as she blushed.

She dismissed the thought of Evvy and instead considered her invitation. School concluded for the year on Wednesday. She'd be back in Rehoboth in plenty of time for a Thursday-evening golf match. Alex cleared her throat and assumed the appropriate attitude to respond to such a well-heeled woman. "I'm sorry to hear about your partner's

cancellation, but as it happens, I'll be available and would be happy to play in her place."

Evvy smiled and lowered her chin so her gaze up to Alex was even more dramatic. "I think I'm going to enjoy my round with you, Ms. Dalton."

As Evvy walked away, Alex seated herself at the bar, where Bree patted her on the back and said, "I think it's going to be a great summer."

Alex considered her golf match the following week, and it pleased her to know she'd have another chance at Ann Marie. Apparently the ladies of the league knew what she was doing and were all happy to allow Alex to step in for them and bring her down. What they were doing was completely legal, and her part in it made Alex feel wonderful. She'd never done anything like this before. More typically, she avoided confrontation and was happy to play her own game. Beating Ann Marie that first night had sparked something within her, though, and now she was on a mission. And apparently, so was the league.

Alex let her thoughts drift for a moment. She pictured herself driving her Jeep, the wind blowing her short, wavy blond hair and the sun warming her face. She also saw herself spending days on the beach with Kim and Tam, and nights with Anke. Yes, Alex had to agree with Bree. It was looking to be a great summer.

Chapter Two

A Whole New World

The stillness was perhaps the most overwhelming feature of this night in the mountains of Brazil. It was black, with not much of a moon to brighten it and no artificial light coming from the buildings in this part of the world, where access to electricity was the exception rather than the rule. Because they had only burning lamps for light, the people of this region kept a very functional schedule, rising with the sun and retiring with it as well, and the quiet was complete, without even the sounds of nature interrupting.

Britain Dodge had grown up on another mountain, thousands of miles north of this one, and she was accustomed to the noises of the night—wind blowing through the leaves of trees, animal footsteps in the forest, insects calling out to each other across great expanses of crisp air. This mountain was different, though, and its stillness was almost frightening as she imagined all other life vanquished from the planet as she was left alone to fend for herself in the wild.

At the moment, she felt alone. She had no job, no money, no plan. She'd always been a planner, a highly organized and efficient creature who needed to know what to look forward to. Since she'd finished college, she'd been in limbo, and she hated the insecurities and fears that seemed to pop up out of nowhere. What if she was in a car accident? How could she afford a new car? What if she wasn't smart enough to impress the powers who'd interviewed her? What if she failed?

She'd always been a winner, but here in this vast and simple place, where she'd come to offer help and perhaps find some inner peace, she felt defeated.

Saddened by the thought, Brit listened intently as she imagined a sound behind her. Her heart raced and she was suddenly fearful, for the privacy that had caused her to choose this isolated spot to brood also made her vulnerable. The sound came again, closer this time, and she turned around to see a flashlight in the hand of someone approaching from the direction of the village. She wasn't sure if she should be relieved or more frightened by the presence of another human.

"Who's there?" she demanded of the darkness.

"I thought I might find you here," a husky but feminine voice replied.

"Syl, you scared the crap out of me." She'd scolded her, but she wasn't really angry. Syl was a welcome companion, and just hearing her voice improved Brit's mood. Syl was the single best thing about Brazil, and Brit looked forward to the time they spent together as much as she once enjoyed the electronics she'd forsaken to come.

Instead of acknowledging her comment, as was Sylvia's habit, she pursued the topic she had on her own mind. "Luke is in love with you."

Whispering into the darkness, Brit turned in the direction of the flashlight. "I don't know why! I've never done anything to encourage him, but he's like a puppy, following me around all the time."

"I'll tell you why," Syl said, and she sat so close to Brit their shoulders touched. Brit knew this was a friendly gesture and nothing more, just like the soft kiss Syl planted on her cheek. Syl was married to Marianna, another aid worker, but that hadn't stopped her from forming an instant and wonderful friendship with Brit when she arrived in South America.

"It's because you're beautiful, and kind, and smart…must I go on?" She was teasing her.

"Shit," Brit said. "I was able to avoid him at school, but here— we're together twenty-four seven. It's a bit more difficult."

"Why don't you just tell him you're a lesbian?"

Brit pulled back and turned her head sharply in the direction of Syl's voice. "My sexuality isn't a topic of conversation."

"And why is that? Do you think it's some great secret?"

Brit sighed. She'd never told Syl. In fact, she'd only told a handful of people, her closest friends and the women she'd dated. "How did you know I'm gay?"

"A million reasons, I guess. But mostly just being gay helps me to

pick up on other people's vibes. That and my connection to the spirits," she said, and Brit wasn't sure if she was joking.

She'd met Sylvia on her arrival in this small village, more than a month before. Brit came with a team of volunteers, all with varied backgrounds, from medical workers and teachers like her to engineers and carpenters. They'd come to help improve the lives of the people who called this place home and intended to complete construction of a town hall, which would serve multiple purposes—a medical clinic, a classroom, a meeting place. Sylvia was a Californian, but an ancestor long ago had roamed these same paths. She'd made it her life's work to help the people of the village by bringing the resources of the world to this far corner of the planet. She worked tirelessly in the completion of paperwork and the hauling of wood, in the cradling of babies and the cooking of meals. A more dedicated woman didn't exist, except perhaps Marianna, who'd led a medical team to a remote village earlier in the day. As if where they were wasn't remote enough. Her smartphone couldn't even get a signal out here.

"It's not that I don't want people to know. I just haven't told them." She was lying.

"You must find your voice, and your courage. Otherwise you and those you love will only get hurt." Even though she was American, Sylvia spoke like a native goddess. And with her flowing black hair, big chocolate eyes, flawless skin, and radiant smile, she looked like one, too.

"I'll take that under advisement."

"Come, now. Let me walk you back. We all have a long day ahead of us. Besides, it's not good to be here alone. What if Luke had found you?"

"Oh, he's harmless," Brit said as she stood and wiped the earth from her shorts.

"Everyone has a limit, and when he reaches it, he might not be so docile anymore."

"I hadn't thought of that."

They walked in silence and Brit was happy for the lull. It allowed her to indulge in the exploration of her thoughts, a leisurely activity she'd been enjoying frequently in this land without electronics. She thought of Luke, wondering if she should begin avoidance tactics. In spite of her respect for Syl, Brit wasn't ready to leave the comfort of the

closet and come out to him. Once she told him, everyone in her world would know the truth she'd been so carefully guarding. And she wasn't ready to be out. Not yet, anyway.

And then another thought occurred to her. If Syl could so easily determine that she was a lesbian, could others tell her secret as well? She was still dwelling on the question as she drifted off to sleep that night and found no inspiration in her dreams. In the morning, the unanswered question lingered, and as she hammered and hauled wood, then read to students and helped them form their letters, she wondered which of them sensed that she was different. She inwardly cringed as she looked from face to face, studying them.

Hopefully the one who *didn't* divine the meaning of her instantaneous and powerful bond with an openly gay woman was the cardiologist on the team, the one whom the others called Dr. Dodge but whom she called Dad.

He returned to the village late in the day, just as the preparations for dinner were under way. The warmth of his smile told her she hadn't needed to worry. "Hi, Daddy," she said.

"Hello, my dear. Tell me about your day," he commanded her as he settled his long frame into an uncomfortable wooden chair. He crossed his legs at the ankles, and Brit smiled as she watched him, knowing how much she resembled him. Her two older sisters favored her mother, with dark features, but Brit seemed to have inherited all of her father's genes—blond hair, blue eyes, endlessly long limbs.

Brit described working with the village children, and he listened intently, happily.

"Perhaps you should have chosen elementary ed instead of high school, Brit. You seem to love the little ones."

She'd debated it for a while, in the end choosing to teach biology to high-school students, and she was happy with her choice. "Don't mess with my mind, Dad," she warned him.

"Just teasing."

"How about you? Did you get a chance to talk to Mom?"

Brit knew the trip to the village took the group through a larger town, where phone service was available. Her dad had planned to call home, and Brit was eager to hear the mundane details about her family that a month away transformed into interesting topics.

"There was a phone call for you."

"From whom?" Brit asked, knowing that all of her friends and family knew she was out of the country.

"You've been hired!" he told her.

"Ahhhhhh!" she screamed, and jumped into the arms of the only man she'd ever love. Brit had applied for jobs in every school district in the state, or so it seemed, and was hopeful for just a position as a substitute. Only six weeks out of college, she wasn't optimistic. She'd briefly contemplated an overseas job, teaching English in China or as a missionary in Africa. It wasn't in her to do that, though. The cause was noble, for sure, but Brit wasn't. She wasn't spoiled, but she did need a few creature comforts, and, more importantly, the security of her family and friends close by. She could live like this for a month, but that was about her limit, and if her father weren't on the trip, she probably wouldn't be either.

"Where? What school?" she demanded as she danced in circles.

Her father, ever calm in a crisis, responded evenly. "Oh, Brit, I have no idea. But who cares? You have a job!"

"I'm really a teacher, Dad," she said as she fell into his lap and hugged him, her trouble forgotten, at least for the moment.

CHAPTER THREE

BORROWING FOR TOMORROW

P.J., I'm leaving in five minutes, with or without you." A loud thump on his bedroom door punctuated his mother's warning.

Her voice was like a bullet piercing his brain, and seeking the protective cushion of his pillow, P.J. Blackwell pulled it over his head. Why couldn't she just leave him alone? He'd been up late listening to the baseball game and was fucking exhausted. The game started at eight p.m. on the West Coast. By the time it was over, it was two in the morning at his home in Clarks Summit, Pennsylvania. That was only four hours earlier. By the time he was able to relax enough to doze off, an hour had passed. How could he function on three hours' sleep?

The pillow trick must have worked because the next thing he knew, the grumbling garage door startled him back to consciousness as it retracted into the floor beneath his bedroom. Leaping from the bed, P.J. suddenly forgot his fatigue as he raced from the room and down the hallway and stairs, then back across the length of the house. Bursting through the garage door in time to see it closing, he turned and pounded his fist into the wall. "Fuck!" he screamed.

"What's goin' on?" his brother asked as he walked into the kitchen.

"Wes, I need your help!" P.J. caught his brother's eye and tried not to sound desperate, afraid he'd raise questions that he wasn't prepared to answer. At the same time, he needed Wes to know how vital this matter was to him. "It's important."

His arms crossed against his chest, Wes studied him with well-founded skepticism. "What's so important?"

"Mom left me without a car and I need a ride to work."

"No way! Gas is four bucks a gallon, and I'm sick of wasting it by hauling your ass all over."

P.J. was sick of worrying about money. Life had been a good, simple, and uncomplicated adventure for his first fourteen years, but the last three had been miserable. His dad had lost his job, gone on unemployment, and was forced to take a job in retail management to make ends meet. It paid far less than he'd made as an engineer, but jobs in his area were hard to find. With P.J. and Wes still teenagers, his parents didn't want to move and force them to change schools. So P.J.'s mom had gone to work as well, and after a lifetime of having her at home, he and his brother were suddenly left with the responsibility for cooking dinner and washing laundry. And if that wasn't enough, the Blackwells demanded that their two sons get jobs as well. Wes was interested in computers and was able to get a cool job with a repair service, even without experience. Because he was only fourteen, though, P.J. was forced to go to work for their neighbor in a mom-and-pop store where the owner paid him off the books and made his life a living hell.

"I'll give you five bucks for gas when I get paid, Wes. But if I don't show up for work, the boss will kill me. He'll fucking tear me apart. The Man is crazy, Wes. I'm not kidding. You've gotta help me."

Wes sighed. "Is he really that bad?"

"You have no idea what my day is like," he said, and the irony of his words threatened to turn the corners of his mouth up into a grin, but he was truly too worried to smile.

"I'm leaving in ten minutes. If you're not down here then, you're out of luck."

Wearing his hair short and his razor stubble long came in handy on mornings like this, and P.J. paused only to pull on a respectable shirt and jeans and then brush his teeth before he was back downstairs with three minutes to spare.

"I need one more favor, bro," he informed Wes as they were pulling out of the circular drive and onto the quiet, tree-lined street.

Wes groaned. "What now?"

"Can you lend me five bucks for lunch?"

"No. No way!" Wes took his eyes off the road and turned them onto him. "Are you doing drugs, P.? You must spend your money on something. It's not food and it's not gas and it's not clothes, so what is it?"

"I only make five bucks an hour. It doesn't go far."

"Well, too bad. I'm not lending you any more money."

P.J. tried not to smile at Wes's response, but it was difficult, for not only was this the answer he'd expected but also the one he hoped for. Finally, something had gone right on this awful morning. He didn't want Wes to lend him the money, because then he'd have to think up another plausible explanation for his next request.

"Well, then drive me to Papa's house. He'll give me five bucks."

Wes snapped. "P.J., Papa isn't your personal bank. Stop taking advantage of him."

"Please, Wes, spare me. Papa has more money than the U.S. Treasury." His grandfather had been born in the wake of the Great Depression and was brought up by parents who remembered a life with not enough to eat. He was raised to save his money and live within his means, and he certainly did. His house, a hundred-year-old Victorian, hadn't been renovated in years. Wes and P.J. and their dad did the yard work and upkeep, but the old man wouldn't spend an unnecessary dime. His car was made by a company that had gone out of business years ago, and even though he could no longer see well enough to drive, he refused to give it to his grandsons, who would have made good use of it. He pinched every penny, and as a result, he had quite a few pennies to spare. Getting them out of him was the trick, but P.J. had mastered it.

"Fine, okay. But don't be long."

Their papa's house was on the way to P.J.'s job, with only a few turns necessary to point them in the right direction. Five minutes later, Wes pulled his old Toyota into his grandfather's driveway. Even though it was close to his neighborhood, this one was worlds away, with older homes situated on tidy little lots, and smaller cars parked in driveways instead of hidden away in four-car garages.

"I'll be right back," P. J. said, hoping his brother's concern for the time would keep him in the car. It did.

Sliding his key into the lock, P.J. opened the kitchen door and prayed it wouldn't squeak and announce his arrival. It didn't. Water was running in the bathroom adjacent to the kitchen, and the light was on there. In the kitchen, shades still drawn from the night before provided the cover of darkness he needed. He tiptoed across the worn wooden floor and quietly opened the cupboard door. A box of Cheerios, so yellowed it practically screamed to get a thief's attention, was his

primary focus. Opening it, he reached inside and closed his hand around the cool, crisp pile of cash inside. There was so much money stuffed into the box his grandfather would never miss it. Besides, P.J. planned to pay it back. Someday.

He pulled out a few bills just as the water turned off and his grandfather appeared in the kitchen.

P.J. held his breath and stood absolutely still, watching as the old man turned away from him and toddled off to the living room. Seconds later, the house was filled with the sounds of a cowboy movie.

"Whoa!" P.J. whispered to himself as he replaced the box's lid and returned it to its proper place. "That was close!" He exited by the same route and with the same care he'd used when he entered the house just a few minutes before.

"Well? What did he say?" Wes asked as he pulled out of the driveway.

"What?" P.J. had been thinking about other things and forgot what he'd told Wes.

"Did Pop give you any money?"

"Oh. No. He said he couldn't afford it."

Wes chuckled. "That doesn't surprise me. But I wish he'd given you enough to pay for my gas."

P.J. tried to hide his smile. The bills in the cereal box were all hundreds, and although he hadn't taken the time to count them before stuffing them in his pocket, he guessed, based on past experience, that he was sitting on about a thousand dollars.

P.J. frowned. "Yeah, it's too bad. If he'd given me anything, I'd have split it with you."

CHAPTER FOUR

BIRTHDAY BASH

"Hi, Dad!" Alex said as she popped her head through the door of his office. This had once been *his* father's office, in the rear of the building that housed the flagship dry cleaner's that had opened long before her birth. In fact, Alex suspected that some of the paperwork scattered about the clutter might be from the same era. Not that the condition of his work space reflected on her dad—his mind was uncluttered, clear and calculating, capable of running multiple businesses and recalling minute details that were never written on paper.

"Hello, sunshine! What a nice surprise! Come in, have a seat," he said. There was no room for debate in his tone, or in most discussions with him. Before she could do as she was told, though, he was out from behind his desk, pulling her into a bear hug that could have broken ribs. Like her, he was tall and blond, and he looked down at her and grinned. "How are you?"

He broke the hug and pushed Alex in the direction of a worn leather chair opposite his desk, and as she sat he returned to his throne behind it. From there he ran a dozen dry-cleaning stores and twice as many car washes and Laundromats.

"I'm great, Dad! How are you?"

"Perfect. I'm so glad you're here early. Your mother will be delighted to see you. And I'm sure she'll put you to work."

Alex had left the sanctuary of the beach to come home for her mother's sixtieth birthday party. An intimate affair for a hundred of her closest friends and family would be catered in the backyard of their home later the next afternoon. To guarantee her arrival in the midst

of shore traffic, Alex had decided to return the day before. As much as she loved the beach, she did miss her parents when she was gone for the summer, and she could tell from their recent conversations that her mother was stressing over the party. Alex's presence would calm her, and her dad was right—a million small tasks would need to be completed. Because she was efficient and skilled, Alex was sure her mother would assign each and every one of them to her.

Not that it'd been easy to get away. Alex was used to her freedom, and this morning as she'd packed her bag and her car, she'd had to deal with a jealous, brooding Anke, who suddenly wanted to take the weekend off to attend the party. Explaining all the reasons why that was a bad idea had only fueled Anke's anger, and Alex had left the beach on such bad terms she wasn't sure they'd be able to patch things up when she returned. It wasn't until she reached Philly and stopped to stretch that the sting of Anke's harsh words began to fade. When she passed through the Lehigh Tunnel, and the flat planes of the valley magically transformed into the mountainous landscape she loved, Alex finally began to relax.

"That's why I'm here, Dad. Whatever she needs."

"Good, good. How are you feeling?" He didn't look at her but instead shuffled some papers before him.

"I'm great. My summer's been a blast and my batteries are recharged."

Now he did look, with squinted eyes that tried to understand the inconceivable fact that someone so young and healthy-looking might really be sick.

"Good! That's good!" he said, and smiled with obvious relief.

Changing to a more comfortable topic, Alex asked about his business, a subject she knew would both brighten his spirits and occupy the conversation for the foreseeable future.

"Not good, sunshine, not good at all. All of this wash-and-wear and casual work attire is killing the dry-cleaning business. Thank God for kids who throw up in bed. We can still get forty bucks a pop for cleaning bedding! The other businesses are fine. They've become our bread and butter."

Sitting back in her chair and assuming a comfortable pose, Alex looked at the joy on his face even as he talked about business going down the drain. She'd heard it all before, from her grandfather, and

from her dad, yet here they were thirty years later, still going strong. She humored him, though.

"Will anything be left for Andrew to inherit?" she inquired about her older brother, who'd worked for their father since he was big enough to walk, or so it seemed, and had essentially never left. He'd attended the local college for both his bachelor's and master's degrees, married a local girl, and settled into the same neighborhood as their parents.

He sighed. "I don't know, sunshine. Probably not much future in dry cleaning. But I'm looking into a couple of liquor licenses."

Alex knew the Commonwealth of Pennsylvania was investigating the sale of their liquor monopoly. Under the current system, the state owned all of the hundreds of stores that provided liquor to both the public and private sectors. The governor was looking to privatize the system. Good arguments on both sides of the debate made the decision a difficult one. Revenue from alcohol sales funded everything from building roads to paying state salaries. Those who supported the sale of the stores touted the economic opportunity for people like her father.

"That's good," Alex replied. "Where do you buy those?"

He laughed. "They're only going to award a handful. You need to have money to get one. Lots of money. And you need the right political connections. But I've contributed to the campaigns of every senator and congressman and representative in the area, and you know—it's all who you know."

Alex studied him for a moment, choosing her words carefully. She'd never agree with him about things like this, but she didn't want to offend him by expressing her opinion too strongly. "That doesn't seem very fair, Dad. I mean, shouldn't they sell licenses to people who've lost their jobs and give them an opportunity to make a living?"

He squinted again, appearing confused. "They couldn't afford them."

"Maybe they could, if they dropped the price."

Again, the squint. "Then how would the state make money?"

"Just sell more licenses. Give everyone a chance."

Waving a dismissive hand, he shook his head. "That would never work, Alex. If the little guy spent, say, fifty grand on a license, it'd be a waste of his money. The outlet liquor stores would undercut the prices, and everyone would go there. Sure, people would go to the corner store to pick up one bottle of wine for dinner, but if they were having a party,

buying a dozen bottles, or if they owned a restaurant or a bar—they'd drive a few extra miles to save money. And your little guy would be out of business in six months *and* fifty thousand dollars in debt."

Alex tried not to show her anger at her dad's logic, but it reflected his sense of entitlement, which infuriated her. He wasn't a bad man, though; in fact he was a good one. Quite generous with his wealth, he supported local causes like children's basketball leagues and the animal shelter, his employees had good salaries and health-care benefits, and he was a fair employer.

"Dad, do you really think that's right?"

"Sunshine, it doesn't matter what I think. It's the way it is. And if I don't buy the licenses, someone else will. Then they'll be making all the money and I won't. It doesn't matter if they're wearing casual clothes to work. They're still going to happy hour afterward, and booze is always going to be a moneymaker."

It was pointless to argue, and besides, this trip was supposed to be a happy one. She decided to change the subject. "I don't suppose you can get out for nine holes before I report for duty with Mom?"

Shaking his head he frowned. "Not today. But let's get some lunch. I won fifty bucks on the Yankees game last night."

Alex smiled. Her dad had always been a gambler, and while he'd probably lost more than he'd won over the years, he'd always spoiled her and Andrew with the winnings. "And how is Mr. Merck?" Alex asked as they stood to leave. Mr. Merck was a friend of her dad's, a jolly man who owned the largest bakery around, as evidenced by his enormous waistline. He also ran an illegal gambling operation.

"Not so good. He hasn't recovered from his bypass and was forced to turn the business over to Greg."

"It's too bad about Mr. Merck. But I'm sure Greg will do well." Greg Merck was two years older than she, but they'd grown up at the country club together, playing tennis and golf in the mornings and attempting to drown each other at the pool in the afternoons. A dozen of them were in that age group, a year or two older and younger than Alex. The parents were all friends and the kids got along as well. Alex was sure the Mercks would be there to celebrate her mother's milestone.

"Shall we invite your mother to lunch?" he asked as he guided her from his office.

"Let's just make it a special date for us, Dad."

Her car knew the way to the country club, and they took a table on the massive covered patio overlooking the eighteenth green. On the way they were greeted by a dozen members, most of them women who were friends of her mom or whose husbands did business with her dad. He'd grown up here, as she had, and served on the board, and knew everyone.

"I love it here," Alex said as she wistfully looked out at the golf course and to the forest beyond, the hills slowly rising, blending into the Endless Mountains in the distance. A group was teeing off on a picturesque hole that climbed the mountainside, its green carved into the trees at the end of the fairway. She loved that hole and all of them at Mountain Meadows.

"You could be the pro here, Alex, if you just said the word."

She laughed. "I couldn't kiss that many asses, Dad."

He laughed, and as the waiter took his order, Alex watched a beautiful drive sail down the middle of the fairway. She was itching to play. Maybe she could talk her mom into it, after the party.

Their lunch was pleasant, and after promising to see each other at home later, they went their separate ways. As expected, her mother was delighted to see her. She quickly put Alex to work taking care of the little things that needed to be done for the party. And what a party it was. Rather than lawn tents, the catering company actually set up a series of gazebos on the back lawn, some designated for the service of food and cocktails, others with bench-style seating and tables to allow people to eat without fear of attack from insects in the grass or the sun overhead.

Alex saw people she hadn't seen in years—the parents of her friends, local doctors and lawyers, a judge, a congressman, businessmen and women—all the important people in Lackawanna County. The number one hundred had been mentioned as an estimated total of guests, and Alex wasn't sure if anyone was counting, but she must have given out at least twice that many hugs before the night was through.

Cleanup was part of the package with the caterers (as well as restoration of the lawn trampled by human feet and gazebo floors), so without an ounce of guilt Alex sought the solitude of her childhood bedroom overlooking the quiet, tree-studded front yard, while the party was still in full force in the back. The sheer size of the property and the thickness of the old leaded windows combined with the soothing hum

of the air conditioner to create for Alex a sanctuary a world apart from the one she'd escaped.

After showering, she stretched out in her bed and closed her eyes, thinking about the night. Her mother had been radiant, charming guests with her warm smile and kind words, and her father had entertained everyone with stories and off-color jokes. They were a remarkable couple, still happy after thirty-five years together.

Her parents were already married when they were her age, and while Alex wasn't concerned with finding a wife, she found herself envying them—the companionship they shared, the obvious love, the comfortable life. Would she ever have that?

When she was younger, it was something she'd never thought of. After her diagnosis, it was something she couldn't think of.

Uncomfortable with these thoughts and suddenly feeling quite alone, Alex rolled over and pulled her blanket up under her chin, desperately fighting the impulse to call Anke.

CHAPTER FIVE

CREPES AND DATES

The first rays of the morning sun were lending their light to the day as Brit climbed onto her Trek and began pedaling. As she headed north out of Bethany Beach, her view of the sunrise was blocked by the rows of houses to the east of Route One. All manner and size of beach homes had been erected over the years, from cottages that had been handed down through generations of families to multimillion-dollar dwellings housing the summer visitors from Philadelphia and Washington, D.C. She passed a gas station, empty at this early hour, and a twenty-four-hour pharmacy, which was surprisingly busy. The coffee-shop lot was filled.

How different this place was from Brazil. She hadn't had long to recover from her service trip before embarking on her family vacation to the beach, and it was still shocking to see the evidence of civilization around her. It didn't last long.

After a few miles Brit entered the Delaware Seashore State Park, and the development came to an abrupt halt. Suddenly, nothing obstructed her view of the waves of the Atlantic crashing on the shore except the grass on the dunes. Britain sucked in a breath, not from the effort of her exercise but from the sheer beauty before her. The waves shimmered as the bright rays of morning sun danced on their peaks. She was close enough to see the spray of water as the waves shattered on the beach. Under cover of darkness the ocean had delivered the treasures children would spend their morning discovering—petrified wood, seaweed, human trash, and seashells, broken and chipped and priceless to little seashell hunters.

She hadn't encountered much traffic at this hour on a Saturday morning, but her return trip would be more hazardous, as Route One swelled with thousands of cars filled with families heading south to Ocean City. She'd take her time on the way back, stopping at the state park to watch the fishermen and venturing across the road to the bay where she could observe the wind surfers practicing their craft.

She didn't usually rise this early, but she was conditioned from six weeks in South America, and lately, opening her eyes in the morning was an easier task. Since coming back home she'd discovered a love of the peace she found when the world was still asleep. It was as if she'd awakened from a coma and all the stimulation was putting her brain into shock. Even before she'd had time to adjust to the climate and the noise and the new apartment she'd rented, she'd left with her family for their annual vacation, and a day at the beach house, crammed with kids, was like a normal day on LSD. As she imagined it, anyway. She'd never actually tried the drug.

Her family had been coming to Bethany Beach since before she was born, but since her sisters had married and had children, the small beach house had become quite crowded. She loved her family, she truly did. She wouldn't have traded her sisters Sam and Jordan for the world. Their husbands, Mike and Mike, were tolerable. Her nephews were the lights of her life. She loved her parents. Even though they all expected her to give up her vacation for them, she didn't mind. Sometimes, she liked the kids better than the adults. So, she'd babysit while they all went out and enjoyed a nice dinner, or had their nails painted.

It was what was expected, and it had always been this way, and so had Britain. She was the devoted daughter, the dependable sister, the spirited aunt who was fun to be around. It had never seemed to bother her before, but now, for some reason, it did.

Brit felt like she didn't fit in with the family she loved so much, and this new reality troubled and saddened her. They'd always been her anchor, and now she felt like she was drifting away.

She knew it was her and not them, yet she could do nothing to quiet the restlessness that had overcome her. So much in her life was changing. Her priorities were certainly different after spending time with people who had so very little but gave so very much. Listening to

Sam whine over her car's entertainment system malfunctioning, and Jordan's concerns about the highlights in her hair, made Brit feel like a stranger to them. Work was scary, too. Getting hired for a full-time job was exciting but, at the same time, a little unnerving. She had absolutely no experience, but in just a couple of weeks, she'd be responsible for the education of hundreds of impressionable teens.

Was this angst just fear that she wouldn't be the teacher she hoped to be, unable to connect with her students? Would she handle the pressure of working every day and of being responsible for a bunch of unpredictable kids? Any one of those could have caused a nervous breakdown, she mused.

Or was it the responsibility of living on her own that was scaring her? She'd leased an apartment and already moved in, and she was enjoying decorating it and choosing furniture. But would she remember to pay the rent and could she afford the expenses and what would she do when she ran out of milk for her cereal?

It was all so overwhelming, and perhaps it wasn't any one of the things she'd thought of, but the combination of all of them. All of them, and the little secret about her sexuality she was so carefully hiding. Spending time with Syl and Marianna in Brazil had thrilled her. Working so closely with two women who openly proclaimed their love was inspiring. Yet it saddened her a little, too, because she knew it would be difficult for her to enjoy that same freedom. Her family wasn't like other people. They were the ultra-conservative, super-Catholic sect and generally viewed homosexuals in the same light as terrorists and murderers. Coming out to them wasn't an option. One day, when—if— she met the right woman, she might tell them her truth. Until then, she saw no sense in causing a family crisis.

The property line at the edge of the state park was marked by the reemergence of development along the shore. With the homes and shops came more traffic—car and bicycle and foot—as vacationers and residents began their days. Brit weaved through the congestion, taking some back roads through Dewey and into Rehoboth Beach to avoid the chaos. On Delaware Avenue she turned right, and when she reached the beach block she parked her bike and secured it. Then she traded her helmet for a baseball cap and, after stretching her trembling legs, began walking toward her destination.

Brit loved Rehoboth Beach. The quaint shops lining the main streets had always drawn her, with their array of unusual gifts and art, beach clothing, and souvenir trinkets. The restaurants offered everything from gourmet meals with vintage wine to pizza by the slice served with fountain soda. For the past few years, she'd watched the women here, so many of them coupled, walking hand in hand, or in groups strolling the boardwalk and Rehoboth Avenue. She could spend her entire day people watching, if only she had the time, but soon her family would miss her and one of her nephews would call her cell phone asking her to toss a ball or fly a kite.

Brit headed into Penny Lane and wasn't surprised to see the long line gathered at Café Papillon, the tiny shop where fresh crepes were made to order. She'd been in this line every day since she'd been at the beach, and still, she never tired of the delicate French pastries. Every day she ordered a ham-and-cheese crepe, but she always chose a different type for dessert. Nutella and bananas. Nutella and bananas with nuts and whipped cream. Nutella with strawberries. Peaches and cream. The combinations were endless and each more delectable than the other, and as she stood there gazing at the handwritten menu, contemplating her options, she couldn't help feeling like she was on a quiet Parisian street.

She was so distracted by her mental vision of the Eiffel Tower that she was startled when someone touched her arm. She turned to see a smiling face she hadn't seen in months. "Now that you have a job, I expect *you* to buy *my* coffee."

Brit smiled and spread her arms to embrace the woman who'd been her preceptor during her collegiate days of student teaching. When Brit graduated, Sally Conklin had jokingly told her it wouldn't be the same at school without her and promptly retired. Brit knew there was more to the story, but she'd received no further explanation and hadn't probed.

"Sal!" she said as she hugged the taller woman more closely.

"So, you got my message?" Brit had phoned with the good news as soon as she returned from Brazil but hadn't heard a reply.

"I did. I just got back in the country myself, so I'm not quite caught up on my messages. But how are you? Excited?"

"I'm a nervous wreck. The closer it gets, the nervouser I get!"

Sal laughed and pulled back. "They didn't hire you to teach English, did they?"

"Fortunately, I'll be sticking to biology. But I think God himself arranged this meeting, because I really do want to talk to you."

"Yeah, sorry about not getting back to you. I was on a cruise. I've spent most of my waking hours doing laundry and cleaning my house."

"Do you have some time to talk now?" Brit asked.

"I do."

"Then I'll buy you that coffee, and a crepe, too." At the coffee shop near campus, it was rumored that Sal spent all of her salary on coffee and pastries for her students. During her four years of college, Brit guessed they must have shared a thousand cups of coffee and an equal number of baked delights.

As they reached the counter and placed their orders, Sal chose the strawberries and cream, while Brit took bananas with caramel, nuts, and cream. Both took their coffees in large cups. As promised, Brit paid, and they squeezed into the two last seats at a wobbly table under the canopy.

"So, you were on a cruise? What was that like? Where'd you go?"

"It started in the British Isles and then went everywhere in the Mediterranean. It was fantastic but exhausting. It's good to be home."

"And is this home for you now? At the beach?"

"Yes. I bought a house here a long time ago but decided to finally make the move. This is home base now."

Brit swallowed a bite of her ham-and-cheese. "I'm surprised. I didn't realize you were considering retirement. You seemed so happy with your job."

Brit realized that she knew very little about Sal's personal life, which saddened her. From the first day they met, when Brit was a freshman majoring in Education, they had shared so many common interests and insights, and Brit felt a special connection to Sal that was rare in her life. Yet even though they shared so much, Sal kept her personal life private.

"I was," Sal said after a moment. "But my partner, Susan, had a heart attack."

Sal paused, and Brit sensed Sal was searching for some reaction from her, not to the awful news about Susan but to the confession about her sexuality.

Brit gave her only encouragement to continue. "I'm so sorry to hear that. Is she okay now?"

Sal smiled. "It was just a little heart attack, but we heeded the warning. We won't live forever. So we assessed our finances and decided we could afford to quit working. Now we're living the good life, having fun and spending all our money so our families can't fight over it when we're dead."

Brit laughed. "So I'm at the beginning of my career, and you're at the beginning of your adventure! How exciting." Brit smiled at Sal, happy for her, and happy that she'd chosen to share such private information.

Brit suspected that deep inside she might have known that Sal was a lesbian, but they'd never discussed the subject. When she was in college and just beginning to understand the meaning of all the little clues she'd been ignoring over the years, she didn't feel comfortable talking about it with anyone. She didn't date. She didn't join any gay clubs (not that there were any on her Catholic campus). She didn't seek out women. If not for the first woman she dated, a woman who, much like Sylvia, immediately tuned in to Brit's sexuality, she'd probably still be waiting for her first kiss. That first date had led to a few more, but even as Brit grew more comfortable with her identity, she still wasn't comfortable sharing it. Even though Sal had opened the door, Brit was still too scared to walk through.

"So tell me about this career you're starting!" Sal's eyes twinkled with pride.

"I start the day after Labor Day. Students report on Wednesday."

"Did they give you any guidelines about what they expected? Have you reviewed the textbook you'll be using?"

"Yes, and yes. I met with the principal and another teacher. I'll be teaching all of the sophomore classes and some senior ones. They pretty much have the curriculum set up, and they're using the same textbooks from the past few years. They're fine. I've gone through the books and made an outline of what I want to emphasize and the order I'd like to present things."

"So what are you nervous about? It sounds like you've already got it ready to go."

Brit shrugged and stared into her coffee, allowing a small sigh before answering. "I'm not sure."

"You. Will. Be. Great! All your reviews were fabulous, and the students and faculty will love you…just wait and see. It'll be a piece of cake."

Brit gave a reluctant smile, not sure she believed Sal but grateful for the encouragement. "You're always so supportive. Thank you."

"Now where are you going to be teaching? Which school?"

"That's what's so cool. I'll be at your old school, Endless Mountains."

Sal sat back in her chair and began laughing. Her salt-and-pepper hair fell casually across her forehead, and wrinkles gathered at the corners of her half-closed eyes, yet Brit marveled at how lovely she looked.

"Small world." She laughed again.

"Yes, it is."

"Even smaller these days. Remember the girl I told you about when you were in school? The one who played basketball at EM?"

Britain nodded. Since basketball was one of their many common interests, she and Sal had talked frequently about the game. Sal often spoke of her greatest former player, one who'd gone on to a stellar college career at a big Division I college. She'd often said she'd like to introduce them, but it'd just never happened. "Alex?"

Sal nodded. "Yes, she's been teaching English at EM for the past few years. She's been the assistant girls' basketball coach, too, and this year she'll be taking over as head coach."

"No way!" Brit was shocked and thrilled at the same time. If she could make a friend at school it would make this transition so much easier.

"Yes. How about that?"

"Oh, wow! I'd love to meet her. If you give me her number I'll call her as soon as I get home. Maybe we can meet and talk."

"I can do even better than that. Why don't you come over to my place tonight for dinner? I'll invite her, and the two of you can get to know each other."

"She's here?"

"Yeah. She spends the summers here, hanging out."

Brit pursed her lips. This was the last night of her sister Jordan's family time at the beach, and it was expected that she would watch Jordan's sons so she could enjoy some time with her husband. Normally,

Brit wouldn't have given it a second thought. She'd have just stayed home to babysit. But not this time. This was too important.

"That would be fantastic. What time should I come over?"

"How about six?"

"Perfect. What can I bring? Wine? Cheese? Dessert?"

"Sue and I love to cook, and we have too much wine already, so no more. But you can pick up dessert."

"Anything special?"

"You decide."

Brit pulled a pen out of her fanny pack and wrote the address on her napkin. "And you really think Alex can come?"

Sal pulled out her phone. "Let's call her and find out."

Brit waited anxiously for the other woman to answer, hoping this meeting would work out. But the phone rang until it went to voice mail, and both she and Sal were a little disappointed. Brit listened as Sal left Alex a message instructing her to be at her house by six for dinner. Noting Brit's look of disappointment, she smiled reassuringly. "Don't worry. She'll be there. She's still afraid of me."

They finished their coffees and left the table for others to use, then said their good-byes. With Sal's home address tucked safely into her pack, Brit strode confidently along Rehoboth Avenue, elation buoying her as she watched the town awaken. Workers opened doors and wiped down benches, pulling goods onto the sidewalk. Marquees were updated with the current day's offerings. Parents trailed behind scampering children, and teenagers went their own way.

After taking a seat on a boardwalk bench, Brit closed her eyes and just breathed. Around her the activity continued, but now as she focused on the sounds of the surf and the seagulls as the sun warmed her, she experienced a peace that had been elusive for weeks. Seeing Sal had been good for her. Calming. Reassuring. Comforting. She was going to have a great night, and looked forward to seeing Sal again and to meeting her friend Alex. But first she had to tell her family she wouldn't be the sitter tonight. She didn't look forward to that conversation.

CHAPTER SIX

BEACH BUM

A lex heard her phone ringing even through the pile of laundry in which it was buried. As she had attempted to answer a call the night before, Anke had plucked it from her hands and tossed it into the laundry basket before throwing Alex onto the bed. Both the phone and its owner were in essentially the same positions nearly twelve hours later.

"My phone," Alex asked helplessly, teasing and pleading with her lover.

"No vay! Zis are my last minutes vis you. I'm not sharink!"

Even if she wished to challenge her, Alex wouldn't have been successful. Anke had bound both of Alex's wrists to the headboard and was having her way with her. Alex watched as Anke slid her hands down her arms, across her nipples, down her abdomen to her hips, where she was perched atop Alex and enjoying her power. "I vant you zoo rememba me, foreffa."

Trembling, Alex moaned as Anke's mouth found her nipple and her teeth gently rubbed across it, back and forth in a steady rhythm. She could never forget this woman. Their sexual connection was phenomenal.

Since they'd met on Memorial Day weekend, she'd spent many of her nights in this same position. Anke was in the United States on a work visa, spending her university break employed at a restaurant on the boardwalk. Theirs was a perfect summer fling. They shared some free time on the beach because Anke's job allowed it, and if the weather wasn't suited for sunbathing, they rode bikes or kayaked. Mostly,

though, they stayed in bed in the mornings having fabulous sex. When the summer ended, both of them would have exciting memories of a great summer.

Although Anke had had similar relationships in the past, Alex never had. A parade of girls had filled her time, but she hadn't been with anyone consistently until now. She had been a little leery in the beginning, concerned about possible unpleasantries if their experiment failed, but to her surprise, she found it an absolutely wonderful arrangement.

Knowing she would spend the night with Anke had filled her summer days with a quiet calm. She didn't have a frantic need to find a girl, just the happy reality that no matter what she did after the beach— whether she played golf or tennis or rode her bike, whether she was alone or with friends, at a bar or on her patio—at the end of the night Anke would be in her bed.

Now Anke was leaving, returning to her home in the Bavarian Alps, and it seemed to Alex that she had done everything in her power on their last night together to ensure that her wish to be remembered did in fact come true. Shuddering with delight as Anke's hands and mouth magically licked and caressed her, Alex managed to speak. "I won't forget you, fräulein."

When Anke finished, she slid from the bed and stood, untying the knot that bound Alex's wrists. Rubbing the sore muscles of her arms, Alex watched Anke dress, admiring the curves of her breasts and her ass, the muscles of her shoulders and back, the beautiful face. Alex's appreciative glances were rewarded with a smile.

"You vill email to me sometimes, yes? Maybe in a sevfral monce."

This statement, like most of Anke's communication with Alex, was a command. Alex didn't mind the assertive role her lover played— she just chose to ignore her when Anke's wishes didn't suit her. But in this instance, she agreed. Alex would have been a fool to just let Anke walk away without leaving a window open for a possible reunion if they both summered in Rehoboth again the following year. "Yes."

"An if I ever come zoo U.S. again, maybe I vill see you, yes?"

"Yes."

"An if you ever come zoo Europe and you don have jealous girlfren vis you, maybe I vill see you, yes?"

"Yes."

"Okay. I say goo-bye, now. Please don call at my home. I have maybe a jealous boyfren who does not like me zoo be vis za girls."

Alex stood and pulled on her shorts and a T-shirt, fighting back a laugh as Anke held out her hand to shake. "I go now. Zank you, Alex, for rememberable summer in U.S."

Alex accepted the proffered hand, but instead of shaking it, she placed a gentle kiss on the palm. "It was my pleasure, Miss Bavaria." Anke was the former Miss Bavaria, and Alex loved using the title.

At the door they shared a small kiss. "Auf Wiedersehen," Alex whispered as Anke turned and walked to her friend's waiting car.

As she watched Anke leave, probably forever, an unfamiliar and not very pleasant feeling came over Alex. Sadness? Regret? She stared after her for a moment, then turned and closed the door. The summer was winding to a close, and she planned to enjoy every minute she had left.

Fishing her phone out of the laundry basket, she dialed her voice mail, changing into her bathing suit as she listened to her messages. She deleted them all, then dialed Sal's number as she sat to pull on her sneakers. "Hey, Coach," she said. "How was the cruise?"

"Exhausting. I'll fill you in later if you're free for dinner? I want to introduce you to someone. A girl I used to mentor just got a job at Endless Mountains, and I think you'll get along great."

"Really? That's a coincidence. What's her name?"

"Britain Dodge."

"I don't think I know her. What does she teach?"

"Science."

"A brainiac, huh? Is she cute?"

"Alex!"

"Okay, sorry. You said six, right? Can I bring anything?"

"Come at five. You can help cook. And all you have to bring is your charming personality. Oh, and if you'd like to bring Miss Munich, she's welcome, too."

"It was Miss Bavaria, Coach, but she just left. She's heading to the airport as we speak."

"Is that a good thing?" Sal asked cautiously.

Alex smiled, knowing that it was, but she understood that Sal didn't have a good handle on Anke. No one did. Even though she managed to see Sal and Sue often, Anke had been scarce on those occasions. Her

job required her to work nights, and their sex life had kept her busy in the mornings. And this sort of relationship was so atypical of Alex that everyone was scratching their heads.

"It's okay, Coach. We knew she'd be leaving. We decided to stay friends. You can never have too many friends."

"Truer words were never spoken. So be on your best behavior tonight. I think Brit will be a good friend for you."

When they ended the call, Alex began humming as she carefully packed her bag for the beach. A sand sheet and flip-flops went in first, followed by water, an apple, a peanut-butter sandwich, and a bag of pretzels. She covered everything with a small towel. After tucking her book into one side and her sunscreen in the other, she zipped the bag closed.

In the bathroom she peed and brushed her teeth, then splashed some water onto the short mop of blond curls atop her head. She ran her fingers through them, then pulled her Phillies cap low over her forehead.

She retrieved her Trek from the garage along with her beach chair, which had a sling that allowed her to ride with the chair strapped to her back, an incredible invention for beach bums like her. After anchoring the backpack to the handlebars, she closed the door and began pedaling.

The condo in Oyster Bay was just across Route One from downtown Rehoboth, and Alex took the back way into town, riding under the bridge on Route One to avoid traffic. It was only ten, but already the tourists were heading toward the shopping outlets near the condo, people walked toward the restaurants and the beach, and all of the coffee shops she passed were jammed with patrons.

It was the end of August, and the season should have been dying down, but the weather was perfect and no one seemed to be leaving. Except Anke, of course. But she'd purchased her ticket well in advance and had important things like university luring her back to Europe. Even if they hadn't had an agreement, she would have been on that plane today.

Alex cut across Rehoboth Avenue at the lighthouse and avoided the congestion of downtown, riding along the canal and toward the northern part of town, toward the women's beach at the state park. This day was going to be a scorcher. She liked to get to the beach early, before the crowd brought a lot of noise and activity and before the sun

began baking the sand. She'd settle in and read, and in a few hours when her roommates staggered from their beds, they'd join her. Before the day was through, she'd find her solitude delightfully disturbed by a dozen friends who made their way to the state park.

Sure enough, the beach was nearly empty when she arrived, and she set up her camp in a favorite spot, where her friends would be sure to find her later. She pulled her book from the bag, but instead of reading, she leaned back into her chair and simply stared at the beauty of the ocean. To her left, the waves crashed into an outcropping of rocks, breaking each solitary wall into a million tiny pebbles of water scattered in every direction. Before her, a family of porpoises swam two hundred yards from the shoreline, and she watched as they playfully jumped through the waves.

A feeling of peace settled over her. In a way, she was happy that Anke had left, so she could spend this last week of summer relaxing, with no obligations, enjoying the sunshine and the company of her friends. This was it. Another summer was drawing to a close. After this weekend there was just one more before she left her college roommates for another year. She wanted to make the most of it. Hopefully, they'd be at the beach before she had to leave for dinner with Sal.

Tam had already started back at school and would leave Rehoboth on Sunday afternoon for Maryland, where she taught kindergarten. Kim would start school after Labor Day, like Alex, but because she lived in Philly and her aging uncle owned the house they shared, she'd be spending weekends here all year round, checking on the place so he didn't have to. In November, they'd meet up when they all returned for the film festival, but with her basketball schedule, Alex would have a short trip.

Her friends didn't disappoint her. She hadn't even started her second bottle of water when Kim arrived, pulling a cooler the size of a bathtub. Tam wasn't far behind, toting their chairs and an umbrella. "Should I get the horseshoes? Or do you feel like Frisbee?" Kim asked.

"I feel like relaxing. It's too hot to show off my athletic prowess for all the beautiful girls."

"Your what? Speak English. Aren't you supposed to be an English teacher?"

Alex laughed. "As a matter of fact, I am. Full time, with benefits. And I also happen to be the head girls' basketball coach."

Kim opened the cooler and offered Alex a beer. "It's about time you stopped slacking. Now here's a benefit I'm interested in. You want one?"

"No, thanks. Too hot." In truth, when it came to alcohol consumption, Alex was a lightweight compared to her friends. This fact had become very evident to all of them in college, and after a short time their circle of friends was happy to have Alex as the sober, responsible party who could steer them all in the direction of the proper dorms and, later on, function as their designated driver.

"I saw Miss Bavaria sneaking out this morning," Kim said as she flopped down into the chair she'd placed next to Alex's. "I thought she was leaving."

"She did. This morning."

"I'll miss seeing her around the house." Kim laughed and took a long pull on her beer. In true European fashion, Anke was fond of topless sunbathing. And topless everything.

Alex grinned and nodded. "Me, too! So what are you guys up to tonight? You want to come over to Sal's with me for dinner?"

"I just want to have burgers on the grill or something like that. Relax for a while after the beach, then head over to the Frogg Pond," Kim replied.

"Yeah, me, too. I'll take a rain check on Sal's," Tam replied. "But don't be too late. We have to have our traditional end-of-summer beer."

"I'm not doing that till next week," Alex said. "The summer isn't over yet."

"Tell that to my principal. How was Sal's trip? Are you going for the slide show?"

Alex laughed. "So that's why you don't want to go!" The year before, Sal and Sue had been on safari in Africa and had been a bit too zealous in sharing the photos of their trip.

"Busted," Kim confessed.

"Well, there'll be no slides tonight. I'm going to meet someone."

"Oooohhhh, you slut! Miss Bavaria isn't even back in Deutschland and already you've lined up her replacement!" Kim teased her.

"I've let down the women of the Eastern Seaboard this summer, but I have a week to make up for it!"

Tam shook her head and laughed. "Alex, you don't fool me. You can sleep with all the women in Rehoboth, but I know you really just

want to settle down with one. You were happy with Miss Bavaria. I could see it."

Alex was going to make a playful retort, then decided against it. She could have told them she was just meeting a new colleague, but she decided it was more fun to let them make their own assumptions. And she could never tell them the truth; they wouldn't understand. They were her friends and they loved her unconditionally. But would *a lover* ever truly love Alex as she was? They all loved the basketball star and the coach, and the golfer, but would they love the imperfect person she really was inside? Alex had no point of reference. She'd bedded many women, but none of them had really ever gotten to know her.

Her first lover had been a high-school classmate who'd played the part of seductress to perfection, and their relationship was all about sex. Both knew they were heading in opposite directions after graduation, and much like her relationship with Anke, the ending of that first affair had been written at the start.

In college, where Alex was known on campus from the moment she arrived, it was much the same. Girls wanted to know her and wanted to sleep with her, and that had been fine with Alex. She wasn't in school to find a wife; she was there to learn a thing or two and to shoot a basketball. The women who so eagerly accompanied Alex to her bed were just a bonus.

One-night stands had been the norm for her, and it wasn't until this summer with Anke that Alex actually had more—conversation, discussions about plans and food and television and not just sex. It was new and different, and if Alex was asked under oath, she'd have to admit she'd enjoyed the summer.

That didn't mean she was heading for the altar, though.

She tuned out her friends and allowed the beauty of the Atlantic to push all those complex thoughts from her mind.

CHAPTER SEVEN

WORKIN' WEEKENDS

Unsold pastries and bread were piled into a large cardboard box, counters and tables were wiped clean, and the dishwasher running as P.J. flipped the light switch that officially closed the bakery on this Saturday afternoon. All that was left to do was tally the money and slip it into the safe. Then he'd walk down the hill behind the bakery to the Viewmont Mall, where his dad was also working, pick up the car, and head to Lake Winola for the party. His friends were already there and had been since noon when it started.

He spilled the contents of a large bank envelope onto a table in the staff lounge. The room was vacant, just like the rest of the building that housed the actual bakery, the coffee shop, and the business office from where his boss ran his operation. Vacant was good. He couldn't do what he needed to do with witnesses around.

All denominations of bills scattered on the laminate surface of the table, along with dozens of slips of white paper. There wasn't much money to count. Mid-August wasn't a busy time in the sports-betting business. The NFL pre-season wasn't wildly popular in the area, and NCAA football was still a couple of weeks away. Baseball's pennant races hadn't really started yet, and most of the teams with local fan bases weren't having banner years, so betting was down. The FedEx Cup Playoffs had started, though, and dozens of golf fans had placed bets on the tournament in New Jersey. The big event by far was the Little League World Series, held just a couple of hours away in Williamsport. All of the media coverage generated excitement, and all the gamblers with nothing else on which to wager were betting on twelve-year-old kids to make them money.

After placing all the paper slips into neat piles, P.J. counted the money he'd collected. Just under three thousand dollars. Then he counted the bakery receipts. He shook his head and frowned. He'd spent ten hours serving coffee and pastries, selling cakes and pies and fresh hard rolls, and the bakery had only brought in a thousand dollars. That was the gross profit. After expenses, including his paltry salary, the profit was probably only half that. It didn't take a genius to realize the illegal activity was much more profitable than the legitimate business. And the illegal profits weren't taxed, either. It made him wonder what he was doing, working and studying to get ahead in the world. Crime was the way to go.

What would he do with all that money? Buy a fucking car, for one thing. He was so sick of bumming rides and riding his bike, missing out on things like the party at the lake because he had no way to get there. Even though he lived close to most of his friends and classmates, work put him on a different schedule in a different town, and it was nearly impossible to find transportation. Thankfully, his mom had agreed to pick up his dad after work, and they allowed him to borrow the car. It would be so nice to hang out and have fun for a change. He hardly saw his friends anymore, and they'd all be at the lake. So would Justina, the smartest girl in his class. They'd been friends since kindergarten, but lately, on those rare occasions when he saw her, she seemed to be paying him more attention. And, he'd heard from a reliable source that Justina thought he was cute.

He rubbed his hands together excitedly. He couldn't wait to get to the party!

Skimming through the slips, he searched for bets that weren't likely to pay off. Long shots. Someone named Frank M. had bet twenty bucks that all ten of the baseball teams he'd picked would win that day. If they did, he'd win two hundred bucks. Chances were, they wouldn't. P.J. took Frank's twenty-dollar bill and the accompanying slip and set it aside. He found several other slips with similar wagers that were likely losers. He set those aside as well. When he was finished, he had two hundred dollars in the extra pile.

Taking a blank slip from the bank envelope, P.J. set it on the table and studied it for a moment. What team to pick? The Yankees were almost as unreliable as the Phillies. The Orioles were playing well, though. He'd bet on the Os. It was a gamble, but it wasn't his money. It

belonged to Frank, and the other losers who'd bet on long shots. If he won, he'd come away with a few hundred bucks. If he lost, no big deal. Unless, of course, one of the long shots won. Then, he'd be in trouble.

P.J. wrote his dog's name on the slip of paper, stuffed the extra pile of slips into his pocket, and made his way to the large safe bolted to the floor in the midst of the industrial ovens. He slipped the envelope into the opening at the top of the safe, and prayed that none of the long shots would win.

Chapter Eight

Coaches' Meeting

As directed, Alex arrived at Sal's house an hour early. Hiding a bouquet of flowers behind her back, she waited impatiently at the door, tapping her feet to mark the time. The sun was hot, and she'd been a direct target of its rays in the topless Jeep as she battled traffic for most of the ride. The heat and the sun didn't usually bother her, but she suspected she might have overdone it on this glorious day.

Frantic barking heralded the door's opening, and Alex knelt to rub the Yorkie's head before it scooted through the opening and ran into the shrubs to water them.

"Hello, gorgeous." Alex greeted the woman who opened the door. Like her partner Sal, Sue was in her late fifties. Her red hair was now streaked with silver, but not a freckle had faded from her face. A bright smile spread across it when she saw Alex.

"Come in before you melt," Sue said and waited until Alex had crossed the threshold before hugging her. "How are you?"

"I'm great." Alex handed her the flowers and hugged her back, happy to see this wonderful woman who'd meant so much to her over the years. They'd met in a Pilates class when Alex was still in high school, playing basketball for Sal. Even then her back had bothered her, and they'd developed a friendship based on mutual sweat and pain and a desire to make it through the class. For Alex, a conditioned athlete, it was difficult. Sue—who was fifty pounds overweight and terribly out of shape—was incredibly limber and able to do amazing things, but only for short periods of time. They worked together, encouraging each other, and both came out feeling better and stronger both physically and spiritually. They'd been friends since.

Sue pretended to look over Alex's shoulder. "Is it safe to accept these?" she asked with a smile. "I don't want Miss Berlin knocking my lights out."

Alex shook her head. Apparently, everyone knew about Anke's jealousy. "She's back in Germany. I think it's safe."

"Well, in that case, I'll take them. They're beautiful."

Sue called the dog and they made their way into the house.

"Do I hear Alex?" Sal called from the other room, and Sue led her in the direction of Sal's voice.

Sal was cleaning up the kitchen and wiped her hands before hugging Alex. "Let's have a seat," Sal suggested, and they moved to the living room. They caught up and shared the photo book from their cruise, and Alex chuckled as she thought of the photos from their previous trip the year before. "Not a single baby elephant this time. How disappointing."

"I can still make you run laps," Sal said with a menacing glare. "Or worse yet, tell Britain the truth about you."

Unconcerned, Alex glanced at her watch. "Speaking of Brit, what time will she be here? I'm having my annual farewell drink with the girls tonight."

"So you can't stay?" Sue asked, disappointment written on her face.

Alex would stay for dinner, of course. How long she stayed depended on Britain. If she was totally boring, Alex would skip out. If not, she might stay a little later. But either way, she was meeting Tam and Kim at the Frogg Pond, and making that announcement now gave her the freedom to leave later.

"I'd never skip one of your dinners. I'm just saying I need to leave early."

Sal eyed her suspiciously, and Alex worried her mentor knew her real motives. She seemed to weigh her response, then let it drop.

"So how are you feeling?" Sue seemed to inspect her from head to toe.

"I'm good. Great, really. How about you?"

Sal laughed at the way Alex had expertly redirected the conversation. "I'm great, too."

"No chest pains or anything?"

"Not a one."

"Excellent."

"You must be happy to see Miss Berlin leave. You still have a week of summer to enjoy."

Alex leaned back into the soft leather of the chair and breathed deeply, studying the ceiling. "It's funny, about Anke. She was actually a good playmate. I kind of liked having her around."

"But you didn't ask her to stay?" Sal asked.

"No. I didn't really want her to. I couldn't have a relationship with her, you know? We're too different, and we'd argue all the time. But it was nice to have…someone. To talk to. To hang out with."

"Someone?"

"Yes."

"Alex, you may be growing up right before our eyes," Sue said.

"It's about time," Sal replied.

"No arguments from me," Alex said. In fact, for the first time in her life she agreed. Maybe it was time for a real partner instead of just a sexual one.

"How about a little sun?" Sal asked. "I think it may have cooled off enough to enjoy the patio."

Alex went to fill the ice bucket with drinks. She'd just reached the patio door when the dog began the frantic barking that heralded the appearance of a visitor. Alex looked up to see a lovely blonde approaching. Her hair was pulled back, and she waved as she made her way down the path, her hips swaying seductively with each step of her long, toned, tanned legs.

Maybe I will hang out for a while, Alex thought.

"Bogie!" Sal yelled. "Calm down!"

Brit heard a chorus of voices yelling at the little dog who so bravely came to meet her. She approached the patio slowly and pushed her sunglasses up on her forehead as she knelt to allow the wriggling pooch to sniff her hand.

"Hello, you ferocious beast. I'm sure you scare away all the bad guys with that bark," she told him as she scratched the fur behind his neck.

"His AKC papers claim he's a pure Yorkie, but we're convinced he's really part Doberman." Brit looked up to find a woman smiling at her. Beside her, Sal watched Brit playing with her dog. As she started to rise, Brit stopped her.

"Don't get up for me, please."

Sal ignored her. "Britain, this is my partner, Sue," she said, and walked across the patio to pull Brit into her second hug of the day.

Brit nodded and smiled. "Hi, Sue."

"Welcome," Sue replied, and she started to stand but sat back down when Brit made the suggestion.

Brit followed Sal across the patio. The house was a sprawling one-story of glass and stone, and the patio was massive, with two levels looking out at Rehoboth Bay. Brit exchanged pleasantries and was about to inquire about Bogie's name when a sliding-glass door opened and a woman stepped through.

Bright blue eyes met hers and held for a moment before Brit forced herself to look away to study the rest of the picture. The woman's blond hair was cut short and fell in loose waves around a perfect, oval face. High cheekbones, a chiseled nose, and full red lips completed the picture. She wore a ribbed white tank top that hugged her lean body and outlined her generous breasts, and flattered the toned arms and shoulders. Navy-blue cargo shorts hugged the long legs that drew Brit's eyes all the way down to the tops of her running shoes. Brit was five-nine, and she guessed Alex must be at least three inches taller than her.

Over the years, Sal had mentioned Alex Dalton a number of times. And Brit had heard of Alex even before meeting Sal. They'd grown up in neighboring counties, but Alex was the star senior heading off to college when Brit was a timid high-school freshman just breaking in, and the two of them had never faced each other on the court. The local news station's coverage included both areas though, and Brit had seen Alex on television enough times to recognize her.

If Alex noticed Brit's appraisal, she did nothing to acknowledge it. Instead, she gracefully carried an ice bucket of beverages to the patio table. As she set it down, Sal pulled back from her and turned toward Alex. "Britain Dodge, I'd like you to meet Alex Dalton." Spreading her arms as if conducting a symphony, Sal looked from one woman to the other, smiling.

With two easy strides, Alex stood before Brit and locked those brilliant eyes into hers as she offered her hand. Brit cleared her throat as she extended her own, surprised at the slight tremor that coursed through her entire being, lucky to find the outstretched hand while her eyes were glued to Alex's. The firm grip with which Alex shook her

hand broke the trance, and Brit turned her attention to the fingers she suspected could be broken. In spite of the pain, she managed to squeeze back.

"It's nice to finally meet you." Alex smiled, and if Brit was off balance from the vision of Alex, the reaction her smile caused was downright dangerous.

It took a second to find her voice in the clutter of her brain. She cleared her throat. "Yes. You, too."

Alex found herself falling into the warm pool of Brit's eyes. They were wide and welcoming, and she couldn't help herself. They seemed to capture Alex and suck her in, causing vertigo that made her reach for the chair to steady herself.

"Would you like a drink?" she asked, trying to make conversation.

"I'm good right now, thanks," Brit said, and took a seat where Sal indicated.

"So, I hear we're going to work together." Alex set the bucket on the table and took a seat on a glider across from Brit's chair, wanting a good place from where she could talk to Brit and check out her sexy legs. Sal hadn't mentioned that Brit was gorgeous, which she was, or gay, which Alex suspected from the way Brit had checked her out. She was distracted from her gawking by the unexpectedly exuberant response to her statement.

Brit's smile was huge, and she seemed to be bursting with happiness at the prospect of her job. "Yes. A full-time teaching job!"

Alex laughed, remembering her own reaction when she was hired not so long ago. She looked at Brit again and realized it wasn't so much her beauty that was the attraction, but the light in her eyes. Brit seemed to glow from within, which drew Alex like bugs to the zapper on a warm summer's night. And Alex sucked in a breath as she realized that she had, in fact, been zapped.

Everyone laughed, and Sue replied, "Well, your first job certainly is exciting. Congratulations."

"Thanks. Sue, were you a teacher, too?"

She laughed. "Nothing so exciting. I was a stockbroker. A long, long time ago. Now I'm retired."

"How's that going?" she asked.

Both Sal and Sue laughed. "It's exhausting," they said in unison.

They told her about their agenda of golf leagues, volunteer work, gardening, and exotic vacations.

"And you live here full time?" Brit asked.

"Yeah, this is it. With our parents gone, we decided to move toward friendlier, warmer skies. And we're close enough to home that we can visit—but quite honestly, our friends prefer to come here."

Brit gestured to the water beyond their tree-lined yard. "I can see why."

Sue wiped a bead of sweat from her brow. "It is lovely, but I've had enough of it for today. I need a change of venue," she said, and looked at all of them. "This heat is getting to me. Let's take the party inside."

Sal looked like she might argue but then suddenly stood. "You're right, Suzie. It's too hot out here."

It was technically evening, and although the sun had begun its westward descent, it still cast powerful rays across the open space of the patio. Sal stood and offered Sue her hand, and with Alex once again carrying the drinks, they headed indoors.

"You have a beautiful home," Brit said as she looked around. Inside the sliding-glass doors was a dining room, with a wall of glass facing the water. On the opposite side of this large, open-style room was a couch with two chairs, a television, and all the furnishings of a living room. It, too, had a wall of glass looking out at the patio, the landscape, and the cove beyond.

Sal beamed. "Thank you," she said, and pointed them in that direction, where they all made themselves comfortable. Seated in a chair where she could easily watch the other three women, Britain chose a bottle of water from the collection in the oversized bucket, ignoring the soda, beer, and wine coolers she saw. She wanted to keep her wits intact, to make a good impression, and she suspected the intoxicating Alex Dalton could fluster her even without the assistance of alcohol. If she started drinking, Brit would be in trouble for sure.

Brit waved toward the wall of glass. "What a view."

"Well, yes, it is. It was the main reason we bought the house."

"Why Rehoboth?" Brit asked, although she suspected she knew the answer.

"It's gay. We wanted to be somewhere where we're the rule instead

of the exception. And besides, we have great restaurants, a nice beach, and a dozen wonderful golf courses."

Brit agreed on all counts. "Where do you play?" she asked.

"Oh, all over. We're in a league, but otherwise we don't limit ourselves. How about you, Britain? Do you play?"

"Yes, as a matter of fact, I do."

"So you live in Bear Creek? Do you play at Wilkes-Barre Muni? That's in Bear Creek, isn't it?" Alex asked.

Brit met her gaze and nodded. Sally must have mentioned her hometown to Alex. The Wilkes-Barre Municipal course wasn't actually located in Wilkes-Barre, but just a few miles from Brit's parents' place. "Sometimes. Mostly I play at Red Fox Run. I'm in the league there."

Alex raised an interested eyebrow. "I love The Run. Do you play the team matches? You may have played against my mom," Alex said.

Shifting her position to see Alex more easily, Brit smiled. "As a matter of fact, I do. What club does she play for?"

"Mountain Meadows."

Brit nodded. The Meadows was one of her favorite courses, and she told Alex so. "What's your mom's name? What group is she in?"

"Liz. Liz Dalton. I think she's in the second flight."

Pursing her lips, Brit tried to place the name. "I don't think I've met her. Is she tall like you? I'd probably remember that."

Alex nodded. "I can look at my mom and tell what I'll look like in thirty years."

Their eyes met again, and Brit couldn't help the slight upturn at the corners of her mouth. "Then we haven't met." Brit definitely would have remembered a woman who looked like Alex, even a slightly more mature model. Brit realized she was flirting but couldn't help herself. Alex was gorgeous and, so far, seemed able to carry on an intelligent conversation. Was she single? More importantly, was she gay?

Then Brit remembered her manners. She wasn't in the habit of throwing herself at women, even if they were gorgeous, so she wiped the smirk off her face and thought of her mother's prim-and-proper demeanor. It wasn't Brit who responded, but her inner mother. "Do you play, Alex?"

"Yes, as much as I can. Perhaps before the weather turns, you can join me at The Meadows. It's not far from school."

Brit loved the idea of playing at one of her favorite courses, and she'd like the chance to spend a little time with Alex and get to know her better. "I'd love to."

"Alex was a sub in the league this year, and she kicked butt," Sue offered.

Brit laughed. She'd only been in Sue's company for a few minutes, but already she could tell that comment was out of character for the sweet and refined lady.

"Really?" Brit asked.

Sal told the story about Alex teaming up with the league to bring down the cheater. "Three-quarters of the way through the summer, when Ann Marie realized she had no chance of making the playoffs to defend her championship, she mysteriously injured her shoulder and withdrew from the league."

Brit offered her knuckles to Alex in congratulations. She hated cheaters, too. They violated the spirit of the game, and no matter what the sport, integrity was important. It carried over to all aspects of life, and people who cheated at sports couldn't be trusted off the field, either. The thought of her personal life flashed across her mind, and the lies she was telling her family, but she quickly buried it. That was different.

"You guys rock," she said. "So you spend your summers here, too?" Brit asked, directing the question at Alex.

"Yep. I come down the day school lets out and basically stay the summer."

"That must be a lot of fun. Maybe I'll get a job here one day so I can spend the summer at the beach."

Alex looked at her intently with those bright blue eyes. "Who says you need a job? Just come."

Brit laughed. "Well, Alex, I'm used to sleeping in a bed and bathing in a tub. If I didn't have a job I'd have to sleep on the beach and wash in the ocean, because I'm pretty much destitute right now."

"Well, I have a place that's very reasonably priced, so if we're still speaking at the end of the school year, I can hook you up."

Brit opened her eyes wide. What a great time that would be, spending the entire summer in the town she loved so much. There were so many rainbow flags and people like Sally and Sue. And Alex. Whether she could afford it was another matter, and she was sure

Alex was just making conversation when she suggested Brit spend the summer in Rehoboth, but still, the thought was intoxicating. "Sounds good to me," she replied.

Alex offered knuckles again. "It's a date," she said.

Brit flushed from her head to her painted toes peeking from her slides. Alex was flirting with her, and while it wasn't unwelcome, it was unexpected. She'd come to Sally's house to meet a friend, nothing more. Alex's good looks and flirty manner had thrown Brit off balance. She needed to change the subject.

"Do you work down here?" Brit asked.

"No, I'm just a beach bum," Alex said, without a hint of defensiveness.

"Where do you stay when you're at the beach?" Sue directed her question to Brit, and Brit told them about the house her family had been renting for years.

"Do you ever come with friends?" Alex asked. "Stay in Rehoboth?"

Brit shook her head. She felt uncomfortable with Alex's questions. Even though they seemed innocent enough, Brit felt like Alex was looking a little too closely at her, examining her. Why did that bother her? Women didn't usually affect her in this way. The need to switch positions and tuck back the stray hair behind her ears, to clear her throat—they were all suddenly irrepressible urges. This unrest was unsettling. Brit needed to ask more questions and answer fewer. "Where do you stay, Alex?" she asked.

"I share a condo." Alex told Brit about the house she shared with her friends and listed half a dozen reasons Brit should spend the next summer in Rehoboth. With some playful coaxing from Alex, Brit admitted it sounded great. Then Sal gave them the history of their house hunting and how they'd come to find their dream home beside the Rehoboth Bay, and Brit's anxiety dissipated.

Brit commented on the layout of the house. "This is perfect for entertaining."

"And we do," Sue said. "There's a kitchen to die for just behind us."

"Really?"

"Yeah. Do you cook?"

Brit shrugged. Her dorm and college apartments hadn't lent themselves to cooking much more than simple dishes, and while her

parents' house featured a gourmet kitchen, it also had her mother at the helm. Brit could cook, but she simply wasn't allowed to. "I'm okay."

"What do you like to cook?" Alex asked, her blue eyes focused intently on Brit in a way that made her feel naked, as if Alex could see it all—the dorm-room Crock Pot, the aged oven in her off-campus apartment, and the Thanksgiving turkey at her mother's house. Instead of intimidating her, Alex's interest gave her the confidence to speak.

"Everything. I like watching cooking shows and finding recipes in magazines. I like to try new things. I'll eat anything that's not still moving, so I try to cook all kinds of foods. How about you?"

"Peanut butter and jelly is about it. But I love to eat, so I tend to find friends who can cook. We may just make a good team."

Brit shook her head. "No, no, no. That's not how it works. You have to help if you want to eat, Alex."

"But I'd hurt the food. Its own mother wouldn't recognize it when I was done with it."

Brit laughed. "You can be the sous chef."

Alex shook her head and pointed at Sue. "No, she's the Sue chef. I'm just the food taster."

"And a great cleaner-upper," Sue said, defending Alex's honor.

"Yes. I'll clean everything and put it all away. I'm very talented at dishwashing."

"I'll let you show off your skills in a little while. Are you ladies getting hungry?" Sue asked.

Glancing at the clock, Britain was surprised to see it was nearly seven. They'd been talking for an hour. "Yeah, I guess I am."

In the dining room, Sal served fruit in chilled glasses and they switched to a light chardonnay. Brit decided to have a glass of the wine. It was one of her favorites, and she'd relaxed enough to know she could enjoy a glass of it. Dinner consisted of pasta with shrimp, and more fruit—this time in a tart—followed for dessert, compliments of Brit.

Brit studied the tart for a moment before piercing a raspberry with her fork. "I can't ever get mine to stay crisp like this. The crust gets soggy."

"So you bake, too?"

"Oh, yeah. I love to bake."

Alex smiled. "That sounds perfect. I like to eat. Baked goods, I mean."

Brit swallowed, flushed under the intensity of Alex's gaze. Was Alex really flirting with her? Seriously? Their eyes met, and Brit felt breathless, immediately regretting the wine. It was making her woozy.

"Well, let's get this stuff put away," Sal suggested, breaking the spell. Brit was again surprised by how quickly time passed as they cleared the dinner table and retreated to the living room. They'd been talking and laughing and sharing stories for nearly three hours.

"So, tell me about your name," Alex suggested to Brit as she looked at her with mischief in her eyes. This was definitely flirting, Brit thought. They were once again relaxed in the comfy leather chairs, separated only by a cocktail table. "I suspect there must be a story behind it."

Brit rolled her eyes. "Yes, lucky me. I'm named after the trip to England my parents canceled because of my impending birth."

Sue looked perplexed. "What happened?"

"My mom's due date was early summer. She would have been in labor in London while my dad was at Wimbledon watching tennis."

"Fortunately, they didn't name you Wimbledon," Alex said.

"London? They could have gone with London," Sal suggested.

Brit chuckled. "I think I lucked out with Britain. Most people call me Brit and never know I'm not just another Brittany."

"It beats Wimmy and Lonny. I like it," Alex said. "It's sophisticated but fun at the same time."

"What about you? Is Alex short for something else, or are you just Alex?"

Alex seemed to contemplate her answer. How hard could it be? It was her name, after all. Or maybe she was debating whether she should answer. Brit was still wondering why when Alex's voice surprised her. "Alexis."

Brit pursed her lips and studied Alex, suspecting from the hesitation she wasn't thrilled with her parent's choice of baby names. "It sounds goddess-like."

Sal and Sue burst into laughter and Brit just stared, until Alex began laughing, too. "Okay, what did I miss?" she asked finally.

Alex frowned. "I'm not much of a goddess, Britain."

Brit studied Alex for a moment. In her fitted tank and cargo shorts, with lean muscle visible on every inch of exposed flesh, she did appear to be quite the goddess.

"Just what goddess would you be? Alexis, the Golf Goddess?" Sue asked around the wineglass hovering at her lips.

Alex bit her lip and shook her head, taking the teasing in stride.

"How about Nike, the Goddess of Victory?" Brit suggested, and Alex pierced her with those eyes yet again as her gaze shifted. And then they turned light again, and Brit could imagine laughter in Alex's mind.

"I thought Nike made basketball sneakers," she retorted.

They stared at each other for a moment, until Sal broke the silence. Brit felt grateful.

"Speaking of basketball, when does your season start, Alex?"

Alex nodded. "Thank you for changing that subject, Coach. I owe you," she said, and she shared her schedule with them.

"This must be so exciting for you," Brit added. Although she had no experience coaching, basketball was one of her great passions. Since first dribbling a basketball at the age of five, she'd never stopped. She'd played at every level and held more records than she could count. Yet she was twenty-two now, out of college, and with the exception of the recreational leagues, she wouldn't have much opportunity to play. If she wasn't ready to toss the sneakers in the can and grow up, coaching would be the next logical step in her basketball career. She loved the game and envied Alex that she was still so much a part of it.

"Yeah, it is."

"You're starting your career at such a young age. You have a chance to win a thousand games, just like Pat Summit." Brit's tone was teasing, yet Alex took it to heart.

"I'll be very pleased if I finish with a winning season." Alex appreciated Brit's enthusiasm, but in fact, she was quite concerned about winning. There had been tremendous pressure from one school board member to hire a more experienced coach, one who happened to be his relative. It was only with Sal's strong recommendation to her friends on the board that Alex would find a whistle around her neck in the fall.

Pushing her fear aside, Alex gave them the details about her upcoming basketball season. She'd been hired a few months earlier, after the previous coach had retired. Alex had been the assistant for two years, and she knew the players, and the system, so the transition was predicted to be manageable, but she was nervous, anyway. Suddenly, it all fell on her shoulders—the responsibility to get a dozen teenage

girls on the right bus, and to the right gym, and make sure their algebra homework was completed and their grades stayed in the comfort zone. They needed to learn plays and execute them and score and play defense, and win. Sportsmanship was important and grades were important, but in the end, if her team didn't win, she'd be tanked. Her athletic director had already told her as much.

"Will the team be good?" Sue asked.

Alex didn't want to get her hopes up, but she was excited about one particular player. "If the center has a good year, we might be okay. She's big, but she's not real confident."

"Who's that?" Sal asked. "Kelsey Kincaid?"

Alex knew Sal had never stopped following the team.

Suddenly Brit leaned forward. "Wait a minute. Kelsey? Like six-two Kelsey with short black hair?"

Alex nodded at Brit's description. "Yeah, sounds like. Do you know her?"

Brit pursed her lips. "Maybe. I've been playing at the park by my apartment for the past couple of weeks with a girl named Kelsey. And if this is your center, Alex, you have no worries. She's phenomenal."

Alex frowned. "That doesn't sound like my Kelsey. Mine's marginal."

Brit shrugged. "Well, this girl's going to be a senior at Endless Mountains, and how many six-two Kelseys can there be in one school? It has to be her. And she's great. She went to camps all summer and told me she worked hard on her game."

"Maybe it is her. I can only hope." Truthfully, Kelsey was the key. If Brit was right and this was the same player, it could make the difference in the season.

"Well, that would make things easier, huh, Coach?" Sal asked.

"It sure would. That and an assistant coach."

"So you haven't found someone yet?" Sal asked.

Alex sighed. "No such luck." Alex had asked half a dozen friends and associates, but for one reason or another, all had declined. She needed an assistant, someone she could depend on, someone who'd be there in those first days and weeks and months of her career—someone to talk with and bounce ideas off, and to share the triumphs and failures. Not to mention scouting opponents and helping run practices.

Sal looked directly at Brit and pursed her lips. "Brit," she asked finally, "what about you? Any interest in coaching?"

Britain's jaw dropped. She looked from Sal to Alex, her eyes wide open, but she said nothing.

Alex leaned closer to Brit, filled with excitement. During dinner they'd talked basketball, and Alex was aware of Britain's accomplishments on the court. She'd be perfect. "What do you think, Brit?" she asked.

"I have absolutely no experience," she confessed.

"Hey, neither do I!" Alex retorted, and they all laughed. Leaning back into her chair, Alex smiled hopefully. Hiring Brit would not only solve her problem, but it also would give her the opportunity to get to know her much better. During the basketball season, they'd spend most of their free time together, at strategy sessions, practices, and games. She only hoped she'd be able to concentrate on basketball with Brit around. She'd spent the evening trying hard to follow the conversation and ignore the distraction of Brit's big eyes and smile. Sticking to business would be a challenge, but one worth taking.

Sal tried reassuring Brit. "Brit, you played the point. You know the game. You know how to teach. You'd be a great coach. A natural."

"Alex, are you serious? Are you offering me the job?"

She turned her eyes to Alex, and at that moment Alex would have given her anything she asked—money, sex, her grandmother's diamonds. Anything for the beautiful woman with the great smile. A job was easy. Alex nodded, embarrassed that she hadn't thought of the idea herself. "Yes. It's a great idea."

Brit smiled. "Then, yes, I'll do it." She answered with such enthusiasm they couldn't help laughing. They talked for a few more minutes before Alex announced with regret that she had to say good night. "I'm meeting my roommates for a drink and should already be there."

"I should get going, too," Brit added.

"Hey," Alex said, addressing Brit, "would you like to join me?" The thought of extending her time with her new assistant appealed to her. They'd shared a really fun evening. Besides, she was curious about Brit's sexuality. Taking her to a bar where lesbian couples were openly affectionate would give Alex a chance to get a better read on her. Since

the bar had a large straight crowd as well, it wouldn't be uncomfortable for her either way.

Without seeming to give it any thought, Brit smiled and replied. "I'd love to."

CHAPTER NINE

TOO GOOD TO BE TRUE

Parking at the beach is a limited resource no matter what continent you're on, and such was the case in Rehoboth on this Saturday night. Brit had followed Alex to her condo, and she'd parked her car for the night, figuring she'd catch a ride home with her roommates. In a pinch, she could always walk. Now they circled the block around the Frogg Pond, trying to find a place for Brit's car.

"Turn right here," Alex suggested after they found no parking spots on the main street. The side streets were no different. In the end, they had to hoof it six blocks to the bar, and Britain suggested writing directions to help her find her way to her car. "Do you have any string?" Alex asked playfully.

Brit smiled. "Theseus?"

Alex nodded, impressed. "Very good. But you don't need a ball of string. I'll get you back safely."

The bar was crowded and noisy, and immediately they were thrust together as they stepped through the front door. Both of them looked down to where their arms touched, and then up. Their eyes met, and for a shocking moment Alex thought of kissing her, but then she was jostled from the side and the moment ended. And she was relieved. As much as she would have liked to, Alex thought kissing Brit wouldn't be such a good idea. Brit wasn't like any girl she'd ever met, and after just a few hours, Alex suspected she couldn't act with her the way she usually did. Brit wasn't going to be interested in a single night, and Alex was reminded that she didn't want that anymore, either. She'd enjoyed what she'd had with Anke. Maybe she was ready for the next step.

Looking over the top of the crowd of mostly women, Alex spotted her friends. The serious thoughts were disconcerting, and she suddenly felt the need for a little bit of space, and Kim and Tam would provide a great buffer. Then, without thinking, she grabbed Brit gently by the elbow and led her to a corner of the bar. "I see them."

Tam and Kim were seated at a cocktail table and already occupied the only two chairs in sight. A bucket sat on the table, and bottles of beer peeked through the blanket of ice that filled it.

After introductions, Alex took a beer for herself and offered one to Brit, who declined with a sigh. "I'd better stick to water. It's a long drive back to Bethany."

"Hey, you can crash at our place if you'd like," Kim offered.

Alex choked, and Tam, who was seated closest to where she stood, began beating on her back. "What happened? Are you okay?" she demanded.

Playfully, Alex pushed Tam's arm away. "I will be if you stop beating me up." She coughed a few more times to clear her airway.

Only Kim seemed to notice that Alex's choking happened when she suggested Brit stay the night. As Tam engaged Brit in conversation, Kim eyed Alex suspiciously.

"What?" Alex whispered defensively.

Kim shook her head, smiling. "If only I had your luck."

Alex feigned confusion but couldn't help smiling. As nonchalantly as possible she scanned the crowded bar. It was a typical mix—mostly young people, some in their thirties and forties, and an equal blend of gay and straight. At the table next to them, a woman had her arm draped casually around the waist of the woman beside her, and as Alex watched, the first playfully kissed the other's neck. At another table, a girl was sitting on the lap of her female date, and their intimacy level was way beyond casual.

Alex looked at Brit, who was talking with Tam while she scanned the crowd. She showed absolutely no reaction to the behavior these women displayed. Either she was very comfortable around lesbians or...well, she was obviously comfortable around lesbians. Did that mean she was gay, too? Alex could only hope.

A waitress approached, and when Brit ordered water, Alex took advantage of the interruption to engage her. She'd been chatting with Tam since they arrived at the bar, and Alex felt jealous. Because of

the noise level, conversation required very close proximity. "Are you having a good time?" Alex asked, leaning far into Brit's personal space.

Much to her delight, Brit moved even closer. "I'm having a wonderful time. Your friends seem very nice."

"They're okay." Alex smiled affectionately at them.

Brit asked, "How long have you known each other?" and leaned still closer to hear the answer. Alex was grateful for the noise that forced Brit to bridge the gap between them. This time Brit placed her hand gently on Alex's forearm as she spoke, and Alex had trouble answering the question as she focused on the heat of Brit's hand.

After another sip of beer, Alex told the story about how she'd met her friends in college. They laughed as they talked, and Brit couldn't help but think of her own college friends.

Would she have chosen the same friends if she'd been aware of her sexuality earlier, or would she have sought other lesbians, as Alex had done? She loved her friends, and it pained her to think of not having them in her life. Yet, it was even more painful to deceive them, pretending she understood their dating rituals and shared their attraction to men. She was attracted to women. Wouldn't it be wonderful if she could share that with the friends she loved so much, just as Alex did?

There was something comforting in the vision of the two casually intimate women at the next table. She'd felt the same way with Syl and Marianna, and at Sue and Sal's, and watching them interact had filled her with happiness. She definitely needed more lesbian friends, people who shared this aspect of her life.

"Do you guys want to get out of here?" Kim asked after yet another attempt to communicate over the background noise. "I can't hear myself think."

Alex looked to her for an answer, and Brit nodded. It was really loud, not to mention hot.

They left money for the waitress and then squeezed through the crowd and out the door and onto the sidewalk. The crowd was noisy outside as well, so they had to walk a ways just to be able to speak.

"Do you want to go back to our house?" Kim asked, "I think it's the only quiet place in town."

"No! It's too early," Tam exclaimed. "And it's our last night together. Let's go for a walk on the beach."

The night was perfect for a walk. It was still warm, but down by

the water it would be cooler, and Brit knew that above the glow of the streetlamp a million stars were twinkling in the night sky. She'd seen them at Sal's house where there were no distracting lights.

They all agreed with Tam's idea and began their stroll toward the ocean, stopping on the narrow sidewalks to allow others to pass. At the boardwalk they melted into the large crowd and headed south. After a few blocks, when the wooden planks beneath their feet ran out and the noise of the mob began to fade, they removed their shoes and continued their journey. The sand was cool and soft as it flowed between her toes, and Britain loved the freedom of being shoeless in the moonlight.

Before long they were at the water's edge, and to her surprise, Brit found that they had split into pairs, with her and Alex in the lead, matching strides as they dodged waves sneaking onto the shoreline. Brit was amazed at how right it felt to be beside Alex.

How right the entire night felt, from the moment she'd arrived at Sal's house. She'd enjoyed their company, and landed a new job. Now she was walking on the beach with a beautiful woman, under a sky full of stars and a big bright moon. That woman was amazing—tall, intelligent, funny, with an interest in sports and summers off to travel and play golf. Alex was perfect.

"So, do you come here often?" Brit asked, breaking the silence and steering her thoughts from a place she feared they were heading too quickly.

"Surprisingly, no."

"Really?" To Britain, walking on the beach was the best part of a beach vacation, especially in the evening, on nights like this, following a path laid out in the heavens. Of course, she was usually alone.

"Yeah. I guess when you're here all the time you just take it for granted."

"So you don't go to the beach at all?"

"Oh, no, of course I do. Every day. I was just talking about the moonlight walk. That, I never do."

Brit felt a sudden heat at Alex's confession. "I'm glad you've made the exception for me."

The bright moon lit their path, and Brit could discern the magnificent features of Alex's face. She snuck a glance her way and caught Alex looking back.

Alex quickly looked down and spoke. "Me, too."

They were quiet for a moment before Alex spoke again. "So, tell me why you decided to become a teacher."

"Hmm. I think the answer keeps changing. I used to think it's because teaching is important. America is way behind other countries in science and math, and that's going to cause problems for us all one day. We can't follow the rest of the world and still be a leader."

"Is it just science and math?" Alex asked. "Should we learn literature and music, too? Do we need to be leaders in those fields?"

"We should try to excel in every way we can. Each of us has different gifts and strengths, and we should all find ours and use them."

"If it were so easy," Alex said softly.

"Yeah, I hear you. But we can do this, Alex. We're so much better off than so many other people. We just don't realize it. We focus on what we don't have and what we want and forget our blessings. I did a service trip to Brazil this summer. We went to this small village and built a town hall with a classroom. They just wanted their children to learn basic math so they can count the money they make from their crops and not be cheated. They live in little huts and have no shoes, and they're happy anyway. Probably the happiest people I've ever known."

Alex was silent for a moment. "Were you tempted to stay?"

"Not at all!" Brit confessed her need for creature comforts, and Alex agreed with her.

"I try to live my life very simply, but I'd have a hard time without electricity and running water."

Brit laughed. "It was an eye-opening experience, that's for sure. But a good one. I feel more grounded now. Like I have my priorities in order."

"That's great. I try to live each day, not getting caught up in the worries and the what-ifs and money and prestige. I infuriate my parents."

"What do they do?"

"They're capitalists. They own car washes and Laundromats and dry-cleaning stores, and they're filthy rich. How about you?"

"My dad's a doctor. Cardiology. My mom was once a nurse, but she retired when she was thirty to focus on her career as a devoted wife and mother." There was no way she could keep the sarcasm from her voice.

"How'd she do?"

Apparently, Alex didn't notice the sarcasm, and Brit let it drop. Even though her mom tended to be tough, Brit loved her, and she had to admit she was a good mother. Mostly. "Fine, I guess. None of us are in jail."

"Hey, you two," Tam called from behind them, "if we don't turn around soon, we'll have to call a cab to get back."

Brit had been caught up in their conversation, watching the starry sky and the moonlit waves, with an occasional stolen glance at the woman beside her, so she was surprised when she looked back to see the lights of the boardwalk so far in the distance. They were on a quiet stretch of beach, the only light coming from the decks and windows of the houses a hundred yards back from the ocean, and of course that big, bright moon.

Alex looked up at the sky and then to her friends. "Let's sit for a while," she suggested. She wanted to go anywhere but back. This night had been so perfect she never wanted it to end.

They huddled a little more closely as they sat on the sand, but Alex kept a respectable distance from Brit, while her friends sat a few feet away. The sand was cool compared to the night air, but not uncomfortably so. Alex sat with her legs crossed, and Brit sat on her butt, knees bent and pulled up close, and long arms wrapped around them. She rested her head on her knees, and when Alex turned to her, their eyes were nearly level.

"This is nice," Brit said.

"It is." Alex smiled, feeling something unfamiliar and exciting and delightful. She liked Brit. In fact, she couldn't remember the last time she'd enjoyed another woman's company as much as she had this night.

She turned her gaze back to the ocean, forcing herself not to stare at Brit. Her long hair fell across her shoulders, glistening in the moonlight. Those same moonbeams kissed her nose and her cheeks and her lips. Perfect, inviting, they called to her. She'd never wanted to kiss someone so badly, yet she knew she shouldn't. She turned her focus to her friends.

"Can I lean on you?" Tam asked Kim.

"Sure," Kim replied, and Tam rested her back against Kim's chest and shoulder.

"Why don't we do this every night?" Tam asked.

"We should," Alex said softly.

Kim chimed in. "No argument from me."

"I do this every night," Brit told them. "Except there's no ocean. Just my deck and some trees and a clear, bright sky full of stars."

"We don't have stars in Philly," Kim informed her.

"I don't think I've ever seen this many," Tam said.

They were quiet again, and Alex's every sense was heightened as Brit reached her hand across the foot of space separating them. With a feather-like stroke, she touched her arm and whispered, "Thank you for inviting me to come with you tonight."

"You're welcome." Alex didn't even twitch, lest her action prompt Brit to move her fingers from her arm. Brit's touch was electrifying, but Kim's voice broke the spell.

"Tam, I need you to move," Kim said. "My arm's falling asleep."

"What? I thought you were strong."

"I am. You're just…"

"What? What? Were you going to say I'm fat?"

Alex stared, disbelieving, as the scene unfolded before her. With the fluid motion of a seasoned wrestler, Tam pushed Kim onto her back on the sand and twisted her own body to a position atop her. Kim didn't fight. Alex saw their eyes lock, and they stared at each other in the moonlight, seeming to forget the company that shared this section of beach. Then their lips met in a tender kiss.

It was an unexpected turn of events, not at all unpleasant, but Brit momentarily forgot her manners as she stared for a moment. Then she turned away, once again seeking the comfort of the ocean.

Alex's voice barely registered. "It's about time," she said.

Brit heard Alex move beside her and looked to find Alex's outstretched hand beckoning her. "Let's go, Brit. We'll give these two a bit of privacy."

Britain accepted the proffered hand and grabbed her sandals. She was effortlessly pulled to her feet, delighted that for a few seconds Alex didn't release her hand. But then she did, and they began to walk back toward civilization.

The steady rhythm of their tandem steps was comforting. It had been a whirlwind of an evening, and Brit was still spinning. She'd reconnected with Sally. She'd gotten a job as a basketball coach. She

was walking on the beach with the most attractive woman she'd ever met, who just happened to surround herself with lesbians.

"Sorry about that," Alex said after a few minutes.

Brit was genuinely surprised. She was anything but sorry about the way her evening had unfolded. "About what?"

"About the PDA."

Brit laughed and searched her mind for an appropriate rejoinder, something that would ease Alex's concerns and perhaps indicate that her own desires ran in a similar vein. Amazingly, after just one evening, Brit felt comfortable enough with Alex to reveal something people she'd known her whole life didn't know. "It's not quite as exciting as kissing a girl yourself, but watching two girls kiss isn't bad."

Alex threw her head back in laughter and made her own confession. "I wholeheartedly agree."

"What just happened?" Brit asked after a moment.

Alex explained.

"You mean they're not a couple?" Brit asked when she heard the story.

"Well," Alex said as she shrugged. "By now they might be."

"I wouldn't have guessed. They seem so sure of each other, so in love."

"Well, there you go. You've known them for an hour and you see it. I see it. Everyone but those two has known it all along."

Alex stopped walking, and talking, too. They'd reached the boardwalk, and it suddenly occurred to her that they had no plan, no destination in mind. It was after midnight yet she didn't feel a bit tired. In fact, the opposite was true. The new friendship forming between them had energized her, and she could have gone on talking to Brit all night. She didn't want their time together to end.

Taking the lead, Alex turned to Britain and raised an eyebrow. "Where to, Coach Dodge?" she asked softly, inviting Britain to dictate the night's direction.

Laughing at her new title, Brit bent to put her shoes back on, but before she could respond, a hand grabbed Alex's forearm and spun her around. Anke stood before them with a snarl on her face and fire in her eyes. Alex was stunned.

"You kick me out of your bed zis morning, and already you have somevon new zis night?"

Brit stared at Anke and stepped back.

"What are you doing here, Anke?" Alex couldn't disguise the surprise in her voice. "I thought you were leaving!"

"Obviously!" she hissed. "How long has zis bin goink on?" she demanded, nodding in Britain's direction.

"Anke, nothing's going on!" Alex said.

Brit looked scared as she started backing away. Alex wanted to tell her to stop, to wait, but before she could say anything, Anke began screaming.

"You are a whore!" Anke shouted as she raised her hand and tried to slap Alex. Only Alex's quick reflexes allowed her to block the blow. She held on to the arm that had tried to strike her, and Anke began wrestling to free it.

"Let me go! You're hurtink me!"

Stunned, Alex released her grip but stepped back, out of Anke's reach, and Anke abruptly turned and began marching down the boardwalk. "Anke, wait! Wait! Let me explain!" she shouted at her back.

Totally off balance, Alex turned to Brit, who'd already distanced herself by a few feet. "I'm so sorry, Brit. I have to go talk to her. I'll see you at school." Without waiting for Britain's reply, Alex turned and began running after Anke. She didn't owe Anke anything, not even an explanation, but she felt she needed to give her one anyway. Even though they'd agreed they could date other people, it was important for Alex to let her know she hadn't.

Wearing loafers, it didn't take Alex long to catch Anke, who was wearing slip-on backless sandals. Beside her, she slowed her stride and raised her arm to Anke's shoulder. Anke shrugged it off and kept walking. Alex tried again. "Anke, she's my new assistant coach! I just met her tonight!"

Anke stopped and turned to face Alex. "You jus meet her? She's your assistan and you take her for moonlight walk on the beach? You zink I'm stupit?"

"Yes! No!" Alex stammered. Flustered, she ran a hand through her hair. She felt like a rug had been pulled out from beneath her and she was lying stunned on the hard floor, looking up in confusion.

Although what she told Anke about Britain was true, Alex somehow felt she was lying. It seemed as if she'd always known Brit

and felt like she always wanted to. When she was walking with Brit on the beach, Alex wasn't sure where their night was heading—and she didn't care, as long as Britain continued to talk to her, and laugh with her, and make her feel lighter than air. But, now Britain was gone and probably thought her a total ass. A whore, as Anke had so eloquently described her.

Alex was left alone and disoriented, forced to deal with an irate former lover whom she had no desire to talk to. She sighed in frustration.

Seeming to sense Alex's emotions, Anke softened her posture and her tone. Motioning to a bench on the boardwalk looking out at the Atlantic, Anke sighed as well. "You vant to go sit and talk?"

Alex nodded, but before she moved she glanced down the boardwalk to where Britain had stood just a minute before. Of course, she was gone. Resigned, Alex walked beside Miss Bavaria, the envy of every unattached lesbian in the world, feeling anything but enviable.

❖

Standing on her deck, Britain studied the moonlight reflecting off the white tips of the waves that crashed on the shore before her. The moon was still bright, but the sandy beach no longer beckoned her. She was close enough to hear the sounds of the ocean, yet so very far away that she heard nothing at all.

The roads were virtually deserted at this late hour, and it had taken her less than forty minutes to find her car and navigate it back to Bethany Beach. Yet she felt like years had passed since that moment on the boardwalk when Anke had appeared. It surely had been a lifetime ago that she began pedaling her bike into the sunrise and met Sal on Penny Lane. Too much had happened in that span for it to have only been one single day.

Britain's head was spinning. Spending the evening with those women, dining together and sharing stories, she'd felt more comfortable than she'd ever felt in her life. More than with her closest friends, from whom she'd been hiding her sexuality. Certainly more so than with her family.

Alex had seemed to be not only an ally who would help show her the ropes at school, but perhaps also a friend. Perhaps much more than that. Brit had felt an attraction to Alex she'd never felt before, and she

knew Alex had felt something, too. Alex had been flirting with her from the first, and Brit had flirted right back. It had been wonderful.

Then the magic carpet they'd been riding had come crashing down. The wind had been knocked out of her, and she couldn't seem to catch her breath.

Brit stood there watching the waves but seeing Alex's face, misery squeezing her heart with the thought that Alex was already attached. And why shouldn't she be? With all her assets—the looks, the brains, the wit—she was every woman's fantasy. Even more disturbing to Brit was her own poor judgment, for she hadn't seen the crash coming. She was normally cautious, especially with her heart. She should have known Alex had a girlfriend. She should have asked.

What a fool she'd been to think a woman as attractive as Alex would be interested in her. She wasn't interested in anything but a fun night. Alex had been playing with her. *Where to, Coach Dodge?* had clearly been an invitation, and if Anke hadn't showed up when she did, Brit just might have accepted it.

How could she have been so stupid?

Brit sighed. She had a tough decision to make. Could she really coach beside Alex, knowing how expertly Alex had played her? Could she sit beside her on the bench for an entire season and still keep Alex at a safe distance from her heart? Remembering the attraction she'd felt, Brit wasn't sure she could.

CHAPTER TEN

THE COWBOY AND THE RUSTLER

Two hundred miles to the north, the same stars lit a clear sky in the Pocono Mountains. Keeping to the shadows, P.J. parked his bike next to the back porch off his grandfather's kitchen. It had been a bitch of a ride over four miles of dark, hilly roads, but the ride home would be mostly downhill. And his pockets would be holding just a few more of the dollars he needed so much more than his grandfather did.

How did he ever get messed up in this gambling business? It had started so innocuously, taking bets at the bakery. Customers came in, handed him their slips of paper with a ten or a twenty, or, occasionally, a hundred-dollar bill. Then he'd begun wagering himself, only a few dollars at first, usually on his favorite teams, like the Phillies and the Eagles. As time went on his bets grew, until he was borrowing money from the cash register at the bakery and his grandfather's cereal box. Sometimes he won, most times he didn't. Then there were times like this, when he lost really big.

One of the long shots whose bet he'd pocketed had actually won. Some fucker named Liam Walsh had bet a hundred bucks that he could pick the winners of ten college football games. Against the odds, he'd done it. He had a thousand-dollar payoff coming, and not only did P.J. lose the hundred-dollar bet he'd placed with Liam's money, but he also had to pay Liam from his own pocket. Hence this middle-of-the-night trek to his grandfather's house.

What a difference those four miles made in the landscape of the neighborhoods, P.J. observed as he hugged the house, careful to stay hidden away from the eyes of the neighbors who'd been watching out for each other during all the years of their long lifetimes. Only a

dozen yards separated the lovely old homes on this street, the trees the occasional sentinel standing watch over an expansive front lawn. In his new, modern neighborhood, his house was surrounded by trees, built into a small clearing in an old forest, just like the other twenty houses in the development, and the only evidence it existed from the vantage point of the road was the mailbox posted at the entrance of a narrow swath of driveway. As he skulked through the night, he enjoyed a sliver of satisfaction knowing that if he ever had to rob his own house, he could do the job with considerable more ease than this one.

Inside the kitchen door, he turned on the flashlight he wore on the band around his head. Its narrow beam of light pointed directly at its target, and he walked purposefully toward the cupboard and the Cheerios box within. Just as he had on a half-dozen prior occasions, he opened the door and the box and felt within his fingers the refreshingly cool texture of the money he so desperately needed. And as he had on prior occasions, he didn't bother to count. He just closed his fist around the money and pulled it from the box. This time, though, something different happened. He was shot in the eyes by the bright waves of light that suddenly flooded the kitchen.

Startled, P.J jumped back and turned his head. If he hadn't been so tempted to cry, he might have laughed at the sight before him. His eighty-year-old grandfather, dressed in a cowboy hat and Western shirt, was pointing a very long gun at him. His feet were covered by embroidered cowboy boots and propped up on a chair, and the gun rested in his lap. The scene reminded him of a cowboy movie, but the gun was real, and probably loaded. His grandfather kept it for protection against intruders. Like him.

But P.J. wasn't *really* an intruder. He was his grandson. Thinking fast, P.J. attempted to humor him. "What's goin' on, Papa? Do you think you're starring in a Western?"

Playing the part, his grandfather snorted and turned his head so that only one angry eye met his. "Some rustlers have been movin' through these parts, makin' off with my money."

P.J. was shocked. His grandfather could barely see, as evidenced by the patches of facial hair that went untouched by his razor and the spots of food P.J. had to wash from the clean dishes left in the sink to dry. How in the hell could he count money? Why would he think to do it? P.J. had been very careful.

As if reading his mind, his grandfather elaborated. "I've been saving my money since I was your age, P.J., and countin' it is one of my few pleasures. A few months ago I noticed two hundred dollars missing, and since then I've been tracking you and studying your methods. I've made it hard for you by putting that television in here and staying in the kitchen during the day, so I figured you'd have to plan a covert night mission. Since I can't see too well at night, no one can blame me if I drill you full of holes."

"Papa! You can't shoot me! I'm your grandson."

"And a lousy excuse for one, if you ask me. If you're startin' a life of crime at your age, there's goin' to be a jail cell in your future. I should do you and the world a favor by puttin' ya down right now."

"Papa, please!" P.J. looked around nervously, searching for an avenue of escape. The front door and all the windows would only take him closer to his deranged grandfather, and a run toward the back door through which he'd entered would equally expose him. For the moment, staying put and outsmarting him seemed the best option.

"Give me one reason why I shouldn't pop ya full of lead!"

P.J. shouted the first thing that came to mind. "Mom and Dad would be devastated!"

Rheumy eyes hooded by bushy, furrowed brows studied his for a moment, and then he nodded and motioned to the table. "Sit down and tell me what's goin' on. Why does a spoiled rotten kid have to steal?"

Now P.J. was pissed. He didn't even try to keep his voice low. No one else was in the old house, and now that he was inside, the thick walls and windows would filter his voice from the neighbors' ears. "Spoiled? Are you kidding me? I guess you haven't noticed, but I haven't been spoiled in a long time, Pop. I have a job while my friends are out playing sports. I don't ski anymore, because the lift tickets are too expensive. There's no Hummer parked in my driveway, and we haven't had a family vacation in three years. My friends went to Colorado for the summer, and I'm selling friggin' donuts to buy school clothes!"

Those old eyes hadn't moved, and apparently his grandfather hadn't been either. His tale of woe didn't arouse any sympathy. "What I'm hearin' isn't so much about you, P.J., as it is about your friends. It's not your concern what they're doin'. You have to worry about what you're doin', and where you're goin'. Yes, your parents made you get a

job—to teach you responsibility. And if they weren't responsible, if they hadn't saved their money and managed it all these years, they would have lost that big house you live in. The bank would have snatched it faster than you can blink an eye.

"But you still have a house, and clothes on your back, and food in your belly. And you have one more, important thing—a future. You have a chance to make whatever you want out of your life. Your parents have worked hard to give you that, and it's the most important gift anyone can have. Opportunity. Why the hell are you screwin' it up by stealin' my money? What if I call the police? You goin' to get into college with a police record? Or do you wanna make a career in the donut business?"

P.J. knew his grandfather wouldn't understand if he told him, and he couldn't help him in any way other than financially. He was frail, old, and apparently crazy, with cowboy fantasies. But maybe, just this once, he could help. And then P.J. would get it together. He'd straighten out. His grandfather was right. He did have a future, if he chose not to fuck it up. "It's a girl, Papa. I needed money for an abortion, and I borrowed it, and now I have to pay it back, with interest."

Using the gun for support, his grandfather stood. "Put your hands in the air!" he commanded, and for the first time, P.J. realized he was still holding the money he'd intended to steal.

"Leave my money on the table," his grandfather ordered him.

He nodded toward the door. "Walk!"

At the door, P.J. hesitated.

"Open it!" his grandfather ordered him again.

P.J. turned, his hands still raised above his head. "Please, Papa. I'm gonna get hurt if I don't have that money!"

"You weren't raised to steal or to kill babies, kid. If you figured out how to do all that, you can figure a way out of this mess. And one more thing, in case you're thinking of addin' murder to your resume—I talked to my lawyer and told him you were stealin' from me. He recommended I turn you over to the police to teach you a lesson. He's probably right. But I'm not goin' to. I don't ever wanna see your face again, though. And if anything funny happens to me, you'll be the first one they look for. Now, get outta my sight!"

On the porch, P.J. sat and buried his head in his hands. What the fuck was he going to do now? If he didn't have a thousand dollars in

the morning, he'd have a few broken ribs instead. Running his fingers through his hair, long overdue for a trim, he pondered his options. Rationalizing with The Man wasn't an option. P.J. had seen people attempt that approach and fail miserably. His parents would probably react much the same way as his grandfather had, or perhaps they'd do something even more drastic, like try to speak to The Man themselves. No, he couldn't go to them with this problem.

Then a possible solution occurred to him. Wes would help. His brother loved him, and he was smart. He'd figure out what to do.

Pedaling hard through the night, P.J. was back home twenty minutes later, and, sitting beside his brother on the bed, he told him everything. For the first time since his problems began, he unburdened himself with a cleansing confession, and as he'd hoped, Wes approached the problem not with anger, but with the analytical mind that made him so good at problem solving.

"Let's talk to him," he said after a few minutes.

"What? No! He doesn't want to talk. He wants to hurt people!"

"I understand that, P., I do. But he's a businessman, and businessmen do business. Let's see what we can offer him. Maybe it's a payment plan, or maybe another job we can do for him. We'll figure it out."

P.J. looked at the clock. It was just after two in the morning. He'd never sleep, but he should try. Apparently, his brother thought the same thing. "We'll talk to him in the morning," Wes said, and then ran a loving hand through P.J.'s hair. "Get some sleep now."

P.J. didn't sleep, and for once he was ready before anyone else in the house. "I won't see you tonight," his mother said. "I'm working a double. There's leftover lasagna for dinner. Bring home some fresh bread and you'll be fine."

"Okay, Mom," he said and suddenly felt guilty for what he'd done. She'd gone back to nursing when his father lost his job, and at fifty years old, those doubles weren't easy. But she did them anyway. And his father now used his mechanical-engineering degree in a department store, a job that was both a demotion in pay and stature, but he happily went to work every day, and some nights, too. This so the family wouldn't have to move, so P.J. wouldn't have to switch to a lower-ranked school and lose his friends. So his life would be better. To give him an opportunity. And how was he repaying them?

Promising himself he'd turn his life around, he read the morning paper, waiting for Wes. The headlines didn't interest him much, but he read them anyway, stalling until he read the sports scores.

"Ready?" Wes asked half an hour later.

P.J. nodded, and they climbed together into the old Toyota Camry that had been his father's last car. "What are we going to do?" P.J. asked a moment later.

Wes shrugged. "I'm not sure, but we'll do it together."

Suddenly, P.J. was filled with dread. This had been a stupid idea, recruiting his wimpy, nerdy brother when he needed a linebacker or a hockey player. But he really had no other ideas, and the wheels were already turning, taking him to whatever destiny was in store for him.

The drive was short, and they didn't speak again. He sensed his brother was as nervous as he was. P.J. told him where to park, and they looked at each other. "Ready?" Wes asked, and P.J. nodded. He had to do this.

Wes followed him through an unlocked side-entrance door, down a series of corridors, and stopped when P.J. did, in front of an open door.

"Hey, Little Man! You're here early." The Man's greeting was playful and light, but P.J. knew he could grow dark and dangerous very quickly. As Wes pushed him aside and faced The Man, P.J. feared he was witnessing such a transition now. The Man's face contorted as he looked from brother to brother and back again.

"Who the fuck are you?" he demanded, studying the potential threat before him.

"Weston Blackwell, IV. I'm P.J.'s brother."

"Oh, nice to meet you. But I'm not hiring right now."

"I'm not here about a job. P.J. has a little problem. Tell him, P."

P.J. swallowed and blurted out the details of his crime before he had a chance to change his mind.

The Man leaned forward in his chair, and pointed a finger at Wes. He squinted and his face contorted in anger. "You think you can say you're sorry and all will be forgotten? That's not the way it goes, Little Man. There's always punishment when you screw up."

Wes spoke. "See, the thing is, P.J. is only seventeen. He doesn't make much money, so he can't pay you back. Not today, anyway. I came with him to see if we could work out some sort of payment plan."

The Man shook his head and laughed, softly, staring at points

high up on the unadorned wall. Then his laughter became louder and sinister, and his gaze focused on Wes. "There's no payment plan. I get my money or he gets hurt. And maybe you do, too, for butting into my business."

Wes swallowed, and P.J. watched, helplessly mute as his brother dug at his own cuticles, a sign of his anxiety. "If you hurt my brother, you'll never get the money. And maybe my parents might even find out and go to the police."

The Man pounded his desk and sneered. "I own the police," he boasted, and P.J. sensed the truth in his statement, for how else could an illegal operation like this thrive right out in the open?

Wes nodded. "There must be some service you need that we can provide. I'm asking this because he's my brother." Wes nodded at P.J. and shrugged. "He's young and stupid, and it's up to people like you and me to teach him the ropes. You're teaching him a good lesson, you know?"

Apparently, The Man liked the praise or the image of himself as a role model, for suddenly his posture relaxed and his expression softened. "What kind of skills do you have? What can you do for me?"

Chapter Eleven

Let's Be Friends

"H ey, how are you?"

Alex turned toward the voice she'd heard playing in her mind for days. The eyes that met hers were indeed as blue as she remembered. The smile was hesitant, and for that, Alex knew she was responsible. Thoughts of Britain Dodge had haunted her for all of the minutes and hours and days since she'd run from her on the boardwalk, and if she weren't so totally humiliated by the end of that evening, she would have called Brit the next morning to see her again. But the evening had ended badly, and Alex had needed this time to recover her dignity and figure out what to do next. In fact, she could probably use another decade or so, but here she was, in the auditorium of the high school, facing the only woman on the planet who made her nervous.

The entire morning had been consumed by an in-service meeting at the high school. Arriving early so she could speak with Brit hadn't worked out. Alex couldn't find her anywhere. Filled with a sense of dread, she worried Brit might have changed her mind about the job. Silly, but the thought of not seeing her turned Alex's mood sour. During a minute-long pause between speakers when she'd stood to stretch, Alex had spotted her in a small group at the back of the room. At her height, Brit literally was heads above the rest.

When the break was announced, Alex should have sought her new colleague in the horde of teachers exiting the high-school auditorium. Instead, she'd held back, choosing to delay the inevitable meeting. Part of her regretted offering Brit the coaching job. Just a small part. She really wanted to coach with Brit. That wasn't the problem. That she wanted to spend time with Brit was the problem. That she'd been

consumed by thoughts of her was the problem. That she longed to do things to take that hesitant smile and turn it into a vibrant one of welcome—that was also the problem. The way their last time together had ended was perhaps the biggest problem of all.

It amazed her that she'd lived so long and had never fallen in love, had never even really had a significant romantic relationship, yet in just a few hours Brit had sent her world spinning. In that short time frame she'd managed what others hadn't accomplished in many years. She had Alex thinking about more. To hell with her illness and freedom and no commitments. Britain Dodge had truly zapped her.

Brit had known this moment was coming, but she still found herself unprepared for meeting Alex again. In fact, she'd been avoiding her. If their evening on the beach had ended any other way, Brit would have called Alex. Perhaps they might have driven to school together, or met for lunch to talk about the upcoming year. Enjoyed that round of golf at Mountain Meadows. But after it all went wrong, Brit didn't have the heart to do that to herself. The memories were bad enough—being with the woman who'd burned her with so quick and hot a fire was just asking for more pain.

In her mind, she'd replayed the scene on the boardwalk a thousand times, still dumbfounded by how quickly she'd gone from the elation at meeting such an attractive woman as Alex to the dejection she felt after Anke appeared. Battling the attraction she'd felt for Alex would be a huge challenge, and Britain wasn't ready for it. She wasn't sure if she'd ever be ready to look into those eyes and keep her heart at a distance. She'd reconsidered the coaching job. She'd reconsidered the teaching job. Hell, she'd even reconsidered her friendship with Sal. There was nothing she wanted from Alex. That was about all she could handle.

Yet those eyes were so blue, and instead of the gentle rebuff she'd planned when they met again, she felt her heart melting under the heat of Alex's gaze. "Hi," she said simply.

"I am so sorry about the night on the boardwalk," Alex told her, and her eyes turned a darker shade of blue as emotion welled within them.

"You don't have to apologize, Alex," Brit replied, and offered a small smile of understanding before she looked away.

"What would you like?" the woman making sandwiches in the cafeteria lunch line asked them. The lunch was free today, with a salad

bar and made-to-order sandwiches, pasta salad, and fruit. They gave their requests.

Gently, Alex held Brit's elbow to stop her from advancing along the deli counter, to stop her from running away. Alex had to make it right with Britain again. She'd felt an attraction that night she'd never felt before, and if she had any sense at all of women—and Alex liked to think she was an expert on the matter—Britain had felt it, too.

"Alex, honestly, you owe me nothing," Brit said, her voice very neutral as she stared ahead.

"Please. Meet me after the in-service. We can just talk." Alex knew she sounded desperate, and she'd never had to beg for a woman's attention before, but she would if she had to.

Alex held her breath as Brit studied her, searching her face for something. Then she reluctantly agreed to meet Alex at South Abington Park that afternoon and left Alex staring after her as she walked away to sit with her new colleagues. When the in-service resumed after lunch, Alex was there in body only. It was impossible to concentrate on the school district's official sexual-harassment policy and changes in the health-insurance plans offered. Inclusion and curriculum changes went right over her head. All she could think of was Brit.

When the conference adjourned for the day, Alex was surprised to find Brit waiting at the back of the auditorium. She hadn't seemed eager to meet her, so Alex just assumed she'd see Brit at the park.

Brit studied Alex as she approached the rear of the auditorium. Wearing a T-shirt and golf shorts with her sneakers, Alex looked relaxed, yet Brit sensed her tension. When she spoke, though, even her voice was strained. "Congratulations, Brit. You've finished your first full day as a teacher."

Brit smiled as the reality of Alex's words hit her. She looked around the large auditorium with its cushioned seats, three sections on the main level and two balcony areas in the rear. It was decorated in green and white, the district's colors, and behind the stage, the word FALCONS was printed in large letters on the drawn curtain. The podium on the stage was adorned with the school's emblem. *Her* school's emblem. It was official. She really was a teacher. "Thanks," she said as she looked around again.

"Do you want to follow me?" Alex asked, wasting no time.

"Sure," she answered, and they began the brief trek to the faculty

parking lot. They walked in silence, and Brit was even more aware of Alex's angst. This tension in Alex definitely hadn't been there at Sal and Sue's, or at the Frogg Pond, or on Rehoboth Beach. Was it the back-to-school blues? Or trouble with Anke? She was tempted to break the silence, to ease Alex's concern, but she just wasn't sure what to say. And then they were at their cars, and the moment passed.

"This is me," Alex said as they reached a black SUV much different from the Jeep she remembered from Sal and Sue's house.

"New car?"

"Nah. Just more practical. I leave the Jeep at the beach so I can have fun all summer."

Brit pursed her lips in contemplation. Before she could catch herself, she replied, "I'll bet you do have fun."

Alex cringed, but Brit smiled and then turned away. Watching as Brit walked to her car, she exhaled some of the tension that had built up on the short walk from the school. She needed to tell Britain what had happened that night on the boardwalk or she would explode. She was still reeling from the confrontation with Anke, and the days that had passed hadn't helped.

The drive from the high school to the park took just a few minutes. Parking spaces were scarce, and by the time Alex had parked the car and walked to Brit's, Brit had changed from sandals to sneakers. With the capri pants she wore, the sneakers were perfect. After locking her car, she and Brit entered the flow of pedestrian traffic moving toward the park's center.

A baseball and soccer complex took up the entire space on one side of the park, while volleyball and a picnic area formed another border. Beyond were basketball courts and a children's play area. Many of the people were bypassing all these options and heading over a covered bridge and into the woods to enjoy the walking trails. Without discussion, the two of them gravitated in that direction.

Brit glanced at the basketball courts where she'd been playing lately. They were jammed with players, but none of them looked familiar to her. Kelsey, the young woman she'd met, wasn't around today, but the thought of her reminded Brit that she needed to inform Alex that she'd changed her mind about coaching. She just wasn't sure she had the courage to say the words. Her evening at Sal's house had convinced her she wanted to coach, and in spite of her concerns

about Alex, the job offer was hard to turn down. But there were other basketball teams, and she'd already made a few inquires. Perhaps she wasn't ready to coach basketball with Alex, but she could still get back in the game somewhere.

Alex seemed to be equally troubled. In spite of her invitation to talk, Alex was quiet as they made their way toward the woods. Brit decided to open the dialogue. "So how's Anke?" she inquired. *Where the hell did that come from?* Alex's personal life was really none of her business.

Sighing in relief or frustration, Alex replied. "I think she's safe and sound and back in Germany."

Britain looked to Alex for clarification. "I don't understand."

"She was only here for the summer, to work at the beach."

"Oh." Brit looked down as she walked, attempting to divine the meaning of Alex's statement. After a minute of silence, broken only by the voices of the other people walking along the trail and the birds flying in the trees above, Alex spoke.

"Brit, what happened on the boardwalk totally shocked me. As far as I knew, Anke had left the country that morning."

They'd crossed a covered bridge and turned on a path carved into the mountainside and began walking along the stream winding at its base. Ahead and behind them they saw others out doing the same thing—walking, talking, seizing one of the last days of summer and enjoying it. Many of the people were pulled along by dogs of various sizes and breeds, and Brit couldn't help smiling as she watched the canines introduce themselves to each other, circling and sniffing butts.

"So you'd broken up with her because she was leaving?" Brit wasn't judging Alex; she was simply trying to understand what happened. Why would Anke say such things to Alex if they'd already broken up? How could Alex flirt with Brit, and seem so ready to move on, when she'd just broken up with her girlfriend? Shouldn't she have been sad and spent the evening talking about her girlfriend, how wonderful she was and how much she'd miss her? Instead, she and Alex had locked eyes and shared smiles a hundred times during the night, and although Brit was still a virgin, she wasn't stupid. Alex had been flirting with her. And yes, Brit had been flirting back. But Brit didn't have a girlfriend, and apparently, Alex did. Because, if they'd broken up as Alex claimed, why hadn't anyone informed Anke?

Brit's inner turmoil must have been written on her face, because Alex reached out and gently held her forearm, and her speech sounded pressured as she spoke, as if her words were exploding from somewhere deep inside her.

"We were never a couple. When we met at the beginning of summer, she'd already booked her return flight to Germany. She was very clear that she was leaving in August and was only interested in a summer fling. And that was fine by me. I didn't want a relationship, either."

"A fling?" Brit asked, mystified. While Brit had no sexual experience, she did possess a very active imagination. She wasn't a prude, yet she had difficulty understanding this type of relationship. A one-night stand, where an alcohol-fueled fire burns hot and then burns out—that was understandable. But the concept of a summer-long fling baffled her. How do you give yourself to someone—all of yourself—and then take it back when the calendar ran out of pages? How do you not feel something? "How can you just have sex without becoming emotionally involved, Alex? How do you prevent women from falling in love with you?"

A bench at the side of the trail beckoned them, and again without discussion, they took a seat and looked out over the stream. Alex had to be honest with Brit, to tell her everything so they could start over. Because Alex liked Brit and was attracted to her, and for the first time, she wanted something more than a fling. She feared it was already too late for her and Brit, but that didn't change her desires.

"I guess that's what happened with Anke," Alex sighed. Their eyes briefly met before Alex turned to study the stream. "She wanted more. I didn't. But I'm not opposed to more. I've just never met someone intriguing enough to pursue."

"So girls generally pursue you, not the other way around?"

Alex squirmed a little. Why did this feel like an interrogation? "No, not always. Sometimes I ask girls out. But I usually don't ask them out twice."

Brit nodded as she seemed to be processing the information. "What exactly did happen that night in Rehoboth?"

Alex relaxed. This was the easy part, because the facts clearly demonstrated her innocence. "Anke left for the airport that morning. We said good-bye and I thought I'd never see her again. But she

developed second thoughts about leaving Rehoboth. During the drive to the airport she realized that…she was in love with me. She managed to get bumped from her flight and came back looking for me."

"And she couldn't call you?"

"My phone was dead. She got a ride to my house, stole Kim's bike, then spent the day wandering all over looking for me. We left the beach early because it was hot and went for drinks in town. Then I left early for Sal's house. It was all just bad timing."

"I'll say. So you didn't make up on the boardwalk? She still left?"

Alex cringed. Anke had no place to stay, so Alex had offered her lodging. Of course Anke wanted to sleep with Alex. Alex couldn't do it, though. Her mind was filled with thoughts of Brit. Angry that Alex refused her, Anke once again accused her of an affair with Brit and attempted to strike her. At that point Alex had piled Anke's luggage into her car and driven her back to the airport.

She was so exhausted by the ordeal that she decided to come home and hadn't been back to the beach since. After arriving back in Clarks Summit, Alex had spent the past days cleaning her apartment and putting her school clothes in order, getting ready for the new school year. And all the while she was thinking of Britain and wondering what she could say to erase the horrible memory of those few moments on the boardwalk.

"Yes, she still left. I didn't want her to stay, Brit. I don't love her. It was really just an arrangement."

Brit frowned and the color seemed to drain from her face.

"It sounds awful, doesn't it?"

Brit turned toward Alex and looked over her shoulder to the stream and the trees. It was a beautiful place, a romantic spot to walk with a lover or a dog, or to bring kids for a picnic. Not a place for flings. Brit wasn't a fling person, and no matter how eloquently Alex pleaded her case, Brit would never be able to understand her actions. Mindful of her manners, she replied cautiously.

"Well, to me it does," Brit said. "I guess I'm a little old-fashioned. I believe in love and commitment." She looked at Alex and shrugged. "You know—the white house with the picket fence and the growing old together."

Alex was quiet as she stared into the distance, and Brit feared she'd been too judgmental after all. It saddened her, for the loss of what

might have been, but in the end, it was really none of her business who Alex slept with or just what arrangements she made with her lovers. Brit placed her hand on Alex's knee. "I'm sorry, Alex. I shouldn't have said that. There's nothing wrong with other people having flings, it's just not what I would want in a relationship. I guess everyone just needs to understand the rules. And if that works for you and your girlfriends— who am I to judge you?"

"I guess the problem is that with women, sometimes the rules change," Alex said.

Brit laughed. "Or not everyone wants to obey them. I guess that's what happened with Anke, huh?"

Alex nodded in agreement.

"Has this ever happened before? Where someone expected more than you were willing to give?"

Alex shrugged, and her action suggested that she took no responsibility for the outcome of her previous affairs. Brit might have had many things in common with Alex, but relationship goals weren't one of them. As much as she found Alex beautiful, as funny and intelligent as she knew her to be—all she could hope for was friendship. The bright day seemed somehow dreary as Brit admitted the facts. Alex was only interested in the one thing Brit wouldn't give her. Sex. Trying to lighten the moment, Brit attempted a joke.

"You should be flattered, Alex—women can't help themselves from falling for you."

Brit suddenly realized what she'd revealed and recoiled until she noticed the comment had gone right over Alex's head. *Whew.*

"Well, the other night on that beach—I kinda thought there was some falling going on," Alex said hopefully. Flirtatiously. "I like you Brit. I was hoping that we might…" She didn't finish the statement, but let it hang in the air between them.

Suddenly, Brit was quite serious as their blue eyes met. There could be no more flirting. She wouldn't do anything to mislead Alex. All playfulness disappeared from her tone. "That night was a fluke, Alex. Too much wine and too many stars, I guess."

Alex looked crestfallen. "So…?"

Brit shook her head, not just to convey her thoughts but so they actually might stick and take hold in her own mind. "I can't…" she finished the thought with a frown and a shrug.

Alex didn't reply for a moment as she seemed to contemplate Brit's words. "You'll still coach though, right?"

Alex turned, leaned forward, and put a hand on Brit's knee as her eyes sought Brit's.

Brit looked away. "Alex, I don't think it's a good idea."

Alex's grip grew firmer. "Brit, please. I really need you. I'm desperate."

Brit chewed on her bottom lip for a second. She really did want to coach. And while she might get a job somewhere else, it would be so easy to coach at Endless Mountains, where she would be teaching. She wouldn't have to rush to get to after-school practices in another town, and make a long drive home afterward. It made perfect sense. She was a big girl. She could stick to business and coach with Alex without letting Alex's charms affect her.

"Okay. We're going to teach together and coach together, and I think we'll be great friends, Alex. But let me be clear. I'll never trust you with my heart."

Alex sat for a long while after Brit left her, watching life happening around her. People walking, talking, laughing. Dogs prancing. Birds flying through tree branches and a brook burbling nearby. It was all so mundane and normal and perfect, and she would never be any of those things.

The stunning irony of the situation wasn't lost on her, and if she wasn't so looking forward to a good cry she might have laughed. How could she have met a woman who finally made her consider changing her lascivious ways, and said woman would have nothing to do with her because of her past?

It had been a foolish idea to reconsider her decision to remain single. Brit's rejection had been a good thing. A relationship would have been wrong. Alex knew it. She just needed to figure out how to convince her heart.

CHAPTER TWELVE

HAPPY HOUR

Whizzing by, the first few weeks seemed a blur to Brit as she packed her bag at the end of school one Friday toward the end of September. It amazed her how easily she fell into the routine of teaching, how good and natural it was for her to be in front of a class of students.

They were great, the students. She had the typical problems that every teacher faces—tardiness and inattention, a few rogue troublemakers—but they were a clear minority. The majority of her pupils were intelligent and interested in the subject matter, eager to fill their brains with all the knowledge she could pass their way.

She saw Alex every day, and they were friendly but didn't have much time to talk at school. Their classrooms were on different floors and they monitored separate lunch periods. If things had gone differently for them, Brit might have sought Alex out, but they hadn't, so she had been trying to keep a respectable distance. It was hard, though. In spite of what she knew about Alex, she couldn't help thinking about her. She couldn't deny the attraction she felt. Fortunately, she had the distraction of school to occupy her mind.

Alex had shared the news of her hiring with the team, and over the first days of school, all of the players introduced themselves. She was teaching nearly every player in either her introductory or senior biology classes. As she walked through the halls each day, some of them greeted her. "Hey, Coach" had begun to sound pleasingly familiar, and she was happy she'd stuck with her decision to coach.

A sense of peace came to her as she was settling into her job and

into her life. Slowly, Brit was defining her future rather than allowing others to do it for her. New stories were being written, and it was refreshing to not simply reread the same old ones she knew by heart. It never would have occurred to her that she was sad before, but now, feeling happy for perhaps the first time since college, she realized she had been.

"Miss Dodge? Do you have a minute?"

Brit looked up from her desk into the questioning eyes of Erica Drummond, a sophomore student in her biology class. It was 2:50, the closing bell had just sounded, and a flurry of students was making as hasty a departure as possible, eager to begin their weekends. What could possibly bring Erica to her door at this time?

Brit saw the concern in her student's eyes, though, and immediately invited her to come in. "What's going on?" she asked.

Erica's eyes filled with tears and she bit her lower lip. Brit walked a few steps toward the door, closing the gap between them, and gently squeezed the girl's shoulder. "What is it?" she asked, more gently this time.

Brit's alarm was growing by the second as she waited to know what was troubling Erica. She really didn't know her that well and had only spoken to her in the confines of the classroom. Whatever it was, though, it had to be serious.

"It's about my eyes. They're blue. You gave us our homework for the weekend and told us to figure out the genetics of our family members. I started working on it in study hall last period. My eyes are blue, Miss Dodge, and my parents' are brown. My three brothers have brown eyes. I must have been adopted, or my mother had an affair!" Erica burst into tears when she finished speaking.

Sighing in relief, Brit pulled Erica into a tight but brief hug. "Relax. Sit down," she said. "I'll show you how it works."

Grabbing a pen and paper from her drawer, Brit began to draw the grid of genetic combinations for eye color that had been the homework assignment. "So, Erica, you have blue eyes. What does that tell us about your genes?"

"I'm recessive."

"Exactly. Blue-eyed people know their genes for sure, because they must have two blue alleles to have blue eyes. They get one gene from each parent." Brit drew the chart that depicted Erica's family

genes, filling in the two blue alleles for her, and also one in each of her parents' eyes.

"So your parents both have brown eyes?" Erica nodded. "What can we say for sure about someone with brown eyes?"

"They're dominant?"

"Yes. They must have at least one brown, dominant allele. But they don't have to have two brown alleles. They could have one brown and one blue." Brit wrote the combinations down for Erica to study. "See?" she asked, and when Erica nodded again, Brit filled in the blanks on her parents' charts, giving both of them a brown-blue genetic combination. "So, here you have it. Your parents can both have brown eyes and have a twenty-five percent chance of having a blue-eyed daughter. Understand?"

Erica continued to study the paper, and Brit watched the relief of comprehension wash over her face. Then she buried her face in her hands and mumbled, "I. Am. So. Stupid."

Brit laughed. "No, you're not. It's just a little confusing at first, that's all. You'll get it now, though, I'm sure."

Erica looked again at the drawing Brit had made. "My family is actually perfect, I guess. They should have had three children with brown eyes and one with blue, and they did."

"You're right. Feel better?"

Erica sniffled. "Much."

"Good. Now go home and have a nice weekend."

Erica seemed to overcome her embarrassment as she smiled. "Thank you, sooooo much!"

"No worries, Erica."

It was now three and Brit figured it was time to head home. There were numerous routes to the teachers' parking lot, and one of them—which wasn't the shortest of her choices—took her past Alex's classroom. She was surprised to see Alex's door open. What was Alex doing here late on a Friday? Surely she had a busy social calendar that required a hasty Friday afternoon escape from school.

Alex was seated at her desk studying paperwork and didn't immediately notice as Brit walked in. She supposed she should have knocked, but seeing Alex sitting there looking absolutely gorgeous caused Brit to forget her manners. Alex's curls fell loosely around her face, and as she looked down at the paper that held her attention, her

face tilted just a little, her full lips pursed, she was a breathtaking sight. Brit stopped and swallowed before she spoke.

After a moment she found her voice. "Hey."

Alex looked up, and Brit could tell from twenty feet away that her blue eyes had become turquoise to match the silk shirt she wore. She smiled in greeting, placed her paper on the desk, and leaned back in her chair. "How's it going?"

"Well."

"Tell me about it," Alex suggested.

Brit sat at the edge of Alex's desk and shared a few of the joys and triumphs of her first weeks of school. If only she could calm the pounding in her chest, the bundles of nerves that frizzled when she was around her. If she could quiet the attraction she could work on being friends. But the pull of Alex's eyes drew Brit, the warmth of her smile and her laughter so inviting Brit felt herself leaning back so she didn't fall into Alex's arms.

Alex watched Brit thoughtfully. The happiness in her voice was as unmistakable as the twinkle in her eyes. Alex added her opinions and comments where she thought necessary, but otherwise she just sat and allowed Brit to talk, only half listening. Whenever Brit was around, Alex's concentration wavered. And since Brit had made it clear how she felt about Alex, she had to gain control of her hormones or she was in for trouble.

After ten minutes of babbling, Britain brought her hand to her mouth, obviously dismayed. "Oh, my God! I sound like a five-year-old on Christmas morning. I'm sorry."

Alex shook her head. "Don't be silly. I was the same way. It's good to see you so happy. And if it means anything—the students love you. They have nothing but positive things to say."

Brit's eyes flew open wide, and her mouth followed, displaying perfectly straight teeth. "What are they saying?"

Alex laughed. "Oh, no. You're going to have to buy my information. I'm not just handing it over so easily."

"Name your price, Dalton."

"A beer."

"A beer?"

"Yeah, you're a biology teacher. You must have heard of it. You ferment a little barley and it makes a great beverage."

"I do remember something about that from college."

Alex smiled and nodded. "I'm pleased to know your education was up to standard."

Brit successfully suppressed a smile. "When would you like this fermented barley?"

"Well, it is Friday. This would be a perfect time." Kim was driving up from Philly for the weekend, but she wouldn't reach Alex's place until much later. Alex had hours to kill and hadn't a clue about how to fill them, until Brit had appeared like an angel at her door.

Brit had a busy weekend planned. This was the night of a bachelorette party for a girl she knew well, but she wasn't enthusiastic about going. Feigning interest in all the marriage plans and guy talk was draining. She planned to make it an early night. In the morning she had a tee time with her father and then the late-afternoon wedding and reception. On Sunday she had a standing date with her family for mass and dinner at her parents' house. For the next few hours, though, she had no plans and no good excuse to refuse Alex's invitation.

Unless, of course, she was avoiding Alex. It would be smart to avoid her, but they could be friends, right? What harm was there in having a beer with her colleague? Other than the fact that she hated beer?

Finally, after what seemed like an endless mental debate, Brit agreed. "Peyton Pub?" She named the only local place she could think of that served beer.

"Fine choice."

"I'll meet you there," Brit said as she rose and turned to leave the room. Then, remembering that Alex had to walk to her car as well, she stopped and laughed. "I can wait for you."

"Good. We can talk on the way. We have a basketball season to plan, Coach."

Brit nodded. "Yes, Coach, we do."

Alex gathered her things, and they'd hardly gotten through a discussion of the roster when they reached the parking lot. It seemed to be the case with Alex—time flew. Brit followed Alex to the restaurant, and because it wasn't quite yet happy hour, they easily found parking places. Inside, they had their choice of tables, but they agreed to sit at the bar. It was only going to be one drink, right?

"So what's your preference of barley?" Brit asked, noticing the

signs for several popular brands. But Alex was looking at her, rather than the menu or the advertisements, and seemed unconcerned about her drink. It was unsettling. Brit nervously pushed the hair back behind her ears, then folded her hands in her lap to keep them quiet. Yet Alex had a ready answer to Brit's question, and her easy manner helped calm Brit's nerves.

"Sam Adams. How about yours?"

"Ah, I must confess I don't drink beer."

Alex turned to her and squinted, studying her suspiciously. "What? That's not possible."

"I think it's some sort of genetic defect that prevents me from liking beer. My parents are the same way. The only thing they ever drink is wine. And cocktails. But cocktails make me stupid, so I'm a wino."

Brit knew she was rambling, and averted her eyes to refocus. Why did Alex make her feel so nervous? It wasn't as if she was a potential date. She was just a beautiful, intelligent, fun…friend. Colleague. Coworker. No need for anxiety. Brit stretched in her chair and willed herself to relax.

Alex leaned closer and tried not to smile at Brit's fidgeting and rambling. Was Brit feeling as nervous as she was? Alex's heart sped up a little at the thought, and she willed it to slow. Friends. They were just going to be friends. Brit was adorable, though, so how could Alex not notice, not react? She cleared her throat before she spoke. "I don't know anyone who doesn't drink beer. What do you do at softball games?"

Brit nodded her pointer finger at Alex. "That's why I don't play softball."

"You don't play softball?" Alex asked, and then, after turning her head to assure no one was in earshot, she lowered her voice and asked, "Are you sure you're a lesbian?"

Brit hunched her shoulders and laughed, then looked up to meet Alex's gaze. "I'm quite sure."

The heat in Brit's eyes set Alex on fire, and she forced herself to quiet a retort that would have been too telling. Swallowing hard once again, Alex averted her gaze. "Well, at least you play hoops."

The bartender arrived to take their drink orders. "A Sam Adams," Brit told him, nodding toward Alex, "for her."

"Bottle or draught?" He looked at Brit for the answer, and she in

turn looked at Alex. "I'm going to say bottle. With a glass." She smiled at the man.

Alex nodded her approval again. "Good choice." Alex turned her gaze toward the bartender and spoke. "And for my friend, I'd like a cabernet."

He looked to Brit for her approval and she gave a nod.

"The house special?"

"Uh…Help me out here, Brit."

"What do you have?" Brit asked the bartender, and both of them listened as he named several varieties.

Brit picked the last brand mentioned.

"Equally good choice," Alex said when the bartender had left them.

"I'll let you know in a minute," Brit said.

"That's a wine, right? Cabernet?" Alex smiled to tell Brit she knew the answer.

"One of my favorite reds, as a matter of fact."

"But you've never had this brand before?"

Brit shook her head.

"So you're willing to spend eight bucks on a glass of wine you may not even like?"

Brit nodded. "Yep. I'll chance it. I like most wine, some more than others, but it'll be fine."

"This is why I drink beer. I know what a Sam Adams is going to taste like. It's always the same. And it's always good."

Their beverages arrived and they raised their drinks in a toast. "To the Falcons," Alex said.

Brit nodded as their glasses met midair. "And to new friends. Now tell me, Coach Dalton, what are they saying about me?"

"Don't you want to talk about the season? Discuss the game plan, what offense we'll run, how we'll play the defending champions?"

Brit shook her head as she swallowed her wine, then waved her glass dismissively. "I'm not talking hoops until you tell me what my students are saying about me."

"How's the wine?" Alex asked, ignoring her plea.

"Fine. Tell me what they're saying, Alex, please."

"Eight bucks and it's only fine? That seems so unjust, because my four-dollar beer is fabulous."

"Alex! Please?"

"Well, I won't name names," Alex said, shaking her head. Leaning back in her seat she glanced sideways at Brit. "But I will tell you what they're saying. Sweet. Funny. Tough. Oh, and hot."

Brit took a sip of her wine, then placed the glass on the bar before looking at Alex. "That's it?" she asked, incredulous. "Just hot? Not incredibly hot? Not smokin' hot?" Flirting with Alex just a little couldn't hurt anything, could it? Besides, Alex had started it.

"Well, I didn't want to inflate your ego…but yeah, it was totally hot. They said totally hot."

"They?" Looking over the top of her wineglass, Brit's eyes met Alex's, and although she would never get used to the vertigo she felt at such moments, it no longer surprised her.

"Well, yes. They." Alex ignored the glass Brit had ordered and took a long pull of her beer directly from the bottle.

"They who?"

"Well, let's see." Alex studied the stamped tin ceiling in the old bar. "The janitor with the black greasy hair. The cafeteria lady who makes the sandwiches. The principal's assistant."

Brit pursed her lips. "The short janitor or the fat one?"

"You'll have to buy me another beer for that information."

"You're tough, Coach." Brit shook her head and then sipped her wine.

Unexpectedly, Alex reached out to Brit and squeezed her fingers gently. "They like you, Brit. The students say you engage them in the classroom. You discuss instead of lecture. You listen. You make them think. They're learning."

Brit's mouth opened in surprise. "Really?" Teaching was the profession she'd aspired to since she was in kindergarten, and it was wonderful to finally be in the classroom. To hear such great things said about her was much more, though. It touched her heart and filled her with an unimaginable joy.

Brit was shocked at the tears that filled her eyes, and they came so quickly she couldn't stop them. She wiped them away with a knuckle as Alex graciously looked up at the television, giving her a moment to collect herself. After a few minutes of silence, Alex suggested they order appetizers.

Filled with an array of emotions—joy, fear, excitement—Brit felt

almost as dizzy as she did when she looked at Alex. The wine only amplified her vertigo. It was a bad idea to stay and eat with Alex, yet she would have enjoyed nothing more. If she had a business dinner with Alex and discussed basketball, she had a valid excuse for missing the bachelorette party. By mentally arguing that she needed time to recover from the wine, she was able to justify her decision. When she caught the bartender's eye, she asked to see a menu.

CHAPTER THIRTEEN

SACRIFICES

P.J. left school along with a thousand other students, but instead of going home and getting ready for the big football game that night, he went to work. With the recent change in his job duties, his need for a car had become critical. Greg understood and had procured one for him, but instead of feeling happy about finally having his own ride, he just felt miserable.

Waiting to pull out of the school parking lot after selling a bunch of exams, he saw a group of underclassmen walking home. They were laughing and talking, no doubt making plans for their weekend. It would have been much more fun walking with them than riding alone.

He'd never felt so alone. He had no time for anything except school and work, and his friends had gotten so used to him declining invitations they'd stopped asking. Even Justina, who'd been his partner for science projects since grade school, seemed to give up on him. When he'd seen her in the library earlier in the day, she was huddled with another student, studying the diagrams in a textbook. When he approached, she told P.J. the young man was working with her on a physics team project.

Ouch! That had stung. It wasn't just that he was smart and used to everyone asking *him* for help. It was Justina. He'd always had a secret crush on her, and had seen her a few times since the party at the lake. They'd been talking more at school, and texting for a while, but now that seemed to be over. Like everyone else in his life, she'd moved on. He had no friends, no life, and not even a secret girl crush to make him smile.

P.J. followed the line of cars from the high school into downtown Clarks Summit, making his usual stops. He spent almost three hours driving around, making his deliveries, collecting money. When he finished his work, he followed a winding country road through farms and forests of the Lackawanna Valley. As he approached Olyphant, he slowed and turned into a well-concealed driveway cut into the woods. A hundred yards in, he stopped at a security gate. "It's P.J." he said when a raspy voice demanded to know his identity.

A second later, the gate lifted and P.J. drove through, then followed the road another two hundred yards into the woods. There, the trees had been cut away, and a large block structure filled the clearing. He drove toward the door, and before he was even close, it began to rise. He drove inside the building and parked his car along the right side, fifth in the line of cars driven here by other teenage couriers working for The Man.

Turning off the engine, P.J. glanced around. He'd been in the building a few times already, but the sight still amazed him. Dozens of trucks formed a convoy, ready to exit in the morning with early deliveries. They were an impressive sight, but nothing like what stood opposite them. At the very front of the building, as if waiting to escape as soon as a door opened, stood a collection of sports cars that made P.J. stop and stare. Antique Corvettes and Mustangs, a Porsche, a McLaren, an Aston Martin. On his first visit, P.J. had sort of floated toward the cars, unaware of anything else around him except the utter opulence of those machines. He'd knelt to study the hood ornaments and the tires, not daring to touch them. The Man had approached him and laughed. "Maybe one day, little man," he'd said.

"Do I have to worry about my collection?" The Man asked as he approached P.J., pulling him from his daydreams of *one day*. "You look a little jealous."

"No, I, I..." P.J. gulped and began to shake. Ever since he and Wes had confronted The Man, he'd been acting weird. It seemed he was trying to intimidate P.J., and it was working. Staring him down, standing a bit closer than necessary. Cracking his knuckles. P.J. and Wes were working with him, paying off the thousand dollars he owed, plus another thousand dollars The Man had decided on to cover incalculable losses, but it still seemed The Man was unhappy. P.J. didn't know how

much more they could do. He had no time, no energy left for anything after he gave his pound of sweat to The Man.

The Man laughed and slapped him on the back. Hard. "Let's go count my money," he said, and P.J. followed him, carrying a backpack stuffed with envelopes of betting slips and twenty-dollar bills. Business was booming.

CHAPTER FOURTEEN

ASSISTS AND TURNOVERS

As usual, Brit spent Sunday with her family. Awakening early, she arrived at the church in plenty of time to sit quietly and reflect and argue with God about all the injustices of Christianity, the most important of which, to Brit at least, was the church's position on homosexuality. The arrival of her family interrupted her silent debate, and after that she heard little of the celebration of the mass as she distracted the youngest of her nephews. When it was over, she chauffeured them to her parents' house for dinner.

After throwing her first load of laundry into the washing machine, Britain joined all of the women in the kitchen. The aroma of roasting beef filled the air, and around the table the female members of her family were peeling, dicing, and otherwise preparing vegetables. Not a male of any age was in sight—and that was just how they all preferred it. This time in the kitchen gave mother and daughters a chance to catch up on what they'd missed during the week.

They had been celebrating their family with Sunday dinner for as long as Brit could remember. Her fondest memories of childhood were of those long-ago Sundays, when both sets of grandparents visited and her father was home instead of at the hospital. The dining-room table was always a dynamic place, alive with gossip and stories, with the faces and seating arrangements changing over time as older members of her family died and new ones were born or connected by their marital ties.

It was a rare occasion when the sanctity of their family time was broken and outsiders were invited to join them. If she weren't so distracted by the constant thoughts of Alex playing like background

music in her mind, Britain would have raised an eyebrow when her mother announced they were expecting company for dinner. But she'd been thinking of Alex's blue eyes and her full lips, hearing a reel of her laughter playing over and over for only her ears, and she'd paid vague attention to the conversation as she'd prepared potatoes.

As a result, Brit was totally taken by surprise when, an hour later, she heard the doorbell ring and saw her mother running out of the kitchen to answer it. That surprise was surpassed when, a minute later, her nephew appeared in the kitchen and summoned Brit to the living room. And the surprise of the day—and perhaps the year—occurred when she arrived in the living room to find her parents chatting with the Thornton family.

Dr. Arthur Thornton was one of her dad's partners in his cardiology practice, and Brit had known his family her entire life. Emily, his wife, had been a friend to her mother. Their son Tommy, who was now in his third year of medical school in Philly, swam with Brit at the country club. He stood before her now looking uncomfortable but trendy in a corduroy blazer over a button-down shirt and a pair of skinny jeans.

Not forgetting the manners that had been drilled into her for two decades, Britain hugged all of the Thorntons in turn before sitting beside her father on the couch, feigning interest in the conversation as the former colleagues caught up. What was going on? Why were the Thorntons crashing their family dinner party? She was oblivious to the banter as she looked around the room and began to understand the situation. As she sat seething, silent and seemingly attentive, anger oozed from her pores.

They were trying to fix her up with Tommy! How could they do this, after she'd told them she didn't want or need their help in finding a husband? Her parents' obvious meddling in her love life, their failure to respect her declinations to the offers of dates with their friends' children devastated her. Even if she weren't gay, Tommy Thornton was about the third-to-last person on the planet she would have dated. He was full of himself and had no sense of humor, and was so smart that half the time Brit needed a translator in order to have a conversation with him.

When she thought she'd spent the correct amount of time to satisfy the requirements of proper social etiquette, Brit excused herself to return to the kitchen. They stopped talking as she entered the kitchen, so Brit knew her sisters were in on the fix.

"How could you?" she asked, looking first at Jordan and then at Sam. Then, raising a defiant middle finger and waving it from one sister to the other, she further spewed, "I am so pissed! No more free babysitting for either of you."

"Oh, baby sister, lighten up. They love you and just want you to be happy." It was Jordan defending their parents.

"I am happy!"

Sam walked closer and hugged her. "Brit, they're not getting any younger. Daddy's going to be seventy this year. They worry about you being alone when they die. They want you to have someone."

She turned to Sam and sighed in frustration. She was tempted to tell them the truth, right then and there, but this wasn't the right time. She had met someone—someone who excited her and delighted her and made her feel and want things the young man in the living room never could. "Sam, it's not my fault they waited so long to have kids. They can't just marry me off to anyone who comes along so they can die in peace."

Sam playfully messed up Brit's hair. "You're right, Brit. I'm not arguing that. I just want you to understand their point of view."

Still angry, Brit pulled away and announced her own surprise. "Well, it's a good thing for me that I have to leave right after dinner." She looked at her sisters' startled faces and knew they didn't believe her. When they started to protest, Brit silenced them with her hand.

It was unlike their well-behaved little sister to rebel, but they'd better get used to it, because she refused to tolerate this nonsense anymore. By allowing her family to push her around for so many years, she'd been a fool. But if she ever wanted anything to change, she had to start somewhere. It might not be the right time and place to come out, but it was the perfect time and place to tell them all to shove it. "I have a meeting with my head basketball coach."

Brit wasn't lying. She and Alex did have a date to meet that evening; that much was true. Alex was beginning to feel nervous about her coaching debut, and Brit had agreed to meet so they could start planning their practice schedule. A typical day at her parents didn't end until the late afternoon, so they'd agreed to meet at six. She didn't tell her sisters that, though.

"Oh, Mommy's going to be pissed. She's really excited about you and Tommy."

"*I'm* pissed, Jordan. *Mommy* doesn't even know what pissed is."

At that moment her mother burst through the swinging door that separated the kitchen from the pantry. "Britain, let your sisters finish dinner, dear. Tommy wants to talk with you."

Brit forced a smile. An argument with her mother wouldn't do anyone any good. Dinner would be uncomfortable—or more uncomfortable—and her mother's embarrassment in front of Dr. and Mrs. Thornton would be a deep wound to her mother's pride. But that didn't mean Brit intended to allow this ambush to proceed. As soon as she'd swallowed her last bite, she was heading for cover. For now, though, she'd be the polite young woman her mother had raised. "Okay, Mom. Just let me get my clothes out of the dryer before they wrinkle."

Her mother pursed her lips and her tone was curt. "Don't keep him waiting."

As her mother marched out of the kitchen in one direction, Brit went in the opposite. Fuming, she quickly folded the wet clothes from the washer and placed them in her laundry bag. She was going to have to find a Laundromat close to her apartment so she could be less dependent on her parents. Didn't Alex say her family owned Laundromats? She'd ask when she saw her. Brit added the already-dry clothing to a pile on top of the bag. The laundry was ready when she made her escape. If she hadn't been out of clean socks, she'd have left the entire wash to rot in the laundry room.

Making the greatest of efforts so as to not embarrass her family, Brit managed to pay attention to the dinner conversation. She laughed when it seemed appropriate and posed thoughtful questions. An occasional nod indicated her interest in what the others around the table were discussing.

After dessert was finished, Brit stood and, to the surprise of everyone in the room—including herself—announced her departure. She wasn't totally sure she'd find the courage to defy her parents, but as the dinner wore on and she imagined Alex sitting across from her, her resolve was fortified. Dinner with Alex would have been perfect. It was exactly what she wanted. As she sat there understanding it was something she'd likely never have, Brit could no longer tolerate the disgust she felt at herself for lying, or for her homophobic family for putting her in a position where she had to.

"You can't leave, dear," her mother insisted. "We have company."

"I'm so sorry about this," Britain addressed the Thorntons, "but I'm having my first team meeting today. It's mandatory. I forgot to tell Mom and Dad."

Whether any of them believed her, she wasn't sure. Nor did she care. She only knew she needed to get out of her parents' house before she started screaming at someone and making a fool of herself. After collecting her laundry, she was about to make a clean getaway when both of her parents cut her off.

"You can't leave without kissing me good-bye," her dad teased her.

Even though she knew he was in on the set-up, she suspected he was an unwilling participant in his wife's caper. Brit couldn't be mad at him. "Of course I can't."

He pulled her into a big hug and kissed her cheek. "Drive carefully, honey. Call us when you get home."

"I'll get Tommy's cell phone number for you," her mother offered. "He'll be home for a few more weeks, and you two can get together."

"Okay, Mom," she replied as she hugged her mother and kissed her cheek. At the moment, she had no more strength with which to argue. She'd save that battle for later.

Once in the car, she began breathing to control her anger, deep breaths that made her dizzy after a few minutes. Then she thought of calling Alex. Maybe she'd like to meet early. Alex would be able to fix her foul mood by simply being there.

"Hey, Brit," Alex said.

"Hey, yourself. I got out of dinner early. Any chance you'd like to meet now?"

"Kim just left, and I was just about to shoot some hoops. Care to join me?"

Brit thought of all the times she'd taken a ball in her hands and felt the weight of the world lift from her shoulders. The concentration she needed on the court allowed no other thoughts but basketball, and by the time she finished her game or her practice, Brit would find herself feeling a million times better than when she started. Basketball therapy was exactly what she needed.

They agreed to meet at the park, and after stopping at her apartment to change clothes, Brit headed directly there. The calendar indicated that fall had officially arrived, but no one had informed Mother Nature.

The sky was clear and blue and the temperature in the mid-seventies as she pulled into the park. On this sunny Sunday afternoon, parking spots were as hard to find as they'd been on her previous visit. Fortunately, a family in a minivan was leaving, and Brit maneuvered her car into a generous-sized parking spot they'd vacated. Bouncing her ball, she walked toward the courts where she'd played with Kelsey before she learned she'd be coaching her.

Alex was on the closest one, looking quite the player in a jersey, long shorts, high socks, and high-top sneakers. She was practicing foul shots. "Hey," Brit said as she shot a jumper from the wing. Alex paused for a moment, but when it became evident that Brit was more interested in shooting the ball than conversing with her, she resumed playing as well.

After twenty minutes of silence, each of them shooting independently, Alex finally spoke. "Are you up for some one-on-one?"

Brit had already thought about whether she wanted to play head-to-head against Alex. Alex was taller and had been a big college star. Brit knew her skills, and she knew she could play the game, but she didn't want to embarrass herself by challenging someone with more natural ability. She suspected a game might be a one-sided fiasco. In the end, though, it didn't matter. She just wanted to play basketball and forget what had happened at her parents' house.

After establishing the rules, she headed toward the half-court line to inbound the ball. Alex had granted her first possession. She tossed the ball to Alex, who stood about five feet away and tapped it right back. Game on. Brit started toward the right side as she glided toward the key. Alex maintained her distance, guarding against a drive to the hoop. When she reached the three-point line, Brit stopped, jumped, and fired an uncontested shot. It rattled around the rim before dropping through the net. Her eyes found Alex's. "Three-nothing," she announced with a smile.

Alex didn't respond. Instead, she took the ball out of bounds and tossed it back to Brit. Brit didn't allow Alex the breathing room she'd been granted, and that was her first mistake of the game. Alex dribbled to the right and with lightning speed shot past her and took the ball to the basket for an easy layup. "Three-two," Alex said as she caught her own rebound and politely handed the ball back to Brit.

The first three-pointer hadn't scared Alex a bit. She allowed Brit

the same clearance as she had on her first possession, and again, Brit drilled a three-pointer. "Six-two."

Brit had learned from her first embarrassing defensive show. This time she gave Alex some room and tracked her as she dribbled toward the right, spun, and tried to break to the basket. When she couldn't shake Britain she pulled up and shot a jumper that rattled around and fell through the net for two points. "Six-four."

Brit couldn't believe that Alex still didn't guard her behind the three-point line, but she again found herself alone out there. Of course, she took the shot, and again it went in. "Nine-four."

"Can you shoot from anywhere else?" Alex asked, her tone sarcastic.

"Not unless I have to."

Alex started to the left this time, drew Brit across the key, then fired from just inside the foul line. The ball hit off the back of the rim and popped out of the cylinder.

"Hey, Alex," Brit said as she stood dribbling the ball. "How many letters are in the alphabet?"

Alex smirked. "Twenty-six. Why?"

"Not in your alphabet. You have no D." Then Brit exploded left.

Down five with the chance to go even further in the hole, and perhaps challenged by Brit's teasing, Alex began to showcase her talents. She guarded Brit closely, forcing her to back off and shoot an off-balance jumper that bounced weakly off the front of the rim. On her own possession, she copied Brit's game plan and knocked down a three. After another stop and another basket, the game was tied.

They played for an hour, with the lead changing hands on nearly every possession, until finally Brit made a three that Alex couldn't counter and declared herself the winner. Both were drenched in sweat as they walked on wobbly legs to the courtside bench to cool down. Toasting with energy drinks from a vending machine, they touched their bottles, saluting the great effort they'd put forth. "I can't believe you didn't play DI hoops, Brit. You're better than half the girls I played against."

"I was a late bloomer. Small in high school. But I grew three inches when I got to college, and I worked hard on my game. I did okay."

"I'll say."

They sat in silence for a few minutes before Brit spoke. "Thank you for the game, Alex. I needed it."

"Bad day?"

"Awful."

Alex turned toward her, pulling a long leg up on the bench. "What happened?"

Brit took a deep breath as she debated telling Alex. It wasn't that she didn't feel comfortable enough to talk to her—in fact, quite the opposite. She just didn't know if she wanted to get into it again. She was feeling relaxed and didn't need to remind herself of how awful her family dinner had been. Yet, she wanted to share this with Alex, just as she wanted to share everything with her.

The look of concern on Alex's face convinced her. "They tried to fix me up with a guy. They invited him to dinner."

"What?" Alex reached out a comforting hand to Brit's knee—the closest body part—and looked at her with an expression of disbelief.

"Yep. My sister told me my parents want to marry me off so they can die in peace."

"Hmm. That's gotta be awkward. Why don't you just tell them you're not into guys?"

Brit sniggered and shook her head. "I have the most religious parents on the planet. My father's a Eucharistic minister. My mother hasn't missed mass in fifty years. I have aunts and uncles who are priests and nuns. They're not going to handle this well."

"So what do you do, then? Lie to them?"

She shook her head. "Not really. I just don't talk about it."

"So no dates for holidays? You and your girlfriend go your separate ways?" Alex sounded flabbergasted.

Sighing in frustration, Brit looked into Alex's big blue eyes and frowned. "I've never cared about anyone enough to bring them home. So I've never had a reason to come out to my family."

Alex squeezed Brit's hand and held it. "I think you do now, my friend."

Brit looked at her, her heart beating faster. For a moment she thought Alex was insinuating there might be a future between them—a reason to tell her parents.

"They won't stop until they understand why they have to." Alex's

expression was sympathetic, and Brit realized she wasn't hinting at anything.

"Why can't they just mind their own business?" She pulled her hand away and instantly felt cold where Alex had heated her.

"They don't understand that there's a problem. Only you do."

"You sound so sure of everything, Alex." Brit looked at her, needing some reassurance. Suddenly, her world and her life seemed to be a big, scary place. Her thoughts and emotions were in constant flux, and she just needed some sense of calm.

"Not about everything, but about this I am." Alex looked sad, and Brit wondered why. Alex seemed so cocky and confident that Brit couldn't imagine what would cause her insecurity. She couldn't ask the question, though. A wall seemed to go up, and Alex leaned back, her body language telling Brit she wasn't open to probing.

"So I take it you're out to your family?" she asked, hoping this was a safe topic.

"Oh, yeah."

Brit laughed. Her tone told her the outing had been eventful. "Do tell."

"I was caught in a rather intimate position with my high-school girlfriend. My mother walked in on us."

Brit brought both hands to her face. "Oh, no! What did you do?"

"Well, fortunately, my mother handled it well. She told her it was time to go home, and then she told me she didn't allow my brother to have his girlfriend in his room and the same rules applied to me."

"Wow! That's all I can say."

"Yeah, me, too."

"How old were you?"

"Seventeen."

"Does your dad know?"

"Yep. No secrets in my family. My brother figured it out even before my mother."

Brit smiled. "It must be nice having that kind of unconditional love."

Again, Alex squeezed her, this time on the upper arm, a ticklish spot above her elbow. Yet she didn't feel like laughing.

"I know we haven't known each other very long, Brit, but I feel like I know you well. And everything I know about you, I like. I

wish I could tell you that your family will give you the same kind of understanding mine gives me. But I can't. I've seen parents disown their kids. It's unbelievable, but it happens. I hope it doesn't happen to you, but if it does, you'll be okay. Because you're going to find some amazing woman who knocks your socks off, and then nothing else will matter."

Brit smiled, though she wasn't sure if she should. She supposed Alex's words were meant to reassure her, but the fear of her family's disapproval was all too real. She couldn't imagine a love grand enough to compensate for the loss of all the people who mattered so much to her. Maybe she should just stay single forever. She'd become an old maid, babysit her nephews on Saturday nights instead of dating, and spend every Sunday with her parents. Then she'd never have to reveal this secret.

Brit's apartment seemed lonely compared to the park, and she couldn't help feeling anxious. Needing a distraction, and some comfort, too, she turned on the oven and pulled a large mixing bowl from her cabinet. Using a large knife she sliced a block of butter and threw it into her microwave to soften. Crack, crack, crack. The eggshells split neatly and she separated their contents, saving the whites. With a whisk, she blended the butter and yolks with sugar and vanilla until the mixture was smooth, then began to fold in flour. She felt the tension leaving her body as the dough flowed through her fingers, growing heavier with each scoop of flour she added.

What a day! She didn't know what stressed her more—the pain her family caused her or the ease with which Alex seemed to handle it. Alex being so perfect was not good. She was a colleague, and a friend. Nothing more. Why had she called Alex in the first place? With so many friends to choose from, one of them was likely to have answered the cell phone if she called to complain about her mother's antics. Meg, her former roommate, was always eager to talk and would have provided a sympathetic ear. There were half a dozen others, too.

Instead, her first instinct had been to call Alex Dalton, and spending time with Alex had been exactly what she needed. As always, dribbling a basketball had taken her mind off her troubles.

Even the conversation after their game, which was unsettling, had been something Brit needed to hear. Someone else telling her that the discussion with her parents was overdue made it more difficult for her to deny it, and like it or not, she needed to do it.

What had her upset now, pounding her fists into a ball of cookie dough, was her simple desire to call Alex. The instinct to call Alex. And the fact that calling Alex, the woman who had flings instead of meaningful relationships, had turned out to be the absolute correct call.

She sectioned the dough, taking a half-cup-sized scoop and putting it directly into the ice chest in the freezer. After washing her hands, she put her headset in her ear and dialed Meg's number. She needed to hear Meg's voice and ground herself. She needed to spill the mass of confusion and let Meg help her sort it out. Meg had been her best friend all through college, the first one she'd gotten drunk with, and the first one she'd come out to. She was a source of good advice and a soft shoulder. Meg would help her. She always did.

Meg answered after a few rings, her voice a breathless sigh. "I had to run in from the garage to catch the phone, but since I knew it was you I figured it was worth the heart attack. What's up, stranger?"

Since meeting Alex and dealing with all the feelings that had blossomed, Brit had been more reserved than usual, not reaching out to her friends. With all the anxiety she was carrying, she did indeed feel like a stranger to her best friend.

"Not too much, getting in the groove of working every day. It's sort of exhausting."

"At least you'll never have a tax season."

"Ah, but soon I'll have a basketball season."

"Then you'll know exhaustion."

"So how are the wedding plans going?" Brit poured some walnuts into her blender. "Hold that thought, I have to chop for a second." *Rrrrrrrrrrggghhhh.*

After thirty seconds, the noise stopped.

"What are you baking?" Meg asked.

"Gramma Cookies." She scooped the finely chopped walnuts from the bottom of the blender.

"Oh, no. What's wrong?"

"I called to talk about your wedding, not my troubles."

"If you're baking Gramma Cookies—your ultimate comfort

food—you must be stressing. So give it up, Dodge, or I'll hop in the car and come eat all your treats."

Brit sighed. "My parents invited the Thorntons to dinner today. They tried to fix me up with Tommy." Her voice was soft, full of sadness and despair. Sitting at the table now, Brit further divided the dough into sections and began wrapping them for freezing.

"Oh, yuck! Is he still a jerk?"

"Yes, but close to being Dr. Jerk, which is very important to my mother."

"So what did you do?"

Brit finished the dough while she told the story, then retrieved the frozen section and began rolling small balls from that allotment.

"Do you think this is my fault? I mean, is she pushing you to get married because I am?"

Brit had enough dough to create seven little balls, which would become an equal number of mouth-watering cookies. Into the bowl of egg whites they all went, and then she rolled them into the crushed walnuts. "Oh, I don't know. When we were in Bethany, the subject of your wedding only came up about a thousand times. So I wouldn't say she's obsessed with it or anything."

"Sorry, Brit. Your mother's just a…bit pushy, I guess. And I wish I could say that telling the truth would take the pressure off you, but I'm not sure it would."

"It might even make things worse, you know? Excommunication from both church and family."

"You'd still have me, babe."

Brit used her forearm to push back her hair and smiled gratefully. "And I'm lucky. Don't leave me, or I'll be all alone."

"What are you doing to change that? Any prospects for the title of Mrs. Right?"

The cookies were going into the oven, neatly spaced on her grandmother's cookie sheet. "Yeah, there is. Maybe." She spoke softly, hesitantly. She'd hardly acknowledged her attraction to Alex to herself, yet here she was telling Meg.

"Ohhh! Yeah!" Meg squealed with delight. "Tell me, tell me! Who is she?"

Leaning against the oven door, taking comfort in its warmth, Brit found her courage. "It's Alex Dalton."

After a moment of shocked silence, Meg responded. "Oh, wow. Is this something new or has it been going on since the summer?"

Brit laughed. "It was love at first sight, until her girlfriend tried to rip out my eyeballs on the boardwalk. So I backed off, but since I've spent time with her, I've come to realize I really like her."

"What about the girlfriend? Are you into that kind of thing?"

"No, it's over with her." Brit told her about Alex's arrangement with Anke and didn't mention how much it bothered her. She still questioned why it did. What was wrong with what they'd done? They were two consenting adults. Maybe, Brit realized, she was a prude after all.

"It would just be me—if Alex could be monogamous, which is a big IF. I don't know if she can, and I'm kind of scared to be the science experiment."

"Well, you'll have plenty of chances to explore this, Brit. Practices together. All those overnight games, sharing a hotel room. Endless possibilities."

"Uh, Meg...this is high school. We can walk to the away games. They're in the next town. There're no hotels involved here."

"Well, still. You'll be together a lot, just like tax season. That's how it happened for me and Steve, when I interned at his office. I'm so happy for you."

"So, I take it you think I should throw caution to the wind and all that stuff?"

"You can't remain a virgin forever, girlfriend. Even if she's not the one...she could be the one for now."

"Stop it!" Brit feigned irritation.

"You know I love you. When can I meet her?"

Brit sighed, exasperated. Meg was often as energetic and flighty as one of her nephews. "Meg, I didn't actually say I was dating her. Or going to date her. Just that I like her."

"Brittzy, listen to me. Life is short. I know you have this romanticized vision of love and happily-ever-after and a Catholic church wedding...but I don't want to watch you grow old waiting for everything to be perfect. So she's slept around, so what? Most of the world has, honey. It doesn't make her bad. It probably makes her normal."

Brit checked the oven. She needed a cookie to lighten the despair

that came with understanding that she was, in fact, the abnormal one. The tops were just showing a hint of color. Another minute at 350° should do it.

"I'm just taking this slowly, Meg."

"As long as you take it."

Brit wanted to take it, she really did. But what if it didn't work out? Alex was definitely attracted to her, she could tell, but could she handle it if Alex's feelings suddenly changed? They'd have to see each other at school and work closely together at practice. It would be humiliating. More importantly, she would have given her heart to someone and have to take it back all broken to pieces. When it came back, would it even be fixable?

Brit pulled the tray from the oven and quickly transferred the cookies to a large plate. Without waiting for them to cool, she took a bite of buttery, sugary comfort and felt better instantly.

"It's scary, Meg," she said as she sat down, thinking there weren't enough cookies in the world to help her find the courage to go on a date with Alex or to tell her family if she did.

❖

Alex stared into the refrigerator as it glowed in the darkness of her kitchen. The shelves were nearly bare. A few condiments were lined up neatly on the top shelf, along with milk and yogurt and some fruit, and a half gallon of orange juice. There was nothing atypical about the sight, until Alex turned her gaze to the crisper at the bottom and pulled out the syringe filled with the poison that kept her body moving. It was a powerful biological agent, one that shut down her immune system to prevent the autoimmune disease destroying her body from doing any more damage.

The plastic was cold, and she stared at it for a moment, watching a bubble in the liquid bob as she turned the instrument in her hand. It was time for her dose, and for the first time in many years, she was debating whether to take it.

When she'd first been diagnosed, her doctor gave her a sample pack of the drug, and Alex had been amazed that, in less than a week, a single shot had taken away the pain she'd had in her lower back for nearly a decade. Two weeks later, when she injected herself for the

second time, she felt normal. And then she stopped, just to see what would happen, and the pain came back with a vengeance. That was five years earlier, and since then, other than the few occasions when she'd been sick, she hadn't missed a dose.

Did she really still need it? Yeah, she had then, when she was playing competitive basketball every day. Perhaps now that she wasn't so hard on her body, her pain might be improved. And maybe her disease was in remission now. She'd heard of that happening. Maybe she could do without it. She could sure do without the worry of contracting fatal infections and cancer, fears that constantly floated beneath the current of her thoughts and periodically surfaced and stabbed her with reminders of the medication's side effects.

Closing her eyes, Alex sighed, a deep breath of frustration that left her dizzy. She just wanted to be normal. Why did she have to have this fucking disease, and to worry about taking her medication, and to fear the pain she'd have if she didn't, and fear dying if she did? What had she done to deserve this? Why couldn't she just be like everyone else and have a normal life and a girlfriend who loved her and not have to be a fucking science experiment?

Opening her eyes, Alex stared at the syringe again and bit the inside of her bottom lip in frustration. Then she put it back in the bottom drawer and closed the door, and walked through her darkened apartment to the bed where she'd try to fall asleep while thinking of the woman who'd made her so anxious to live.

CHAPTER FIFTEEN

TIP-OFF

The sound of dozens of basketballs bouncing echoed throughout the gym as Alex watched Brit make her grand entrance, her first official appearance as assistant girls' basketball coach. Alex knew Brit was as nervous as she was—they'd been talking almost every day—but she looked confident and beautiful as she approached, her hair in a ponytail and her trim body wrapped in a black sweat suit with teal-blue accents. Alex smiled as she noted the sneakers in the same color and thought it so typical of Brit—both delightfully feminine yet athletic, too.

Discussing their practice schedule and goals over the course of several meetings had led to the development of the agenda that Alex posted on the wall near the girls' locker room. She watched as Brit checked it and smiled. Again, typical Brit—methodical and perfectionistic, double-checking Alex's work. If someone else had been checking up on her, it might have bothered her. Brit was so nonchalant about being super organized it didn't bother Alex a bit.

Both of them thought it a great idea to keep the players informed about what they'd be doing at practice and to give them ideas about what they could work on during their free time. Alex had listed ball-handling skills as one of her top priorities for all players, even the ones who didn't routinely have to bounce the ball. Brit wanted to focus on foul shooting. Their practice plan included time to work on both skills, with rewards offered to the players on both JV and varsity who had the best performance of the day as well as the one who showed the most improvement.

Watching Brit approach, Alex tried hard to focus on the words spoken by the girl who was likely to be the team captain. Sidney Stone was a senior guard who'd been the leading scorer the year before and was admired by her teammates for her attitude and work ethic. She was a good student and stayed out of trouble. Sid wanted to talk about the practice agenda—she had her own thoughts on the matter—but all that filled Alex's brain was the image of Brit as she approached.

Snap out of it! she told herself and forced herself to concentrate on the conversation. Sid described a ball-handling game she'd learned at a summer camp and Alex agreed to implement it. With a bounce in her stride, Sid walked back to the court and joined her teammates in the warm-ups. Alex's spirit soared as she watched her players, the young ones scared and eager and the older ones confident and casual. Remembering the first day of her high-school basketball tryouts, she knew the adrenaline rushes these girls were experiencing—and she felt a bit envious that she was now the coach and no longer the player.

"Excited?" she asked as Brit approached.

"Yes! I didn't realize how much I missed being in a gym until just now."

"Kind of wishing you were out there instead of over here?" Alex almost sighed the words.

"Was that a question or a statement?" Brit asked with a smile.

"Busted. I don't think I'll ever get tired of playing."

"Well, I think our games at the park have been fun." The weather had been clear, and though sometimes cool, it wasn't enough to keep them from the court at South Abington Park. At least twice a week they went head-to-head. It was a great workout and great competition.

"Yeah. When the snow comes I guess we'll have to bring our game in here."

"It's a date," Brit said before she could stop herself, but she quickly recovered. "How are you? Nervous?" Alex had confessed she was jittery, and Brit knew about the pressure from the school board, but she always seemed so together. She looked great—tall, blond, beautiful, well dressed, and always with her head held high and a purpose in her stride. Confidence seemed to ooze from her, yet in their private times, Alex gave Brit clues that she was human, too.

Alex made a sort of comical frown. "Petrified."

"Well, it doesn't mean much—but I got your back."

Alex turned to her and smiled. "Actually, Brit, it means a great deal."

Brit answered her smile. "Did they look at the agenda?" she asked. Brit loved to have a plan. She needed it. If she didn't know what was happening it set her off balance, and knowing how they'd be spending their two hours of practice, and their week, and their month helped to ground her. If Alex thought it odd that Brit wanted to work out their practice schedule, she didn't mention it. She did ask that they remain flexible and make adjustments as needed, and Brit agreed.

"Yeah, they're all talking about the skill games, and Sidney actually just suggested another one. I think they'll be into it. It'll psych them up."

"That's great. That's the point, right?"

"Yep. I have something for you."

Alex reached into her pocket and pulled something out. It was a shiny new whistle, fastened onto a beaded, blingy lanyard. Brit laughed as she saw it but tried to hide her delight as she studied it. It was absolutely perfect for her, and she loved it. As she turned it over, she noticed an inscription in small, script letters. *Coach Britain Dodge.*

"Oh, Alex, this is perfect. And so sweet of you." She looked into Alex's sparkling eyes. "I love it."

"You're welcome. Now see if it works. We need to get this practice started."

"Wait a sec. I have something for you, too." Brit reached into her pocket and pulled out a small cardboard box of the size typically used for presenting earrings. She bit her bottom lip, trying to hold back her smile as she handed it to Alex.

Without delay Alex lifted the lid and stared at a whistle nearly identical to the one she'd given Brit. Hers had a green-and-white lanyard, matching the school colors. Alex held it up. Like Brit's, it was inscribed, but hers had just one word. *Nike.*

Alex laughed as she placed her new gift around her neck. "Do you want to get this practice started, Coach?"

Brit blew her new whistle, and within seconds the gym grew quiet as the players stopped bouncing and chatting and made their way toward their coaches.

Two hours later, as members of the boys' team began filtering into the gym, Alex blew her whistle and congratulated them all on

a great first practice. As the girls began their exodus, Alex and Brit turned to each other with triumphant looks. Not only were the veterans in great shape and in possession of enviable talent, a freshman guard named Melissa Black had dazzled them. She hadn't been a great junior-high-school player, but she'd had a growth spurt and spent some time working on her game, and it showed. She was the total package. And Kelsey was, without a doubt, destined to be a star.

One of the problems with the high-school gym was a lack of office space for the coaches. Alex's was a 4x4 converted closet and not conducive to a long conversation. With the boys now bouncing balls all over the court, the building was too noisy for Brit and Alex to talk. "I can't hear myself think," Alex complained.

"Do you want to grab some dinner?" Brit suggested. "A restaurant has to be quieter than this place."

"I'm not sure about that. How about a pizza at my place?"

Brit hesitated for just a moment. Did she really want to be alone with Alex at her place? They'd been spending much of their free time together since their first game of one-on-one, but Brit had never been to Alex's. Would it send the wrong message? What was the right message? When it came to Alex and her feelings about her, Brit just didn't know what to think. But they were friends, right? Coworkers who needed to cowork. "Okay," she answered, finally.

They met the men's assistant coach as they headed back to the locker room. "How'd it go, Coach?" His question was directed at Alex.

Maintaining a neutral expression and tone, Alex responded. "Even better than expected."

"Well, hopefully you do a better job than your predecessor."

Brit winced at the venom in his voice but was impressed by Alex's composure as she responded. "Yes, well, I hope so, too. Have a good practice," she said, walking away, Brit on her heels.

"What the hell?" Brit asked.

Alex shrugged. "He was the other finalist for my job. He's been the men's assistant for ten years, and with such a young head coach ahead of him, he's not likely to ever see a promotion. I guess he's holding a grudge."

"I'll say," she said, and patted Alex's back in support. "But I don't have any concerns about the board's choice. You're going to be great." Brit had watched in awe for two hours as Alex ran their first

practice, commanding the attention of every player and eliciting great performances from all of them.

Alex nodded. "Thanks," she said, but there was no smile on her beautiful face. Brit found herself wanting to change that. "Want to follow me?"

Brit followed Alex through residential neighborhoods, where the houses became bigger and bigger the farther they got from the center of town. They passed Mountain Meadows Country Club and then turned onto one narrow road, then another, and finally into a winding, tree-lined drive that opened into a clearing. In front of her stood a Tudor-style home that could only be described as a mansion. It had the typical half-timbering, black-and-white look, with mullioned windows and pitched roofs with dormers, and seemed to have been built as a series of additions off a large main building. As Brit was studying the expansive house and landscaping, one of the four garage bays opened and Alex pulled inside.

Brit pulled up behind her and parked in the driveway, feeling a bit awed by the house before her. When Alex stepped out of the garage, Brit questioned her immediately. She knew Alex didn't live with her parents—how could she afford a house like this on a teacher's salary?

"You live here?" she asked, incredulous.

Alex laughed at the reaction. "Actually, no. I live in the apartment above the garage."

"What a cool place. Who owns the house?" Brit asked as they walked into the garage and up a flight of stairs at the rear. She couldn't help noticing that the other car parked in the garage appeared to be a small convertible. The details were indistinguishable through the canvas tarp covering it.

"Pauline Fielding. Do you remember the Fielding grocery stores?"

Brit nodded. It was a successful local chain that had recently been sold, but everyone who'd lived in Northeastern Pennsylvania in the past fifty years had shopped at Fielding's at one time or another.

"Her husband was the founder. She's about ninety now, and she refuses to give up the house. She winters in Florida and doesn't want to leave the house completely empty. So I live here for free, in exchange for checking for rodents and leaks in the roofs and keeping burglars at bay. The only drawback is that I can't have parties in the main house… and my boyfriend can never spend the night."

"What a sacrifice!" Brit replied, laughing.

They'd entered into a small foyer, and Alex shrugged off her coat and hung it in the closet. She reached for Brit's when it was offered and hung hers as well. The foyer opened into a living area that took up the entire width of the garage, and beyond Brit could see a small kitchen. A door in a clear space toward the front of the room presumably opened to Alex's bedroom.

"I called for the pizza. It should be here in a few minutes. Can I get you a drink? Soda? Water? Or are you ready to drink your first beer?"

"Not quite there yet. Just water, please," she replied, looking around. "This place is magnificent." The Tudor theme she'd seen on the house's exterior extended to the interior, with a steeply pitched ceiling supported by huge wooden beams. There was hardwood throughout. On one wall a giant television was hung, another housed a bookcase, and at the front and rear were those magnificent windows. A comfy-looking leather couch sitting on a braided rug took up the middle of the room, and a sofa table behind it supported a lamp, which Alex promptly switched on. It cast the room in a warm, inviting glow.

"Have a seat," she directed as she headed for the kitchen. She was back a minute later with two waters. Leaning back into one corner of the sofa, she twisted the cap from hers and looked to Brit. "Well, what do you think?"

"Of the team or the house?"

"The team, silly. You've already told me how you feel about the house."

"Wow! That's how I feel. Melissa's fantastic. Kelsey is, too, but I already knew that. All of our guards are fabulous. I know we can't play four guards, but I can't imagine which one we'll bench."

"Every coach's dream," Alex smiled and sipped her water.

"How do we make cuts?"

Alex explained the process of selecting the varsity team. The players would have just one week to prove themselves before the final decision was made. Alex pulled her clipboard onto her lap and found the roster sheet. She began naming the players and they both graded them on several categories—speed, agility, ball-handling, shooting, rebounding, passing. Before they'd made it through a quarter of the list, Alex's cell phone rang. She glanced at it and jumped from the

couch. "It's the pizza," she informed Brit as she walked toward the door. "There's no doorbell on the garage."

She was back in a minute and placed the box on the coffee table. Carrying on their mission while they ate, by the time they finished the pizza they'd made it through the entire field of girls. Her hunger satisfied, and her job nearly complete, Brit found herself relaxing for the first time since the last time she spent with Alex. Easing back into the supple leather couch, Brit took the opportunity to study Alex. She was making notes on the clipboard, her head cocked as she bit her lip in concentration. A curl fell onto her forehead. Her long legs were tucked beneath her, and her strong hand gently cradled the clipboard on her knees.

Desire overcame her so suddenly that Brit gasped, and Alex looked to her, obviously as surprised as Brit. "You okay?"

"Yes, yes, I'm fine. I just need to use the restroom." Alex nodded to the appropriate door, and once safely behind it, Brit leaned against it, admonishing herself for that lapse in judgment. Alex Dalton wasn't a woman who had relationships, she reminded herself. It was okay to think about Alex once in a while. That was harmless, and probably inevitable. But she couldn't allow her fantasies to get out of control. While she was attractive and attentive and engaging, she was also a shark. She'd devour a little fish like Britain with a few snaps of the jaws and then spit out the leftover bones.

No matter how appealing she was, Alex was trouble. She could be her friend, but that was it. Friend, friend, friend, she told herself before exiting the bath.

She returned to the living room to find Alex talking on her cell. "It's Tam," she whispered.

"Tell her I said hi." Although Brit knew she'd visited the mountains, she hadn't seen Tam since the night they'd met.

Alex nodded. "Tam, Coach Dodge says hi."

Brit heard Alex groan. "You tell her. I'm going to put you on speaker," Alex announced.

"How are you?" Brit asked. "How's Kim?"

Brit's question led to a five-minute recital about the status of their relationship. They were dating. Taking it slowly. Getting to know each other. Sleeping together, with all of their clothes on.

Brit felt herself blushing from her head to her toes, and Alex seemed to notice.

"Uh, Tam. I think maybe this is TMI for Brit. She's not your BFF just because you shared a drink at the Frogg Pond."

Tam was silent for a second and then asked, "So, how was your first practice?"

Both Alex and Brit laughed at the sudden change in topic and told her about their team.

When they stopped talking, Tam wished them luck, then abruptly changed the subject again. "So, Brit, are you a film fan?"

"Film, like movies?"

"Yeah, like movies."

"I love movies. Why do you ask?"

"How about coming to Rehoboth for the film festival? Since Kim and I are sharing a room these days, we have an empty one. Why don't you join us?"

A few years before, Brit had discovered the program for the Rehoboth Beach Film Festival in the bathroom of her parents' beach house. She was awed by the schedule, which included tons of lesbian and gay films, and late at night, as the house slept, she meticulously recorded the names of the movies she'd put on her watch list. She was able to see most of them on her computer, and while some were lacking, others were phenomenal. In the back of her mind she'd filed away the film festival as a destination to visit when she finally found a girlfriend. She supposed Alex, Kim, and Tam would do until then.

"I'd love it!"

Across the couch, Alex gave her a thumbs-up. "Tam, will you be in Rehoboth at all before then? Can you send me the program?"

Tam laughed. "Sorry. You'll have to look it up on the Internet."

Brit spoke up. "Yeah, they have the entire program on the website."

"Have you been there before?" Alex asked.

Brit hesitated, feeling a little awkward. If these women only knew just how little experience she had in all aspects of life, they'd probably cancel the invitation to the beach and spend their time laughing about her. "Actually, no. I've never been. I just haven't been able to free my schedule. But I usually check out the program, and then I watch the movies from home."

"Yeah, us, too," Tam said. "It's hard to get time off from school,

so Kim and I usually miss the first two days. If we're lucky, we get to the beach on Friday and maybe see a late movie, but more often we just end up seeing one or two on Saturday. Then we rent the ones we want to see."

They spent the next few minutes talking about movies from the previous year's film festival. Brit had seen a number of them. She was pleased to see that she had another thing in common with Alex and her friends—they were all film aficionados. Not just the obvious lesbian titles, but classics as well. For a moment she allowed her mind to drift, and the image of Alex snuggled up beside her in her bed as they watched *Imagine Me and You* played on the screen in her head, filling the rest of her body with a flushing warmth. The desire to escape to the bathroom again suddenly overcame her.

Admonishing herself for these recalcitrant thoughts of Alex, she forced herself to rejoin the conversation. Alex and Tam hadn't noticed her absence. After a few minutes more, they told Tam good night.

Alex leaned back into the couch and pulled a blanket onto her lap, and Brit knew she must be tired. It'd been a long day—seven hours of school, two of practice, and then another two rehashing the day. Brit was so charged by the events of the day, she hardly noticed the fatigue. Yet when she took a moment to sink into the leather couch beside Alex and relax, her exhaustion became evident, and she suspected Alex felt the same way. She was about to announce her departure when Alex confirmed her suspicions.

"If it wasn't a school night, I'd invite you to stay and watch a movie," she said as she reached across the space between them and placed her hand gently on Brit's knee. "But, even if it wasn't, I don't know if I could stay up long enough to see the end. I'm beat."

Alex seemed to melt into the couch, totally relaxed, yet her eyes sparkled, spilling over with joy, excitement, and unmistakable desire. Brit saw it, and she knew she should fear it, but it was becoming more difficult to deny the attraction. It was clearly mutual. But how did she explain to this woman with so much sexual experience that she had none? How could Alex, a woman of many flings, understand Brit's desire for love and commitment?

She couldn't expect Alex to change. A sexual relationship would be on Alex's terms, with no candlelight dinners and bubble baths, or walks in the woods on snowy days. It wouldn't involve romance; it

would involve passion. It would be hot and heavy and physical, until it was over.

Looking across the couch at Alex, Britain wondered if she herself could change. Could she be happy with a fling, happy to have a little bit of experience under her belt? She smiled at the pun. She didn't know if she could, but if anyone could motivate her, Alex surely could.

Brit refocused her thoughts as she heard Alex's voice. Seeming to read her mind, Alex asked, "Are you dating anyone, Brit?"

Why was Alex asking? Brit's heart was pounding as she felt paralyzed by Alex's gaze. "Um, no," she managed to get out, clearing her throat.

"Do you date a lot?"

Brit felt uneasy and suddenly self-conscious about her lack of experience with women. Once she'd been proud of it, an old-fashioned ideal in a modern world, but now it just seemed lame. "I'm rather particular," she said at last.

A smile formed at the corners of Alex's mouth. "Hmm. Do you have criteria? Like she has to have blue eyes or be taller than you?" Alex stretched out, pulling her legs up, and stuffed them into the space between the couch at Brit's thighs.

Brit looked down to see if she could see something to explain the tingling that started in her leg and shot directly to her crotch. Then she looked up to see Alex grinning and realized Alex had given a description of herself.

Brit swallowed, then cleared her throat. She shifted on the sofa, but instead of alleviating the pressure on her leg, Alex slid farther down into the space left vacant by her butt. She stared across the room, focusing on the painting on the far wall. It was a portrait of a nude, probably a copy of a Renoir.

"Nothing like that," she said after a moment, taking care not to go down the path Alex was guiding her toward. "There needs to be a spark, though. Something that inspires me. I don't date just to get out of the house. I'd rather spend my time and my money doing something I enjoy rather than trying to make magic where there isn't any."

Alex nodded in support of Brit's philosophy. "Makes sense. How's it gone for you? Have you found much magic?" Alex's voice was a soft caress to her ears, husky and sexy.

A moment of vital importance had snuck up on her, and Brit

contemplated her response. She wasn't sure what she wanted from Alex. She wanted her, she knew that. But what did she want after the night of passion that usually brought an end to Alex's time with a girl? Could she sleep with Alex and move on, or would she need to have something more? She wished she knew the answer, but she didn't. She suspected she would never discover it by thinking about it, though. She needed to talk to Alex about it. She decided to tell her the truth.

"I have found absolutely no magic. None." Brit's eyes bore into Alex's, trying to convey the cryptic truth in her words. "Until now."

Alex took a deep breath, a look of confusion on her beautiful face. She tilted her head and studied Brit carefully. "Exactly how many women have you slept with, Britain?"

Brit whistled softly as she rolled her eyes heavenward, pretending to think. Then she looked at Alex again. "None."

Alex leaned forward, closing the space between them. "Oh, my God. You're a virgin?"

Brit wasn't sure what response she was hoping for, but she wasn't prepared for this one. Alex might as well have said, "Oh, my God. You're an alien." Or "You're a child molester." At least she was focusing on her lack of experience, though, and seemed to have completely missed the other morsel of truth Brit had spoken. Brit tried to blow it off and make light of it, hoping to regain some of the dignity draining from her body. "Yeah, well, like I said, I'm kind of picky," she said, and stood to leave.

Alex leaned back, the shock still evident on her face.

Brit needed to get out of there, and fast. "Hey, it's late, Alex. Time for me to go home. Thanks for a great day."

"Yeah, it was a great day," Alex said as she stood and walked her toward the door.

Brit slipped into her coat and was halfway down the stairs before Alex even reached the landing. "I'll see you tomorrow," Brit called over her shoulder, and as she walked into the cool night, she felt a chill that had nothing to do with the cool October air.

CHAPTER SIXTEEN

CLEAN SLATE

P.J. wiped two sweaty palms on his jeans as he approached his boss's office. For the past few months, any contact with The Man made him extremely nervous, and on this occasion it was doubly so. According to his calculations, his debt was paid, and he couldn't be happier. He'd learned a big lesson in his dealings with The Man, and P.J. vowed to stick his nose in his books and keep it there. The life of crime was too stressful.

Since he'd been on his repayment plan, he'd been setting his alarm for five every morning and working before school, then for hours after school. Some nights he didn't have a chance to begin his homework until very late, and with the college-prep curriculum he studied, laden with math and science, he felt like he was drowning. Fortunately, he caught on easily and could absorb most of what he needed simply by paying attention in class. If not for that, he'd be flunking out of high school.

Yes, he was happy to be done with this. He held his head high, feeling suddenly proud that he'd made the decisions he had and been able to start righting the wrongs he'd done. He'd even worked on a repayment plan with his papa. His knock was answered with an unfriendly growl, but The Man smiled when he saw it was P.J. who dared to disturb him.

"Little Man! Come in!"

It bothered P.J. that The Man referred to him as Little Man, that he seemed to think of him as his protégé. Following in his footsteps was the last thing P.J. wanted. Getting as far away from him as possible was his most immediate goal.

P.J. stood behind the chairs arranged before The Man's desk, for he hadn't been directed to sit. "Can I talk to you?" he asked.

"Of course. Tell me how everything's going. School? How's school?"

This line of questioning startled P.J. The only interest The Man had ever paid him was in angling for information, to learn how he might better use P.J. and his brother. And suddenly, the hair on the back of his neck stood as he wondered what The Man was thinking.

"School's tough. I have some hard classes. And with work...well, not much time for studying." P.J. smiled and shrugged to soften the impact of his words.

The Man's eyes narrowed as he looked at him. "It's a good thing you're so smart, Little Man. Studying comes easy to you. It wasn't like that for me. If it had been, I might have chosen another line of work. Anyway, what brings you in to see me?"

"I think my debt is paid. I calculated the percentages we agreed to, and with last night's sales, it looks like we're square." P.J. handed him a spreadsheet filled with initials and dollar amounts, and after looking at it for a moment, The Man inserted the report into his shredder and waited while it chomped the paper to bits.

Then he looked at P.J. "You're a smart cookie, Little Man. Why the fuck would you put this shit on your computer?"

P.J. was alarmed by The Man's tone and stammered in reply. "I...I...I needed to keep track, so I'd know when the debt was repaid."

The Man shook his head. "Do I look like an idiot to you, Little Man? I know exactly what's going on with my business. I'll tell you when your debt is paid. Now, where'd this spreadsheet come from?"

"I made it."

"No fucking kidding! Desktop? Laptop? Please don't say school computer or I'll throw something."

"No, no, no. Laptop," he stammered.

"Good. Bring it to me. I'll reimburse you for it. But I can't have records of my business floating around, Little Man. And don't ever, ever do something so stupid again."

P.J.'s knees threatened to buckle. "Okay, fine. I'll get you my laptop. But, um, now that, uh, my debt is paid, I think I'm just going to stop working and concentrate on school. I just wanted to tell you."

A menacing smile spread across The Man's face and he leaned

back in his chair, throwing his head back and letting out a laugh that would have rattled windows in his office if there'd been any. But The Man's office was in the center of the building, insulated from the world, and had no windows to rattle. P.J.'s eardrums were another story though, and his hands began to tremble to match their beat.

"Little Man, you're such a comedian."

P.J. swallowed hard. "Whatta ya mean?"

The Man smiled at him again. "You can't quit. I need you. Where would I find a replacement for you in the middle of the year? No, no, no. No quitting. Now that your debt's been paid, though, *you* get paid. You and your geeky big brother."

Before he could reply, his words were frozen on his lips by the sight of the money The Man pulled from his desk drawer. The roll was bound by a yellow rubber band, and when the man pulled it free, the pile of hundred-dollar bills seemed to dance in his hand. He quickly counted ten and placed them on the front of the desk, near P.J. He counted ten more and placed that pile beside the first. He nodded toward one and then the other. "For you, and for your brother."

P.J. had been paid minimum wage for all the hours he'd worked for the man. He hadn't earned a penny in his two months of criminal work. Now the man was offering him two thousand dollars for nothing. He wasn't even tempted, though. He'd had enough, and he shook his head to let The Man know. "No, thanks. I appreciate it, but now that my debt is paid, I just want to go back to my normal life."

The Man shook his head. "P.J., you're a criminal. You'll never go back to a normal life. What would the police think of what you've been doing? And how about those colleges where you're applying? Do you think they want juvenile delinquents roaming their campuses? I don't think so. And how about your brother? How long would he last when the police find out what he did?"

P.J. noted how he'd addressed him. He called him P.J. instead of Little Man, because it was P.J. who was doing The Man's bidding. Little Man didn't exist in the halls of his school and the businesses of his hometown, only in this office. It was P.J. who'd go to jail if he was caught. Fuck. He needed to get out of this while he still could. "But you said I'd be clear when I repaid you."

The Man let out a deep breath and shrugged. "A miscalculation on my part. You're too valuable to let go. I don't need your brother

anymore, so there's no need for you to tell him what's going on. Give him the money or keep it. Whatever you want. But I can't let you go. Not until you graduate. So get used to it, kid. You're working for me."

P.J. fought to swallow the bile that had risen in his throat, drowning his voice. He'd watched him operate for nearly three years, and he knew The Man let nothing stand in his way. He knew he'd be hurt, maybe killed, if he resisted. What could he say? He turned and was through the door before The Man called him back.

"Don't forget your money, Little Man. You earned it."

CHAPTER SEVENTEEN

CONFESSIONS

Alex was troubled by the thought she wanted something she couldn't have. Britain.

How could she ever have a relationship with someone, dreaming of a tomorrow that might never come? How could she ask that of someone she loved? How could she do that to someone she loved? She couldn't, and so her relationships with her bed partners had always been superficial. She'd been content with that, until Anke had opened her eyes to something different, and then Brit came along, unleashing within her a hunger Alex had only read about in romance novels. Now she was forced to ask herself the hard questions "What if?" and "Could we?" The answers were as elusive as a cure for the illness that was a focal point of her life and caused all her worry.

Even so, they'd been growing steadily closer since the school year began. They'd become friends. At least they had been, until Alex blew it.

Brit had shared something so personal, and Alex had reacted with such utter and total insensitivity she didn't see how Brit could ever forgive her. And it didn't appear she would. Since she'd admitted her virginity, Brit had been avoiding Alex. She was always friendly, always upbeat and enthusiastic, but that night at her apartment had been the last dinner they'd shared. It was the last social time they'd spent together, and Alex couldn't blame her.

She'd apologized for her rude reaction, but the more she tried to explain, the deeper a hole she dug. She wasn't judging, or perhaps she was, but it was great to know someone with such principles. Alex

hadn't known any virgins since her first girlfriend. No one that admitted it, anyway.

Brit was special. She deserved someone extraordinary, not someone like Alex, who slept around and didn't commit, who took no sides and rocked no boats. The impossibility of her fantasy had hit her at that moment as she sat across from Britain on her couch, and all she could do was silently watch her leave, because nothing she could say would equal Brit's words. And her inadequacies did nothing to quench the thirst she still had for Brit. The fire still burned. She wanted something she didn't deserve, but she wanted it nonetheless.

And she'd done something else, too, equaling the profound stupidity of her reaction to Britain, perhaps even surpassing it. She'd stopped her medication. Within a week, her back had started aching, and now every sudden turn she made resulted in shooting pain from the base of her spine to the back of her thigh. Even pain patches and pills gave her little relief. She could find no comfortable position for sleeping, and the sleeplessness made her miserable.

But it was time for her six-month checkup with the rheumatologist in Philly, and she hoped to talk to him about an alternative therapy. Perhaps one that wouldn't kill her but would give her some hope for a future, if not with Britain, then with someone. This was the most important doctor's visit she'd had in years, and, now, again, Brit was right at the heart of Alex's thoughts. She'd never had to answer to anyone, but now, she knew she'd have to explain her absence in a way that would appease Brit's curiosity. She couldn't just skip school without Brit asking why.

Someone cleared his throat, and Alex looked up at the group of students focused on the exams before them and wished for a moment she was back in school with them, without these worries. In high school all she'd had to worry about was bouncing a ball and finding ways to sneak her girlfriend past Andrew and into her bedroom.

Her gaze traveled to the window and she was shocked to see snow flurries. It was freakin' October. And then Alex sucked in a breath as she realized she hadn't bothered to check the forecast. Snow in the mountains would make her morning trip to Philly a nightmare. Pulling out her smartphone, she tapped the WeatherBug icon and checked the news. Fuck! It might snow.

Alex rubbed her hands over her temples. She couldn't cancel her appointment. It would take months for another one, and her back was in no shape to wait. She'd have to leave tonight. After practice she'd pack a bag and make the drive. The spare room at Kim's was always available, and she'd make good use of it. What would she tell Kim, though?

They'd been friends for seven years, and Kim knew about the backaches and the freaky rash on her left foot, about the headaches and the occasional pain in her ankles, and the pinkeye that plagued Alex from time to time. She'd never put it all together, though, and since Alex tried to minimize her symptoms and didn't complain much, her friends hadn't pressed for details. Kim would wonder about this trip, though, and wouldn't be put off with a simple answer either. Would she lie? Or was it time to finally come clean?

Discreetly, so her students couldn't see, she sent Kim a text telling her she'd be in Philly later in the evening and asked if she could spend the night at her place. Within seconds, Kim replied.

Of course. What's up?

Alex answered her.

I'll explain later. Wanna meet for cheesesteaks?

Kim's response came a few minutes later. Apparently she was paying more attention to her class than Alex was.

Call me from Allentown. ☺

Alex sighed as she put away the phone and glanced at the clock. It was already after two o'clock. She'd be in Philadelphia at seven.

She had five hours to decide.

The students began standing and stretching and handing in their tests. Alex stood and reminded them of the ticking clock, and just a few minutes later she was heading to the gym for practice.

The idea of changing her clothing for practice seemed impractical. Brit always did, emerging from the locker room in coordinating sweat suits and sneakers, and Alex always looked forward to seeing Brit's

variety of practice gear. Sometimes, she even changed her earrings if the colors contrasted. Alex merely changed from loafers into sneakers and coached in the same pants and shirts and sweaters she wore during the day at school.

"Nice pants," Alex said when she saw Brit.

They looked like they were covered in confetti, and Brit wore a lime-green fleece that magically made her blue eyes look green. The shirt pulled the green from both the pants and her eyes, and although Alex couldn't have imagined it if she hadn't seen it on Brit, the effect was stunning.

Brit nodded, acknowledging the color coordination of the blue shirt and blue pinstripes in the pants she'd chosen. "You, too."

Alex looked down at her black pants and nodded. "I'm a wild one, all right. But, hey, at least we don't clash too badly." In fact, the blue and green went together nicely.

"I don't think we clash at all, Alex."

Before she could catch her tongue, the words slipped out. "Then why are you avoiding me?"

Brit just stared at Alex, literally speechless, and Alex felt like the fool she was. "I'm sorry. I shouldn't have said that. Forget it. But I want to tell you something."

Brit's eyes opened in surprise and she turned to Alex, studying her. "What's up?"

"I just wanted to let you know I won't be in school tomorrow. I'll still be at practice—don't worry. I wouldn't abandon you. I just didn't want you to be concerned."

Brit touched Alex's arm. "That's so sweet of you, because I would have been. What's going on?"

"Ehhh. Doctor's appointment. Nothing exciting."

"Is everything okay?" The look on Brit's face nearly melted Alex's heart, made her want to pull Brit back into the locker room and tell her everything, and kiss her senseless, too.

"Yeah, everything's fine. Just a checkup." Which was technically true. This was her regular appointment.

"Oh, wow. You go for checkups? Maybe I should do that, now that I have insurance. I never thought of it before."

Alex swallowed a laugh. "Maybe you should."

"Who do you go to?"

Just then an errant ball came flying their way, and only Alex's quick reflexes protected Brit from a concussion, so the issue was forgotten. Relief washed over her when practice ended and she was finally in her car, heading home. It took only a few minutes to pack her bag, and a yogurt appeased her growling stomach before she was on the road. As instructed, she called Kim from Allentown, and by seven thirty they were at Dalessandro's enjoying cheesesteaks.

"So why are you here? What's her name?" Kim's tone was light but her gaze piercing.

"Diona." Diona was the name of Dr. Prejean's nurse.

"Is she hot?"

Diona was wider than she was tall, but with a beautiful face and a heart to match. She'd been guiding and counseling Alex for nearly five years.

"She's lovely," Alex said truthfully.

"So how did you meet her?"

"She's a nurse. She works with my doctor."

Kim chewed, and then the words seemed to register. Her forehead wrinkled as the question formed in her eyes. "What doctor?"

Alex sighed and put on a brave smile. "Kim, I have to tell you something."

Kim cleared her throat and put her sandwich back into the little plastic serving basket, then took a sip of her drink. She wiped her mouth and waited, not looking at Alex.

"Kim?" Alex asked.

"So, tell," she said at last, finally turning to face her.

Alex made it short and simple. Kim already knew the symptoms. Alex just needed to fill in the diagnosis to give her a glimpse of the big picture.

"How long have you known?" she asked.

"Five years."

"So why tell me now?"

"Your place is cheaper than a hotel, and I can't sleep under your roof and lie to your face."

Kim laughed. "I guess I can't argue with that logic." She cleared her throat again.

"And maybe it's just time to talk about it."

"So, are you…okay?"

Alex nodded. "I'm okay. I'm good. Just a little stiff after the ride."

"That's…good."

They both laughed, and Alex pulled out her wallet and paid the bill. Twenty bucks for a night in Philly was very reasonable. Much more reasonable than the overnight parking fee at the garage closest to Kim's downtown apartment. From there, though, Alex could walk to the hospital in the morning and have no worries about the time.

When they were both changed into their most comfortable sweatshirts and pants, they reconvened in Kim's living room. "Are you up for a movie?" Kim asked.

"Sure."

"Or do you want to talk?"

Alex leaned back into the couch and hugged a big squishy pillow. "Let's talk. How's my friend Tam?" It was unsettling to think that the three of them had lived together for nearly three months every summer and then could go weeks without having a significant conversation once Alex became engulfed in the chaos of basketball season.

"She loves me." Kim sighed and leaned back into the opposite corner of the couch. Both of them had their feet up on the hassock, and Alex gave Kim's a soft kick.

"I know that, silly. She's always loved you. But what's happening now? Who's moving where? What china pattern have you picked out?"

"Huh? How do you know about this shit?"

"Andrew. I bought them a sugar bowl for their wedding shower. It was the least expensive gift on the bridal registry, and it still cost me fifty bucks."

"Well, if we register you'll be the first to know. As far as a move goes…I think we should sleep together first. What if we're incompatible?"

Alex waved her hand in disgust. "What is it with people not having sex anymore?"

"Who else isn't having sex?"

As Alex looked at Kim, she realized her error. That she was practicing celibacy on the off chance Brit would someday go out with her was absurd. At times she couldn't believe it, and at other times she was tempted to call someone up or go out to a bar and find someone for

a few hours of fun. Just as fast as the thoughts came to her, though, they left and she was alone with her daydreams of the only woman she'd ever wanted who didn't share her desire.

"No!" Kim practically screamed. "Not you, too?" She buried her face in her hands and faked a sob. "My hero has fallen."

"Shut up!"

"Seriously, Alex, you're not having sex? Why?"

Alex pursed her lips, trying to decide if she should tell Kim her feelings about Brit. She'd never disclose the confidence Brit had shared with her, so how could she explain all of her insecurities without divulging their cause? But this was Kim, and she'd already revealed something much more significant than a crush on Brit.

"Because I met someone."

"Someone who doesn't like sex?"

"No, you big jerk. I'm just taking it slowly."

"Why?" Kim asked, the confusion written all over her face.

"You're so dense. I like this girl. I don't want to seduce her. I want to date her."

Kim leaned back and studied Alex, pursing her lips. "It's Brit, isn't it?"

Alex swallowed and nodded. "Is it that obvious?"

"Well, I didn't figure it out until you told me it was someone special, but it makes sense. You've been spending most of your time with her."

"I don't think she likes me."

"What? How could she not? You're tall, gorgeous—don't make me say any more or I'll get sick. All the women love you, Alex."

"She's different, Kim. I know she's attracted to me, but I actually think she's holding my torrid past against me."

Kim nodded. "I can see that. She's looking for more than one night, huh?"

Alex smiled. "You know what, Kim? I think I am, too."

"A lot of other shit goes with a relationship, though. It's not just having someone around to keep you company. You have to compromise on every aspect of your life." Kim pointed to the dark-green walls. "The colors you paint your apartment." She pointed to the couch. "Leather or fabric? Leather's too cold for some people and fabric gets dirty. What's for dinner? What movie do you see? What game are you going

to watch? Where are you traveling? It's all compromise. Then there are the problems—not enough money to do everything you want, so how do you choose? What if you don't like her friends, or she doesn't like yours?"

"That's not possible, but I see why it could be a problem."

"A huge problem."

"So, is all this compromise giving you second thoughts about Tam?" Alex asked, concerned.

"Absolutely not. I think I'm going to give up teaching and work as a chemist. I have a dual degree. I almost have my master's. I can move to Maryland and live happily ever after."

"Even with pastel-colored walls?"

Kim nodded. "Even with."

"Wow. That's serious."

Kim smiled.

"So I should overcome my anxiety and just ask her out, huh?"

"What do you have to lose, other than pride?"

Alex pursed her lips. "There is the matter of this disease, Kim."

"What about it?" Suddenly fear flashed into Kim's eyes. "What, Alex?"

"I've been well controlled, Kim. But the medication's really a bitch. It suppresses my immune system, so I'm at risk for infections. And cancer."

"What kind of infections? What kind of cancer?"

"All kinds of infections, and lymphoma. It doesn't really seem fair to go into a relationship with someone knowing I'm probably going to die."

Kim jumped up, the fear on her face evident. "What the fuck are you talking about? You're going to die? I thought you said you were fine?"

"I am now, but who knows what could happen?"

Kim stared at Alex. "So what are we talking about here? Like a one-percent chance of death, or a ninety-percent chance?"

"Single digits."

Alex could see Kim's eyes cloud over as she thought about this. "We're all going to die, Alex. Car accidents, school shootings, cancer. You can't let this possibility stop you from living your life."

"It doesn't seem fair to ask this of someone."

"Well, this is America and people are free to make their own choices. If she thinks you're worth it, then it's her choice. If not, then fuck her."

Alex laughed. Could it really be so easy? Of course not, because even if Alex decided to go for it and pursue a relationship with Brit, there was the tiny little matter of Brit not wanting anything to do with her.

❖

"You are such a sweetheart, Alex," Diona said as she unwrapped the box of Gertrude Hawk chocolates Alex had given to her. They were her favorite, and unavailable in Philly, so Alex picked up a box from the store near her house before each doctor's visit.

"How are you feeling?" she asked as she bit into something luscious.

Alex shrugged and sighed. "I stopped my meds."

"I have a mind to put you over my knee and spank you."

"I hate it," she said, trying to control her emotions. "I just want to be normal."

Diona shook her head. "I understand, Alex. But a war's going on in your body, and this medication is helping you win it. Think of a bomb going off, of all that destruction. That's what's happening to your connective tissue. Little by little, it's getting destroyed, until one day, your back won't move. Then there's nothing you can do. The damage is irreversible."

Just then, Dr. Prejean walked in. "It sounds like I'm interrupting a serious discussion."

Alex tried to smile but couldn't. She listened as Diona told the doctor about her latest concerns.

Dr. Prejean patted Alex's leg and looked her in the eye. "I can't guarantee anything, Alex, but this is what I predict. If you take your medication, there is a very small chance you can get sick and die. If you don't take it, there is a huge chance you'll live to regret it."

"Is there a different med I can use? One that's less dangerous?"

"No. This is working. It's the right drug. Why change something that works?"

"I guess I don't have much choice, do I?" The doctor was right.

She felt good on the medication, but since she'd stopped, she had a little more stiffness and pain every day.

"I know it's scary to have this disease. But you're lucky, too. We can treat this. A hundred years ago…I'm glad I didn't have to practice medicine then."

Alex just stared at her.

"The chances of getting sick are very, very, small. You can't dwell on it, Alex. Take your medication, live your life. Every day is precious, for all of us, whether we have an autoimmune disease or not. You're never getting today back. Make the most of it."

"I understand about today. But what about tomorrow? How many tomorrows do I have?"

"How many do I have? None of us knows that, Alex. But you're not terminal. Stop acting like you are."

Chapter Eighteen

Trick or Treat

B rit followed the commands on her GPS deep into the forest, wondering if she'd made a mistake. This was a long way to drive just to get away from Alex, and she hoped she'd find her way home along these dark, deserted country roads.

But she needed to get away from Alex. She needed a diversion. She was so attracted to Alex, and until the night she'd told Alex she was a virgin, she was fairly certain the feeling was mutual. Alex hadn't handled that news well, though, and it had been a tough battle for Brit to appear unfazed by Alex's rebuff. The attraction was still sizzling, which confused her. What was Alex really feeling? What was she really feeling? Until she decided what to do about it, she was trying to keep a little distance. A dozen times in the past weeks Brit had declined Alex's offers for dinner after practice. Other than that one time, Alex hadn't questioned her, and each time she graciously accepted the rejection as if it were of no consequence.

And that was another problem. Brit wished it was of consequence for Alex. She wished she saw a question in Alex's eyes, some bewilderment at the sudden rejections. She longed to see a sag of her shoulder indicating disappointment, or a frown, or a sigh of frustration—anything to show that she cared. But Alex showed no response, and in the last week, she actually seemed happier. She had a bounce in her step and a twinkle in her eye, and Brit wondered if she'd started dating someone. Or at least met someone. Alex's actions proved that she meant nothing more than a potential fling, just like Anke.

To get away from Alex, she'd decided to attend a Halloween party, where her friend Candace promised a plethora of single women with

whom she could mingle. A fellow teacher, Candace and she had met the year before when she was student-teaching. Candace and her partner lived an hour away from Brit, and Brit had never met most of their friends. It was the perfect escape.

Her GPS directed her to the appropriate driveway, and she was thrilled to see a dozen cars already there. She loved a big crowd, had always enjoyed talking to people and hearing stories. After parking, she followed the parade of jack-o'-lanterns to a chalet constructed of logs. Candace and her partner had built the home themselves, and she was eager to see their handiwork.

A sign directed her to the sliding-glass doors around the back, across a fieldstone patio, and a petite brunette named Rose, who introduced herself as Candace's partner, greeted her at the door. After taking her coat, Rose guided her toward the back of the room, where she saw Candace working behind a well-stocked bar.

Along the way, they passed women shooting darts, shooting pool, shooting hoops, and playing air hockey. Others were seated at a sectional couch, talking, as a huge television played mutely in the background. A musical group Brit didn't recognize provided the soundtrack to the numerous conversations occurring all around them. Memorabilia from every sport covered the walls. There were jerseys, pennants, framed balls, pictures, and posters, some old, some new. The room was the ultimate girl cave.

Candace came out from behind the bar to hug her and immediately offered introductions to the three women who sat there, drinking beer and mixed drinks and munching goodies from the bowls of snacks on the shiny glass surface. "Nice." A woman dressed as a police officer complimented her on her Minnie Mouse costume, and Brit blushed the color of her shoes as she saw the woman's eyes follow her legs from the top of her skirt down to the shiny red pumps. She was tempted to run away, but she didn't. She'd driven an hour to meet people, and she wasn't leaving until she did.

After regaining composure sufficient for speech, Brit spent a few minutes critiquing their costumes. The cop looked genuine, and a wicked thought flashed through Brit's mind as she noted the handcuffs dangling at the woman's hip. The wicked thought included Alex, and she quickly pushed it away. A hockey player's costume was complete, from the blackened eye and missing teeth to the skates she was actually

wearing. Hopefully the woman could handle her alcohol, but if she lost her balance and fell, the woman in scrubs could offer some first aid.

The group was friendly and welcomed her to their conversation, which at the moment involved a debate over which female vocalist's voice provided the most stimulating background for a romantic encounter. Candidates for the crown included a few women Britain had never heard, so she didn't feel she could offer a fair vote, but the group agreed to throw out those few. Adele, Carrie Underwood, Faith Hill, Whitney Houston, Cher, Norah Jones, and Alicia Keys were all in the running. When the late Ms. Houston's name was suggested, the police officer suggested an entirely new contest for the best *late* artist. The hospital-worker-in-scrubs pulled out a smartphone and began searching for demo songs, which prompted a call for yet a third contest—this one for a specific song to set the mood.

As she laughed and debated with these three very funny women, Brit marveled at the luxury of feeling so relaxed in a social setting. She fit right in, no longer the round peg in the square hole. Just as she was congratulating herself on her decision to make the long drive to the party, Britain looked up and gasped.

❖

Alex finished wiping the last of a dozen folding chairs and leaned it against the wall. She'd been assigned this job when it became apparent to Rose and Candace that this Halloween party was going to have a record attendance. Her job had been to trek through the yard to the pool house at the rear of the property and retrieve additional seating options for the partygoers. Her friend Erin had been transferring their hoard inside, while Alex was busy in the alcove adjacent to the rear doors, cleaning off several months' accumulation of dust and cobwebs until the seats were suitable for use. After the crowd began arriving, the large basement had grown quite noisy, and Alex was enjoying the break away from the cacophony of music and voices.

Two weeks after restarting her medication, she was beginning to feel human again. Doing physical work felt good after a month of difficulty with simple tasks like tying her shoes. But something was wrong, and she couldn't name it. She didn't feel sad, and in fact, she felt happier than she ever had in her life. Classes were going very well.

Her team was going to be fantastic. She had a new friend named Brit who had an ability to make her heart pound in a most delightful way.

The doctor's words had been a great comfort to Alex, just the tonic she needed to soothe her spirit. She wasn't dying. She needed to live.

Could that life include someone like Brit? Since seeing her doctor, she'd been trying to find the courage to talk to her, but Brit was still avoiding her. Sure, they talked every day at school—but not about what was really important. They spent three hours every day, six days a week, either at practice or discussing practice. But every time Alex said those six words, "I need to talk to you," Brit backed off like a frightened kitten. Now Alex spent most of her free time thinking about Brit in one way or another. In spite of her caution, Alex still thought Brit was feeling a similar attraction. The heat between them singed Alex. Everything she knew about women told her it wasn't one-sided. But had she blown her chances with Brit in that one moment of supreme insensitivity?

Alex didn't know what to think, or feel, and so when her friend Erin had called that afternoon to invite her to the party, she'd gladly accepted.

Carrying the last two folding chairs, Alex followed the noise back into the great room and set them up near the couch. Then she had a seat and pulled a cold beer from the ice bucket conveniently located beside the couch. Two beers, that was the limit her doctor had given her, and she intended to enjoy them thoroughly. The group seated here consisted of her closest friends at home, a bunch of jocks with whom she'd been competing since she was a teenager. They'd all played softball together, and some of them still did, although Alex had given up the game in favor of her summers at the beach. Some played on the same basketball team, a few of them golfed, and all of them liked to hang out and watch sports. They were opinionated, vocal, sometimes crude, and always fun. Alex adored them.

"So let's do Rock-Paper-Scissors," one friend suggested.

Another waved a dismissive hand at the suggestion and frowned. "There's too many of us. How about we pick names? We can use a hat." Someone was dressed as a New York Yankee.

"I see straws on the bar. We can draw straws," someone else suggested.

"Straws are good," a few of them said.

"What are you guys talking about?" Alex queried after taking a sip of her beer. Apparently she'd missed something important while she'd been on chair duty.

"We've spotted an unidentified hottie at the bar. We're devising a fair plan to see who'll get to talk to her first."

Alex turned her head in the direction of the bar, and her heart skipped a beat as she looked into Britain's beautiful blue eyes. She sucked in a very loud breath.

Her friends laughed. "That's what we said, too, Alex," someone commented, but Alex was too distracted to notice who it was.

"So, I'll get the straws," another offered.

Rising, Alex stopped her friend. "Oh, no, you don't. This one's off limits." Without saying another word, she walked across the room, her eyes locked into Brit the entire time. They'd just seen each other hours before, at their nine a.m. practice, yet the unexpected sight of Brit here sent Alex off balance. When she reached the bar, Alex instinctively opened her arms and drew Brit into a hug. Protective, possessive, she pulled her close and was startled. Brit's body against her felt good, right. Alex forced herself to shorten their contact before the heat set her on fire.

Pushing Brit back a few inches, Alex surveyed Brit and then once again met her eyes. "Hello, Ms. Mouse. You look quite adorable this evening. Talk about a small world."

Brit nodded and forced a smile. "It is indeed, Captain." Brit couldn't believe her luck. Bad luck. She wanted to meet people, to meet women. To forget about Alex Dalton, the very one who had swaggered across the room as if she owned it, looking sexy as hell in a pirate's costume. The one who made her mouth dry and other places very, very wet. The one who spun her head and electrified every one of her senses. The one who had bedded so many women she'd been mortified to the point of speechlessness when she learned of Brit's inexperience.

"So what brings you here?" Alex asked.

"Oh, I just needed a change of scenery."

"Are you alone?"

She might have been embarrassed if someone else had posed the question, embarrassed that she'd had so very few dates in her life, but in answering Alex, she felt no shame. Alex already knew the truth, so what did it matter? She was, in fact, relieved that she was alone.

"Yes." Alex touched her arm and a spark seemed to shoot through her. It was not a welcome jolt.

Since timing is everything, Candace returned to the bar at that moment, accompanied by another woman dressed as Sponge Bob, sparing Brit from any further intimacy with Alex. She just couldn't handle it. Why did Alex affect her so? Brit glanced at the newcomer. A handsome face, with dark features and a wide smile, was the only physical feature evident in the bulky costume, other than height, which Brit noted was about the same as Alex's. Why did she compare everyone to Alex?

"Brit, I want you to meet my friend Marissa. Mar, this is my friend Britain."

Alex stepped back reluctantly as Candace and Marissa encroached on the personal space she'd been sharing with Brit. And I'm Alex, she thought, but held her tongue. This was obviously more than a casual introduction, and Alex was unsure if Candace, Brit, or both had planned this meeting. Knowing how things had been going with Brit, none of the options would have surprised her.

"Very nice to meet you." Brit's tone was friendly, as always.

"This is my friend, Alex," Candace offered reluctantly. And then, before Alex could even respond, she felt the firm pressure of Candace's grip on her elbow, leading her away. "Let's get a few more chairs, A," Candace suggested.

"What the fuck?" Alex asked when they were out of earshot. "We were talking!"

"Don't go there, Alex. Do. Not. Go. There."

Alex pulled up and turned to face Candace. "What are you talking about? She's my new assistant coach."

A hand flew to Candace's mouth. "Oh, A. I'm so sorry. I thought you were putting the moves on her, and I'd promised Mar I'd introduce her. I didn't know."

Alex was stunned. Offended. Humiliated. "And what if I was putting the moves on her? Are you some sort of guardian angel or something?"

"A, don't even joke about it. Britain is a *nice* girl. The last thing she needs is a player like you."

Alex shook her head in disbelief. "Oh, thanks, friend. Is that what you think of me?"

Candace looked sorry, sort of. She screwed her face into a look that begged forgiveness and extended her arms, palms up. "Well, Alex, you do have somewhat of a reputation."

Alex was silent. After all, what could she say? Candace spoke the truth. "There are no more chairs," she said, changing the subject.

"Oh, that's okay. We don't need anymore. I just wanted to get you away from Britain."

Alex didn't speak. She just turned and walked away, toward the back of the house, through the alcove, and out onto the patio beside the pool. A significant part of their acreage had been cleared to allow for Rose and Candace's swimming pool. The missing canopy of trees allowed in the light of a bright moon and a million stars, and as she leaned against a lamppost, Alex glanced up toward them. It was a spectacular sight, and as she stood contemplating Candace's stinging barbs, she barely heard the door sliding open behind her, the soft steps of the woman gliding up beside her. Only when the heat of Brit's hand seared her shoulder did she return to earth. She whirled around to see who'd joined her but instinctively knew it was Brit even before she saw her. She quickly turned her eyes back to the sky.

"Are you okay?" Britain asked her. "What happened?"

"Oh, nothing. I'm fine. Just needed a little fresh air."

"Good. I was worried." Brit sighed but didn't move her hand, then followed Alex's gaze. "Wow! What a view."

Alex looked down, away from the stars to Brit's beautiful face, and then, before she could stop herself, before Candace's words could shackle her or her own insecurity could paralyze her, she pivoted and seized Britain's shoulders. She stepped forward and pulled Britain toward her, claiming her lips as she'd wanted to since the day they met.

Brit's lips were soft, and warm, and as her tongue peeked through them, they were suddenly wet and welcoming. Alex dropped her hands to circle Brit's waist and pulled her closer. Flames of fire, flames of desire shot from Alex's feet to the top of her head, and she seemed to melt in the heat, molding her body in an embrace that seemed to weld their separate forms into one.

She collapsed against Brit, and they held each other upright. Brit's tongue was inside her mouth, tickling hers, then on her lips, teasing them, too. Alex fought to control the beating of her heart as it pounded in her chest.

Their lips eased apart, yet they stayed connected, their foreheads meeting and their arms clinging as their breaths came in desperate gasps. Alex was weak with desire. She'd never wanted anyone more.

"Why?" Brit whispered after a moment.

This wasn't the question or the command she'd expected after such an earth-shattering kiss. "Huh?" Alex stammered, confused by the intoxicating kiss and the intoxicating woman and the strange question.

"Why did you kiss me?" Now Britain pulled back and in the faint light looked expectantly at Alex. "What do you want?"

Alex ran a hand through her hair, jumbled thoughts running through her mind. What kind of question was that? "What do you mean?" She paused, then said simply, "I want you."

Britain groaned. The kiss had left her dizzy and definitely longing for more. The proof of her desire was tangible in her weak knees and wet sex. She wanted Alex. So why was she fighting her feelings? Alex had proven to be more than the woman on the boardwalk in Rehoboth. She'd become a friend. A playmate. Brit knew if she said the word, they could be lovers, too. Maybe it was time to stop avoiding Alex and talk to her, see where this might lead. If not, she'd go mad simply from the memory of the kiss they'd just shared.

A relationship with Alex was a risk, like driving the lane with the ball in her hands. She could miss the shot and lose the game. She could get flattened by the opposing center and sent sprawling to the floor. Or she could make the basket and be a winner.

Trophies and awards on her parents' mantel proved she'd been a winner on the basketball court. They'd once made her feel important, accomplished. None of them really mattered anymore. She wanted and needed something more, and that something was standing before her, not even playing defense. It seemed that Brit just had to make an uncontested layup. Did she have the courage to take the shot?

Maybe, but first she needed to know the rules of the game. She needed to share her feelings. And she needed to know Alex's feelings as well. She rested her head against Alex's shoulder and spoke into her jacket, still holding her arm.

"Alex, you're an English teacher. You're good with words. You've got to come up with a better answer than that."

"I don't think I understand the question," Alex said.

Brit leaned back and found Alex's eyes. "What are you after, here?

You know me. I'm not some girl you can just play with and then cast aside. I'm not fling material. So what do you want with me?"

Alex stammered, finding her courage. She sniffled, the cold air causing an inopportune runny nose. Then she spoke the truth of her heart. "You make me forget everyone else in the world, Brit. No one else is on my mind or in my heart. I want to be with only you. It doesn't matter what we're doing. If we're doing it together, I'm happy."

"But what do you want? Are you looking for a new best friend? Someone to hang out with? Someone to bike with? A new golf partner?"

Alex shook her head. "All of those. But a lover, too. I want a real relationship, Brit. With you."

"You were somewhat put off when you found out I'm a virgin. What's changed?"

Alex shook her head, reached for Brit's hand. "Oh, no, Brit. I wasn't put off. I was just shocked." Alex paused and looked heavenward, unable to find the courage to look at her. "I feel unworthy of you," she whispered.

The confession shocked Brit. "You?"

"Yeah, me."

Brit took Alex's hand and squeezed it. "Look at me, Alex."

Brit waited until Alex looked down at her. "I've never felt such an attraction to another human being. It's so powerful I feel like I'm flying most of the time. But I have to know this means something more than sex to you. If not, I can't do it. Maybe, if we didn't work together, I could have a little fling. Because, honestly, you turn me on so much I think I'll die soon if you don't touch me. But I can't make love with you and walk away and pretend each time I see you that it didn't happen."

"Didn't you hear me? It's not about sex! I want a relationship with you." The way Alex tripped on the words made Britain laugh, and Alex joined her. "I'm nervous. You make me nervous."

Pulling Alex closer, Brit once again folded herself in her arms as she attempted to reassure her. The heat of Alex's body was the perfect remedy to the chilly night. The combination of Alex's firm muscles against her and the gentle way she held her made Brit feel safe. How could Alex ever hurt her?

Emotions overwhelmed her—fear, happiness, desire. She thought she might cry. This was exactly where she wanted to be, and it felt right.

She knew she had to say something to Alex, but for a moment she just stayed silent and enjoyed the perfection of the moment.

Then stroking Alex's back, she tilted her head, kissed along her jaw until she found her ear. "I don't imagine you're nervous very often. But if it makes you feel any better, you should know that I share your jitters."

"It does," Alex said, and she kissed the same place on Brit's ear. "So what now?" Alex asked.

Brit felt exhausted as heat seemed to soften the resolve of her muscles. It took a few seconds to think about Alex's question. She had no idea what came next. A kiss was the last thing she'd imagined as she'd followed Alex's retreating form onto the patio. But then she thought of her fantasies, of how she'd always imagined it would be. How it should be.

"Why don't we go on a date?" Brit said.

"A date?"

"Yes, a date. You pick me up, we do something fun together, you drive me home afterward."

"And we don't have sex."

Brit laughed. "Not until the second date."

Alex pulled Brit close again, and their mouths found each other in the darkness. This kiss was slower, wetter, deeper. Hotter. They pulled away breathless.

Alex dropped her hand to hers and pulled her toward the house. "Do you wanna get out of here and go on a date with me, Ms. Mouse?"

Her heart soaring at the words she'd never really thought she'd hear, Brit smiled.

"I'd love to, Captain."

CHAPTER NINETEEN

FILM FESTING

It was the second Friday in November, a cold, clear, crisp evening. Snow flurries had been dancing outside Alex's window earlier in the day, threatening their plans, but they'd dissipated without a trace, making way for a magnificent sunset. An orange sun was just falling off the mountain's top as Alex rushed in the door from practice, deposited one bag and picked up another, and threw some food into a cooler before heading back out the door. She drove to Brit's and announced her arrival by phone, then waited for her in the parking lot.

This was the weekend of the film festival, and they'd scheduled practice to allow them forty-eight hours of downtime. It was crazy, the idea of driving two hundred miles just to watch a few movies, but they were doing it anyway. The movie previews were exciting, and they'd see Sal and Sue and hang out with Kim and Tam.

Alex was eager for her friends to spend time with Brit. Their opinions meant a lot to her, and even though she wouldn't give up on Brit if they suggested it, their stamps of approval would make her feel better. She and Brit were both looking forward to seeing Sal. Since reconnecting at the beach, Alex knew Brit had been speaking to Sal weekly. Sal had taught for more than thirty years and was a great source of advice for everything from handling tardiness to developing test content. And her basketball knowledge was superb. They often put the phone on speaker as they talked hoops and Sal shared her ideas for plays and drills to help her players develop. Sal was important to both of them, and now that they were dating, both she and Brit wanted to share the news in person.

"All set?" Brit said as she opened the rear door and put her bag on the seat.

They talked nonstop during the trip, even through their quick dinner at the service plaza in Allentown. In truth, they'd been talking for two weeks. Since that moonlit kiss beneath the canopy of stars, so much had changed between them. Before that, neither was sure of the other. But they'd made a pact, sealed with a kiss and witnessed by the moon. Conversation had always been easy for them, but now it was more relaxed. They were talking about feelings and making plans instead of basketball and school and the weather.

"Yep," Alex replied, and after leaning over to give Brit a kiss on the cheek, she started the car. Dating. They were dating. They looked for each other at school, and walked by each other's classrooms, and slipped each other notes. Taking advantage of every opportunity, one or the other of them always reached out to touch a shoulder or an elbow when they were in close proximity. Once in a while, their eyes would meet, and they sent messages that way. *You look great. It's nice to see you. I want to kiss you again. And again.*

Alex was smitten. But since that first, scorching, life-altering kiss, there had been only a few follow-ups, and Alex was frustrated. Brit's comment about sex on the second date had clearly been a joke. They'd watched a movie at Alex's place the night after the Halloween party and kissed good night in the driveway when Alex walked her to the car. Short, sweet, and intoxicating—that kiss had just left her hungry. After practice a few days later, Brit made Alex dinner, and another solitary, fabulous kiss occurred. They'd spent Saturday together, gone out for dinner with friends, and kissed in the car before Brit retired to her apartment, alone. Again during the week, Brit kissed her at the door. All of these one-kiss nights were driving her crazy. The need for more was driving her crazy.

Alex was amazed at how her priorities—and perhaps her needs—had changed. In her life before Brit, she would have laughed at the idea of dating. She wanted and expected sex, and she found plenty of partners who thought like her. Now though, she'd be thrilled to just cuddle, and to hold Brit, and to kiss her for hours. Sure, she wanted to make love, but sex was a big commitment for Brit, and she was willing to wait until Brit was ready. They'd occupy separate bedrooms in Rehoboth—or at least that was the plan. Alex was eternally optimistic.

When they grew restless with the stops and starts of Friday-night traffic, Brit turned on the stereo, and as they listened to the *Kinky Boots* soundtrack the miles passed quickly. Alex had seen the show, and Brit wanted to, and they both knew all the words and sang along. They seemed to float on the fun lyrics and happy ending. It was after ten when they pulled into the parking lot of the condo. Kim and Tam had decided to take in a movie, so they wouldn't see them until later. Alex and Brit were alone.

The thought made Brit shudder. Sure, they'd been alone dozens of times before this night. This was different, though. Rehoboth was a vacation of sorts, meant for them to relax and let loose. Just what did that mean to Alex? In the past, it had meant sex. What now that she was with a woman who wasn't such an easy conquest?

The condo looked small from the outside but had an open layout and was quite roomy inside. On the first floor was a small study, with a stocked bookshelf and a large couch and chair flanking a reading lamp. A kitchenette opened to a spacious combined living and dining area. Up a flight of stairs were three bedrooms. She and Alex deposited their bags in rooms separated by a shared bath. Alex showered first, and after slipping into sweatpants and a long sleeve T-shirt, Brit joined her on the couch. Alex looked comfy in sweats, too. They were still alone, except for a bottle of red wine, a corkscrew, and two wineglasses sitting on the coffee table.

Raising a questioning eyebrow toward Alex, Brit picked up the bottle. It was the same cabernet she'd enjoyed on their first…date? "For me?" she asked.

"You liked that label, didn't you?" Alex queried.

"I did. Thank you!" As Brit began peeling the foil wrapper from the cork, the significance of the second glass registered. There was no beer or other beverage on the table in front of Alex. "And will you be joining me?"

"I thought I might broaden my horizons."

Pouring just an inch of wine in each glass, Brit showed Alex how to swirl the wine and inhale the aroma before taking her first sip. "Now let it flow slowly across your tongue, from the tip to the base, so you can pick up all the flavors."

Tipping her head down and her eyes up, Alex laughed. "I don't know if this is appropriate conversation for a chaste date."

Brit's shoulders shook with laughter, and she gasped and began choking on her wine. She handed the glass to Alex as her eyes watered and she coughed and sputtered, desperately trying to regulate her breathing. Meanwhile, Alex was slapping her back with an open palm. When it was over, once again Brit burst into a fit of laughter, and leaning forward, Alex pulled her into her arms, their lips meeting as they both giggled. The laughter quickly faded as the kiss deepened, setting Brit on fire and melting her, and then breathless, they pulled apart.

"This is why I drink beer," Alex explained, and Brit fell against her and began laughing all over again.

Brit turned slightly and gently ran her fingers down Alex's cheek. Shifting her face into Brit's hand, Alex kissed the tips before she slowly lowered them back to Brit's lap. Before either of them could speak, before Brit could close the gap between them for another kiss, they heard a key in the door and the muted tones of human voices.

Clearing her throat but not turning away from Britain, Alex announced, "We're in here." She sounded both disappointed and relieved that their friends had arrived.

Brit quickly distanced herself from Alex, smoothed her clothing, and then sipped her wine. Alex stood to welcome her friends.

They all exchanged hugs, Kim got a beer for both her and Alex, and Tam poured herself a glass of the cab. "How was your trip?" Tam asked. "Traffic, huh?"

"Awful," Brit replied, "but the company was nice."

"Hmm, so I hear. You two are dating, is that it?" she inquired, and Brit was sure she saw amusement somewhere in the depths of Tam's eyes.

"Dating, yes. We're going to tiptoe into this rather than run full steam."

"Kind of like what we're doing," Kim interjected.

"Yes, exactly. How's it going for you?" Brit asked them.

"Very well. In fact, we decided to take this to the next level. We're going away for a few days at Thanksgiving to get better acquainted." As Tam said the words, Brit could see the color rising in Kim's cheeks, like mercury in a meat thermometer.

"Stop pressuring me, Tam," she interjected, and they all laughed.

"Well, let me explain," Tam said. "When we do it, finally, we

won't be able to get out of bed for probably days. So we have to wait for a holiday, or we'll both lose our jobs."

"Good thinking," Alex said, nodding as she sipped her beer. "I've heard of things like that happening. It could be a disaster if you don't plan it properly."

"Shut up, Alex," Tam retorted as she flipped the third finger of her left hand in Alex's general direction.

"Where's the romance? Where's the spontaneity?" Alex demanded.

"Oh, I promise it'll be romantic. But as far as spontaneity goes—we don't have time for that right now."

"Not to change the subject, but how's school?" Brit asked and took a sip of her wine and leaned back into the cushions.

"You won't believe what happened to me." Tam said.

"Do tell," Brit replied, leaning forward.

"I was getting ready to leave school the other day and couldn't find my phone. I looked *everywhere*. It was gone. So, I went onto the computer and tracked it with this app I installed. It was five miles away. I hopped in the car and went to the address, and who should answer the door but one of my students! The little bugger stole my phone. He's only five years old."

Brit shook her head in disbelief and Alex shrugged.

"That's pretty cool though, that you found it. What's that app?"

Tam promised to download it for her before they left at the end of the weekend.

They spent the next hour huddled around the coffee table, talking and laughing, until the chorus of yawns prompted Kim to suggest they call it a night. Although they'd missed the movies that night, their agenda for the next day was full, and Alex and Brit had plans for an early breakfast with Sal and Sue.

Theirs was the first room at the top of the staircase, and they all hugged good night at the door. Brit's room was next, and she barely noticed the familiar fluttering in her chest as she anticipated kissing Alex. Since their first kiss, they'd shared a few others, but they'd been limited. She wanted more. More kisses, more everything. Thoughts of this moment had occupied her mind since they'd decided to come to Rehoboth. What if Alex asked to come into her room? What if she didn't? Brit didn't know which thought scared her more. Yet she'd never been happier. "I've had a wonderful evening," she whispered.

Alex was standing a foot back, but then she smiled and opened her arms and pulled Brit into a tight hug. "You're a fun date, Coach Dodge," she said in a teasing tone. Then she pulled back so they could look at each other.

Brit craned her neck and her eyes met Alex's before wandering lower to her lips. They were full, and wet from the tongue Alex had just run across them. With her eyes still focused on her mouth, Brit pulled Alex's head lower until their lips were touching. Alex brushed her lips back and forth across Brit's, barely touching, creating incredible sensations of tingling and pleasure. Then she pulled closer and their lips closed in on each other's, and their tongues met again.

And then, just as suddenly, Alex pulled back, placing her fingers where her mouth had just been. "Good night, beautiful lady," she said before she turned and walked eight feet down the hall to her own bedroom door.

Alex held onto the door frame with one hand, and with the other, she waved.

Britain stood watching, then waved with a simple flick of her wrist and let her hand hang suspended in midair, as if awaiting something more.

"Good night."

❖

The morning was bright and sunny, and Britain was dressed and waiting when Alex descended to the kitchen at seven thirty.

"How was your sleep?" Brit asked.

"Wonderful. How about yours?" Alex leaned against the counter, looking sexy in jeans and a sweatshirt, and Brit nearly forgot the question before she could formulate the answer.

"Um, okay," Brit said. In truth, sleep had come slowly as she wrestled with the knowledge that Alex was only a few feet away.

Alex didn't seem to notice the hesitancy of her answer, and Brit was grateful. What could she say? I couldn't sleep because I was wondering what you were wearing? If I had come to your room would you have made love to me?

"Okay, then, let's get movin'."

Alex drove, heading north out of Oyster Bay and west on Route

24, toward the Delaware farmlands. Traffic was sparse and they made the trip easily, then found Sal and Sue awaiting them at the door.

After sharing hugs, they retreated to the living room. Looking at the leather club chairs, Brit remembered her first visit here—talking to Alex, seeing her smile, thinking how attractive she was. They'd arrived separately that day, but this time they walked through the door side by side, and it felt perfect.

"So, thanks for bringing winter with you!" Sal said.

"Sal, be nice. How was the drive?" Sue asked.

"Uggh," Alex replied.

Sue grinned. "Yeah, I kind of remember that. I'm glad I live at the beach now and don't have to risk my life every weekend commuting."

"Maybe someday," Alex said.

Sal answered this time. "I won't say I don't miss teaching. Especially at this time of year when the season's so full of promise."

"Yes, at this point we still have hope," Brit deadpanned.

"Oh, c'mon. I thought you said they were going to be good?"

"I think we will, I really do. We just won't know until we actually play."

They talked about the schedule and the team before Sue changed the subject a few minutes later.

"Sal, can you give me a hand in the kitchen?"

"Absolutely not," Brit exclaimed. "I've been dying to get into that kitchen since the last time I was here."

Sal laughed. "Wellll, if you insist."

"You two can handle cleanup," Brit reminded them.

Alex watched as Brit disappeared into the kitchen, and when she turned her attention back to Sal, she discovered she was under surveillance. Sal's lips were pursed and she was squinting.

"What?" Alex asked, feigning innocence.

"So, when did this happen?"

It was Alex's turn to purse her lips. When did it happen? That amazing first kiss had occurred two weeks earlier, but it was the result of what had been building up for weeks and weeks before. "I guess it happened right here," Alex said, spreading her hands to indicate Sal's living room.

"Really?" Sal asked, seeming surprised. "She hasn't said a word."

"Well, perhaps I should clarify things. Nothing's really happened. We're dating, that's all. Getting to know each other better. Exclusively."

"I'm not surprised to see you two together."

"Why did you wait so long to introduce us?" Alex asked. Lately it'd occurred to her that Sal might have had something more than a business relationship in mind when she introduced her to Brit.

"You weren't ready for someone like her, Alex. She's much more mature than you are. You needed to settle down." Sal's words were harsh but spoken without criticism. They were just the truth. Still not easy to hear, though.

Alex frowned.

"Don't take that the wrong way. It's not a bad thing. Look at all the heterosexual couples who get married at a young age and then divorced. They're too young. People need to experience life and see the world before they decide what part of it they want to call home."

"Do you think Brit's done that?"

"In her own way, she has. Just because she's done things differently than you have doesn't mean she wasn't living her life."

"And you think I've lived enough to settle down?"

"Alex, I don't think it's been a matter of living. I think you just needed to accept your illness and realize that you're still quite lovable, even if you're not as perfect as you seem. And Brit's just the sort of well-grounded, good person to make you see that. What did she say when you told her?"

Alex looked to the ceiling, avoiding eye contact, wishing she could sink into the chair and disappear from the intensity of Sal's gaze.

"Oh, Jesus, Alex! Don't tell me you haven't told her."

"I haven't told her, Sal."

"What are you waiting for? The wedding night?"

"I don't know."

"You have to tell her."

"I know."

"So what's the problem?"

"I don't know."

"Alex, that's pathetic," Sal said, but her voice was softer, concerned.

"I know."

"What do you know?" Brit asked from the doorway.

"That I'm lucky to be seen on the same side of the street as you."

Brit's jaw dropped. "You told her? I wanted to tell her!" Brit didn't sound angry, just surprised.

"She didn't need to tell me, Brit. All I had to do was look at you. It's written all over your faces."

Brit smiled. "Is it really?"

"Oh, yes. There's no hiding this."

"We're not hiding, Sal," Brit said, walking over to kiss the top of Alex's head. "I just wanted to tell you in person."

"Tell her what?" Sue asked from the doorway.

All three of them looked her way, and they all laughed. "What? What did I miss?"

When the laughter died down, Alex answered. "Brit and I are dating."

"Oh, no kidding. I could tell you were going to wind up together when you met right there on my patio."

"Well, I wish you'd told me," Alex said. "You'd have saved me a lot of time."

They enjoyed a wonderful breakfast of fruit and yogurt and applesauce waffles, and talked about the film festival. After breakfast, as promised, Alex and Sal cleaned up while Sue and Brit sat and shared recipes.

"What's on your agenda?" Sal asked when they were all seated in the living room.

"Movies. And we have a seven o'clock reservation at the steak house. You're going to join us, right?"

"Of course. We'll meet you there. What movies are you seeing?"

Alex groaned. "I have no idea."

"We're going now to see what's available." The only way to pre-order tickets was by purchasing an expensive pass, one that Brit couldn't afford. They'd have to settle for the less-popular movie choices.

"You should get going, then," Sal said.

"Why does time fly when we're together?" Sue asked as they all stood and headed toward the door.

"It does, doesn't it?" Alex said. "But we'll see you soon, right? You're coming for the tip-off tournament?"

Sal beamed. "I wouldn't miss it."

"*We* wouldn't miss it," Sue added.

"It'll be good to see you again," Brit said. And then, remembering the invitation Alex had issued a few months earlier, she replied. "We'll have lots of time together next summer if I spend it at the beach."

All three of their faces showed surprised delight. "Let's make sure of that, Brit," Sue suggested as they walked to Alex's car. The frigid air made Brit shiver, and she rubbed her arms for warmth.

First stop was the big tent behind the theater, where they selected tickets to one of the movies their friends were seeing, and another two features that looked somewhat promising.

"Do you think we have time to stop by the beach? Just for a few minutes? I don't think we'll have time tomorrow," Alex asked as she pointed the car toward the condo.

"That sounds great."

Unlike their last trip to Rehoboth Avenue, this time the place was deserted. Alex found parking close to the beach. Off-season in Rehoboth also meant little foot traffic on the boardwalk. They easily found an empty bench and sat hand in hand, staring out at the ocean. Down on the beach a photographer was taking advantage of the clear sky to shoot pictures, and farther down the boardwalk two men were engaged in conversation, the proximity of their bodies suggesting an intimacy beyond friendship. Otherwise, they had the Atlantic Ocean to themselves.

"I like it like this, when it's quiet," Brit said.

"Yeah, me, too. It's peaceful. Remember our last time here?" Alex asked.

Brit turned to her, horrified.

"Yikes. What a stupid question." Alex said, grimacing. "I meant before *that*. When we were sitting on the beach. There must have been a million stars in the sky that night."

Brit nodded. "I didn't want to stop walking. I wanted our time together to never end."

"I was wondering if you were gay."

"Me, too. The evidence was mounting. Sal and Sue, The Frogg Pond, Kim and Tam."

"I almost forgot. That was the night they kissed on the beach."

"Yeah. It seems to be working for them. They seem happy."

"They're perfect for each other. It just took them some time to figure it out."

"That's what dating's for."

Alex smiled and pushed a stray hair behind Brit's ear. "Yeah, that's what I hear."

"How do you think it's going? The dating, I mean? *Our* dating."

Alex was surprised by the question and not sure she knew how to answer. Slowly? And then she silently chastised herself, because she knew she was enjoying this experience. Getting to know Brit was a delight. "It's going well, I think. The girl I'm dating can't keep her hands off me, though, and I'm not sure what to do. I think she's only after me for my body."

Brit appeared thoughtful. "I can hardly blame her. You're a hottie."

Alex only smiled in response, looking out onto the water, and Brit leaned into her. Alex shifted slightly, and draped her arm over Brit's shoulder.

A minute later, Brit spoke again. "I never thought I'd date you, after that night. I thought we were too different."

"What made you change your mind?" Alex asked, turning her head to look at Brit.

Brit paused before she spoke, and turned her head up to Alex's. Her eyes held a devilish twinkle when she finally did. "That kiss."

Alex nodded in understanding. "I knew you just wanted me for my body."

They were quiet again, but now they looked at each other, their eyes locking. After a moment Brit spoke again. "You know we really aren't that different, Alex. We have the same passions. We have the same values. You just hide them well."

Brit knew Alex was a good person, just as she considered herself to be a good person. And she was beginning to see that she was more like Alex than she ever would have guessed. Suddenly, since that kiss, Alex's naked body was all Brit could think of.

The night before, all she'd wanted was to be with Alex. She'd tossed and turned, thinking of Alex in the next room, wondering what would happen if she just crawled in next to her and began kissing her. It wasn't the first time she'd fantasized about making love with Alex, but it was the first time the fantasy could have come true. Just holding

Alex would have been great, though. What would Alex think if she told her that?

"I had a rough night," she confessed at last.

"Really? Why?" Alex sounded concerned.

"I was tormented by the thought of sneaking into your room, just to be with you."

Alex studied Brit. "That would have been okay."

"Really?"

"Really."

"We could just cuddle?"

"I'd love to hold you, Brit. And I can't think of anything better than falling asleep with you in my arms. Well, except waking up next to you."

Brit wrinkled her nose. It seemed that Alex always knew exactly the right thing to say. Was that a natural instinct or something she'd learned? "You're so charming, Alex."

"I've never said that to anyone before, I swear."

"I wasn't accusing you. I was just observing."

Alex nodded, and they were quiet for a long while.

"So, Alex. Tonight? Can we spend the night together?"

Alex again pushed the wayward hair behind Brit's ear. "I'd like that. Your room or mine?"

"Hmm," Brit said, thinking. "Have you ever had a girl in your room?"

Alex rolled her eyes in admission of guilt.

"Then let's make it mine."

And so later, after meals and drinks had been consumed and movies had been watched and showers had been taken, Brit sat on her bed, waiting. She jumped at the knock. "Hi," Brit said, holding Alex's gaze for a moment before scanning her long frame approvingly and stepping away to allow her in. She gently closed the door behind her.

"So, I'm nervous," Brit confessed when she turned to face her. She'd spent the day in a state of controlled anxiety, constantly monitoring her breathing and willing her heart to slow down. She couldn't believe she'd invited Alex to her room, and she wasn't sure how she could back out of the offer, or if she wanted to. But the thought of sleeping in the same bed with Alex—even fully clothed—terrified her. The act seemed so intimate, and it was, really. How much more vulnerable could you

be than unconscious? Yet the night before, she'd thought of nothing else but falling asleep in Alex's arms, and she wouldn't spend another night wondering.

"Would you feel safer if I let you tie me up?"

Brit bit her lip and suppressed a smile. "Well, that would be a memorable first night together." But the joke managed to relax her, and she suspected that was just what Alex intended. Somehow Brit willed her feet to move until she was standing before Alex, and then she was in her arms. It was a sweet, warm, loving hug. Alex wore fleece sweat pants and a long-sleeve T-shirt that was soft and welcoming, and Brit seemed to melt into her.

Alex wanted to give Brit the reins, but she sensed her faltering. After a minute, she pulled back and kissed Brit softly on the cheek. "Let's go to bed," she said, and without waiting for a reply, she took Brit's hand and led the way. Pulling back the big, fluffy comforter with one hand, she crawled beneath and gave a tug to the hand she still held with the other, beckoning Brit. Brit gracefully sat beside her, then pulled her legs onto the bed and rested her head on the pillow next to Alex.

Alex rolled onto her side, facing her, and Brit did the same. "Welcome to my place," Brit said.

Alex moved closer, until her face was in Brit's hair and her arm fell across her middle. Wiggling and squirming, they adjusted positions until they were both comfortable, and Alex closed her eyes and allowed her senses to fill with Brit—her smell, her softness, the sound of her breathing. Brit was tense, but as they lay beside each other, Alex could feel her relax, hear the change in her breathing, and after a few minutes of quiet, Alex thought Brit had fallen asleep. When she tried to place a chaste kiss on her cheek, though, Brit turned her head so it was her mouth Alex met instead.

Alex took what was offered, but from the moment their lips met she knew she had to stop quickly, because the contact caused a flood of wet and heat and throbbing. It had been building for so long, Alex couldn't stand much more torment.

Pulling away, she thought of something she knew would quiet the fire burning within her. She had to tell Brit the truth.

Since her conversation with Sal that morning, it had been on her mind. She'd planned to tell Brit at the beach, but she'd chickened out.

Watching the movies, she'd only half followed the plots as she saw her own personal drama unfolding instead. Thoughts of the conversation looming ahead of her would haunt her until she told Brit. It was time.

Looking at her, Alex pushed the hair back from Brit's forehead and kissed her gently. She sighed, and her words seemed to float on her breath. "I have to tell you something."

Brit seemed to sense Alex's anxiety, because the passion in her eyes died, replaced by fear. She pulled away, and sat up, studying her. "Alex, what is it?"

Alex wished she could quiet it, but what she had to tell her might only make it worse. Instead of trying to protect Brit by offering false words, she cleared her throat. "Have you ever heard of ankylosing spondylitis?" she asked.

Confusion replaced the fear, as if she didn't understand the question.

"Noooo."

"It's an autoimmune disease. I have it."

As Brit sat up, her eyes flew open and her jaw dropped. "You have an autoimmune disease?" she whispered.

"Yeah."

"Are you sick? I mean, obviously you're not sick, are you?"

"I guess it depends on how you look at it. I'll always have the disease—there's no cure—but it's under control. My symptoms are in remission."

Brit cleared her throat and reached for the bottle of water on the bedside table. After taking a sip, she offered it to Alex. "So what are your symptoms?"

Leaning back against the headboard, Alex closed her eyes and listed the problems that had plagued her for more than a decade.

"What's the worst thing?"

Alex rolled her head toward Brit and their eyes met. She saw concern there, and fear. "The uncertainty. Not knowing when it may pop up. 'Cause I know it will. Not knowing how bad it might get." Alex closed her eyes again. "Worrying that I'll get sick from the medicine."

"Sick how?"

"The medicine blocks my immune system. I'm more likely to catch everything contagious. I can also get cancer."

Alex opened her eyes again and looked at Brit.

"I don't know what to say," Brit said.

"There's not much to say." Alex smiled sadly. Obviously, she'd been right. This was more than Brit could handle.

"What can I do to help you?" Brit asked after a minute.

"Whatta ya mean?" Shouldn't Brit be running out the door by now, ready to end their fledgling relationship? Or at least be slithering away from her, worried about contracting the disease?

"I mean, what do you need me to do?"

"I don't understand," Alex said.

Brit sighed, a rare display of impatience. "You're my girlfriend. You're dealing with something difficult. How can I help you? Do you need me to clean your apartment because your back is sore, or do you want me to cook healthy foods that boost your immune system, or do you just need me to hold you?"

Alex leaned back again, and before she could raise a hand to wipe them, the tears she'd held for a decade flowed from her eyes. Making good on her offer, Brit slid close to her and wrapped her arms around Alex.

Brit would have done anything to help her, to take away her pain and make everything all right. She couldn't do any of those things, though. So she just lay next to her, holding her, until Alex relaxed and drifted off to sleep. Then she kissed her gently on the lips and slipped out of her arms.

It was hard to imagine that someone so physically fit and strong could be sick. Yet, apparently, she was. As she looked at Alex sleeping next to her for the first time, Brit was determined to do everything she could to keep Alex right there. Forever. Pulling out her smartphone, Brit leaned back against the headboard, her face inches from Alex's. She didn't detect any sign of the strain she'd seen earlier or any sign of the disease that had invaded her body. She was simply beautiful as she lay sleeping, and Brit was overwhelmed with love for her.

After turning on her phone and navigating to the search engine, Brit typed in the words "ankylosing spondylitis" and began reading.

Chapter Twenty

Taking Care of Business

Trying hard to look casual, P.J. paced the corridor outside the girls' locker room, an envelope in his sweaty hands. Even though he'd been in business for more than two months, and had already done this hundreds of times, it was still nerve-wracking. The fear of getting caught had him fumbling and stumbling, jumping at every noise, and he swore if the girl didn't show her face in thirty seconds, he was leaving. Twenty bucks just wasn't worth it.

Out in the parking lot, a dozen students were waiting for him, and every one of them had money for him. He'd be done and gone in five minutes flat. Here, he was a trapped animal and didn't like the feeling at all. They were going to have to make some other arrangements, and soon. P.J. couldn't handle the stress.

He couldn't eat and was losing weight, and even though he was exhausted, his sleep was fragmented, interrupted by bad dreams. After he woke up, his thoughts often prevented him from falling asleep again.

"P.J." Someone called to him, and he turned to see one of his classmates approaching him. Kevin Bennigan was bearing down on him quickly.

"Do you have physics?" he asked.

Shaking off his earlier concerns, P.J. smiled. "Of course I do."

"Can you spot me, buddy? I don't have the cash."

P.J. frowned. He hated when this happened. Kevin was a foot taller than he was and outweighed him by a hundred pounds. He didn't like to tell him no, but he didn't have a choice. The envelopes he picked up from The Man were numbered, and the exams they contained were

printed on copy-proof paper. At the end of the day, he either had to give The Man an exam, or a twenty. No exceptions.

He tried to act tough when he replied. "No can do, pal. You know the rules. No money, no goods."

"Fuck, man, help me out here. We've been friends since kindergarten."

Kevin had never been his friend, but they had played Little League on the same team one year. "Believe me, Kev, if it was up to me, I would. But they're counted, and you don't want to go fucking with my boss."

The door at the end of the hallway opened, and a boy carrying a black instrument case walked through. "P, what's this nerd's name? He's in our class, right? Lyle? Kyle? Who is he?"

"Lance. His name is Lance."

Lance approached with a bounce in his step. "Hey, Lance," Kevin said. "I'm in a bind here, man. Can you loan me twenty bucks until tomorrow?"

P.J. closed his eyes and fought the urge to punch Kevin in the mouth to keep him quiet. Lance was not only at the top of their class in academics, but he was a model citizen and the one P.J. would vote most likely to send him to jail. Lance eyed both of them suspiciously as he pursed his lips.

"I'd consider you my friend for life, Lance. Anything you ever need, man, I'll be there. Anybody gives you any problems, you come to me."

"Wow, really?"

"Yep, you'll be my new best friend."

Lance pulled the wallet out of his back pocket and removed a twenty-dollar bill.

"Thanks, buddy," Kev said as he took the money and escorted Lance the rest of the way to the band-room door. He returned with a sneer.

"A loser's born every minute," he said as he handed P.J. the money.

"You got that right," P.J. replied, and Kevin had no idea he wasn't referring to Lance. P.J. searched his backpack and pulled out an envelope marked "Kane—Physics" and placed it in Kevin's waiting hand.

Kevin practically skipped down the hall. "Gotta go lift, man. Big game this week. Thanks for your help."

"Sure, no problem," P.J. said, but he'd already returned his gaze to the locker-room door. He stopped and leaned against the wall, debating what to do. He didn't want to piss off a customer, but how long could he be expected to wait?

Just as he was about to abandon the mission, the door opened and a girl in a black basketball jersey and shorts came through.

"Jesus, Kelsey, if you'd made me wait another minute I was outta here."

"Sorry, P. Coach Dodge snuck up on me and wanted to talk," she said as she handed him a twenty-dollar bill and accepted the envelope in exchange.

"Well, I can't do this anymore. You're going to have to meet me in town like everyone else. It's too risky."

Kelsey's expression turned sour and her eyes flew open wide. "Don't say that, P. You know I need you. We'll figure something out, okay?"

"I gotta go," he said as he walked away.

"Thanks." She tucked the envelope into her shorts and headed back into the gym.

P.J. pulled his car out of the school parking lot and made his way to the town library, where the lot was crowded with cars, most of them belonging to the students who were waiting for him. He looked around for signs of trouble but didn't spot any security cameras out here, and no suspicious-looking cars. He approached a Mercedes SUV parked farthest from the building.

"Chemistry?" he said to the driver, an underclassman whose name he didn't know. But this was the third chemistry exam he'd sold him in two months, along with biology, history, and algebra. P.J. didn't know his name, but he knew the kid's entire class schedule. "Yeah," the boy said as he parted with the crisp bill and took a copy of the chemistry exam Mr. Lewis would give the next day.

"Thanks," the boy said, and before P.J. walked to the next car, the Mercedes pulled from the lot.

A total of ten exams changed hands at the library, and then P.J. drove to the Dunkin' Donuts a mile away and sold another six, then

to the gym, where he passed along five more. His final stop in this neighborhood was at the park, where another five people awaited him. In less than forty minutes, he'd sold copies of six different exams to twenty-six students and had all the profits in a bank bag in his car.

He spent the next three hours in a similar manner, stopping at a variety of stores and public buildings, ever changing to avoid suspicion and detection, until, emotionally exhausted and nearly starving, he arrived at his final destination. "How much?" The Man asked when P.J. knocked on his office door.

Every night's tally differed. It varied, based on the number of exams given on any particular day. The one constant was the ever-growing popularity of this little business, and P.J. was finding it harder to make all his deliveries. His territory covered four school districts, and each week more students showed up at the predetermined rendezvous points, causing more time to slip through his fingers as he raced to deliver the exams and get home in time to complete his own schoolwork.

"Sixty."

"Whew! Nice job, Little Man. Anything else?"

"Ninety bucks in tickets."

P.J. offered him the bank envelope, a bulging vinyl bag holding twelve hundred dollars, plus another envelope containing ninety additional dollars, plus the tickets declaring the wagers on the football games scheduled for the following weekend. He forced a smile as The Man counted the money and gave two hundred dollars back to him.

That was a bonus; their agreement had been ten percent of P.J.'s collections. Some days his take was fifty dollars, and on others like this one, a few hundred. Since he'd started this business with The Man, he'd been averaging almost a thousand dollars a week. It was more than his father made at the mall, and if business grew, he'd be earning more than his mother as well.

He hadn't spent a penny of it. Even if he wanted to, even if he didn't feel like a piece of shit for doing this, he couldn't start spending that kind of money without raising Wes's suspicions. Since he'd confessed, Wes had taken a bigger interest in P.J.'s activities, as if he needed to keep an eye on his brother. P.J. had lied to Wes, told him it was all over with The Man. He was also saving to repay his grandfather. But he couldn't do anything to redress the situation with all the teachers

he was cheating—people whom he respected and admired, and who thought highly of him. At least, though, he could make restitution within his own family.

"See you tomorrow," The Man said, and sadly, P.J. knew he would.

CHAPTER TWENTY-ONE

FIRST COMES LOVE

Fall was slipping by and the leaves were long fallen from the trees in her apartment complex as Brit walked through her front door on the day before Thanksgiving. School had been dismissed early, and practice had been short. Now Brit had the entire afternoon for one of her favorite activities—baking pies. On this occasion, for the first time in her life, she wouldn't be mixing dough and slicing apples in her mother's kitchen, but in her own. And instead of her mother and sisters beside her, today it would be Alex.

Since she was a little girl they'd made pies, at first with her mother's sister and her grandmother, and lately just the Dodge women. If there were no Alex in her life, she would have been at her mother's house in the early afternoon and up to her elbows in flour shortly thereafter. She'd drink wine while making dough and mixing pumpkin and creating great memories. At night, she'd fall asleep in her childhood bed, exhausted but happy.

But there was an Alex, and Mr. and Mrs. Dalton had invited Brit to Thanksgiving dinner at their house the following evening. Although it would mean lying to her family, she couldn't decline. The expectant look on Alex's face as she'd passed on the invitation had just been too precious to refuse. And then, when Alex told her it was her responsibility to *buy* the pie for dessert, Brit knew she was in trouble. No way could she allow her girlfriend's family to eat frozen pumpkin pie after Thanksgiving dinner.

And so she'd told yet another lie to her family, begging out of their traditional pie-baking party with a false claim about a late-afternoon basketball practice. Her sisters had been sympathetic, but her mother

was livid. Brit feared her reaction the next day, when she planned a migraine shortly after dinner to escape her parents' house in time for a second Thanksgiving feast with the Daltons.

Slinging her briefcase under the desk in her bedroom, Brit slipped out of her sweat suit and pulled on a tattered old sweatshirt and her most comfortable faded jeans. Her fuzzy slippers came next, and then she wandered into the kitchen. The apartment was small but modern, and the kitchen was large enough to accommodate a table and four chairs, which gave her plenty of work surface for baking. Even if she didn't have enough closet space in the bedroom, the kitchen worked out well.

Alex made Brit promise not to start without her, and so instead, she just put all the ingredients they'd need onto the table. They'd make the dough first and let it chill while they mixed the pumpkin and peeled apples for the two pies they'd serve for dessert. Brit had bought a few extra apples and planned tarts to share with Alex that night. Before the pies went in, though, Brit planned to broil a chicken breast for their dinner.

She'd read everything she could find about AS, and as it turned out, Alex actually was eating a very good diet. Even though she lacked cooking skills, she consumed tons of fruit and veggies and avoided red meat and sugar. Her famous peanut-butter sandwiches were a good source of protein. Tonight's menu of chicken Caesar salad was perfect.

Sharing dinner had been one of the best parts of their time together in the weeks since they'd returned from Rehoboth. Alex wasn't a fussy eater, so after practice they'd go back to one of their apartments and Brit would cook something simple, focusing on veggies and minimizing meat. Alex actually liked helping in the kitchen, not just with the cleanup, and they worked together well. They'd analyze their players and talk strategy while they cooked and cleaned up. Inevitably they'd end up on the couch or in bed, kissing and watching television. Most nights, they fell asleep in each other's arms.

Opening the refrigerator door, Brit retrieved their chicken and put it under the broiler. Just as she was setting the oven timer, she heard Alex using her newly minted key. Brit peeked into the living room and studied her as she took off her coat and hung it on the tree beside the door. "Hi," Alex said as she closed the door behind her, and Brit marveled that one simple word, spoken by the right woman, could

cause such havoc to her senses. She strode quickly across the living room and into the kitchen, where Brit stood with her hands in the air beside her. She puckered her lips. "Kiss me, please, but don't touch me. I'm full of chicken."

Alex followed directions and placed a chaste kiss on Brit's lips. "Hi," Brit said. "Let me clean up." She turned toward the sink. Alex was right behind her, and with her arms wrapped around Brit's waist she kissed the back of her neck, working her way forward toward her ear. Brit leaned back into her, enjoying their touch. When her hands were dry, she swiveled in Alex's arms and filled them with her hair, pulling Alex closer until their lips were touching, their tongues caressing, and their bodies sliding against each other.

After a minute, Brit pulled back and rested her head on Alex's chest. "Wow, Alex," she whispered.

Alex kissed her temple. "Yeah. Wow."

"I've been waiting all day for that," Brit confessed. Alex had spent the night with her but left early in the morning to go home and shower before school.

"Me, too. It's hard to see you and not touch you, Brit. It's hard to pretend."

"Do you suppose we're fooling anyone?" she asked.

"I've had questions since the day of the in-service."

"I see the players watching us. I think they're all suspicious." Brit and Alex never behaved any way other than professionally when they were at school, and anytime they were in public, but the chemistry between them was obvious. Kim and Tam had commented on it, and Sal had known about them the first time she saw them together. Brit supposed one only had to know what to look for to see it.

"Does it bother you?"

Brit pulled back and looked at Alex. She was so in love that nothing bothered her. Even though they hadn't made love, yet, Brit knew they would. And she also had no doubt that she would spend the rest of her life with Alex. She was beginning to wonder how to break the news to her family. "No. I don't care who knows that I love you." It was the first time she'd said those words to anyone other than her best friends and family, but Brit knew they were true. It was time Alex knew, too.

Alex swallowed as she stared for a moment, holding on to Brit

for balance and hoping Brit didn't notice how clumsy she'd suddenly become. And then Alex pulled her closer, wrapping her arms all the way around Brit. "I love you, too," she whispered into the softness of Brit's hair.

At that moment, the timer began to buzz, and Brit turned her attention toward the stove. When she turned back she looked at Alex. "Saved by the bell."

"Oh, no. This isn't over. Say it again."

"What?"

Alex began tickling her. "Say it!"

"I love you." Brit giggled, and Alex thought she'd never been happier in her life. So much had changed for her since she met Brit. She was truly a different person, simply because someone so amazing looked at her the way Brit did.

"I love you, too."

"Okay, good. Ready to bake?"

Alex kissed the tip of Brit's nose. "Ready."

After washing her hands, Alex joined Brit at the counter. "What's first?" Alex asked. She was growing more comfortable in the kitchen, thanks to Brit's tutoring, and no longer feared losing a finger when she lifted a knife. They'd never baked pies, though, and because she knew how much Brit loved to bake, she was looking forward to this experience.

"First, the wine. Are you up for a glass of white wine?"

Alex made a face. "No beer?"

"No, sorry. Wine with pie." Brit expertly uncorked the bottle and poured two glasses.

"Cheers," Brit said as their glasses clinked.

"Cheers." Alex tentatively took a sip from her glass. "This isn't too bad," she observed. "What kind is it?"

"It's a pinot grigio. You like?"

Alex sipped again. "I can handle it."

"It's light and crisp. A perfect complement to apples. Now let's bake. First, we make the crust. Roll up your sleeves, Alex. You're going to get messy."

Alex mixed the necessary quantities of flour and salt and shortening and water that Brit poured into a large glass bowl, forming the ball of dough that would be their crust. When Brit was happy with the texture,

she took it from Alex and placed it in the freezer. Then they did it all over again.

"Would you like some music?" Brit asked as Alex washed her hands.

"Sure," she said.

Brit pushed the appropriate buttons on her iPod and the *Kinky Boots* soundtrack began to play again. They sat at the table, a dozen apples of different varieties in a bowl before them, and began peeling.

"Let's go to New York, Alex. I want to see *Kinky Boots*," Brit said as she sang.

"Why should you *see* the show? You already *know* the show. You know every word of every song."

"Yeah, and I've seen most of it on YouTube. But I still want to see it on Broadway."

"Why don't we go in the spring?"

"Why wait?"

Alex tried to appear neutral as she concentrated on her work. She'd already ordered the tickets and planned to surprise Brit with them for Christmas. She rationalized that covering a Christmas surprise was an acceptable excuse for telling a tiny lie. "I'm saving my money for Christmas. I really can't afford a trip to New York right now."

Brit nodded. "I guess you're right. I probably can't either."

"What does your family do on Christmas?" Alex asked.

"Oh, the usual. Everyone goes to my parents' house on Christmas Eve, we go to mass together, then open presents. Lots of presents. Then they all go home for a few hours so Santa can come and are back at noon for a Christmas feast." Brit used her forearm to push the hair back from her eyes and asked "How about you?"

"My family usually has dinner in the evening on Christmas because Andrew goes to his in-laws during the day."

"Just like Thanksgiving, huh?"

"Yeah. So do you want to come to Christmas dinner?"

Brit looked up from her peeling, surprised, hoping her trepidation didn't show, but before she could answer, Alex continued. "Because I know my family's going to love you, and before you leave tomorrow night, my mom's going to invite you for Christmas."

"Oh," Brit said, but she didn't have to think about it for long. There was nothing she'd like more than to spend Christmas Day with

Alex. And since she knew Alex wouldn't be welcome at the Dodges', the Daltons' was the only alternative. "Then I guess I'll be coming to Christmas dinner."

"How will you handle it with your family?"

Brit hadn't told Alex about her plan for the next day. She knew Alex wouldn't approve of the deception, and she found it ironic that while she'd questioned Alex's integrity, now she was the one with the big moral void. Yet she didn't know what else to do. She'd only been invited a few days earlier—she certainly couldn't just spring the girlfriend on her family as the excuse for missing pie baking and then leaving dinner early. The migraine was a much easier solution.

"I don't know. But I'll figure out something. Don't worry. I'll be there." They smiled at each other across the table.

"What did you tell them about tomorrow?" Alex asked.

Brit's heart stopped. At least it felt as if it did. And although she'd been telling a ton of lies lately, she couldn't lie to Alex. "They don't know yet."

Alex tried to hide the disappointment that sprang up inside her. She supposed this was inevitable, and she knew she had no right to any such feelings because Brit had been totally honest with her about her family from the very beginning.

"Look, Brit, if this is a problem, let's just forget it. Dinner isn't that important."

"It is important, Alex. I want to be with you. It's just new, that's all. I have to figure out what to say to them." Brit seemed to understand her feelings, because she smiled sweetly at Alex. "We're going to work this out, Alex. Together. I wish I could say I know what to do and how to do it, but I'd be lying."

The reassuring words relieved Alex. "You're sure?"

"I've never been so sure about anything in my life."

Smiling, Alex sliced off a piece of apple and popped it into her mouth. "Okay. Now what do we do with all of these apples?"

Brit showed her how to slice them, then added sugar and cinnamon to flavor them, and when she was happy with the taste, she set the bowl aside and filled another with all the ingredients for the pumpkin pie. Through it all, Alex was an attentive student, playfully kissing Brit's nose and feeding her apples and dough, but mostly serious about the task at hand.

When the dough was rolled into a perfect size to fit the pie plate, Brit folded it and carefully placed it into the pan. Alex poured in filling, and then Brit carried the pie plate to the oven and gently placed it on the rack. After wiping her hands on a towel she set the timer. While the pumpkin baked, they rolled the other crust, poured in the apples, and placed the top crust over the heaping pile.

"That's it?" Alex asked, disappointed. She'd been having fun.

"Well, we have some extra dough, and some extra apples, so why don't we make a few tarts? I'll let you roll the dough this time."

"I don't think I'm ready for this," Alex said, teasing her, and pulled her into another hug. She'd meant it to be playful but wasn't surprised when Brit's mouth found her neck, and then her mouth. She opened slightly to receive Brit's tongue, and she caressed it with her own, gently sucking, the heat between them hotter than the oven baking their Thanksgiving pies. They both pulled away breathless, and Alex backed up far enough to look into Brit's eyes. Hers were twinkling as she spoke.

"Do you want to make tarts or make out?" Alex asked as she buried her mouth in Brit's silky hair.

Alex could feel Brit trembling in her arms as she whispered, "That depends. Do you want to have an apple tart later or not?"

Alex turned her head so she could see Brit's face and ran her fingers through Brit's hair as she looked into her eyes. "Can't I just have the damn pie? After all, I made it."

Brit shook her head and frowned. "You can have as much as you want—tomorrow at your parents' house."

Alex looked down at Brit and kissed the tip of her nose again. It had taken a full minute to regain focus, but she had it now. "You drive a hard bargain."

Then Brit reached up and tenderly stroked Alex's face. "We have the entire evening, Alex. What's the rush?"

Alex smiled at the irony of Brit's words. There was certainly no rushing going on in their relationship. It was, in fact, maddeningly slow going. But it was okay. This was all new to Alex, too, and she wasn't going to push too hard. At least she was trying not to.

Brit stepped away, happy for an excuse. She'd nearly collapsed in Alex's arms, and she needed to regain control. Apple tarts were a good diversion. Brit instructed Alex on the proper rolling technique,

and soon, they had pieces of dough of a suitable size for the proposed tarts. Alex filled and folded, pinching the edges as directed, then went to work on a second tart.

"You're a quick study, Alex." Brit beamed as she watched Alex, happier than she ever could have imagined feeling. Everything ordinary was so much better with Alex around, and something as routine as baking a pie was suddenly fresh and new and fun.

Alex met her eyes, and offered a piece of apple to Brit. She sucked it in, along with Alex's fingers. Suddenly, her resolve melted as she was overcome with desire, and she moaned as Alex withdrew the sugary thumb from her mouth and ran it across Brit's bottom lip. Brit opened her eyes to meet Alex's and, seeing the heat and the hunger there, had to close them again. She couldn't see but sensed Alex's lips as they met hers, and she felt herself pulling Alex closer, pushing herself into Alex, wanting, needing more. Their tongues tangled and rolled across and around each other, their lips turning first one way and then another as they sought a perfect fit. Alex's knee parted Brit's legs, and she found herself sliding against Alex's thigh, her desire mounting to unprecedented heights.

Biting her lip, Alex pulled away and rested her forehead against Brit's. They were silent, except for the ragged breaths they both sucked into their air-starved lungs. Brit held her tightly, trying to regain control.

"What do you want, Britain?" Alex finally whispered.

"What?" Brit asked, confused.

"You asked me that question a month ago, when we first kissed. You asked me what I want. Now I'm asking you. What's the plan? I mean, do I buy you a ring and plan the country-club wedding because we're never going to have sex before marriage? Or do you have a certain timeframe in mind? Three months? Six months? Valentine's Day? I've never done this before so I'm not sure how it works. But I really need to know what you're thinking, because it's getting so difficult to pull away from you." Alex sighed and was finally silent.

Brit pulled back and looked at Alex. Her blond hair was messed up and dusted with flour from Brit's hands. Her brown lashes rested on her flushed cheeks, and her lips were swollen from the kisses she'd given them.

What did she want? This! A beautiful woman who made her laugh and think and wasn't afraid to get a little flour in her hair. What was

she waiting for? Love? She had it. It was time to stop making excuses and start living. To begin loving the incredible woman who'd won her heart. She stroked Alex's lip with her thumb, copying the caress that had ignited the inferno that now threatened to consume them. Alex's eyes opened, and Brit could see all the love in them. Love for her. "You, Alex. I want you." Brit sucked in her breath and spoke again before she lost her courage. "Will you make love with me?"

Alex's jaw dropped and she pulled her head back. "Now?" she asked, and Brit thought she sounded a little frightened.

Brit leaned around Alex and looked at the timer on the stove. Thirty-eight minutes until the pumpkin was done. "No, in thirty-nine minutes."

Alex reached to the counter, and her hand found a wineglass. Her head was spinning and her knees were threatening collapse at any moment. She hadn't intended to confront Brit on this day; she'd simply imploded. All the kissing over the past month, the cuddling, the caressing—they'd apparently taken their toll. And no matter how many times she used her vibrator to quiet the demands Brit helped raise, she never seemed satisfied. An orgasm or two just wasn't enough. It was frightening, really, to measure the effect Brit had on her.

Somewhere in the back of her mind a voice told her to stop, that this was too impulsive a decision on Brit's part. Paying it no attention, she slid the glass across the counter. She wasn't even sure if it was hers or Brit's, but she put it to her lips and took a big gulp. "Let's get these dishes done."

❖

What seemed like days later, Alex followed Brit to her bedroom.

"Can we light some candles?" Brit asked.

"Yes, of course."

Brit pulled a book of matches from a drawer and a candle from the dresser and handed them to Alex, then vanished into the bathroom, returning a moment later with three more candles cradled in her arms.

It was late afternoon, and the November daylight was quickly fading as one by one the candles began flickering and casting dancing shadows on the ceiling.

"How about music, Alex?" Brit asked. "At the Halloween party I heard that Norah Jones is perfect for setting a romantic mood."

"What?" Alex was perplexed not just by the question but by the calm and routine of the last hour. What were they doing here? Alex had washed dishes while Brit threw together a salad. Sitting beside each other, they ate and sipped wine as if they were planning practice instead of making love. This would be Brit's first time, ever, and she was behaving as if she were following a recipe. First you light the candles, then you put on the music, next remove your clothing, then place a hand on a hip. It was ridiculous.

Alex sat on the bed, facing away from the iPod where Brit was searching for the correct playlist. She was oblivious to Alex's confusion, so Alex just sat there, letting Brit do what she needed to do, until she turned around a minute later.

"Alex, are you okay?"

Alex felt Brit's hand on her shoulder and turned to her. "Sit by me," she said as she patted the bed next to her. Brit did as she was told, but Alex noticed the apprehension on her face.

"Brit, this isn't a recipe. You can't just light candles and put on music and announce that you're going to have sex in thirty-nine minutes."

"Don't you want to, Alex?"

Alex sighed in frustration. How could she explain her hesitancy? She squeezed Brit's fingers as she looked into the eyes that matched her own. "I do, Brit. But this is your first time, and I want it to be amazing."

Brit crawled up on the bed and collapsed on the pillows, her blond hair fanning out around her, her eyes sparkling, a seductive smile on her face. She summoned Alex with her pointer finger. "So come over here and amaze me."

Alex pounced on her, not with a passionate intent but a friendly one. She began tickling Brit, teasingly pleading with her. "This is too much pressure! Stop pressuring me. I have performance anxiety."

Brit laughed into Alex's mouth as they kissed. "I'm betting your performance will be award winning."

Alex smothered the rest of Brit's words with a kiss, deeper this time. She rested her weight on her arms, as she settled on top of Brit, with their legs straddling and their chests meeting perfectly, breasts

mashing against each other through the barriers of cloth separating them. Alex didn't stop the dance her hips did this time. Instead she followed the rhythm they set as they pushed sensually against Brit's leg. And as she pushed her tongue deep into Brit's mouth, she felt Brit's own hips rising to grind against her and Brit's hands pulling her pelvis down into her as her head came up off the pillow to take Alex farther into her mouth. The questions vanished from her mind, and all she wanted was to make love to Brit.

Alex followed Brit's lead, sliding her tongue back and forth across Brit's, sucked Brit's into her own mouth, and surrendered when Brit forced her way into Alex's mouth. Their hips continued the dance that brought clits crashing against thighs in absolute wonder.

Alex pulled back enough to look into the bright pools of Brit's eyes, now hooded with passion. "Brit? Are you sure?"

Brit took Alex's hand and guided it into her sweatpants, into her underwear, and down into the hot, wet pool of her sex. They moaned together at the touch, and Brit removed her hand, leaving Alex's to explore, then pulled Alex's mouth to hers once again. "I'm so sure, Alex."

Alex pulled back from the kiss and slowed down, sucking gently on Brit's bottom lip while she gently squeezed Brit's clit with her thumb and middle finger, sliding in the abundance of wet. Then, as Brit's legs thrust higher, silently begging for more, Alex slipped that finger inside and watched Brit's face contort with pleasure.

It was so good, so hot, everything Alex thought it would be, and it hadn't really started yet. She was nervous, and she knew Brit was, too. Suddenly afraid that Brit would orgasm and lose her bravado, Alex pulled back her hand and smiled. "I think we're overdressed for this occasion," she said as she slipped the T-shirt over her head.

In the split second her vision was blocked by the shirt, Brit had managed to sit up and was shedding her clothes in record time. First the sweatshirt, then the bra, and then the pants and underwear.

They finished at the same moment but didn't bother to pause and study each other's naked beauty. Instead, they pulled each other close, and this time Alex didn't need the guidance of Brit's hand to find the place she wanted to go. They kissed again softly as Alex entered her, slowly sliding her middle finger along the front wall of Brit's center. Brit's legs were climbing Alex, wrapping around her as her hips thrust,

but Alex refused to increase the pace or the pressure of her fingers on all the places that seemed to thrill Brit.

"I want to taste you. Would that be okay?" Alex asked as they looked at each other with longing.

Brit's jaw dropped open and she nodded. Alex moved quickly down the bed, never withdrawing her finger but now adding her mouth beside the thumb that had been teasing Brit's clit. She paused and listened with joy at Brit's gasps of pleasure and words of encouragement as her tongue softly lapped at Brit's clit.

"Oh, yes, Alex…Oh, God…Oh, wow."

Using the inside of her lower lip, Alex began caressing her, up one side of her clit and down the other, and then in little circles all around it, as her finger grew more brazen inside. Brit's hips had grown still in anticipation of Alex's mouth, but now they began to move again, and Alex felt Brit's hands in her hair, at first softly running her fingers through the curls, then grasping, and then finally holding tight to Alex's head, assuring she wouldn't abandon the task she'd set out to complete.

Alex moved her head and her lips and her tongue and her fingers, swirling and licking and stroking until she felt Brit arching beneath her and heard the indecipherable moans and sighs that told her Brit was about to orgasm. Inspired, she licked more frantically at Brit's clit until finally, with a last thrust of her hips toward the mouth that claimed her, she let out a groan that rattled the windows. The hips and the hands that had been so active grew still, and Brit collapsed in a heap on the bed.

Resting her head on Brit's thigh, Alex took a few moments to settle down. Her heart threatened to break through her chest wall, and her lungs were on fire. She was dizzy, and all she could taste and smell was the salty sweetness of Brit. The throbbing in her clit was fierce, and she thought that for a moment, just as Brit was starting to come, that she might, too, from the mere brush of her clit against Brit's comforter. She hadn't, though, and she tried to focus on Brit's pleasure as a distraction from her own need.

Opening her eyes, she studied the neatly trimmed bush of blond hair, a few shades darker than on her head. Her sex was puffy and shiny and inviting, and Alex gently kissed it, barely touching the lips that guarded her entrance. Was Brit a woman of multiple orgasms, or was she a one-and-done kind of girl? Alex wondered if Brit even knew the answer herself.

Shifting her head slightly, but still resting on Brit's thigh, Alex began exploring Brit's sex yet again. She glided her fingers smoothly through the wet folds and sucked gently. Tracing her finger up and down Brit's center, from top to bottom, she began tentatively pushing her finger in, then pulling out before beginning the route again, on each pass venturing in a little deeper. Before her first knuckle was buried, Brit was moaning again, asking for more.

"Please, Alex. It's so wonderful. Don't stop."

Yet again Alex shifted and found herself on her knees, squarely between Brit's legs, her head bent in worship. She began to fuck her more deeply while sucking feverishly on Brit's hard clit. It grew beneath her mouth from a soft nub of nerves to a hard bundle that demanded her attention, and Alex gave it all she had, until she sensed and heard and felt Brit's second orgasm.

This time she withdrew and slid up to the head of the bed, then pulled Brit into her arms. Tears glossed Brit's eyes as they looked at her, and a smile picked up the corners of her mouth. "There are no words to describe that."

In response, Alex pulled her closer. "Shhh. You don't have to say anything."

"Okay, then I won't tax my brain. It seems to have short-circuited."

"I'm glad."

Brit closed her eyes and focused on her breathing. She'd known the wonder of orgasm since figuring out how to pleasure herself as a teenager, but comparing those orgasms to the pair Alex had given her was like watching fireworks on television instead of in person. They weren't in the same category.

They held each other quietly on top of the blankets, listening to the music and feeling each other's heat. Brit tried to take in every sensation to preserve forever this amazing moment. A faint smell of apple pie mingled with the berry-scented candles burning in the bedroom. And with Alex's face so close to hers, Brit detected another smell, a musky, heady aroma she knew was her own. The music was soft and sultry. The candles threw off dancing waves of light. The hot, firm body beside her warmed her. Her own body was totally relaxed, totally satisfied, totally alive. At that moment, their world was a perfect place. It was amazing, just as she'd requested.

"They were right about the music, Alex. Norah rocks," Brit said after a while.

Alex cleared her throat. "I think it was actually me who did the rocking."

Gently, Brit pushed Alex onto her back, and she rolled onto her side, holding her weight on her forearm. Instantly her calm was replaced by desire, and she was wide-awake, charged. With her free hand, she began to trace a line with her fingers, from Alex's own fingertip, along her arm and to her collarbone. Drawing ever-widening circles there, she came closer and closer to Alex's breast, causing Alex to gasp. Brit smiled in response, biting her lower lip. "You do rock. Now I want to rock *you*."

"You already do."

Their eyes met, and Brit shuddered at the thought of what they'd just done. At what she was about to do. And just what was that? She had no idea where to start, what to do first.

Brit slid on top of Alex and kissed her softly, then searched for her eyes again. "I may need some directions."

Arching her hips and pulling Brit into her, Alex smiled. "I think you're doing a great job, Brit."

"I just want to make you feel as good as I do, and…what if I can't?"

Alex sighed and, pulling Brit's hand to her mouth, kissed her fingertips. Their faces were inches apart, and again Alex rocked her hips into Brit's. "I could come like this, Brit. I could come with your fingers inside or your mouth on me. That's how much you excite me."

"You're not making this any easier," Brit said as she began kissing her way down Alex's long body. She paused at the angle of Alex's jaw and again at the front of her ear, eliciting a moan. She slid wet lips along her throat to the hollow at the junction of her collarbones, where she kissed the muscles straining as Alex arched her neck. With her hands, she found Alex's breasts and gently slid across the pebbly surfaces of her nipples, teasing, kneading, and flicking her fingers by turns. With her mouth she continued down until it met her hands, and then Brit pulled the stiffened nipple into her mouth, pushing the rest of Alex's breast, too, trying to take it all in.

"Oh, Brit." Alex groaned at the sensation, and Brit was inspired

to keep going. Such joyous noise could only mean she was doing something right, right? And she wanted to take her time with this; she wanted to repay Alex for all the attention she'd been given, wanted to show her the love that was in her heart. Even if she didn't have a clue about what to do, whatever clumsy attempts she made at lovemaking would be from the heart, and she wanted Alex to know that.

Yet as much as she wanted to linger in the valley between Alex's breasts, she was drawn lower, craving Alex's sex. The need to lick her and taste her and attempt to give her that indescribable pleasure she'd just experienced was suddenly too much to resist. Hastening her descent, she found Alex's clit with her fingers, felt it throbbing as it slid along her forefinger, and felt Alex tremble with pleasure as she moaned yet again. "Oh, Brit, that's so good. It feels so wonderful."

Encouraged, Brit moved lower, through the patch of blond curls, searching for that magical part of Alex she was caressing with her fingers. When her mouth found her hand, Brit sucked Alex's clit and stroked it, moving her head and her hands in tandem with Alex's pelvis, which had pushed her off the bed. She remembered holding Alex's head a moment earlier and understood that need. The thought of what Alex had done with her tongue and what she now was doing to Alex caused a sudden flood between her legs again and an aching that shocked her.

She responded with more pressure, with both her fingers and then her tongue, encouraged by Alex's thrusting and groaning, as well as her own growing need. Brit slid through Alex's wet folds and slipped inside, where it was so hot and wet her fingers were burning. Alex shouted as Brit's finger went deep inside her, and suddenly Alex's hand was on top of hers, not showing her what to do, but holding it in the place that told Brit she'd found home.

Brit could sense Alex's impending orgasm, feeling her need as if it were her own, and she moved her mouth and her tongue and her fingers faster, deeper, harder, until at last, Alex shrieked and shuddered and then grew still beneath her.

Brit held on to her, still, but then feeling quite proud of herself, she began to laugh. "Wow!"

"Yeah, Brit. Wow."

Brit sat next to Alex and stroked her with a fingertip, admiring the perfect features of her face, the sculpted form of her shoulders and arms, the model-like body. "You're so beautiful, Alex."

"You make me feel beautiful."

"Good."

"And you make me feel…needy. If you keep touching me, I'm going to be very needy very soon."

"As in needing another orgasm?"

Alex nodded.

Brit sighed. "Oh, I'm so happy you told me that, because I feel needy, too."

Smiling, Alex sat up and kissed Brit, then began laying a trail of kisses down her body, moving headfirst as she went. "Let's see what we can do about all of these needs," she said as she worked her way down.

Brit gasped as she realized what Alex was doing, sliding along her body, aiming for the triangle between her legs even as she positioned her own sex above Brit's waiting mouth. Brit came in the instant Alex engulfed her, but she continued the motions of her own fingers and tongue until just a moment later when the now-familiar sounds told her Alex was going to that same wonderful, blissful place.

Only when Alex stopped shaking did Brit slow her movements and collapse back onto the pillow, and only when Alex was resting again in her arms did she allow herself the simple pleasure of those three magical words that were all either of them needed to perfect the moment. "I love you," she said softly.

CHAPTER TWENTY-TWO

LET THE GAMES BEGIN

I think it's good to start off playing a great team, Alex. It'll test us."
Alex was pacing the living room of her apartment, looking sexy as
hell in a black tailored suit. Even the scowl on her face couldn't detract
from her magnificence.

"But what if we lose? Will their confidence be shattered?"

The team's schedule had been decided long before Alex was
hired, and by the time she realized their opening game was against the
defending champs of the neighboring county, it was too late to change
things. The team was a perennial power, and to make things worse,
since it was the first game of the year, they hadn't had a chance to scout
them. If they could have seen them play, perhaps it would have eased
Alex's fears. As it was, her anxiety seemed to grow daily as the tip-off
tournament approached.

Now it was just five hours until game time, and Alex was a wreck.
She'd left Brit's apartment on this bright Saturday morning, claiming
she needed to get ready for the game. Brit had been preoccupied with
sorting laundry and cleaning her refrigerator, and it had taken an hour
for her to realize Alex didn't have anything to get ready for. Game time
was five o'clock, and their bus was scheduled to leave the school ninety
minutes prior. Did she really need five hours to change clothes?

Brit had found her at home, all dressed up, watching a video of
their opponent from the prior season.

"What can I do? Would you like a drink?"

Alex ran her hands through her hair as she stood at her window,
looking into the dense forest behind the Fielding estate. Few leaves
remained on the trees, the grass had faded to brown, and patches of

the first snow were scattered across the landscaping. It was a dreary picture, perfectly matching Alex's mood.

Wrapping her arms around Alex's waist, Brit pulled her close, and after a moment, Alex began to relax against her. Then Alex turned in her arms and returned the hug, then bent and began kissing Brit's neck, following it to her jaw until she finally found her mouth. Brit was instantly wet, and as she returned the kiss, Alex grabbed her butt, pulling their centers into each other. "I just thought of another way to relax you," Brit whispered into Alex's ear.

How she'd gone from celibacy to her current state amazed Brit, but she wasn't questioning it. Not too deeply, anyway. She was too busy enjoying herself, having as many orgasms as possible, smiling as the happiness within her bubbled out.

They quickly shed their clothes, and Brit concentrated on Alex's pleasure rather than her own. Within minutes of settling onto the bed, Alex was shuddering in her arms. Brit couldn't suppress a triumphant smile, and Alex returned it.

"That was much better than a drink."

Brit settled into Alex, wrapped her arms tightly around her, and rested her head on Alex's chest. "It's really going to be okay, Alex."

Alex kissed the top of her head. "I've never failed at anything, Brit. Everything's always been easy for me. I just practiced and prepared, and it worked. But this is out of my control. It doesn't matter what I do, it's up to the team now."

"You can't control everything, that's true. But you can call the plays and change the defense, make substitutions. You're not using your physical skills, but you'll be using that amazing mind."

"Stop teasing me. What if we lose?"

Brit trailed her finger across Alex's collarbone, across her shoulder, down her arm. "We'll give them a pep talk, and we go back tomorrow and win that one."

"You make it sound easy."

"Well, I know it's not, but as your girlfriend it's my job to lie to you to make you feel better."

Alex laughed.

"See, it's working."

A few hours later, Brit followed the team from the locker room into the gym. The fans erupted in a chorus of cheers as the players tore

through a green-and-white banner, and Brit quickly found her family in the stands just behind the bench. Even in pumps and a skirt, Brit bounded up the bleachers to greet them. They were all there, all eleven of them, and each of them hugged her and kissed her for luck.

"I'm so proud of you," her dad said, and Brit beamed.

"Good luck, dear," her mom said, and Brit knew her mother was still mad that basketball was keeping her away from her family. In addition to Thanksgiving, when she'd bailed out early, she'd missed the family dinner the week before. Brit couldn't help it; she'd been unable to pull herself away from Alex for long enough to make the drive home. Her entire life she'd spent busy Sundays with her family. Now that Alex was in her life, she wanted nothing more than to spend lazy Sundays with her. She had no reason to feel guilty, and when a little gust of guilt whipped up in her conscience, she quickly squelched it.

Then another emotion, fear, quickly replaced her guilt. As she pulled from her mother's arm, her eyes locked with a pair of blue eyes in the next section. Alex's dad. Brit excused herself and quickly made her way to the Daltons.

Shit! With all the thoughts occupying her time lately, Brit hadn't considered this one. Two sets of parents were operating on two different assumptions. Her family thought she was Alex's assistant coach. And on Thanksgiving, Alex had introduced her as her girlfriend. Under no circumstances could the two families be allowed to meet. Not yet, anyway. Brit wasn't about to ruin her parents' Christmas by coming out to them.

A dozen friends surrounded Alex's parents, and Brit tried to keep her greeting brief. The game was about to start, but the eyes she'd felt following her as she left her family to join the Daltons concerned her. With a promise that she'd talk to them later, and a prayer that neither family decided to introduce themselves to the other at the half, Brit rejoined Alex courtside.

Her foray into the bleachers had lasted only a couple of minutes, but Brit felt like she'd aged years in that time. What was she going to do now?

She stood beside Alex as the national anthem played. Alex looked stunning in her suit, and although Brit knew she was nervous, it didn't show. She chatted with players, joked with parents, talked with

reporters, and made it all look easy. Soon Brit was caught up in the excitement of the game as well, her fears about her family forgotten.

They'd decided on the starting five a week earlier, and Brit felt confident as she watched them take the floor. Then the ref threw up the ball, Kelsey tapped it to Sid, and Melissa broke to the basket and caught the pass in the lane. She danced around the defense and banked her shot off the backboard for the first basket of her high-school career. The play took only six seconds.

All of Alex's worry had been needless. The defending champions were no match for the Falcons, and by the third quarter, the game was over. They won by thirty points, with help from every player on the team.

Rather than head straight to the locker room, Brit met her family as she came off the court. She hoped to dismiss them quickly and join the team, without having to make any introductions. They'd planned to have dinner together, but Brit hadn't counted on staying to scout the second game. It would be another two hours before she could leave the gym.

With a discreet glance in the Daltons' direction, Brit accepted hugs from her family as they congratulated her, then again as they said good-bye. After she promised she'd see them the next day for mass and dinner before her game, they left without incident.

Laughter and loud banter greeted her in the locker room, and Brit's spirits soared when she entered. The players joked with each other as they changed back into their warm-up suits, and Brit handed out pats on the back as she approached Alex.

"That was easy," she said, and Alex smiled from ear to ear.

"Thanks for helping me relax today. That was the key to my outstanding coaching performance."

Brit blushed but couldn't resist a retort. "The pleasure was all mine."

"Ready?" Alex asked.

Brit didn't need to change, but she grabbed her bag from a locker and followed Alex back to the gym. Her parents were waiting. "Congrats, Coach Dalton. Coach Dodge," Alex's dad said, and he hugged her again.

"Yes, it was a great game," her mom added.

CHAPTER TWENTY-THREE

HOLIDAY SURPRISE

Bing Crosby was singing "White Christmas" as Brit started her car and left her parents' house, headed for home. The local radio station had begun a countdown to Christmas on the day after Thanksgiving, playing carols nonstop. Now, Christmas was finally here. It was just after midnight, yet another imaginary migraine freed her from the family obligations that were a constant obstacle in her pursuit of time with Alex. And after they'd first made love—since before that, really— because all Brit wanted was to be with Alex, life had become quite complicated.

Not that she was complaining.

The month since Thanksgiving had been simply magnificent. They were together most of the time and somehow managed to pull their mouths away from each other long enough to complete lesson plans and practice agendas in between talking and cooking and washing laundry, and all the other little things required to run apartments and lives and careers. Each day was new and adventurous, and Brit was savoring all of it. This first love was all she'd ever dreamed it would be. And so much was going on, Brit's head was spinning. Not only did they have the wonder of their new love, they had the magic of Christmas and the excitement of their basketball season to keep everything lively.

And all of it was great. The team was undefeated. Seven girls were good enough to start, which made their bench phenomenal. Kelsey had improved tremendously in the five months since they'd met at the park. At the beginning of the school year, she'd planned to attend a small local college and wasn't even interested in playing college basketball.

After scoring more than a hundred points in her first three games of the season, though, the plans had changed dramatically.

Daily calls were coming in from college coaches, all inquiring about Kelsey's future. Some small Division I schools had offered scholarships, and a few bigger schools had made inquiries about her intentions. Suddenly, she was excited about her future as a basketball player, and her energy filtered through to the rest of the players. They were playing well together, mixing up the offense with jump shots and drives, and working to find a way to get the ball into Kelsey's hands. Their defense was spectacular as well—Kelsey was blocking shots left and right, and the guards were stealing the ball at a record pace.

Conditioning couldn't fix academics, though, and that bothered Brit most. The last thing a winning team needed was to lose a player due to poor grades, so Alex had given her the job of keeping tabs on the players' classroom performance. With a few of them, Brit had her hands full. And of course, because that's the way it usually happens, the player who struggled most in the classroom was Kelsey.

Brit was working with her, taking the first ten minutes of every practice to go over her class work. They would stand facing each other, bouncing balls and talking about history and literature and calculus. Biology was a delicate subject, and Brit tried not to cross the line by discussing her class in too much detail. It didn't matter, though. Kelsey was doing well in biology. And in the month since they'd started their little pre-practice ritual, Kelsey's grades had improved across the board. The time they spent together in the gym was helping her ball-handling skills, too. Brit thought a big part of her success was the confidence with which she moved to the basket. She was suddenly so sure of that ball in her hands that nothing could stop her.

It was wonderful to see the team doing so well, and Brit was proud to be a part of their success. The energy was palpable and put a bounce in all of their steps, but none more so than Alex's. Alex had been sweating about the team when they first met at the beach, but now she was finally relaxed and enjoying the early success they were having. Reporters had interviewed her for the newspaper and television, and the school and the community were beginning to get excited about the team. On a few occasions when they'd been at the grocery store and the mall, strangers had approached Alex to offer their congratulations on

her team's success. Brit was her biggest fan, but suddenly Alex had a horde of admirers.

Even more pleasing, though, was the love growing between them. In typical honeymoon fashion, they rarely got out of bed. Every morning they awakened together—sometimes at Alex's, but mostly at Brit's—kissing each other awake, making love before they went off to school. They'd teach all day, have practice, and then come home and make love again. On Saturdays they squeezed a little shopping and baking into the routine. Brit had skipped two of the Sundays at her parents', insisting she needed time for shopping and putting up her own Christmas tree, a job she shared with Alex.

They'd ventured a few miles into the snowy woods to find the perfect tree at the farm, then hauled it back to Brit's on the top of Alex's SUV. It was like a fantasy, listening to carols and decorating, then making love on the couch in the glow of their first Christmas tree.

Brit couldn't believe what had become of her. For a woman who'd felt virtually no sexual energy for so long, she'd exploded. Sex was on her mind constantly, to the point of distraction, and even if they made love four or five times on a Saturday afternoon, she could have still found the energy to do it again if Alex indicated the desire. And, most often, Alex did.

Alex had proved to be just a hair shy of perfect. She was a tender and passionate lover, an attentive girlfriend, a neat and considerate roommate, and a fun playmate. Brit could imagine spending her life with Alex, which was just one more reason she had to tell her family.

She had to. Since that first game, Brit had been holding her breath, awaiting the collision of Liz Dalton and Joan Dodge. Thankfully, her parents had made it to only one other game, on the same Saturday the Daltons traveled to New York City to see the Christmas show at Radio City. She'd introduced Alex to her family that day, and they were charmed. But she knew her mother, and it wouldn't be long before she insisted on meeting the Daltons. It was just good manners. Her parents knew the parents of all her friends. This situation was totally different, though, and a conversation between their two moms would be a disaster.

It wasn't only the stress of discovery weighing on her, though. It was the lying. How much longer could she make up excuses and pretend to be sick? It was a drain on her energy, and if she told Alex

what she was doing, Alex would be disappointed in her. Alex had no hard feelings about her non-invitation to Christmas at the Dodges', but she'd once again invited Brit to her parents' for the holiday celebration. Brit wanted nothing more than to spend the remainder of Christmas Eve and Christmas Day with Alex, and share dinner in the evening with the Daltons, but her decision to abandon her family hadn't sat well with any of them.

As usual, Brit had awakened that morning with Alex beside her. Their lovemaking had been soft and slow and sweet, and without even trying Alex had brought her to orgasm twice. They did a yoga workout in Brit's living room and then watched *The Santa Clause* in bed before parting ways in the early afternoon.

Once at her parents' house, Brit helped her mom prepare the house and the food for the party, and the entire family attended mass together before coming back to the homestead to exchange gifts. Christmas was a grand celebration for her family, and it was the time of year her parents spoiled them all, showering them with clothing and toys and electronic devices. The boys had too many toys to count, and her parents gave all three daughters earrings and boots and purses. Brit had inherited her love of Broadway from her parents, and she and her sisters had chipped in to buy them tickets and a hotel room for a weekend in New York.

It was a festive time as they opened gifts and sang carols, but Brit purposefully avoided the cocktails that were circulating because she was planning to drive home that evening. When Jordan asked her why she wasn't drinking, Brit used the opening to complain about the headache she'd had all day. Later, after the invaders had retreated, Brit straightened the house from top to bottom, put away the food, and took out three bags of trash before confessing to her parents that she was going home.

"Why, Britain, that's absurd! You can't drive home at this hour," her mother insisted.

"Mom, I feel better in my own bed," she explained.

"Honey, it's such a long drive," her dad said. "Why don't you take your medication and go to bed? We'll be quiet in the morning and let you sleep in."

Guilt tore at her heart, but she fought it, because all she really wanted for Christmas was waiting at home for her. Alex.

"That's the problem, Dad. I rushed out of the house after practice and forgot my medicine."

"Well, maybe I can call in a prescription for you. I'm sure there's a pharmacy open."

Her mother scoffed at him. "Don't be ridiculous. What pharmacy would be open on Christmas Eve? But this basketball all the time is no good, Brit. You need to rest after school instead of practicing all the time. No wonder you get headaches."

Brit bit her lip to suppress a retort. "I love you. I'll see you tomorrow." She kissed them both at the door and smiled. "Merry Christmas."

"It won't be merry at all if you get into an accident," her mom shouted after her.

"Oh, hush," her father said. "She needs to get her medicine."

That's how Brit had left them, and the anxiety about the phone call she'd have to make in the morning, telling them she wasn't coming to Christmas dinner, was stressing her enough to cause a *real* migraine. But she'd do it. Because she had absolutely no desire to spend her day refereeing her nephews, putting together toys, programming electronics, and cleaning up after her sisters. Her Christmas fantasy involved waking up with Alex, having breakfast in front of their tree, and watching a couple of movies before having dinner at the Daltons'. A simple, calm day with the woman she loved. And perhaps they'd even find the time for a little sex, too.

The drive home was easy on this clear evening, and Brit easily managed to carry her packages to the apartment. It amazed her how much money she'd spent on tiny gifts of gold and silicon, enough to fill an entire room with the toys she'd once loved. Just as well, though, because with Alex's clothing now resting beside hers in the closets, there wasn't much room for clutter.

Brit was about to key the lock when the apartment door opened. Alex stood just inside, wearing a Santa hat and very little else. She quickly pulled a smiling Brit inside and into her arms.

"Merry Christmas," Alex greeted her, feeling as merry as she'd ever been. Brit smiled and kissed her softly.

"Are you my present?" Brit asked.

"Oh, no," Alex said, motioning to the tree that twinkled a few feet away. "Santa left you some other things."

"Well, I'd still like you," she teased her.

Alex kissed her again, more deeply this time, and as had often been the case since the day before Thanksgiving, that initial spark quickly ignited a fire that made Alex want to drag Brit directly to bed. Brit was always willing, and it amazed Alex how well they connected sexually. Of course she'd known immediately they were compatible, with similar senses of humor and the ability to make each other laugh. Her parents had taught her that laughter was the best antidote for any troubles, and although their marriage of nearly forty years wasn't perfect, they were happy. If Alex could have what they had, life would be good.

Alex nodded toward the bedroom, took Brit's hand, and led her that way, trembling in anticipation at what she knew was coming. Her. And Brit. Probably twice. Yes, she'd known they were perfect together outside the bedroom, but what she'd discovered between the sheets was absolute bliss.

"Oh, Alex," Brit said as they walked into the bedroom, and she brought her hand to her mouth.

Alex proudly surveyed the scene. A hundred tea-light candles twinkled in the four corners of the room, casting dancing shadows all around them and onto the ceiling. A larger candle on the nightstand filled the room with the unmistakable scent of Christmas Eve. The thick white comforter was pulled down invitingly, and a single red rose lay on Brit's pillow, its stem adorned with a green-and-red ribbon. Kenny G belted out a Christmas tune on his sax, a slow, sultry rhythm perfect for romance.

Alex turned to find Brit looking at her.

Brit was overwhelmed.

"This is amazing," she whispered into Alex's neck, and she wrapped an arm around her waist and began slowly moving her feet in time to the music. They'd never danced together, and the mood couldn't be more perfect for their first time. Brit moved her hips, rolling them into Alex, pulling her closer, growing immediately wet at the contact. Shuffling in step with her, Alex followed the movements, kissing her head as they moved together, pulling each other closer. Leaning back, Brit looked into Alex's eyes and read her feelings. Love, lust, excitement, happiness. Much the same as her own. Even though Alex had experienced many lovers, Brit knew that, like her, this was a first. She'd never really been in love before, either. The relationship

idea was new. And this experience was new. Alex had never, ever spent Christmas Eve with a girl. It was a first for them, and Brit knew in her heart it would be the first of many. Alex was the one she'd spend every Christmas Eve with for the rest of her days.

The song came to a climactic end, and Brit pulled her lover toward her bed—toward their bed. Brit quickly shed her own clothing but decided to leave the Santa hat when she began undressing Alex. Sliding a hand between them, she unfastened the topmost of the buttons on Alex's cream-colored silk blouse. She slid her fingers inside, pushing away the fabric as she kissed the soft skin beneath, then slipped the next button through the fabric, exposing the top of Alex's breasts. Her bra—a lacy affair so unlike the sports bras Alex usually wore—pushed them up, creating tantalizing cleavage that Brit admired for a moment before devouring it. Clinging to Alex's waist to support her trembling legs, Brit explored the cleft between her breasts, darting her tongue inside, sucking on the soft mounds, nibbling along the fabric that still contained them. Gulping air, she paused to look at Alex's face, covered in a mask of desire, and decided to move them to the bed. It just wouldn't do to fall over and break a bone.

Pushing Alex onto the soft, thick comforter, Brit slid between her legs and discovered silky panties in a color and style that matched the bra. She loved Alex the jock in sports bras and gym shorts, but Alex the Victoria's Secret lingerie model was equally hot. "Oh, Alex," she said, slipping a finger into the crotch while she kissed along the lacy band. Alex was wet and accepting, and Brit pushed inside, making Alex buckle. Brit realized she'd gotten ahead of herself; the underwear had thrown her concentration. Cleavage. She'd wanted to explore cleavage.

"You like?" Alex breathlessly murmured.

"I do."

"It goes with the shirt," Alex murmured, then moaned again as Brit withdrew the wet finger and sucked it.

"You taste heavenly. I want more." Brit shifted slightly and began opening Alex's shirt again, this time from the bottom. "But first, I want to see your breasts. It would appear they've been specially wrapped for Christmas."

Alex's stomach was all gooseflesh, and it quivered beneath Brit's hands and mouth as she took her time opening the first of her Christmas gifts. One button popped, and then the next, each revealing more of

Alex's soft skin. Then the final button was undone, and the silk fell away beneath Brit's fingers, exposing the lace and the tops of the breasts it contained. The sight of Alex like this was overwhelming, and Brit closed her eyes as she rested her face against soft material, her heart pounding, her clit throbbing with need.

Pushing up onto her forearms, Brit licked along the top of Alex's bra, darting her tongue down to caress the breasts that threatened to explode from the confines of the thin fabric. The shift in her position put Alex's leg between her own, and she gently rocked her hips for maximum effect. She felt she might explode, and she didn't want that to happen, at least not until Alex did, too. She willed her hips to slow down even as her hands and her mouth picked up the pace, pushing the bra up, freeing Alex's breasts. Brit sucked a hardened nipple into her mouth, grazed her teeth lightly across it, noting again how Alex quivered at the contact. She slid her hand lower, across the hot skin of Alex's belly, across the fabric covering her sex, and found again a way around the barrier, slipping easily inside.

"Uyuuhh," Alex groaned, and Brit stroked her, the moan and the movement causing Brit's excitement to mount, too. Her heart raced from the pleasure of Alex's breast in her mouth and her finger inside her and from the pressure of Alex's leg against hers. The need to come was becoming almost painful, and Brit knew she needed to stop or go, so she pulled back, moved down, covering Alex's clit with her mouth, soaking the fabric of her panties as she sucked through them, fucking Alex frantically and sucking even harder, until Alex's hips rose and her moaning became a cry of release. Still Brit kept at it, until a minute later Alex's lower body collapsed onto the bed and she begged Brit to stop.

Brit slid up the length of Alex's body and kissed her hard on the mouth, rubbing her center against Alex's leg. God, she was hot. On fire, actually. Every cell in her body seemed to burn with lust and she moved her hips. Finally, looking into Alex's eyes, she thrust hard against her and exploded.

Brit collapsed where she was, too exhausted to move, and when she awakened, the apartment was quiet. Kenny G had put away his sax and gone to bed. The candles had been extinguished; at least she hoped Alex had put them all out. Sunshine poured in around the blinds, and as she blinked the sleep from her eyes she tried to focus on the clock. Ten.

They'd slept for eight hours, and Brit was amazed at how refreshed

she felt. The emotion of the holiday and the stress of their schedule had been wearing them out, and sleep had been just what she needed. An entire day with Alex was just what she needed.

Her movements caused Alex to awaken, and Brit immediately ran her fingers through the mop of blond curls. Somehow Alex had ditched the Santa hat, but she was still adorable anyway. "Good morning," Brit said.

Closing her eyes again, Alex smiled, just a small smile, but the peaceful look on her face told Brit how happy she was, too. "Good morning." Then her eyes popped open. "Merry Christmas."

"Yes, Merry Christmas," Brit said as she snuggled closer.

"You feel so good, Brit."

"You, too. I wish we didn't have to move, but if I don't pee, my bladder will explode, and if I don't eat I really will get a migraine."

Alex poked her in the ribs. "Well, I can't help with the peeing, but I can make breakfast. I brought fruit and yogurt and...cheese Danishes."

"Ummm," Brit moaned.

Alex smiled in response. "Merry Christmas."

Brit used the bathroom first and came into the kitchen a few minutes later to find the promised Danishes quartered and plated, yogurt in dessert bowls topped with raspberries, and the water hot in the Keurig. "Be right back," Alex said as she disappeared into the bathroom.

She emerged dressed in sweats and a sweatshirt, and Brit was leaning against the counter, sipping her coffee. "Shall we eat on the couch? In front of the tree? It looks like Santa was here and we have presents to open."

Brit frowned. Since the night before, she'd been dreading this moment—both telling Alex and her parents. But she had to do it, and soon. "I need to make a phone call," she said, and from the look on her face she suspected Alex guessed the reason.

Alex sighed. "You didn't tell them, huh?"

"I wimped out," Brit confessed.

Alex squeezed her arm and tried for a smile. "Well, make your call, then, because I'm not letting you out of this apartment until it's time for dinner."

Brit dialed the phone as Alex watched. She thought of seeking privacy in the bedroom, but she wasn't hiding from Alex. They'd

always been honest with each other, and that was important to Brit. She wished she had the courage to be honest with her family. After the holidays, she'd tell them about Alex. She had to.

"Hi, Mom. Merry Christmas," Brit said. She walked to Alex's side and leaned against her. Brit stood so close that she was sure Alex could hear her mom's side of the conversation.

"What time will you be here? I'd like to get the table set and relax before everyone arrives." Mrs. Dodge asked.

"Mom, I'm not coming," Brit said, and then she sucked in a breath. "My headache's still pretty bad." Alex stiffened.

Then Brit looked at Alex and winked. "I'm just going to spend the day in bed."

Alex sniggered uncontrollably and Brit poked her in the ribs.

"Britain, I've never heard of anything so ridiculous. You can't be alone on Christmas Day."

Brit ran her fingers through her hair, obviously stressed. "I think I just need a break from all the excitement, Mom. Just some down time."

"What you need is to give up that coaching. It takes up too much of your time and it's starting to affect your health. I'm going to make an appointment for you to see Dr. Sigmund next week."

"Mom, Dr. Sigmund's a pediatrician. I haven't seen her since I was in high school. I'll be fine. I'll see my neurologist and get a checkup. Don't worry about me."

"Another ridiculous statement. How does a mother not worry about her child?"

"I'm going to take a nap now. I'll call you later. Merry Christmas. Tell Daddy I love him and I'll call him later.

"Glad that's over." Brit exhaled a loud sigh, disconnected the call, and stepped away from Alex as she placed the phone on the counter.

"Me, too. I'm sorry you have to lie to them."

"I have to tell them soon, Alex. They're going to run into your parents at one of our games. Like maybe tomorrow."

"My parents won't say anything, Brit."

"Maybe not intentionally…"

"No, they won't say anything at all. They know you're not out."

"You told them?" Brit asked, and Alex heard the edge in her voice.

Alex nodded, and then explained. "My mom wanted to invite your family over after one of the games, since they live so close to the school

and your family is so far away. I had to say something, and I thought the truth was best."

Brit nodded. "So what did your mom say?"

"Something distasteful about your parents, although I don't feel at liberty to repeat the exact words."

Brit laughed and hugged Alex. "I wish I knew. I've been sweating about the holiday tournament."

"Well, now there's no worries."

"Thank you."

They carried their feast into the living room, turned on the tree lights, and devoured everything.

"I want to give you your presents and then watch *It's a Wonderful Life*," Brit said.

"And I want to watch *A Christmas Story*," Alex said. "And make love. And take a shower with you. And then eat a very quick dinner at my parents' house and then come right back here and make love again."

Alex was concentrating on breakfast, but noticing a lull in the conversation, she looked up and met Brit's gaze. "What?" she asked, suddenly suspicious.

"It's amazing, isn't it? How compatible we are in bed?"

Alex wanted to tell her just how much she agreed, but she always hesitated to discuss sex in general. Sex in particular, the moments they shared and the things they did—those were easy to talk about. But the generalizations might open the doorway to what had been an uncomfortable issue for them since Anke. Alex was afraid to reference other women, or allude to any others, or compare Brit to them, for even though her sexual connection with Brit was the most amazing one she'd ever had, she couldn't tell her that without reminding her that there had been many others before her. So she kept her answer simple. "Yes."

"I never imagined it could be like this."

And then she didn't need to measure her words, for this reply was so much easier than the last. "Neither did I."

Their gaze never wavered, even as Brit set the mug down on the coffee table and slid across the couch, into Alex's arms. Alex looked up at her, fighting the urge to push her back on the coach and devour her. Instead, she sat quietly as Brit kissed the top of her head, then her eyelids, and finally her lips. She pulled Brit closer and sunk deeper into the couch, with Brit snuggled in her arms. "I love you," Brit whispered,

and they held each other, and Alex could see and hear and feel only Brit, and it was perfect.

"Do you want a present?" Brit asked a few minutes later.

Alex's answer evoked a laugh. "Yes, please."

As Brit slipped from her lap, Alex stood as well and walked to the tree to retrieve several beautifully wrapped boxes. The first was small, the second medium, and the third huge. She'd wrapped them in shiny silver paper and topped each with red bows. Brit returned from the bedroom with a handful of boxes and placed them on the table.

"Three presents each. Perfect. I wanna go first," Brit informed Alex.

"'Kay," Alex answered and handed her the smallest package.

"I want the big one," Brit said.

"Best for last."

So Brit opened the small box and found a pair of silver snowflake earrings. "They're perfect," she said as she slid the stems through the holes in her lobes.

"You next." She handed Alex the medium package, wrapped in blue snowman paper with a big blue-and-white bow.

Just like Brit, Alex was methodical and deliberate, unsealing the tape that closed the paper and then sliding the box out. It was a Converse box, and Alex smiled as she pulled off the lid. Classic black Chuck Taylor high-tops. "They're perfect."

Brit beamed. "Glad you like them. Okay, now my turn," she announced, and grabbed the big box.

"No, no, no, Britain! The medium box is next."

Brit picked it up, seeming startled by its weight. Or lack thereof. She shook it and looked suspiciously in Alex's direction.

"Go ahead, open it."

Brit opened the paper to reveal a shoe box. Flinging the lid to the floor, Brit sifted through the tissue paper, red and green and white for Christmas, and found a red envelope. It wasn't sealed, and she reached inside and pulled out two tickets. Alex watched her closely as she read them and saw the excitement on her face as it registered.

"*Kinky Boots!*" she yelled, and jumped up to hug Alex. "When? When are we going?" she asked, and then she studied the tickets, finding the information before Alex could tell her. "Oh, wow. Sunday!

We're going on Sunday!" she yelled as she kissed Alex. "This is so perfect, Alex. This is the best present ever."

Alex had been bursting with excitement from the day she ordered the tickets, right after the first time they'd made love.

"You are such a better shopper than me, Alex. You got me *Kinky Boots* tickets and I got you sneakers. How lame."

"I love my sneakers. Don't knock 'em. And speaking of presents, umm, don't I get two more?"

Brit beamed again. "As a matter of fact you do," she said and handed Alex another gift, this one a bit smaller than the last. Again, Alex fastidiously peeled the paper to reveal the Disney logo on a small, black box. Flipping up the lid, she looked inside. A watch, with multiple changeable bands—leather, gold, silver—and Mickey Mouse on the face.

"So you'll never forget our first kiss."

"How could I ever forget it?" she asked and leaned over as their lips met in a soft, tender kiss filled with all of Alex's love. "This is beautiful," she said, turning back to the watch. "Thanks."

Brit smiled. "I'm glad you like it. Now I want my big present."

Alex pretended to struggle with the weight of it, but it was just as light as the other box. Brit pursed her lips, and this time she tore off the paper to reveal a U-Haul box. Impatiently, she shifted through tissue paper to find an envelope. Inside was a reservation for a hotel in New York City, and Alex watched another smile form on Brit's face, and then Brit raised her face to look at Alex.

"We're going to New York!" Brit danced around Alex and then pushed her onto the floor and kissed her passionately.

"I guess you like your presents, huh?"

"I do." Brit would have been happy with nothing more than a special day at home with Alex, but the gifts were truly perfect. She was so happy to have Alex in her life, as her lover, to be sharing Christmas morning with her, that she felt as if she would burst from joy. Full of energy, she jumped up. "Let me give you one present, and then I'm taking you back to bed." Brit handed Alex the largest of the boxes, and she was startled by its weight. Brit's present had been big but light, and though hers was small by comparison, it was quite heavy.

The paper gave way to a plain cardboard box, stuffed with packing

peanuts. Within, wrapped in a layer of protective foam, Alex found a marble statue, eighteen inches high. It was a winged, headless, armless form with curves and breasts that were unmistakably feminine. Alex studied it, turning it over and over before finally placing it on the table. The details were remarkable, from the feathered wings to the lines of her flowing robes. "She's beautiful," she said at last.

"Do you know who she is?"

"I don't have a clue," Alex chuckled.

"It's Nike. This is a replica of a statue at the Louvre called *Nike of Samothrace.* It's Greek, and the original is over two thousand years old. She reminds me of you."

Alex studied the statue again, overwhelmed by emotion she couldn't explain. It probably had something to do with the novelty of the gift and how much thought had gone into it, or perhaps because she was so much in love. As if reading her mind, Brit stood and offered Alex her hand.

"Let's go back to bed."

Alex accepted the hand and followed Brit to the bedroom, and after they made love again, they turned on the television and cuddled up together in Brit's bed, watching movies. All of the pillows in the apartment were piled behind them, and the blankets were pulled all the way up as George Bailey and Clarence wandered around Bedford Falls in a blizzard.

"What was that noise?" Alex asked, sitting up and turning her head toward the door leading to the living room.

"Huh?" Brit asked. She'd been paying attention to the movie and didn't catch Alex's words.

"I thought I heard something," Alex said.

She turned her gaze from the television to the doorway just in time to see a well-dressed woman appear there, perfectly turned out with the exception of the expression of shock on her face.

Brit sat up, equally surprised. The fact that she was nearly naked didn't occur to her until she saw her mother looking at the pile of clothing still on the floor from the night before. "Mom. Hi," Brit said, trying to keep her vocal cords from trembling as she spoke.

"Britain, what's going on here?" her mother demanded.

Brit dropped her jaw as she noticed her mother taking it all in—

the candles, the lunch tray beside the bed, the woman in the bed beside her.

"Get dressed, Britain. I'll be in the living room," she said, and she turned around and walked back through the doorway.

"Oh, fuck," Brit said as she collapsed back into the pillows.

Alex sat up and turned to face Brit. Her concern was evident in the creased eyes and pursed lips, and Brit could hear Alex's voice wavering, too. "How could this happen to me twice in one lifetime?" Alex asked.

"I think you got off easy last time."

"Just tell her I came over to keep you company. I brought you food," she suggested.

Brit sighed as she slipped from the bed and reached and pulled some clothes from her dresser. She turned to face Alex, who was also dressing. "You can stay in here if you'd like."

Alex shook her head. "And let you face the executioner alone? Never. We're in this together."

She found a measure of comfort in knowing that, but it wasn't enough to erase the fear that gripped her. But they dressed and then Alex followed her to the living room. Her mom had claimed the recliner but sat on its edge, anything but relaxed. Her sister Jordan was leaning against the wall near the kitchen, silently watching.

"Hi, Jordy," Brit said as she offered a feeble smile.

"Hey, sis." Jordan didn't even attempt to smile.

Brit sat on the couch and Alex walked past her before sitting, erecting a barrier between Brit and her mother. Brit tried to picture her mother taking on Alex, pushing her back onto the couch and attacking her. Somehow she knew Alex wouldn't fight back. Fortunately, Joan Dodge was much too dignified to throw punches. She battled with words.

"Mom, you remember Alex," she said by way of breaking the ice.

A half smile appeared on her mother's face, and Brit knew it was only a gesture to maintain appearances. Her mother was scrambling, and keeping to routine as much as possible would help her regain the control she thought she'd lost. Brit knew her so well, knew how she manipulated people—herself included—and she was so tired of it all.

"Yes, of course. Merry Christmas to you and yours, Alex."

Alex nodded but didn't smile. "Merry Christmas."

This is anything but merry, Brit thought as she pondered how to handle her mother. She spared Brit by taking charge, as she always did.

The smile faded as she pierced Brit with her dark eyes. "Britain, I demand to know what's going on here! I thought you were sick!"

Brit returned her mother's steely gaze and knew she understood the meaning of the bedroom scene. She also knew her mother well enough to know she could deny it and convince her mother she'd been mistaken. Her mother didn't really want to know the truth; she just wanted a reasonable story she could live with. She'd accept whatever ridiculous tale Brit told her to explain why she was spending Christmas Day half-naked in bed with Alex. It would be much easier to accept a lie than to accept her daughter's sexuality.

One little lie. That's all she needed to make it all go away. Brit looked from her mother to Alex, not even bothering to gaze in her sister's direction. Jordan was suspiciously quiet, and Brit didn't intend to complicate matters even more by dragging her into the conversation.

Her mother's look was expectant—hopeful, even. Brit could just imagine her thoughts. *Please tell me something plausible to take away this fear I have about why you've never dated a single one of the many handsome young men I've hand-picked for you.* Brit looked to Alex. It had been only a month, but she could read Alex pretty well, too. *I'm so sorry this is happening to you, Brit. Do what you have to. I'll be okay. We'll be okay.*

Brit didn't seem to have a drop of saliva left in her mouth, in spite of the fact that she'd swallowed half a dozen times as she tried to speak. And then her mother must have sensed her fears and decided that perhaps forgetting the entire episode and avoiding a conversation might be the more prudent course of action. "Britain, pack your bags. I'm taking you home. You need to rest and spend some time with your family."

Now Brit knew she had to say something—to one or the other of them. Her mom was squirming on the chair. Alex looked resigned to the idea that she'd spend the rest of the day alone.

Brit swallowed again and then turned to her sister. "Jordy, would you get us some water, please?" Then she slid over on the couch so that her leg was nearly touching Alex's. Her mother might have thought she was moving closer to her, but Alex sat a little taller and placed her hand

on Brit's back for support. Alex knew, and it only made Brit that much more confident about what she had to say. She finally had to say the words. As much as she loved her family, she had a right to live her life with the woman she loved.

"Mom, I'm not going home with you. I'm spending the day with Alex." Brit looked from her mom to Alex and back again. "I'm in love with her, Mom."

Joan sat forward and waved a dismissive hand in their general direction. "What? That's ridiculous! Pack your things right now, Britain!"

Brit leaned forward just a little and locked eyes with her mother. The anger and fear she saw was startling, but it didn't deter her. Alex's hand on her back was fortifying. "Mom, I'm a lesbian. I'm sorry you had to find out this way, but it's true. I wanted to spend this day with my lover, so I lied to you because I didn't want to ruin your holiday by telling you the truth."

"So you ruined my holiday this way, instead."

Brit accepted the water offered by her sister and took a sip, then leaned back into the couch. "That wasn't my intent. But I know how much you guys love me, so I should have figured you'd come over. Did you bring food?"

Her mother stood and stabbed a finger in Brit's direction. "How dare you make light of this! I'm giving you one more chance to come home, and if you don't take it, I'm not sure what the consequences will be, but I can assure you, there will be consequences!"

Brit didn't stand. She didn't have the energy, and worried her legs would give out if she tried. Instead she leaned farther into the cushions of her couch and looked at her mom and her sister. She knew this would be their reaction. She'd always known it, which was precisely why she'd never come out to them. But going home with them wouldn't change the fact that she was gay and in love with Alex.

"I'm sorry you feel that way, Mom. I really am. But I'm not going home with you."

Her mother didn't waste her energy on a good-bye and didn't even look Alex's way before she hurried through the door.

"Call me later," Jordan whispered. It was the first thing she'd said since exchanging hellos, and Brit knew she'd been right to keep this information from her sister as well. She hadn't come to Brit's defense;

she'd simply stood silently by as her mother threatened her and then ran out the door behind her.

Shifting slightly, Alex turned and silently wrapped her arms around Brit, pulling her closer. Brit had a vague sense of Alex's presence, heard mumbling words and felt suddenly warmer, but she couldn't seem to focus on what was happening around her. Her mind was occupied with her mother's parting words. *I can assure you, there will be consequences!* Brit had no doubt there would be, and understanding her mother as she did, Brit feared those consequences would not only affect her, but everyone else she loved as well.

Her father! She should call him, warn him. Tell him the truth, before her mother did. She found her phone in the kitchen, and sat beside Alex on the couch just as he answered the call. "How's the head?" he asked.

Brit sighed. "It's fine. I'm calling to tell you something. Can you talk?"

"Yes, of course. What is it?"

Brit could hear the concern in his voice. "Daddy, I lied about the headache. I, I just wanted to have some time away, because I met someone special." She paused, gathering her courage. This was so hard, and she wished she wasn't telling him over the phone. "Someone I really care about, and I…"

His voice boomed when he interrupted her. "Britain! Do you finally have a boyfriend?"

"No, Dad. I finally have a girlfriend."

There was a pause as he cleared his throat. Brit could imagine him sitting down, or collapsing onto the floor.

"Dad?"

"I don't understand, Brit. Are you saying you're a lesbian?"

Brit closed her eyes as she clutched the phone. "Yes, I am. I'm sorry to tell you like this, but Mom just stormed out of here and I didn't want you to hear it from her first."

"What happened? Are you okay?"

Brit laughed and wiped away a tear. "Not really, but I will be. She's pretty upset right now, though. I think I ruined Christmas."

"Nonsense. I'll deal with your mother. What can I do for you?" he asked.

"Just deal with Mom. Maybe you can calm her down, and in a few days maybe I can talk to her."

"I'll take care of it. You take care of you, okay?"

Trying very hard not to cry, Brit disconnected the phone and snuggled into Alex's arms. She focused on the Christmas tree, then on one tiny ornament. It was a mouse, resting in a hammock laced with Christmas lights, and had been added to her tree from Alex's collection. To Brit it represented Alex—so laid-back and calm. Nothing like the other woman who'd dominated her life, yet just as strong, and so much nicer.

I can do this! Brit thought. I can. I want Alex, I need Alex, I love Alex, and I can get through this crisis, because Alex is the prize I win if I manage to navigate this obstacle course. And what a prize! She was everything Brit could have hoped for, and for the first time in her life everything was perfect. It had been, anyway, until a few minutes ago, when her mother had forced her to make the most difficult choice of her life.

And she'd chosen Alex. She'd chosen to be herself. No matter how difficult, her choice had been the right one. It had been the only one, really, because she couldn't keep lying and running and hiding the truth. She'd said the word *lesbian* to her mother, and while she was sure her mother had never said the word herself, she certainly understood its meaning. And now she understood that her daughter defined herself in that way, and Brit could do nothing to change that.

The only direction to move was forward, so she took a deep breath and put on her game face. "Let's get a shower, Alex," she said. "I don't want to be late for dinner."

An hour later, they were seated beside a roaring fire in the Daltons' expansive living room. Frank poured a cocktail for himself and his wife, a beer for his daughter, and a malbec for Brit. This was their first appearance at the Daltons' since Thanksgiving, and Brit found them just as friendly and inviting as they'd been on the last visit. Alex made a point of taking her in through the front door to show off the landscaping adorned with lights and a replica of Santa's sleigh sitting on the lawn. And her parents made a point of greeting them at the door, offering hugs even before taking their coats.

"So, Brit, can you give me the inside scoop on the holiday

tournament? I want to bet on the game, and my daughter is very scarce with details."

"Isn't that like insider trading?" Brit asked.

"I can see why you two get along so well," he said in a teasing tone. "Seriously, it should be a great tournament. All of the teams are well balanced, and when you add the element of bloodlust you see with these rivalries, anything can happen."

"I think you're right. Our girls are very excited, and they're going to leave it all on the floor. I'd bet on us."

He grinned from ear to ear. "I will."

"You will what?" Liz asked as she walked across the room and set two trays on the coffee table. One held a cheese board with half a dozen varieties as well as grapes, almonds, and fig jam. The other was piled with stuffed mushrooms.

"Bet on Alex's team."

Liz shook her head disapprovingly as she took her drink and sat beside Alex. "How was your holiday so far?" She looked from Alex to Brit.

Alex winked at Brit and saved her from answering. "Brit and I always have a great time together, Mom. But we've been so busy with practice and games I think we just needed a little down time. We slept in and watched some movies."

Liz lovingly rubbed Alex's arm. "I'm glad you got some rest."

Brit was amazed by the interaction between them. Alex had just told her mother she'd spent a late morning in Brit's bed, and her mom was happy for her. Why couldn't all mothers be like Liz Dalton? Or, at least, why couldn't her mom?

CHAPTER TWENTY-FOUR

WINNERS AND LOSERS

P.J. jumped up in anticipation as Kelsey battled for a rebound and then squeezed her body through a pack of defenders. He pumped his fist to the heavens as the ball fell through the net. He joined the entire student section, jumping up and down, cheering wildly as their team came from behind to tie the score. So much noise filled the gym that the referee's whistle was useless, and he watched the woman gesturing to learn the call.

"Yes!" he shouted. "And one!" The students cheered as the official dropped her arm, her second finger pointing down to indicate Kelsey had been fouled on the shot.

He looked at the scoreboard. Four seconds left in the third overtime period. Score tied, ninety-four, ninety-four. Kelsey on the line, shooting one foul shot to win the game. It didn't get any more exciting than this, and two thousand fans at the Lackawanna College Student Union showed their team spirit. Half of them were screaming and half were biting their nails, but all of them had seen a great game.

The opposing coach called a time-out, and the noise level in the gym grew even louder.

P.J. looked around the sea of students. They were packed into the gym, but no one seemed to mind. He searched for one face in the crowd and found it. Justina was a few rows down from him, sitting with her friends, but he noticed she spent as much time turned around looking at him as she did watching the action on the court. Maybe she still liked him after all. The thought made him smile. All of his old friends were at the game, too. They'd all caught Falcon Fever.

This is what high school was supposed to be like, he thought. Spending time with friends. Cheering on your team. Having fun. Smiling at girls.

He wished he hadn't spent the hour before tip-off in the parking lot collecting bets on this game. He had, though. Students from both schools had bet nearly two thousand dollars on the game. It was unbelievable, but the team's success had created a gambling frenzy as everyone wanted in on the action.

The gym grew silent and he held his breath as the teams took their places around the key. The official handed Kelsey the ball. Her shoulders heaved with the deep breath she took, even as the fans seemed to hold theirs. After calmly bouncing the ball once, she raised her arms and launched it toward the basket.

It hit nothing but net.

The crowd roared with cheers and groans, the opposing team immediately called time-out again, and P.J. caught Justina's eye. She smiled at him. "This is so great," she said above the crowd.

"Yeah, isn't it?"

"Are you going for pizza after?" she asked him.

He wanted to, he really did. He needed to talk to Kelsey after the game, though. The Man had told him he had to, and he wasn't about to piss him off again. And with all the reporters and fans around, it could be a while before P.J. had Kelsey alone. By the time he reached the pizza place, everyone would probably be gone. Worse yet, if they were still there, they'd ask him where he'd been.

He looked at Justina and offered a sad smile. "I can't," he said. "Maybe next time."

CHAPTER TWENTY-FIVE

BLUE CHRISTMAS

B rit smiled into the mirror, studying all thirty-two teeth. She'd just flossed and they seemed to pass inspection, with no particles of food hiding between her molars with tooth decay on their agenda. Although she knew she was overreacting, she felt like this was the only reason she had to smile.

It had been a difficult few days. She'd spoken with Jordan on Christmas night after dinner, and her sister had simply pretended nothing had happened. That was typical Jordan, avoiding controversy at all costs, and although Brit understood the simple fact that they were speaking meant that Jordan loved her, it would have been wonderful to have a real conversation about everything going on in her life. Her sexuality. Her feelings for Alex. The scene with her mother. But nothing was said and never would be, not with Jordan.

Not with Sam, either. She didn't hear from her eldest sister until the morning after Christmas, when her simple phone call to confirm the game time made Brit weep with joy. Both sisters and their families were present in the stands as the team won the first round of the annual holiday tournament, and they all went to dinner afterward. Brit had planned on that time as a way for her family to meet Alex socially before she spilled the beans, but as it turned out, the beans were already scattered on the floor, and she walked into the restaurant with her nerves on edge, unsure of what to expect.

But Sam was her typical self, a much taller and more beautiful version of her mother, and just as controlling. She took charge at the restaurant, not only arranging the seating (she'd thankfully placed Alex beside Brit), but also providing games for the boys to occupy them

during the waiting time. She even made menu suggestions because she'd eaten there before. Their suspiciously absent parents were not discussed, but both her sisters and their husbands were cordial to Alex, and their sons loved her. Conversational topics included holiday gifts, the weather, the game, their clothing, and finally, the food. It seemed they talked about everything except the one issue of importance, and it was maddening. Even if dinner wasn't the right setting to have a heart-to-heart, some mention of it would have eased Brit's angst. If not for one small incident in the parking lot after dinner, Brit might have thought Sam was oblivious to the events of Christmas Day. "I love you, no matter what," Sam said as she pulled Brit into a hug that was just a little tighter and longer than usual. And Brit knew that, like with Jordan, nothing else would ever be said.

She supposed she should have felt grateful they'd shown up at all. She knew her mother wouldn't support their decision to support her, and with all the money Joan gave them and babysitting she provided, they were smart to stay in her good graces. Yet, she couldn't help wishing for more from them. If she were with a male Alex, the sisters wouldn't have shut up about him until Easter, but their discomfort kept them quiet, and Brit couldn't do anything about that. She'd have to navigate the murky water she'd created with her mother with only her own instincts to guide her. And perhaps with a little help from her dad.

Brit met her dad for lunch the next afternoon, and he, at least, wanted to discuss what was happening, even if she didn't feel comfortable telling him everything she felt. He was, after all, her father.

"Britain, are you sure about this?" he asked.

"Yes, Daddy." She squeezed his hands. "I am." Looking across the table at his handsome face, Brit realized he looked tired. His hair had always been blond and the gray didn't show, but it seemed to have turned white overnight. The last thing he needed was a family crisis. More than likely he'd been losing sleep in his concern for her and the grief her mother was causing him.

He simply nodded and looked to the ceiling or maybe to God as he took in a deep breath and squeezed back.

"Would you like to know the details?"

The shocked look on his face made her laugh. "Not *those* details!" she retorted, and his blush made her laugh even more.

But he told her he wanted to know everything about her, because

she was his baby girl and he loved her. And so Brit wiped away a tear and told him how she'd never felt an attraction to boys—or to girls for that matter—until she met Megan.

"Is she—?" her father asked, unable to hide the shock on his face.

"No, Dad. But I did have a crush on her, a long time ago."

And then she told him about dating, and meeting Alex, and falling in love with her.

"So, she's your first...love?" he asked, and although he fumbled over the words, Brit knew he was genuinely interested.

Brit nodded. "Yes."

"What if it doesn't work out?"

They'd both been pushing the food around their plates rather than eating, and Brit suddenly stopped and put her fork down. "Daddy, I'd be crushed if it doesn't work out with Alex. I'm in love with her. But I'll still be a lesbian. That's not going to change."

And even though he hadn't specifically asked that question, Brit sensed that was exactly what he wanted to know. This wasn't about Alex. It was about Brit.

"Well, then, I hope it works out, because you deserve to be loved. Not just loved, adored. And spoiled."

"I'm okay with just being loved. I have you to spoil me," Brit said in a teasing way.

"Well, then I'll buy lunch," he offered, and their stomachs finally settled down enough to eat their food instead of playing with it.

Halfway through the meal, after they'd talked about their family, the topic turned to medicine. Her dad always loved to talk shop. "Daddy, what do you know about ankylosing spondylitis?"

He swallowed and studied her a moment before answering. "It can cause aortic aneurysms and irregular heartbeats. It's treated with biological agents and steroids. There's no cure. Other than that, though, I don't know much. Why?"

Brit had read about Alex's disease, and she already knew everything her father said. It was still scary to hear him say the words, as if having him validate the Internet's information made it more ominous. Nothing about this disease was good, and Brit desperately wished it wasn't waging war in Alex's body. Her father might be able to help in some way, and Brit would have liked to share the information with him. Yet she knew Alex kept her diagnosis private, and she didn't feel she

could share it without betraying Alex's trust. "One of my friends was just diagnosed."

He nodded in understanding. "Well, if she has questions, hook her up with Pete Morgan. He's just finishing up in rheumatology in New York. He'll be joining his father's practice in July."

"Maybe I'll do that, Dad. I'll look him up."

Before they left he told her he wanted to meet Alex, and Brit promised to set up a date for the next week. She knew it would be stressful—because her dad would actually talk to Alex and might ask some questions that made Brit uncomfortable. She could imagine some noble inquiry, such as "What are your intentions with my daughter, Ms. Dalton?" But Brit would handle it. She'd prefer a million questions to the silent treatment her mother was giving her. And her mother wasn't likely to back down. To her mom, this wasn't just a matter of pride (or shame); it was a matter of morality. And in her eyes, Britain was sinning, betraying not just her family and her values, but her god.

Her mood was better after lunch with her dad, but her heart was still heavy as she and Alex boarded a Martz bus for New York on Sunday morning. They'd won the game the night before and had a quiet night at home, but the incident with her mom had definitely deflated the holiday mood. *Kinky Boots* was as good as she thought it would be, and she and Alex strolled through Central Park and window-shopped on Fifth Avenue, just like she'd always dreamed. But in her dreams she was happy, and in reality, she was not.

Forcing herself to eat and smile and talk to Alex was draining, and as New Year's Eve approached, Brit found herself too tired to pretend any longer. "Let's just stay home," she said, and collapsed on the couch with the pillow over her head as Alex called to make excuses to the friends they'd planned to join for a party.

Why did it have to happen this way? She thought she loved Alex enough to endure anything, but as she looked at herself in the mirror, she wondered if that was true. Perhaps she'd overestimated her strength and courage. All she wanted to do was cry, and somehow she felt that crying was immature, because she'd done nothing wrong, nothing to deserve the pain that had been dropped upon her like the weight of the world.

And her world was in such chaos. Maybe she'd been lonely before she met Alex, and she'd definitely been unfulfilled, but she hadn't been

miserable. Now she had the girl and the great sex, and she'd never been more unhappy in her life.

"You've really fucked it all up, Britain," she told the woman in the mirror, and then she turned off the bathroom light and headed for bed.

CHAPTER TWENTY-SIX

TRUE LOVE

Tapered candles flickered in tall candlesticks made of china, casting their light on a beautifully set table. Flowers added color to the crisp white linen. A bottle of Chianti had been uncorked and was breathing beside two glasses. Soft music played in the background, and the smell of spices and spaghetti sauce filled Brit's apartment.

It was the setting for a perfect Valentine's Day dinner, and in spite of the dour mood that had seemed to plague her since Christmas, on this day, Brit was excited. She'd rushed home after practice, asking Alex to give her an hour to make the preparations. She'd turned on the oven, set the table, poured the wine, and now she decided to drink some. She willed herself to be happy.

Sipping the wine, she looked at the scene and wondered how she could feel so sad. Her job was fulfilling and she enjoyed going to work every day. Basketball was exciting and rewarding. The team was winning and their energy was infectious, and Brit couldn't wipe the smile off her face when she was around them. Kelsey seemed out of sorts, and Brit wondered about her. She reminded herself to talk to Alex about it.

Alex. Alex was amazing. A good friend, a passionate lover. Brit couldn't find anything wrong with her, and she wondered why she was trying.

She wanted to be happy. She was trying to be happy. But should you have to try? Shouldn't happiness just be the reward for working hard and living a good life? She suspected the Bible sold it that way, but she saw her share of sad people in church. Maybe she'd talk to her new priest. It never would have occurred to her to talk to her old priest,

the one at her parents' church. But her new church in Clarks Summit was guided by a younger man, one who didn't know her parents, or her aunt the nun, or her uncle the priest. Maybe he could help her sort it all out, tell her what to do.

Or maybe she should see a therapist. A counselor might be able to help, suggest how to deal with this loss that felt like a death. Her mother still hadn't spoken to her, and even though her father was an angel, that didn't make up for the loss of her mom.

Alex's key in the lock announced her arrival, and Brit turned in that direction just as the door was opening. She wore a ski hat, dusted in snow, and her blond curls poked out from beneath it in all directions. In a gesture Brit had come to love, Alex pulled off the hat and shook out her curls, then smiled. "It's really snowing hard. I think school's going to be canceled tomorrow."

"We can play in the snow."

"Or in the bedroom."

Her troubles were forgotten as Alex's smile lit up the darkness in her heart. A few long strides carried her across the room, and she presented Brit with a bouquet of flowers she'd hidden behind her back. "Happy Valentine's Day," she said, and Brit felt the tears forming in the corners of her eyes.

"Hey," Alex said as she wiped them away with gentle strokes of her fingers.

"Will you make love to me?" Brit asked, wanting, needing the connection to Alex that she knew such intimacy would bring.

"I'd love to."

And so they turned off the stove, carried the candles to the bedroom, and slowly undressed each other. Alex wore dress pants and a silky, light-blue shirt that matched her eyes, and Brit draped them from her desk chair when she removed them. Alex wasn't so careful and, when she had Brit naked, pulled her quickly to the bed, as if sensing Brit's need. The hurry ended there, though, and they made love more slowly and tenderly than ever, coming together in a wave of emotional as well as physical release that left them both drained. They fell asleep that way, awakening as the chill of the bedroom set in.

"Hungry yet?" Brit asked when Alex sat up to fix the covers.

"Famished."

They sat down at the elegant table wearing sweats, and Brit's

mood was much better than it had been an hour earlier. She was finding that fabulous sex could do that to her, at least temporarily.

"Have you talked to Kelz?" Brit asked halfway through the meal. She'd stuffed shells the night before, picked up fresh bread on the way home, and tossed a simple salad while she was waiting for Alex. It all came together perfectly. She wished she could settle her mind as easily.

"I talk to her ten times a day," Alex said, but she sat back and studied Brit, seeming to sense more to the question.

"About anything important? I mean, she just seems out of sorts. I know she's probably worried about college, and all of these recruits have to be annoying, but it just seems like something's weighing her down. She doesn't talk to me like she used to, and I think whatever's bothering her is affecting her game."

"She's scoring twenty-five points a game, blocking shots, and pulling down rebounds. What more do you want from her?"

Brit sighed. "I know the stats, Alex. But her scoring's down. Way down from the beginning of the season. It just seems like she's doing stupid things. Shooting from out of her range. If she moves any farther into the corner she'll be making threes. She's out of position for rebounds, too, and she's fouling. But it's not just those tangible things. Her passes aren't crisp, and she's not seeing the plays develop. She's missing the open man. She's a step behind on the break."

"I hadn't really noticed. But you're obviously more tuned into Kelz than I am. You probably see more."

"I used to think we had a connection. I'm not so sure anymore." Brit frowned and shrugged.

Alex reached over and squeezed her hand. "I'll talk to her, okay?"

Brit nodded.

"Did you make me dessert?" Alex raised a suggestive eyebrow. "Or will that be you?"

"Chocolate and me, but the chocolate's optional."

Chapter Twenty-seven

Snow Day

As Alex had predicted, they awakened to a world blanketed in nearly a foot of snow. This wasn't the winter's first storm, and Alex had left her cold-weather gear at Brit's during the last one. After breakfast they bundled up and went walking through the woods. The sky was clear, and the sun reflected off branches and rocks carrying their heavy burdens. Using trees as barricades, they held a snowball war and ended it by calling a ceasefire, sealed with kisses that quickly turned heated.

"I think we should negotiate the peace in bed," Brit suggested.

Back in the apartment, Alex had a message on her cell. "My mom wants us to come for lunch."

"Do you think it's safe to drive?"

"I have an SUV. We'll be fine. Are you up for spending time with my parents?"

Brit nodded. "Of course. I always enjoy your parents' company." Since she'd been skipping family dinner at her own parents' on Sundays, she and Alex had begun a new tradition with the Daltons. Every Sunday evening they shared dinner with Alex's parents, and her brother and sister-in-law. Afterward, they played cards or watched a movie while a load of laundry cycled through the washer and dryer.

Brit took a plate of cookies for dessert and was warmly welcomed by Alex's mother. This time they came in through the garage, and they found her in the kitchen, preparing their lunch. A huge bouquet of flowers adorned the center island, brightening the room.

"How lovely," Brit said as she sniffed the bouquet.

"Thanks. My valentine bought them for me with his gambling money."

"That's sweet."

"I am sweet," Alex's father said as he waltzed into the kitchen and kissed all three of them.

"You must have hit the lottery. That's the biggest bouquet I've ever seen."

"I won a hundred bucks on your team."

Alex's jaw dropped. "You bet a hundred bucks? On a high-school basketball game? Dad, you're insane."

He waved dismissively. "I have confidence in you. And that freshman guard."

Alex laughed. Melissa had hit six out of seven three-pointers and scored twenty-six points in their most recent game. For the first time all season Kelsey wasn't the high scorer.

"I'm fond of her, too," she said.

"She busted the spread wide open."

"Dad, for some reason I think we shouldn't be having this conversation."

And so they changed the conversation to the most reliable of topics, the weather, and Alex and Brit helped her mother set the table while her father watched them all working. After enjoying tomato soup and grilled-cheese sandwiches, Brit served the cookies.

"Alex, you should marry this girl," her father said as he bit into a Gramma Cookie.

Brit's jaw dropped and Alex blushed, but quickly recovered. "Are you trying to get rid of me?"

"Never. But I wouldn't mind having Brit around more."

Brit felt herself blushing. One day she'd like to marry Alex. For now, they needed to think about living arrangements. Brit's lease expired in August, and even though it was only February, she liked to plan ahead. Neither one of them had enough space to accommodate them both. A two-bedroom apartment in her complex would only cost a few hundred dollars more each month but would give them a little more space. If Alex was willing to give up her place. Brit felt like she was ready, but she wondered if Alex wanted to make that commitment to her. She was afraid to ask.

Chapter Twenty-eight

The Bigger They Are, the Harder They Fall

Alex came through Brit's front door carrying a gym bag, a paper bag of Chinese food, and her briefcase, and Brit laughed at her balancing act.

It warmed Alex's heart to hear her laugh. Since her mother had discovered them on Christmas Day, Brit had been struggling with her emotions. Alex knew she tried to stay upbeat, working hard on her class assignments and coaching, cooking for her and keeping up with laundry and chores. Yet when she was quiet and still, Alex detected a certain sadness she knew she couldn't fix. It made her sad as well.

Not to mention stressed. She'd done this, practically forced herself on Brit, and she constantly questioned herself and their relationship. Had she been selfish to push Brit? Maybe Brit wasn't emotionally ready to be in a sexual relationship, and every day Alex worried Brit was going to call the whole thing off. So she went out of her way to do little things to make Brit laugh, to let her know how much she loved her. It was hard, though, to be responsible for someone else's happiness, and Alex hoped Brit would come out of her funk soon. It was exhausting.

Focusing on school, and on her team, was the best way to cope with her stress, Alex realized. It helped that the team was winning and had a superstar on the roster as well. They were working toward a district championship and a ticket to Pennsylvania's high-school championship tournament. It was amazing to see what her team had done! She'd had such low expectations at the start of the season. All she'd wanted was a winning record to prove to the suits in charge that she was competent enough to be their coach. Even if they lost every game for the rest of the

season, they'd still have more wins than losses. They wouldn't, though. There was no reason their success wouldn't continue.

But success caused other issues.

Kelsey's play and the parade of college recruiters at every game had created a frenzy with the local media, and Alex had been interviewed dozens of times by television, radio, and newspaper reporters. Strangers were talking to her and offering congratulations and, of course, advice. Casual acquaintances were suddenly treating her like friends. Business associates of her parents were requesting tickets to the sold-out games, and now Alex had to beg the athletic director for tickets to appease her family. It was overwhelming, but compared to dealing with Brit, coaching was easy.

Even though basketball was stressful, Alex loved it. She loved the practices, loved the games, and loved the attention. What if she really was offered a college job because of the great season her high-school team was having? It would be the most amazing climb in history. From high-school assistant to college coach in only two seasons! Just one of many records she hoped to log in the books before she was done.

"I have dinner," Alex said.

"Good. I have the video ready to go."

They planned to make it a working dinner. Their next contest was against a team they'd played in the first half of the season. They'd had some problems getting into an offensive rhythm during the game, and it had been their lowest scoring effort of the season. If not for some clutch foul shots at the end, they might have lost. They wanted to review the video so they could work on strategy at the next practice.

Alex changed while Brit plated their food, and both found seats on the couch. Seconds later they were watching the previous game.

"Did you see that?" Brit asked a few minutes later, eyes open wide as a play unfolded before them on the television screen.

"I sure did. That was sort of boneheaded."

"I think she does it again."

The subject of their conversation was Kelsey. She'd ignored an open player a few feet away and threw a pass cross-court. It was nearly intercepted. As they watched, Kelsey did the same thing again, and this time, the pass was picked off and taken in for a layup by the opposition.

Instead of scouting their opponent, as they'd intended, Alex found herself watching Kelsey. To her dismay, she realized Brit was right.

Kelz was managing to score, but she wasn't doing it the easy way. It was actually hard to watch all the bad passes that left her teammates off balance. The bad shots taken from out of position. The missed screens. The missed opportunities.

"I can't believe I didn't notice all this before," Alex said.

"It's hard to be focused on the mistakes when she's scoring and the team's winning."

"If she keeps doing this shit, we won't keep winning. Not when we play anyone with talent."

An hour later, they'd pushed their food aside and sat with notepads in their laps, watching and taking notes. When they decided on their game plan, Alex turned to Brit.

"Any chance you have other games I can watch?"

"They're all on there. Which one do you want to see?"

"All of them."

"Alex, would you mind if I get some work done? I have to proof my bio exam and email it to the secretary before morning."

"Sure. Just set that up for me."

Brit pressed some buttons on her laptop and it fed the video into her television, and there they were, back at the first game. "I'll be in the bedroom," Brit said as she kissed the top of Alex's head and left the room.

Alex barely noticed her leaving. Her mind had already moved on. She watched Kelsey's performance carefully, noting the difference between her performance at the beginning of the season and her current play. How could a player get worse over the course of a season? Her mistakes were all mental, as if she'd forgotten the basics. Which, of course, was ridiculous.

Yet there it was, in color. In real time and slow motion, Alex watched Kelsey pass up easy shots and attempt difficult ones, make bad passes and stupid mistakes. A wave of nausea overcame her, and she wasn't sure if it was her dinner or the suspicion brewing that caused it.

Something was definitely wrong with Kelsey, and Alex was determined to learn what it was. She needed more information, and she knew just who to call.

"Dad, tell me about the spread on my team."

"You're giving the other team eight points."

"So we have to win by nine for you to win money?"

"Exactly."

"Do we always give the other team points?"

"Yes. The number of points varies, based on how good your opponents are. That's what makes it interesting. Everyone would bet on you winning. The question is can you win by twenty-five points."

"Do we usually cover the spread?"

"No. The last game was the first time I've won, and I've been betting on you since the holiday tournament."

"So roughly ten games you've lost by betting on me. Even though we're supposed to win."

"Yep."

"Wow. Why do you keep betting?"

"Because you're my daughter. And because you should be able to beat the spread."

Alex nodded in understanding. If Kelsey had played up to her potential, to the ability she showed in the first part of the season, they'd win every game by forty points. They'd beat the spread. But Kelsey wasn't playing up to her potential, and Alex was concerned. If her suspicion was right, Kelsey was shaving points.

❖

Talking to a player in her office with the door closed wasn't all that unusual, so Alex wasn't worried about what the team would think when she called Kelsey in. Brit was used to it, too, and she didn't ask questions. Alex hadn't wanted to share this with Brit. Not until she had proof. Brit adored Kelsey, and Alex knew she'd be devastated by this discovery.

"I know what you're doing," Alex said when Kelsey was seated across from her. Alex leaned forward, her hands folded on her desk, thankful for the barrier separating them. Otherwise, she might have shaken Kelsey senseless.

"What are you talking about?" Kelsey asked innocently, but her eyes began to dart around the small office and she shifted in her chair.

"Point shaving. I know you're shaving points, Kelz. I just don't know why. So that's my question. Why are you doing this? You have so much talent, and so much potential, and a bright future ahead of you. Why would you do something so stupid?"

Kelsey sighed and hid her face in her hands, seeming to search for courage. When she pulled them away, she didn't look at Alex when she spoke, and her voice was so soft Alex had difficulty hearing her clearly. "Have you ever heard about students buying tests?"

"You mean exams?"

Kelsey looked up, and though Alex saw fear in her eyes, she didn't hesitate. Apparently she needed to get this off her chest. "Yeah. You can buy them."

"Old exams, like last year's?"

Kelsey shook her head, and Alex's heart pounded as it sank into her abdomen. This wasn't sounding good. "No. You can get a copy of current tests the day before. Then all you have to do is memorize the answers."

"Jesus. Have you been buying exams, Kelz?"

Kelsey nodded, then swallowed, and tears formed in her eyes. "Since the beginning of the year." She sniffled and wiped her nose before continuing, and Alex felt the need to cry as well. "Now I'm in trouble. The guy who sells them is blackmailing me. He said he'd tell the principal and I'll get thrown off the team, and I won't be able to get a scholarship or go to college. He told me if I shave points, he won't tell." As she said the last words, she began to really sob.

"Oh, shit," Alex said. It was just as she suspected, only worse. She'd imagined Kelsey was betting on the games, making money when they didn't cover the spread. It would have been easy to stop her just with this conversation. The truth was an entirely different matter, and Alex wasn't sure what she could do about it. She ran her hands through her hair and tried to stay focused. How could this be happening? She did everything she was supposed to do with her team. There was no impropriety on her part, and she'd tried from the beginning to teach them about integrity and sportsmanship and character. In spite of the lectures and the threats of dismissal and suspension, the one player who mattered most to her team had seen fit to not only break the team rules, but to get into trouble, too.

Alex could only shake her head in disbelief. "You have no way of holding him to that, Kelsey. He's a criminal, a blackmailer. What makes you think he'd be honest about your agreement? And I don't think this is the sort of thing you can put in writing."

Kelsey crossed her arms on the desk and buried her head in them

and cried again. Alex was silent. After a moment, Kelsey turned her head and spoke. "You're right, Coach. I don't believe him, either. I think he'll just keep hounding me, follow me to college and want me to throw games there."

Alex wondered how someone who'd done something so stupid could grasp such an intelligent concept. Of course he wouldn't let her walk away. He'd hold this over her the rest of her life, and no matter where she went or what she did, he'd still own her.

Unless they stopped it now. If Alex confronted him, would it piss him off and put Kelsey in danger? Or would he walk away, not wanting to risk trouble himself?

"I don't know what to do, Coach."

Alex had no clue, either. "Let me think about this, okay? I'd like to discuss this with Coach Dodge. She's pretty smart, and two heads are better than one."

Kelsey turned pale and her voice cracked. "Please, don't."

Alex frowned. Brit would help her put this in perspective and find the best answer to the problem. "Are you sure? You two are so close. I know how much she cares about you. She's been worried about you and she'll want to help."

"I can't face her, Coach. I've let her down. After all she's done for me—helping me with my game, helping me study—I just can't."

"Kelsey, Coach Dodge is a good person. She'll forgive you."

"Do you still think she'll forgive me when she finds out I was buying her exams?"

Alex's jaw dropped. "Oh. Shit."

"Yeah, that about sums it up."

Kelsey reached into her backpack and pulled out a white envelope and handed it to Alex. It was business size, white, and had two words printed on the front. *Dodge/Bio*.

Alex set the envelope on her desk and stared at it. She was almost afraid to touch it, for all the power it held. If she opened it, there was no turning back. Perhaps there was no turning back anyway.

"So this is tomorrow's exam?" she asked. How the hell did this happen? Brit had just finished it the night before.

"Yes."

"How did you get it?"

"I meet the guy after school, usually before practice."

"He comes in the school?"

"Yeah. He's a student."

Alex was dumbfounded. A high-school student fixing her games and blackmailing her player. What next? Somehow, though, it made Alex feel a little bit better to think she was dealing with a student, a small-time criminal rather than some sinister citizen at large. She had plenty of experience handling students.

"We have to confront him, Kelz. After practice. You and me." Alex decided Kelsey was right about telling Brit. It was a bad idea. Brit would be crushed by this news, and with the stress she'd been under about her mom, this might push her over the edge.

Kelsey nodded. "Okay."

"Do you know where he lives?"

"Yeah. Near Mountain Meadows. He usually sells exams after school, so he might not be home until later."

"How about eight?"

"Okay."

"Go practice."

She closed the door behind her, and Alex crumpled into her desk chair, closing her eyes. This was the worst day of her career. Possibly the worst day of her life. "Fuck, what now?" she mumbled as her phone rang and an unfamiliar number flashed on the screen. Hoping that maybe she'd just won the Publisher's Clearinghouse Sweepstakes, she answered it.

"Coach Dalton, this is Troy Rittenhouse from Florida. I'm calling to see if you're interested in coaching here. And, of course, we'd like you to bring Kelsey with you. What do you think?"

This was about the twentieth call from Rittenhouse. Clearly, he was interested in Kelsey. And her. How quickly would that interest fade if he heard the news Kelsey had just shared? Alex breathed deeply through her mouth as her entire body started shaking. Fortunately, she was still sitting, because she wasn't certain her legs would hold her at the moment. "Oh, hi!" she said in greeting, feigning a delight that was so removed from her real feelings it was almost comical. "It's looking pretty good, Coach."

❖

"How are you? I didn't see you all day, and I'm personally going through withdrawal." Brit's eyes twinkled as she smiled at Alex.

Alex hung up her coat and turned to Brit. In spite of her miserable day, her return smile was genuine. Brit had that power over her. And just maybe, Brit was coming out of her funk.

She still wouldn't tell Brit her plans, though. The news about the exams would crush Brit. And quite probably, Brit would try to stop her from doing what she needed to do.

Alex needed to solve this problem, and she needed a few hours on her own to do it. But how to get away from the woman you love without raising suspicion?

She decided to borrow a page from Brit's book to do it. "I'm feeling a little under the weather," she lied.

"Oh, no! Is it the flu? I heard there were a ton of students out of school because it's going around."

"I don't know. I want to run down to the urgent care to get checked. I don't like to take any chances."

Concern was written all over Brit's face, and it made Alex feel like shit to worry her. Brit's bright eyes narrowed just a little as they studied Alex. "You don't look too bad, but yes, you should get checked. I'll go with you."

Shit! Alex thought. Of course Brit would want to go with her. "No, you don't have to do that. I want to rest for a little while, and then I'll head down there in a couple of hours, after the crowd clears out."

"Do you want to rest here?" Brit asked.

"Yeah," Alex said.

They had leftovers for dinner, and then Alex crawled into Brit's bed. She wasn't sick, but the stress of everything was getting to her, and exhaustion quickly overcame her and she dozed off. An hour later, she was surprised when Brit gently shook her shoulder to awaken her.

She brushed the gunk from her teeth, guiltily kissed Brit good-bye, and met Kelsey as planned near the golf course. Kelsey directed her to a newer development near her parents' house, into a hidden drive of a large house built in the mature woods on a mountainside. Lights were on, and two cars were parked in a driveway that had room for eight.

"That's his car," Kelsey said.

Alex parked and hopped out without speaking. The closer she got

to this moment, the angrier she became. She wasted no time ringing the doorbell, and by the time someone answered the door, she was ready to lock horns.

She was shocked when she saw the face of the young man who opened the door.

"Miss Dalton!" he said.

"Wes. Hi!" She'd taught Wes the year before.

"What are you doing here?" he asked, but before she could answer, the boy she'd come to see appeared behind him.

"I think she's here for me," P.J. announced.

Alex met his gaze. "Are you P.J?"

He nodded.

"Are your parents home? I think it's time I talk to them."

Wes answered. "No, they're both at work. Why? What's going on?" The concern in his voice was evident even as he eyed his brother suspiciously. "P., are you in some kind of trouble?"

"Let's sit down," he said, showing a composure Alex envied at the moment. She was ready to pass out from the stress of the day.

"Yes, please come in," Wes said, and Alex introduced Kelsey.

"P.J.! What's going on?" Wes demanded before they'd had a chance to sit in the formal sitting room just off the main entrance hall.

"The Man is blackmailing Kelsey," he said simply.

"What? Why? Why didn't you tell me?" Wes looked confused.

"He's blackmailing her 'cause she bought some exams. He thinks she's going to be a big WNBA star one day, so he wants to get his hooks into her now."

"Fuck!"

Alex looked at Kelsey. She looked just as confused as Alex felt. "Would you two mind telling us what you're talking about? And do your parents know what you're doing?"

Suddenly, P.J. stood and pointed at Alex. "You can't tell my parents, Coach. You don't understand. The Man is *not* a nice guy. I don't know what he'd do, and it scares me to even think about it."

Alex looked at both of them. "Who's The Man?"

"The guy I work for. I sell exams and collect sports bets for him." He laughed at Alex, who didn't hide her surprise. "What, you think I thought of this racket all by myself? Nah, I'm not that smart. I'm just the courier."

Alex's mouth was dry as her mind raced. It couldn't be, could it?

"P.J., what's this guy's name?" she asked, fearing the answer.

He stared mutely in response.

"It's Greg Merck, isn't it?"

"You can't talk to him, Coach! He'll kill me. He'll think I told you."

"No, he won't. Everyone knows Greg runs the gambling."

Alex's mind was spinning. How could it be that someone from such a reputable family had sunk so low? That someone she considered a friend was fixing her games? Then she realized the novelty of her position. She might have felt less offended if a stranger had been behind this, but she wouldn't have felt as confident that she could handle it. She'd been beating Greg since they were kids—first at kickball and tag and later at tennis and golf. She could handle him now, too.

"Are you sure?" Wes asked.

"I know Greg. I'll take care of this."

P.J. looked at her with a hopeful expression. "Really? 'Cuz he usually doesn't take no for an answer."

"Trust me."

Minutes later, Alex dropped Kelsey off at the club. "I'll see you tomorrow." Then she drove back the way she came, into the same development where P.J. lived, and into the last driveway on the quiet street. The house was a big modern brick structure, boasting of its owner's wealth and prestige. She knew Greg had purchased it just a few years before, and it infuriated her to think how he'd come up with the money. She jumped on him when he answered the door.

"What the fuck are you doing, selling tests and fixing my games?"

Alex was nearly as tall as Greg, but he outweighed her by at least fifty pounds, and as he pushed her aside and slammed the door behind her, she felt suddenly small beside him. It hadn't occurred to her that she might be inviting danger by confronting him, but as she stood next to him, she felt the vulnerability of her situation. She stood tall anyway and met his gaze.

"This isn't your business, Alex!" he said, and the fire in his eyes and bright-red shade of his face caused Alex to step back. She didn't back down, though. She was mad, too.

"The hell it isn't! This is my school and my player we're dealing with! My team you want to bring down."

He held his arms out and his palms up. "Who cares about cheating? Everyone cheats. And no one gives a shit about your little high-school team."

"No? What about education, Greg? Students are there to learn something, to prepare for their futures. And they shouldn't be gambling at their age. That's how they become addicted and ruin their lives."

"I want them to gamble, Alex. That's how I make money. And education is overrated.''

"You make me sick." She spat the words.

"Who cares?"

"Greg, I'm telling you to stop this. Get out of the exam business, take your gambling out of the high school, and leave these kids alone. Leave Kelsey alone."

He glared at her, and she could see the pulse beating in his neck. "That's not gonna happen. But because we're friends, I'll let your girl off the hook. Now get the fuck outta my house and don't you ever interfere in my business again."

Alex shook her head in disgust. "Does your dad know about this? He built the bakery from nothing, and you're risking it all for this? To corrupt kids?"

"The bakery hasn't made money since Wegmans opened twenty years ago! All the money's in gambling. And now in exams. And as far as my dad goes—he turned this business over to me. I'm in charge now, and I'm doing this my way."

Alex shook her head, pleading. "This is wrong, Greg."

"Yeah, well, thanks for stopping by, Alex. I'll see you around."

With one hand on her back guiding her, he practically threw her through the front door. Suddenly anxious to get as far away from Greg as she could, Alex practically ran to the car, and when she tried to key the ignition, she realized how badly her hands were shaking. Minutes later, she had to force her legs to carry her from the parking lot to Brit's apartment. She wanted to call Kelsey, but she didn't think she could dial the phone. Her encounter with Greg had rattled her that badly.

"What did the doctor say?" a worried Brit asked her as she helped Alex out of her coat and kissed her cheek.

"Everything's fine," Alex lied as she wrapped her arms tightly around Brit and tried hard not to tremble.

CHAPTER TWENTY-NINE

NOTHING BUT TROUBLE

A lex was surprised by how well she slept after all that had happened, but she awakened feeling refreshed. That was good, because she had a million things to deal with. She wished she'd never have to see Greg again, and even though it'd be impossible to avoid him totally, she'd minimize contact until the desire to punch him faded. She had to deal with Kelsey, and she wasn't sure what to do. There was no official school policy on buying exams and shaving points, so Alex could really manage the situation as she saw fit. She hoped to use that flexibility to her advantage.

And Brit seemed to be doing better. Alex kissed her good morning, then good-bye, and headed home for her shower. She dressed and was walking into her kitchen for a yogurt when the sight of her brother sitting on her couch startled her.

Alex stopped, her heart pounding in her throat. This couldn't be good. "What's wrong?"

"What the hell's wrong with you? Why would you do that to Greg?"

Andrew didn't raise his voice; they might as well have been talking about the weather. She did, though.

"How can you defend him? Do you know he's trying to fix my games? Pushing gambling in school? And selling tests to kids?"

"Grow up, Alex. He's not pushing anything. He's giving them what they want. And if he doesn't, someone else will."

"Andrew, this is wrong, and it's illegal, and he should stop."

He stood and turned toward the door. "I'm warning you, Alex. Mind your own business."

Alex didn't get it. Why the hell would her brother care about Greg's illegal activities? It wasn't like they were close friends. Sure, they knew each other—all the kids who'd grown up at the club did. And then a sick feeling overcame her. Just as he reached for the doorknob she spoke. "What the hell are you doing? You have a good job with Dad. Why get messed up in something like this?"

He turned his head. "You think I have a good job? Huh, that's a joke. Try living on the sixty grand a year Dad pays me!"

"Hey, that's more than I make and I'm doing fine."

"You live above a garage. For free! I have a wife, and a house, and—unlike you—one day I'll have a family to support. The dry-cleaning business isn't going to do it. And as far as Dad's dream about the liquor licenses—it's pie in the sky. Lots of guys with money contribute to political campaigns. There's no guarantee we'll get a license. I need to take care of me!"

"Then get a job. Start a business, like Grampa did. Don't become a hoodlum!"

"I never thought you were such a prude," he said as he walked through the door.

Her day didn't get any better. Most of the students seemed to linger in snow-day mode, with minds unfocused on class. Every player on the team made her way to Alex's classroom to talk strategy for that night's game, increasing Alex's anxiety about benching her star. Fortunately, the opposition wasn't one of the better teams in the league, and Alex hoped she could pull off a win even if she decided to bench Kelsey.

Before she left for the day, a text caught her attention. It was from Wes. He needed to talk.

What now? Alex agreed to meet him at the coffee shop.

The coffee and pastry she purchased held no appeal, but for the sake of appearances, Alex took a sip as she slipped into a corner booth. "What's up?" she asked.

Wes shook his head, and Alex saw fire in his eyes. "We have to stop this guy, Coach."

"Who?"

"Greg Merck."

"What? He agreed to back off."

"Maybe he backed off on your player, but he's putting the heat on

my brother. I thought P. was done with the exams. That's what he told me, anyway. He only got into selling them because he owed Merck money from gambling. When he paid his debt, he was supposed to be free. Then Merck changed the plan, and what could P.J. do? He had to go along. But that's not bad enough. He graduates in May, and he thought he saw the light at the end of the tunnel. Your friend Merck just snuffed it out."

"How so?"

"P.J.'s been planning to go to Penn State. It's always been his dream, and he got accepted into the engineering program at the main campus in State College. But today Greg 'suggested' P. go to Pocono Mountains University so he can work for him. Greg wants to expand his gambling and exam racket to the local colleges and wants him to run the operation."

"Fuck." Alex thought she'd convinced Greg to lay off the students—and maybe he had. Maybe he'd shift his business to the colleges instead. Either way it wasn't good for P.J.

"You have to help me. Help P.J. Help these kids. They're stealing to get money for gambling. They're getting hooked. They're jeopardizing their futures."

Alex studied him. He looked so much older than she remembered him, but she supposed he'd aged in the past months. Hell, she felt like she'd aged overnight. Knowing Wes spoke the truth, Alex bit her lip and sucked in a breath. Before confronting Greg she'd Googled teenage gambling and was dumbfounded when she learned about the enormity of the problem. Not only were kids getting into trouble, but they were much more likely to become addicted gamblers if they started young. Trouble with gambling would cause them to lose their homes and their jobs and sometimes their lives. Her childhood friend was helping them get started.

Greg had always been a decent guy. Sure, he'd been collecting bets for his dad since he was big enough to walk, but it'd always been an innocent sort of illegal activity. Nobody pressured anyone to bet or had trouble collecting—everyone put their money up front. A five-dollar bet on college football games could win you fifty if all your teams came out on top. Gambling made the games more interesting, and winning was fun. Why did he have to push this into the schools and get kids involved? And selling the exams was completely wrong. While Alex

could bend her ethics to defend the gambling—at least where adults were concerned—no amount of magic or smoke and mirrors could change her view on selling exams. Or trying to fix her games.

"Wes, you should go to the police. It's the only way to get your brother out from under him." Even as she said the words, Alex was doubtful they'd shut down Greg's gambling operation. For some reason, authorities seemed to look the other way when it came to sports betting. But maybe a police report would take some of the heat off P.J. and get him out from under Greg's thumb.

Wes laughed, a bitter sound, and patrons at the nearby tables turned heads in their direction. "Yeah, right! Do you know how many cops bet with Greg? How do you think he stays in business? He gives them Yankees tickets and dinners at Ruth's Chris, and they look the other way. About five minutes after P.J. reports Greg and walks out of the police station, he'll be so black and blue my mother won't recognize him."

"I don't know, Wes," Alex said. "I don't think I should get any more involved than I already am."

Wes studied his coffee for a moment before looking up at Alex. "He's blackmailing me, too. He wants me to sell exams."

"Just tell him no."

"I can't."

"Why not?"

"Who do you think hacked into the EM email account to get those exams?"

Alex looked at him and wanted to scream. This situation just kept getting worse and worse. Before she could, he spoke again.

"It was the only way I could protect P.J. Greg would have broken both his legs."

Alex sipped her coffee and thought about what Wes was saying. She remembered how angry Greg had been when she confronted him and didn't doubt he'd developed a temper, and quite possibly could be dangerous. She'd been scared when she confronted him. Then she thought back to her mother's birthday party the summer before. The Mercks had been there, socializing with all of the power people, schmoozing, no doubt doing just what her father was doing—taking care of business. How many political campaigns did the illegal profits of his gambling business fund?

And then she thought of her own brother, and she set down the coffee. It was quickly turning to acid in her stomach.

Just what did Andrew have to do with this business? If Wes called the police, and they actually listened to him, would her brother be implicated? He'd defended Greg, but was Andrew involved in the business or just standing up for his friend?

Her thoughts turned to Kelsey, and P.J., both good kids reduced to cheating and lying for Greg. She looked at Wes, dealing with a problem he should have known nothing about. How many others were there, stealing to get money for gambling? Cheating on exams, instead of learning to study and work toward their goals. Dozens, probably, or more. So many young kids jeopardizing their futures. She couldn't allow her concerns about Andrew to interfere with her decision to do the right thing. Greg was hurting people she cared about. Her students. Her players. Her neighbors. She needed to stop him.

Alex sighed and looked at Wes. "Maybe you're right. What do you have in mind?"

Alex leaned back in her seat and listened as he told her.

Chapter Thirty

Dirty Laundry

B rit sat down across from Alex at the kitchen table and studied her for a moment. It was only nine o'clock on Sunday morning, but already she'd read the paper, been to mass and the grocery store, and was now preparing breakfast. She'd thought of sleeping in, but she was restless, and rather than disturb Alex, she'd gotten an early start on the day.

Alex was tired, and Brit wondered what was at the root of it. It was the middle of March and they had just a few weeks of basketball left, give or take, depending on how well they did. Considering that the team was still undefeated, making a run deep into the playoffs was likely. Brit prayed for strength. She wanted to win, and she wanted to be a part of such excitement, but it really was stressful, and she wouldn't be sad when the season ended.

The recruits were still beating down Alex's door, even though Kelsey had suffered an ankle injury and was out indefinitely. They'd seen her talent and were convinced she had the ability to play at the highest levels of basketball. Alex had now been offered three jobs— one in Florida, one in St. Louis, and one in California—if Kelz would commit to the schools. Alex downplayed the significance of the offers, but Brit was worried. What if Alex left? Was that on her mind?

Or was it her health? Alex didn't complain, but Brit knew from the way she moved and constantly stretched her back that the cold, damp winter was taking its toll on Alex's health.

Brit tried to help ease Alex's burden by doing as much as she could with the team, running practices and scouting opponents. She gave Alex a break at home by cooking and keeping the apartment neat.

And she'd talked to her friend, the young rheumatologist, who was interested in Alex's case. Even though Alex might feel better when the season ended, Brit didn't want to postpone this discussion any longer.

"Alex, I want you to see another doctor. A rheumatologist—well, almost a rheumatologist—he's finishing his fellowship in a few months. I've known him all my life, and I talked to him about you, and we think you might be misdiagnosed."

Alex flicked at her teeth with her tongue, attempting to remove something that appeared to be stuck there. "Excuse me?"

Brit sighed. "I've been reading all about your disease, Alex, and I'm not sure you really have it. My friend agrees with me, so I'd like you to go see him."

"I already see a specialist, Brit."

"I know, I know. But just read this." Brit pulled some papers from the cupboard. "Your symptoms could be Reiter's syndrome. It's the same gene."

Alex looked from Brit's face to the papers in her hand and tried to focus on the words. Her stress level was through the roof and she was exhausted. All of the lying was getting to her, as were the increasing pressures of coaching her team to an undefeated season and dealing with the madness of college recruiters hounding her. If only she could tell Brit the truth, it would ease some of the burden. But Alex still didn't know what sort of trouble lay ahead and didn't want to put Brit in danger. Better to keep her in the dark. And then, of course, Brit might possibly tear her head off for getting involved in this mess.

The last thing she wanted to talk about was her illness. It was one of the few things in her life under control at the moment. She hardly had any symptoms. These days, she was fine, but getting there hadn't been an easy road. She couldn't count the number of specialists she'd seen over the years, trying to figure out what the hell was going wrong. She didn't want to see another one and told Brit so.

"Alex, would you at least read what it says? If you don't agree with me, then, okay, we won't see him. But if you have any doubt, don't you owe it to yourself to find out the truth?"

Alex studied Brit. Her face was slightly flushed as she leaned forward, talking with her hands as she stressed her point. Her eyes were dark, and they glimmered with their intensity. She was beautiful, and Alex was lucky Brit had fallen in love with her, for many reasons,

but mostly because she was the kind of woman who'd spend her time researching a disease to make sure the doctors had gotten it right.

To be deceiving her hit Alex hard and sucked the wind from her lungs. Brit had given up so much to be with Alex. She missed her family terribly and was spending all of the energy she'd once used on them to take care of Alex. Alex was repaying that loyalty with deception and lies.

Suddenly wanting to do something for Brit, something to make her smile, Alex said, "Okay. I'll see him. If it'll make you happy."

Brit hugged her. "I'm going to get the laundry together," Brit said as Alex began gathering the breakfast dishes.

Brit was thrilled that Alex had agreed so readily. Maybe her friend could help. Probably couldn't hurt, right?

Brit grabbed the towels from the back of the bathroom door, and then the laundry basket from her closet, and began emptying the contents into a large duffel. They were heading to Alex's parents' for dinner, and she'd wash a load of laundry while she was there. Just as she was about to zip the bag closed, she noticed Alex's gym bag on the floor beside the bed. Even though Alex didn't usually change clothes for practice, sometimes she had dirty clothes in there. Brit decided to check. Opening the zipper, she spilled the contents on the bed—two sneakers, two socks, a neatly folded sweatshirt, sweat pants, and an envelope.

It was plain white and business size, inscribed with two words. *Dodge/Bio.*

Without hesitation or thought, Brit opened the envelope that bore her name. And as she pulled the papers out she frowned. It was a biology test, given by her a month before. Why would Alex be carrying around a copy of one of her exams?

That was odd. She picked it up and carried it into the living room, where Alex was reading the paper.

Brit held the envelope in both hands, facing away from her so Alex could read it. "Why do you have a copy of my test in your bag?"

Alex gasped. Wes had needed the original test to check details such as the type of paper it was printed on and the placement of the staple in the upper left corner. Alex had given it to him a week earlier and he'd just returned it, and she hadn't had a chance to hide it somewhere safe. Somewhere away from Brit's curious gaze.

Alex studied Brit for a moment as she held her breath, not daring to move. Did she suspect the truth? Or was she just puzzled? Was this the chance Alex had been waiting for, to talk to Brit, or would it be a mistake to involve her? She ran her hands through her hair as she considered her options.

"Alex?" Brit asked. "What's going on?"

Alex buried her face in her hands as she leaned back into the couch. She felt Brit beside her, the soft hands that knew her body so well clutching her wrist, pulling it from her face.

Alex opened her uncovered eye and studied Brit.

"Hey? You okay?" Brit asked.

What was the point of being in a relationship, of totally giving yourself and committing to someone, if you can't be honest with them? Brit had given herself and committed herself. Alex had, too. She had to trust Brit with this.

Dropping her hands, Alex forced a weak smile. "We have a problem."

Brit sat a little taller and looked at Alex curiously. "What kind of problem?"

Alex sat up, gathering her strength for the conversation. She met Brit's gaze. "It's Kelsey."

"Yeah? What about Kelsey?"

"It started with her buying exams." Alex nodded to the envelope containing Brit's biology exam. "And then the guy selling them started blackmailing her. He runs a sports betting operation and made her shave points so he could make more money."

Brit's mouth was open as she stared at Alex, her eyes unfocused as she shook her head in denial.

"You're joking, right?" she asked after a moment.

"No." And as Brit pulled her knees up in a protective posture, Alex explained everything. Well, not everything. She still didn't feel comfortable telling Brit what she and Wes had planned. Their idea was crazy and might land Alex in jail, or the hospital. She refused to picture herself in the morgue, but that was possible, too.

"I can't believe this. I worked so hard with her and was so proud of all she's accomplished academically. Her grades have been good. Well, no wonder. I assume it's all been a big lie. She's been cheating the whole time."

Alex patted Brit's thigh reassuringly. "She hasn't cheated for the last month. I stopped her once I found out."

Brit's eyes flew open wide and bore into Alex. "Wait. You've known about this for a month? And you didn't tell me?"

The volume of Brit's voice seemed to rise with each word. Alex had never seen her so angry. "Shhh, calm down."

"Calm down? Calm down? Our star is cheating on exams, my exams, and you've known about it for a month and haven't told me, and you think I'm not calm enough?" Brit was practically screaming.

Alex stood, pacing the room, running her hands through her hair. "I'm sorry. I should have told you."

"Duh!"

Alex leaned against the wall. How had she allowed herself to get into this position? She never should have agreed to help Wes. She should have taken the exam to the principal and allowed him to handle the problem, then worried about her own problems—her team, her health, her girlfriend. She looked at Brit and repeated her apology, more quietly this time. "I'm sorry."

Brit closed her eyes and leaned back against the couch. Alex knew her anger was gone when she saw the tears glistening on her eyelashes. "Maybe I failed her. Maybe we all did. I mean, we put so much emphasis on sports that she chose to do these crazy things just so she could play. And in the end, she's probably going to lose her scholarship offers when the colleges find out. She might not even get into college once this gets out."

"That's why I haven't told anyone. It's over. Kelsey made a mistake, and she's sorry for it. Believe me, she feels awful. What good would it do to expose her? It's just going to ruin her life."

Brit's jaw dropped and she scowled. "Are you out of your mind, Alex? She. Was. Buying. Exams! Cheating! You can't just ignore this. What message are you sending her?"

"Believe me, she's sorry."

"Well, that's not enough. She needs to be punished. Suspended."

"She's not even playing right now. Why does it matter?"

"Integrity? Honor? Sportsmanship?"

Alex paced again. What could she say to make Brit understand this? Probably nothing, which Alex realized was the true reason she hadn't confided in Brit. Brit was too moral, too honest, too good to go

along with this sort of deception. But if she couldn't understand, could she at least accept it and just let it go?

"Brit, can you just let me handle this? I promise you, I'll take care of it."

"How? What will you do?"

Alex sighed. "I reviewed the school policy on academic integrity. There's nothing there that says I have to tell anyone. I can handle it how I want, and I swear to you, I'm handling it. Please?"

Brit stared at Alex. "Oh, fuck! Please, Alex, don't tell me this is about you getting some big-time coaching job. Please don't tell me you're that unethical!"

Alex closed the space between them and faced Brit, and suddenly all of her own frustrations and fears burst from the place she'd been containing them for more than a month. "Don't give me your holy, Catholic, ethical bullshit, Britain. I'm sick of it! This is the real world, not the fucking convent. In the real world people aren't perfect. They make mistakes. They have real problems, and they have to deal with them the best way they can. That's what I'm doing."

Brit sniffed back tears as she looked at Alex with eyes that could have frozen the Pacific Ocean. "I can't believe I trusted you, Alex. I let you get close to me, ignoring my instincts, because I thought you really had changed. But you haven't. It's still all about you and your instant gratification. I'm so disappointed in you! But I'm even more disappointed in myself for trusting you." Brit wiped her arm on her sleeve and then pointed to the door. "Get out of my apartment, Alex. Just go!"

Alex knew she shouldn't go. She should tell Brit everything she'd done and why, and ask for her help. But she couldn't. She was angry. Why couldn't Brit just trust her? She was tired, too. She'd been going, going, going since the first day of practice. Physically, she was spent. Emotionally, she was even more exhausted—from putting her heart on the line with Brit, and coaching, and dealing with all of the drama with Kelsey. She didn't have any energy left with which to argue, or discuss, or debate.

Besides, Saint Britain had already made up her mind, and Alex knew she'd been condemned.

CHAPTER THIRTY-ONE

MISERY

It had been a tear-filled, sleepless night, and it showed. Brit looked exhausted. No amount of makeup could hide the circles beneath her eyes, and after a minute, Brit stopped trying. She retreated to her bed and began crying again. Just what her eyes needed, but she couldn't help it.

If she'd thought the rug had been pulled out from under her at the beach, when Anke showed up, she'd been wrong. That was nothing compared to this. How could she have been such a fool? Why had she trusted Alex with her heart after she'd vowed not to?

Falling back, Brit stared at the ceiling, wondering what to do next. She'd wondered all night and was no closer to understanding. How could Alex just blow this off? The question haunted her. She could forgive Alex if she'd only come clean now. But she wouldn't, and how could Brit live with that? She coached and taught to make a difference with kids, to teach them the skills they would use to be successful in the world. It was great to win, but winning above all else wasn't Brit's goal. How could she accept that sort of morality in her lover? It was wrong, and Brit didn't like the lesson Alex was teaching Kelsey, that she could cheat and get away with it if she issued a little apology in the end.

But the personal aspect of Alex's professional conduct concerned Brit even more. If Alex had no integrity as a coach, what sort of choices would she make when it came to things like fidelity and money? What values would she teach their children one day?

Brit had no answers. She had to face Alex and talk some sense into her.

She left her apartment early, and the darkness seemed appropriate to her mood. She and Alex had an hour to talk before they had to leave for school, and they needed privacy, so she drove the familiar roads to Alex's house with hope and dread filling her by turns. The lights were on, and as she pulled into the driveway, she dialed Alex's number. It went to voice mail.

Damn. There was no doorbell. Should she honk the car horn at six in the morning or just pound on the door? She dialed again. No answer. She honked and saw the curtain move behind the window of Alex's apartment. Then the garage door opened, and Alex appeared like an apparition out of the garage into the morning, backlit by a dim bulb on the ceiling.

She stood still, with her arms folded across her chest, wearing just sweats and a hoodie on this chilly morning. She seemed to be waiting.

Brit summoned her courage and got out of the car.

"Hi," she said.

"What's up?" Alex's tone was cool.

Brit tried to ignore it but was instantly on edge. "Can we talk?"

Brit walked closer, close enough to see Alex's stony expression.

"What's left to say?"

"Please, Alex. This is our future on the line. Don't you think it's worth a few minutes of your time?"

Alex nodded and turned, and Brit followed her through the garage and up the stairs to her apartment, as she'd done countless times before. On those occasions, they'd been building a friendship, and a relationship. It seemed so different now. The wonder and joy were gone, replaced by anger and confusion and fear.

"I was just about to make my coffee. Would you like a cup?"

"That would be great."

Brit sat on the couch as Alex disappeared into the kitchen, and as she heard the familiar sounds of the Keurig brewing and coffee being stirred, she stared into the creamy brown leather couch, thinking of the scenes it had witnessed. Coaches' meetings, movies, passionate lovemaking. Tickling and cuddling, reading and talking. In the six months since her first visit to Alex's place, they'd said and done so many things together. They'd fallen in love. She loved Alex with all her heart, and she needed to make things right.

"I'm sorry I threw you out last night," Brit said as Alex handed her the coffee.

Alex sat, putting a noticeable distance between them on the couch. Her sigh was audible. "Don't be sorry. You were right."

"I was?" Brit was shocked.

Alex gave her a crooked half smile. "Yes, I was wrong to keep this from you, and I understand your anger. I'm sorry I hurt you, and I'm sorry I let you down."

Brit sniffled and smiled back. "I'm so relieved, Alex. I knew you'd do the right thing."

Alex shook her head and gave her that sad smile again. "That's where you're wrong, Brit. I'm sorry I hurt you, but it doesn't mean I'm doing anything differently. I can't turn Kelsey in. I can't ruin her life for one stupid mistake."

"But…"

"No buts, Brit. Do you trust me?"

"I…" Brit said, looking at Alex. It seemed like she didn't know Alex anymore. Perhaps she'd never known her at all. What was truly in Alex's heart? Was she really the woman who'd given up flings and doing things the easy way, or was that just an experiment? Alex seemed to have a knack of getting her way, and this was just another example. She cast integrity aside in favor of convenience.

Brit didn't know if she trusted Alex. She needed something from Alex, some concession, a willingness to right this wrong. Yet Alex seemed determined to stay on her crooked course. "I'm not sure. I need you to do the right thing, Alex. I need you to show me what kind of person you really are."

Alex sighed. "I understand, Brit. I need to get ready. I'll see you at school, okay?"

Brit shook her head. "So this is it? It's over?"

Alex shrugged. "It could never work for us, Brit. We're too different. It's best if we just walk away now before we're in too deep."

"Alex, I'm already in deep. I love you! You love me! This is worth fighting for!"

"Not when we have to fight each other."

CHAPTER THIRTY-TWO

BOUNCING

Brit stood as the official blew her whistle to indicate a time-out. The starting five jogged over and sat as the bench players gathered behind them, watching Alex diagram a defensive play. They'd won the league championship and were in the state playoffs. The first game had been an easy win, but now they were down by five in the final minute of the second game.

Brit tried to stay focused, but it was difficult. Alex had stopped talking to her, stopped seeking her advice about which play to run and which player to substitute. And with Kelsey on the bench with her sprained ankle, they had a lot to debate. The worried look on Alex's face crushed Brit, and she wanted to whisper something kind or encouraging, but she couldn't. Alex no longer wanted to hear those things from her.

They'd trailed the whole game. From the opening tip the opponents had controlled the tempo, slowing things down and taking them out of their rhythm. At first, Brit hadn't worried. But now, with only a minute left on the clock, she was concerned. If the Falcons didn't foul, the other team would eat the clock and win. If they fouled, the opponents would have an opportunity to make free throws and increase the lead. The play Alex drew on her dry-erase board indicated they should go for the steal on the inbounds pass and foul if they came up empty. They'd settle for a two-point basket but take a three if they had one.

Their execution was flawless, and Sidney stole the inbounds pass, passed it long, and they scored a layup. Down three, they ran the same defense and stole the ball again, tossed it out beyond the arc, and hit an open three.

Just like that, the game was tied. Thirty seconds left to get another defensive stop and score. No problem.

The opposition called their final time-out.

Brit noticed the opposing coach talking to the official as the players huddled, and she nodded amicably as the coach gestured with her hands. That isn't good, Brit thought. The coach thought she'd seen a foul, and the ref was likely to be watching closely as they inbounded the ball yet again.

"It's worked twice," Alex said. "Let's run it again."

Brit was concerned about the coach's conversation with the official and spoke up. "The coach just complained to the official about something. Maybe we should switch it up. If we hold them for thirty seconds, we can win in overtime. Momentum is on our side."

Alex barely looked her way. "No. Let's stick with this. It's working."

Brit's heart was in her throat as the teams took their positions. The official handed the ball to the opposing center, who passed it to the point guard. The whistle blew immediately. A foul was called on Sidney.

After a time-out by Alex, the opposing point guard calmly sank the first shot. She missed the second, but it didn't matter. Brit's team was down with twenty-eight seconds to play.

Now Alex called a time-out to outline the offensive options. Their eyes met over the heads of the seated players, and Brit could see the anxiety she was trying so hard to conceal. After all their team had accomplished over the season, their future came down to this one play. If her team scored, they'd likely win. If not, their season was over.

"What do you think, Coach?" Alex asked.

"I think you're right." Alex had designed a play for Melissa, the freshman guard. She'd been overlooked in the scouting reports and the defense was underplaying her. She'd likely be open. It was risky, to put your future in the hands of an unproven player, but they knew Melissa had the ability.

"Okay, it's settled then."

They inbounded the ball under the opponent's basket and took eight seconds to get the ball across the half-court line. They only had twenty seconds left to score. The guards passed the ball on the perimeter, running the play Alex had given them. Brit followed the

defense, and there it was, the opening they'd hoped for. Melissa stood unguarded in the corner, her hands up in anticipation of the pass. The point guard threw it, and out of nowhere, the opposing guard picked it off. Before the defense could react, she was at the top of the key, with a host of defenders trailing her. One managed to catch her just as the layup floated off her fingers. It fell through the net, and she made the foul shot that followed, and twelve seconds later, it was all over. They lost by four, and even though they all knew they should have been happy just to make it to the playoffs, none of them were.

On the bus ride home, Brit thought it was an appropriate end to the season. Kelsey had carried them early on, and she'd cheated and broken every code of ethics a student and athlete has. She was on the bench, crippled by her ankle as her team lost. Alex, too, had made the wrong call at the end, and it cost them.

Where had their cheating gotten them?

Brit stared at Alex in the seat across from her, willing Alex to meet her gaze. Alex, though, was busy with her phone and paid Brit no attention.

And that was probably a good thing. Because, really, what could Alex say? The moment that final horn blew, the season ended, and the chance for Alex to do the right thing was gone as well. Now, she didn't have an opportunity to come clean. She couldn't very well suspend a player when there was nothing to suspend her from. Alex would have to live with herself and her decision. So would Brit.

They only ran into each other in school by design. Without the daily practices that drew them both to the gym, and the games that put them together on the bus and in the locker room, they wouldn't have an opportunity to see each other. No chance to talk.

And that realization brought Brit back to her original thought. What would they say, anyway?

CHAPTER THIRTY-THREE

PLACE YOUR BETS

The first Saturday in May was warm, and Alex adjusted the wig she'd pulled out of her Halloween basket. It had only been on her head a few minutes, and already she was sweating. Damn. Long, with dreadlocks, it was intended to go with a hippie costume. Hoping to cool off, she pulled the mane into a ponytail and then topped it with a tie-dyed fishing cap and surveyed the results in the mirror. Not bad.

A car's horn alerted her to her ride's arrival, and she quickly made her way down the stairs and out of the garage, wiping sweaty palms on her pants before opening the car door. This would be the performance of her lifetime, and it had to be good. The first step—her physical transformation—seemed to have gone well. She'd borrowed the baggy sweatshirt, jeans and work boots from her father. Along with the wig and cap, she appeared just as she'd hoped to—like a thirty-five-year-old male hippie.

"Nice ride," she said, and appraised the interior of the powerful Porsche Wes drove.

"Thanks, dear."

His falsetto made Alex laugh. Along with the female voice, he was wearing makeup and a long beaded skirt. He'd let his hair grow in the past months, and he wore it in a feminine style. His toenails were polished bright red and Alex gasped in shock. "What did you do to your feet?"

"Pedicure," he said calmly, as if it was something he did every day.

"Well, you're certainly taking your role seriously." Since Alex was much taller than Wes, the gender switch made sense. It also helped

their disguises. If the events of the day were caught on video, both were concerned about concealing their identities.

"The car can't be traced?" she asked.

"Yep. It can be traced right back to Greg Merck. I thought borrowing one of his cars was safer than borrowing one from someone else. If this goes well, Merck won't be in a position to ask too many questions."

"Hopefully we'll return it in one piece. Are you nervous?"

"Nah. I think our plan's solid."

Alex wished she shared his confidence. She and Wes had been planning this day since basketball had ended in the middle of March. It had been easy to meet with him, to come and go unencumbered, because she no longer had Brit in her life to answer to. And that was good, wasn't it? Alex remembered the days and nights she'd spent with Brit, feeling loved and like she belonged. She didn't think she'd ever let herself get so cozy again. Because, when it had ended, it really sucked.

They never talked. They were avoiding each other, taking different routes around the school to avoid confrontation. Brit hadn't handed in her letter of resignation yet, but Alex had no doubt she'd be looking for a new assistant coach.

The combination of anger and frustration and sadness was unbearable, and it was only by concentrating on her plan that Alex was able to maintain her sanity. Just about everything wrong in her life could be traced back to Greg Merck, and while crucifying him wouldn't change a thing, it would make her feel good. And, as Wes had long ago suggested, just maybe someone else's life would be better because of her.

The Run for the Roses would be under way in just a few hours, and the race was the key to Alex's plan. Bets on the Kentucky Derby were estimated to be in the range of a hundred million dollars, and it was the perfect opportunity for their sting. After months of planning, the day had come. They'd bring down Greg Merck or shoot themselves in the foot trying. Hopefully the foot and not the head.

They'd set things in motion way back then. They'd had fake IDs made, purchased an iPhone and a laptop, and created hundreds of files filled with real data detailing the illegal bets collected by P.J. and others like him on Greg's behalf. They'd also included every exam Wes had hacked from school email addresses. The laptop was backed up onto

a flash drive, which had been copied and mailed to the police. They'd receive theirs in a few days. So would the various news outlets they were hoping would force the police department's hand in prosecuting Greg's crimes. Since he'd bragged about his friends on the force, Alex and Wes were trying to make it hard to bury the evidence.

P.J. was oblivious to their plan. Wes didn't think he'd be able to pull off the deception of working for Greg while plotting to send him to jail. And so Wes and Alex had done all the work themselves. P.J. would likely get arrested, but they hoped the pressure Greg had put on him would cause the courts to be lenient with him. Alex wished there was a way to spare P.J., but they were unable to think of a plan that wouldn't implicate him in some way. At this point, the threat to P.J. from Greg was far worse than anything the justice system could offer.

"Let's do this," Wes said.

Alex's biggest concern was her brother. He'd never admitted involvement in Greg's activities, and she hoped her constant threats over the past months had scared Andrew straight. Just being disinherited by their parents could cost him millions, and in the end, Alex didn't think Andrew had the balls to take a real risk. In this case, Alex was really happy her brother had been spared the burden of courage.

They pulled in front of the Dickson City police station and smiled at each other. "Break a leg," she said. As they walked through the front door, they held hands, more for support than to give the appearance of being a couple.

"Our daughter is missing," Alex said when the police officer asked if he could help them.

"She was at the mall with her friend," Wes said in his high-pitched voice. "And some man forced her into a van."

"It was a Merck Bakery van. He had a gun."

"Please," Wes begged. "You have to help her. She's a diabetic."

"And she has seizures," Alex said.

"She'd never go with a stranger!"

The officer looked at them both, studying them, but then he shook his head sympathetically and offered a seat so he could take their information. They presented their fake driver's licenses and gave a full description of their thirteen-year-old. "We'll get right on this," the officer said a moment later.

"Will you issue an Amber Alert?" Wes asked.

"Yes, of course," he said.

"One more thing," Alex asked, and handed him a piece of paper with a cell phone number and address written on it. "We used the computer to track her cell phone. It's at this address. It's the Merck Bakery up on the highway by the mall."

"That's good police work," the officer said as he looked at the paper.

They watched as he disappeared into another room. Ten minutes passed, ten long, anxious, sweaty minutes, before Alex's cell phone alerted her to a text. She read it and smiled at Wes. "An Amber Alert has been issued," she said.

"I want you two to wait right here," the officer said a minute later when he emerged from the back. "I'm heading up there now. We'll have your daughter back in no time."

"Just you?" Alex asked. "I mean, what if this guy's dangerous? He kidnapped our baby. He has a gun."

"So do I, and the dozen officers who'll be there with me."

They watched as he drove away, his lights flashing and siren squealing. "We're going to get a coffee," Alex said to the officer who remained on duty, and they walked quickly out the door.

"Where to?"

"Feel like a pastry?" she asked.

"I'd only throw it up. But let's go see what's happening."

They couldn't get any closer than a block away. The road was closed, barricaded by state police cars on either side of the Merck Bakery.

"Well, we did our part. Let's hope they find the evidence," Wes said.

"And use it. Now I suggest we get this car back before the police show up at the garage and find yours."

"After getting this far, that would really suck."

Alex removed her wig and ran her fingers through her damp curls. "Then get moving!"

An hour later, as she sat glued to her television, she smiled as she saw the first news reports. Then she turned off the television and hopped in her car. The television in the pro shop at the country club was turned to the news, and all of the workers stood mutely watching.

No doubt they'd all bet with Greg. Some of the caddies had probably purchased exams from him, too.

Not anymore, Alex thought. Not anymore.

Her back felt so good she decided to join one of her mom's friends for eighteen. And the cherry on top of her great day came in the grill room after their round, when Libby Gold announced that her husband was away for the weekend and casually suggested that Alex stop by for a nightcap.

Although she respectfully declined, it sure felt nice to be wanted.

❖

Wes breathed a huge sigh of relief as he keyed the code that opened the gate to the Merck Bakery's garage. In a few minutes, it would be over. In a few days he'd start his final exams, and he looked forward to taking the summer off. He needed a break. Of course, he'd have to work, but that was nothing compared to carrying a full load of classes and plotting his revenge.

It had been hard to concentrate on anything since his brother had dragged him into this mess, and he lived in constant fear of exposure. If his crime was discovered, he'd be ruined—expelled from school with no chance of an education anywhere in the country. He might even face jail time.

With the stress he'd been under, his grades had suffered, and now he worried about losing his own academic scholarship. He'd thought of hacking into the university's mail system to steal his own exams, but that wouldn't be right. It would put him in the same category as Greg Merck, and no matter what happened, he wasn't that low. Perhaps now that it was over, he'd be able to concentrate. He needed to ace his finals to keep his scholarship.

If he didn't, though, at least he had a plan B.

The garage door opened when he pressed the button on the console, and Wes drove inside the building. He quickly closed the door behind him, then parked the car.

It was cool and dark and quiet, and he knew he was alone. Walking quickly, he reached his own car and removed two suitcases. Then he made his way across the garage. He passed a reception area, empty

as always. A door that led to an empty office. A door to the ladies' restroom. The men's restroom. The door to Greg's office. He paused before the vending machine, then used all his weight to push it aside.

Slipping through the small hole in the cinderblock wall, he flipped a light switch and found himself facing the large, black vault door. The video camera he'd installed had paid off, as he was able to watch Greg open it. He entered the same combination he'd watched Greg use, and the huge door opened when he tugged.

His dilemma was deciding how much to take. He could walk away with all of it—Greg would likely not complain to the police. But one day, he'd get out of jail and might wonder who'd robbed him. Better to just take a fraction of the money and hope Greg was unsure of the total. Or better yet, let him think the police had siphoned some.

Wes stuffed both suitcases with boxes of money and zipped them closed. It was a tight squeeze through the hole in the wall, but he and the money made it. He stashed his treasure in his trunk and looked around one last time.

The computer crimes might be traced back to him; he could have left an electronic fingerprint that an expert might find, but he doubted it. There were no direct links to him. Everything he'd done had been with Greg's money, at Greg's office, using dummy accounts, or on the laptop he'd planted in the garage. When Greg went down, he'd look like the mastermind who'd not only planned the crime but executed it as well. Unless, of course, he ratted on Wes. But then, of course, Greg would have to admit to even more wrongdoing, involving the threats to his brother.

It was ironic that Greg would be thought a criminal genius, because he was really stupid, and greedy, which Wes was beginning to appreciate was a fatal combination. How did such an idiot get so far in the world? Wes could only assume Greg had inherited everything, because the way he ran his business, it was doomed to fail. No wonder he'd been pushing P.J. harder into criminal activities—they seemed to be the only way he could make a living. Now, P.J. wouldn't have to worry.

With the money in his trunk, he drove away thinking that he didn't, either.

CHAPTER THIRTY-FOUR

BREAKING NEWS

The first Sunday in May was warm, and Brit had nothing to wear. Everything in her closet was wool and heavy and suited for the winter. Instead of spending yet another day moping, she figured she should put all that stuff away and haul out her spring clothing. Even if she felt miserable, at least she could look good.

Nearly two months had passed since basketball ended, and the last spring snowstorm was now a memory. The sunshine kept trying to force a smile from her, but it wasn't having much luck. Inexplicably, she loved Alex. She loved *her* Alex, the person Alex was when they were together. But that person was an illusion, and she needed to let her go.

Her ringing phone pulled her away from folding sweaters. The tone told her it was Sam calling, and she debated for a second before answering. Then she decided she should. Sam's self-centeredness was just what she needed at the moment to distract her from the misery she'd made of her life.

"What's up, sis?" she asked in greeting.

"Were you one of the teachers whose tests were stolen?"

"Huh?"

"Didn't you see the news? Your school's email was hacked and tests were stolen. Some guy was selling them to students."

A chill coursed through her body as Brit ran to the television and turned it on, searching for a news channel. She couldn't find one.

Shit! What if Alex was in trouble? What if she was, too, because she knew about this but never said anything?

"Where did you hear this?"

"It was on the news. And it's one of the headlines in today's paper."

Brit ran to the front door and opened it. The *Times* was there in a plastic bag, untouched. She'd lost interest in most things, and reading the paper was just one of them. "I wanna read this, Sam. Let me call you back."

Dropping onto her couch, she looked at the headline. POLICE RAID NETS $200,000. She read the first of three related stories.

> In one of the most bizarre new stories in memorable history, a highly profitable crime operation was busted up yesterday in Dickson City. The tale involves a phony Amber Alert, an iPhone and tips to local and national media, who were on-scene to witness the police raid that resulted in the arrest of nine men, the seizure of over $200,000 in cash and recovery of evidence including computers and copies of exams given by local high-school teachers.
>
> Police say they were summoned to the Merck Bakery on the Scranton-Carbondale highway by an Amber Alert, in search of a missing teen whose cellular phone was reported to be at that location. When they arrived, authorities found the suspects counting money bet on the Kentucky Derby. The race was about to get under way at the time of the raid. In just one of the bizarre twists in this story, the minor who the police were searching for apparently does not exist, and a cell phone that led police to the scene is linked to an untraceable post-office box. Police can't seem to locate the couple who claimed to be the girl's parents. The license plate of the Porsche they were driving is registered to Greg Merck, owner of the bakery and one of those arrested.
>
> According to a press release issued by the Pennsylvania State Police, a man and a woman claiming to be Melvin and Martha Waters walked into the police station and reported their 13-year-old daughter, Melody Waters, had been abducted. They traced her cell phone to the location of the bakery and requested the Amber Alert. When police arrived they discovered evidence of illegal gambling, and the suspects were taken into custody. Further arrests are expected in the case.

The Scranton Times *and other news outlets were made aware of the raid beforehand, via the following email, sent on Friday afternoon:*

Dear Reporter:

If you want to be one of the first to report an incredible story, be at 36842 Scranton-Carbondale Highway tomorrow (Saturday) by 12:00. The Merck Bakery is the front for a large illegal sports-betting operation. The manager, Greg Merck, is also the leader of a group selling exams to local high school students. Police will be raiding the bakery just before the start of the Kentucky Derby, when it is expected that hundreds of thousands of dollars in bets will be confiscated.

This is a top-secret raid. Please do not make any inquiries regarding police action or YOU MAY ALERT THE CRIMINALS! Just trust this tip, and you'll have one of the best stories of your career. For a front-row seat, I suggest you buy a coffee and a pastry at the bakery and settle in to watch the race. Police will probably come in through the front door.

Nike

Nike is the name of the company founded by Phil Knight in 1971 and a world leader in the manufacturing of athletic clothing and footwear. It is also the name of the Greek goddess of victory.

The Times' *Cam Kelly was one of the recipients of the cryptic email, and he was on hand to witness the raid. "I figured, why not show up? The worst that could happen was I have a good cup of coffee and a pastry. And maybe I might get a story out of it. What a story!"*

According to Kelly, reporters from The New York Times, The Philadelphia Inquirer, *and a few premier horse-racing papers were also on hand for the action. "When I walked in, I recognized Zam Russell from* USA Today, *and I*

thought this was either one heck of a scam or going to be one heck of a story."

Kelly says he sat and talked with Russell and two other reporters for about forty-five minutes before police stormed the café. One reporter had set up a live video feed and recorded the first twenty minutes of the police action, until officers discovered the camera and disconnected it.

Police are studying a surveillance video from the police station to see if they can identify the couple who initiated the Amber Alert. An anonymous source told reporters the Amber Alert was used to draw the police to the location to bust up the gambling ring. Authorities have been cracking down on illegal gambling in recent years. Video-poker machines netting millions in illegal gaming dollars were confiscated two years ago from local businesses, and our source tells us this bust could be even bigger.

What troubles authorities most about this case is that it seems the criminals were targeting vulnerable teens. Computers and paperwork at the scene tell a tale of a very organized system operating in local high schools. Betting records list initials, but no names, and authorities say it is unlikely the students involved will be prosecuted. "These kids are the victims, not the criminals," said one investigator. Charges for filing a false police report would be considered against the couple who started the ball rolling, but an insider close to the investigation thought it unlikely charges would be filed. "They're heroes."

With regard to exams recovered, police say at least 10 school districts are involved. None of the school officials contacted would speak to The Times *for this story.*

For more information on this raid, see Cam Kelly's story.

Brit sat back and looked again at the letter to the editor. It was signed Nike. Her jaw dropped as she thought back to the evening she'd met Alex at Sal's house.

How about Nike, the Goddess of Sport? Brit had suggested.

I thought Nike made basketball sneakers? Alex asked.

Her whistle was inscribed with those four letters. And then at Christmas, Brit had given her the *Nike of Samothrace*.

Could it be? She shook her head. The idea was ridiculous. It had to be a coincidence. Someone else who was fond of sports had probably gotten involved in the gambling and decided to bring down Greg Merck. Just because Alex knew about the tests and Brit called her Nike didn't mean she was the one behind this. Did it?

And then Brit thought of the night she'd found her test in Alex's bag. Alex had told her she was going to handle it. And the next day, at Alex's apartment, she'd asked Brit if she trusted her. Brit hadn't been sure enough of Alex to stick by her, to learn her plan.

Is this what Alex had meant by handling it? Brit had to know.

CHAPTER THIRTY-FIVE:

THE HAND IS QUICKER THAN THE EYE

A lex climbed down from her SUV and walked around it, grabbing the kayak on the roof and pulling hard. Satisfied that it was anchored firmly enough to make it to the state park four miles away, she touched her toes to stretch her back, then headed into her apartment.

In addition to Greg's arrest, the one thing she had to be happy about was her back. Alex had seen Brit's doctor friend, and even though he'd agreed with the diagnosis of ankylosing spondylitis, he'd suggested a change in her meds. Since the switch, Alex felt better than she had in years.

As she walked into her living room, Alex heard her cell phone ringing. Not just any ring, though—this was a jazzy rhythm she'd assigned to a special woman so she'd always know it was her on the line. So she would know to stop everything and take that call, no matter what. Because, back then, that woman had been the most important thing in her world. She hadn't heard that ring in months, since Brit had stopped calling her.

She picked up the phone to verify what she already knew, and Brit's smiling face appeared on the screen. Cringing at the sight, Alex dropped the phone onto the counter. She had no intention of answering.

In her bedroom she didn't even consider what to wear, just grabbed the first golf shirt and shorts she pulled from the drawer. She needed to get out of the house. The weather was beautiful, and several friends were heading to the park to cook out with real charcoal and toss horseshoes and paddle kayaks around the lake. It would be an excellent diversion for Alex to get away for a few hours and relax. Perhaps she

might meet a cute girl at the lake. A new woman might help take her mind off Brit. She needed to think about something else and to get Brit out of her mind and out of her heart.

Alex supposed in the back of her mind she hoped that when the mutiny was over and Greg was arrested and the exam-selling exposed, she might tell Brit what had happened and see if they could work it all out. Start over. But then she'd realized there was no point in starting over—she and Brit were just too different. And Alex was angry. Brit had done nothing but judge her, from the first. The insults to Alex's integrity were unforgivable. That she didn't trust her, though—that was the worst thing.

The beeping of the phone indicated Brit had left a message, and Alex deliberately walked over to the phone and deleted it without bothering to listen. Now it couldn't taunt her. The message was gone, just like Brit, and she couldn't do anything about either one.

As she walked into the living room, the phone beeped again. This time it alerted her to a text. She sighed as she looked at the screen and saw a text from Brit.

Call me. PLEASE!

Alex had spent the last months trying to forget her, so why would she call? And then she paused and thought about that reaction. Hadn't she actually spent all of that time hoping Brit would call, just to say I do trust you. To say I love you and I'll stand by you? It was a fantasy, to think Brit would blur her moral lines, even for Alex. So Alex hadn't even tried to see her at school or contact her in the evenings. Still, she'd hoped and prayed Brit would come to her senses and give Alex a chance. She'd wanted that, and now Brit had not only called but sent a text, too. Why was she so hesitant to talk to her?

Then another thought occurred to her. *Why* was Brit calling? Had someone died? Her parents weren't young. And accidents happened all the time. Every night the news reported explosions and car crashes and terrorist attacks, all claiming innocent lives. Had one of her family members been in an accident? Or maybe one of their players? Or Sal and Sue?

Suddenly, Alex felt panicky. After all this time, Brit had to be calling for a reason, and it couldn't be good. With trembling hands, she

pressed the green telephone icon next to Brit's name and initiated the phone call.

She answered almost immediately. "Was it you, Alex?"

Alex had expected news of death or dismemberment. This question completely baffled her. But then again, so did Brit. "Huh?"

"Are you *Nike*?"

Alex sighed. So, that was it. The one news report Alex had watched talked about the illegal gambling activity at Merck Bakery and the sale of high-school exams but hadn't mentioned the letter from Nike alerting the media. That must have changed.

She'd put a lot of thought into the email she'd penned to the news outlets, and in the end she'd whimsically recalled the day they'd met, when Brit told her she was like a goddess. Her whistle was inscribed with the name Nike. And there was her Christmas gift, too. She walked into her bedroom and ran a finger across the statue's wings.

Nike seemed generic enough to be untraceable. Except that Brit knew. She hadn't thought about it at the time, but maybe that signature was a way of reaching out to Brit one last time, before Alex finally accepted that it was over and moved on. If that had been the plan, it worked. Brit had called. Now what?

"Yeah," she said at last.

"Arggggggg!" Brit shouted into the phone, and in the best interest of her eardrums Alex pulled the phone away.

"Can you talk now?" Brit asked.

"Whatta ya mean?"

"I mean…Oh, God, Alex. I don't know what I mean. I've just spent the last two months trying to hate you, because you were doing something so bad. How could you do something so good and confuse me so much?"

Alex ran her fingers through her hair. "Was that really a question?"

"Can I see you?"

"Right now?" Alex dropped on the sofa and lay on her side, suddenly overwhelmed. Did she even want to see Brit, who'd rushed to judgment and sentenced her to life without her love? Brit, who hadn't even given her an opportunity to explain. Brit, who'd haunted her day and night. Of course she did. Even if Brit was a jerk, Alex was still in love with her.

"Can you meet me at the park?" Brit asked.

"I was just walking out the door. I can be there in five minutes."

"See you there."

Alex grabbed her basketball on her way through the garage and threw it onto the seat beside her. As promised, she was at South Abington Park five minutes later, and a minute after that, she was shooting at one of the open baskets.

It amazed her how relaxing it was to play basketball. A few bounces and a jump shot, a rebound and put-back, and a reverse lay-up later and Alex was already feeling better. Sensing Britain rather than seeing her, Alex stopped after a missed shot and turned. When Brit held up her hands for the ball, Alex passed it her way.

Brit bounced it once and shot it, and Alex rebounded the miss and tossed it back to her. She tried again and this time hit nothing but net. Before she knew it, Brit was guarding her, and they found themselves in the familiar game of one-on-one. They'd played often since that first time on this same court so long ago, mostly before practices, but sometimes just like this, with the two of them alone at the park. It was always a challenge, and always a workout, and always fun.

This time was no exception; in fact, it was more intense than ever, and Alex soon realized they weren't really playing basketball at all—they were doing battle. They struggled for position and neither allowed a basket unchallenged. They blocked each other's shots and fouled each other all the way around the court. It was if they were taking all of the frustrations of the prior months out on each other now, getting it out of their system so they could move on. No matter who won this epic battle of wills, they would both walk away having said their piece.

Alex finally ended the game, with a three-point shot from the top of the key. Too tired to gloat, she simply walked to the bench and sat, wishing she'd thought to bring one of the water bottles from her cooler. She watched as Brit retrieved the ball and walked to the bench, then sat beside her, facing her.

"Can you tell me what happened?" Brit asked when she'd regained her breath.

"Let's get water," Alex suggested, and they walked to her SUV and pulled two from the cooler. They walked, and Alex told her the entire story, from the moment Kelsey confessed to the moment she and Wes walked into the police station the day before. They were seated on a rock beside the stream by the time Alex finished.

"So, when I found the test, you'd already suspended Kelsey and pretended she'd sprained her ankle?"

"Yeah. I wasn't sure what to do, so I asked Sal the hypothetical question about how to handle a player who'd cheated on a test. She suggested the suspension, but we had to fake the injury so she could still get into college. It might have been dishonest, Brit, but I didn't want to ruin her life because of one stupid mistake."

"I guess I can understand that, Alex. But you blew your chances of coaching in college."

"After this season, I don't even know if I want to coach high school."

"Alex, that's crazy! You were born to coach," Brit said, and she grabbed Alex's arm, forcing Alex to look at her.

Alex smiled in answer. "Well, I haven't resigned, but I've thought about it."

"Don't resign, Alex."

"How about you?"

She saw Brit hesitate, but then she smiled. "As long as you still want me…"

Alex nodded. "Of course I do," and Alex looked into her eyes, hoping Brit understood she wasn't only talking about basketball.

"Alex, this was so dangerous. I can't believe you did it."

Alex shrugged. "I knew Greg wouldn't stop unless someone forced him to. I saw an opportunity, and I took it. It was probably stupid, but I'd do it again. Kelsey's life wasn't ruined. P.J. is free. Wes is free. And lots of other kids will be spared this kind of trouble."

Brit touched the smooth skin of Alex's knee, sending a shiver all the way through her. "I'm so sorry, Alex. I should have trusted you."

Alex turned to face her, locked into those blue eyes, and felt all the same energy that was always between them—the attraction hadn't weakened with time. The sadness they'd both endured hadn't changed the magnetism that drew them together. But could they ever trust each other again? Could Brit trust Alex to be honest with her? Could Alex trust Brit to be fair?

Alex had no idea. Relationships were still foreign to her, and even though she'd learned to be a thoughtful partner who picked up coffee from the store and socks from the floor, even though she'd learned to compromise about movies and food, even though she'd learned to

discuss feelings and ideas, she had no idea if they could move on from what happened.

"Why didn't you?"

Brit sighed, and when Alex looked at her, she saw tears flowing down the beautiful face of the woman she loved. Longing to wipe them, she instead shifted, sitting on her hands to keep them still. It wasn't her place to wipe Brit's tears. Not anymore.

"I don't know, Alex. I don't. I'm new at this, too, remember? But maybe it was a combination of things. I was frustrated about my mom, and maybe I was blaming you for that. If I didn't have you, I could go back into the closet and hide where I was safe and my mother still loved me. It sounds ridiculous, but I think a part of me believed that. And then there was the fear of losing you. I'd just found you and was madly in love with you, and then you started getting offers to coach on the other side of the planet. I was afraid you'd leave me, so maybe I left you first.

"Maybe I'm not ready for a relationship—for giving and taking and compromising. I don't know. I just know that what felt so right back then, when I thought you were dishonest and unprincipled, feels terribly wrong now that I know the truth. It didn't feel right to be with you under those circumstances. Even if I loved you, I wondered if I knew you. Would you cheat on your taxes and go to jail? Would you cheat on me? They seemed like valid concerns then. Now that I know the truth, none of it's relevant."

"I still can't believe this happened. It's so unreal. I keep thinking I'm going to wake up from a dream. Or perhaps I should say a nightmare."

"Couldn't you have trusted me with this, Alex? I wouldn't have told anyone."

Alex patted her knee, and she nearly shuddered at the contact. Again, it was as electric as ever. She sighed. "I know, Brit. I know. It's easy to see it now. But I worried it might be dangerous, and I didn't want to drag you into that. And I didn't think you'd approve of the plan, and you would have tried to stop me. I was pissed, too. I was mad at you for the way you acted, and I just wasn't thinking clearly."

Brit leaned back until she was lying flat on her back, staring up through the canopy of trees at the brightness that lingered beyond, seemingly just out of her grasp. It was a metaphor for her life, she thought as she closed her eyes. For a brief, shiny month she'd been

blissfully happy, but now that seemed so long ago. And Alex, who'd seemed so far away, was suddenly beside her again, but as unattainable as the warmth blocked by the dense foliage above her.

Sensing they'd said all they had to say, Brit prepared herself to sit up, to stand, and to walk away. This time, it would be forever. When she'd kicked Alex out of her apartment they'd been angry and hurt, and Brit had hoped it was just temporary and Alex would come to her senses. They'd make up and carry on. This, though, was much different. They were both harder now, and Brit supposed they were wiser, too.

Understanding that they'd talked the topic to death, Brit knew it was time to say good-bye. But what if she didn't? What if she said something else, words that might open a window instead of closing a door? What in the world did she have to lose? Alex was already gone. Nothing else mattered.

Still on her back, with her eyes closed and her heart shut to all the world except Alex, Brit spoke. "Alex, if you admit that you weren't thinking clearly, can you possibly understand that I wasn't either?"

Perhaps it was the sound of Alex moving, but Brit thought it was actually a feeling that told her Alex was beside her, as if the electrical charge of the atmosphere suddenly changed, causing her skin to tingle.

"What exactly are you asking?"

Unsure if she'd really heard the words, or just imagined them, Brit opened her eyes, and sure enough, there was Alex, beside her, watching her expectantly, awaiting a reply.

"Can we try again?" Brit whispered.

Alex closed her eyes. This was all she'd wanted for so long. She'd wanted Brit from the moment she saw her, and she still did. The months they'd been friends had been some of the happiest of Alex's life, surpassed only by the months they'd been lovers. Could they work out their issues and forget the pain they'd caused each other? Alex had no idea. But she never would if she didn't at least try. She had to try. She owed it to Brit, and she owed it to herself.

She said nothing, though, because she feared her voice would crack before she could give it life. So, in answer, she simply took Brit's hand and squeezed it, then placed it below hers, right over her heart.

CHAPTER THIRTY-SIX

WHAT A DIFFERENCE A YEAR MAKES

B rit could hear her phone ringing as she stood before the bathroom mirror, struggling to corral her unruly mass of hair into a thick band of elastic. It was early, but she had so much work to do to prepare for the summer, to get the beach house ready for the summer invasion. She was living the dream, spending the summer in Rehoboth Beach, and she had a *girlfriend*. Alex. She and Alex were dating again.

Brit knew where she wanted her relationship with Alex to go. Perhaps it was frustration, or insecurity, or inexperience, or perhaps it was something else altogether that had caused her to doubt Alex at the first possible chance. It didn't matter. What mattered was that she—Brit—was different, now. She'd loved, and she'd lost, and she'd wept and mourned over what she'd had and what might have been. Miraculously, she'd been given another chance with Alex, and this time, she wouldn't blow it. She'd treasure Alex and talk to her more about her feelings and insecurities. She'd trust her.

"Brit, your phone is ringing," Alex said through the closed door.

"I know. I'll call them back."

"It says *Mom* on the caller ID."

Brit opened the bathroom door and looked at Alex, whose worried expression surely must have mirrored her own. Why would her mother be calling? Of the multitude of possible reasons, all of them involved death or dismemberment. Not a single word had passed between them since Christmas, and Brit had started to become used to life without her mom. Her relationships with her sisters were strained, because of course they were worried about pissing off their mother. Her dad really didn't care who he offended, so they were getting along better than

ever. Her mother, though, had been stonewalling, and this call was the last thing Brit expected as she prepared to celebrate the Memorial Day holiday at the beach with her friends.

Brit accepted the proffered phone and quickly slid her thumb across the screen. Neither she nor Alex moved as she spoke. "Mom, hi. What's wrong?"

"Why does something have to be wrong for me to call my own child?" her mom asked, and Brit felt the months disappear. Nothing about Joan's arrogance had changed. Yet, still, her mother had called her, and unless she was delivering a death announcement, that was progress.

"Well, nothing has to be wrong. It's just that you haven't called me in six months, so I'm just assuming the worst."

"Five months, Britain. It's been five months. It won't be six months until June twenty-fifth, which brings me to the point of my phone call."

Brit was holding her breath, and Alex had walked her into the bedroom and was now holding her, which was good, because Brit was more than a little shaky. She still had no idea what was going on. She tried to lean back into Alex's embrace, but it was impossible to relax until she knew what trouble lay ahead.

Her mother wasted no time in telling her. "For the past twenty-two years, I've made your birthday cake with my own hands. And as long as my heart is beating in my chest, I intend to continue that tradition. So I'm calling to make plans for your birthday."

Brit's birthday was still a month away. She and Alex were down for the weekend to help prepare the house for the summer, but as soon as school was out, they'd be back for good. "Mom, I'm staying at the beach this summer. I'll be here for my birthday."

Her mother tsked. "Well, I suppose if you can't be troubled to drive home, the rest of your family can come to Delaware to see you."

Brit's jaw dropped, and she turned and looked at Alex. "She wants to see me," she mouthed.

Alex gave her a smile and a thumbs-up.

Concentrating again on the conversation with her mom, Brit decided to tease the woman who wasn't known for her sense of humor. "Well, it *is* my birthday, Mom. The least you can do is drive a few miles."

"I see. Well, then, we will. And I'll bake the cake. Do you think

you can pick out a restaurant for dinner? You know Rehoboth better than I do."

"Yes, of course, I can handle that."

"You should make a reservation, Britain. A table for thirteen isn't easy to come by."

Brit immediately corrected her mother. It had been twelve of them, for the three years since Samantha's son Brandon had been born. "Mom, it's twelve. Sam's five, Jordan's four, you, me, and Dad. Five plus four plus three. Twelve."

She heard her mother sigh. "Are you saying that your...Alex won't be joining us for dinner?"

Brit stood when she heard her mother's invitation, overwhelmed. Relief and happiness combined to form a wave of emotion. Her mother was inviting Alex to dinner! It had taken five months for her to come around, but Brit would have waited five years for this. Fortunately, she didn't have to. She knew her mother was stubborn and principled, but apparently her love outweighed those other factors. Brit wiped away the tears that suddenly flowed down her face and cleared her throat, and sat down again, hovering on the edge of the bed. "She's right here, Mom. Let me ask her."

Brit smiled at Alex and their blue eyes locked. Alex winked at her in solidarity. "Alex, my mom would like to know if you'd care to join my family for dinner to celebrate my birthday. Next month. June twenty-eighth."

Alex's grin lit up her face, and Brit couldn't resist running a hand through her golden locks. "I'd love to," Alex replied as she kissed Brit's forehead.

Brit's heart was ready to burst, and she stopped trying to stop the flow of tears, instead allowing them to run down her cheeks unchecked. After sniffling, swallowing, and wiping her eyes on her sleeve, she finally answered. "She'll only come if it's the strawberry cake, Mom."

"Well, obviously, you two have a great deal in common."

"Yes. Yes we do."

She heard Joan clear her throat. "I won't pretend to understand this, Britain. But you're my daughter, and if she's a part of your life, then I suppose I have to accept her into mine."

Brit sighed and finally relaxed into the arms that were wrapped around her, holding her tight. "Thanks, Mom."

"Please call me with the details as soon as you've made the reservation."

"'Kay. I love you," Brit said.

"I love you, too." Her mom's declaration brought on a fresh wave of tears.

Alex slid back on the bed, pulling Brit with her, and gently wiped away her tears. Then she smiled. "Do I need to get my calendar out and start booking reservations for your time, Miss Popularity?"

"You have a standing reservation."

"I'm so happy for you, Brit." Alex sighed. She was happy. And relieved. Although she'd come to truly believe that Brit loved her and had the guts to stick it out this time, she knew that the love and support of her family would make their relationship that much stronger, and she told Brit so.

"I love you even without my mom's approval, Alex."

"I know, baby. And so this is just the icing on the cake."

"On the birthday cake," Brit reminded her.

"Yes, the strawberry birthday cake. I'm glad that your mom reminded me, since I only have a month to plan. How would you like to celebrate your birthday? Do you want to play golf, or go deep-sea fishing, or go for a long bike ride?" Alex was so in love with her she'd have done anything in her power to make Brit's birthday special.

Brit bit her lip, suddenly serious. Apparently, she didn't need to think about the answer. "I'd like you to make love with me."

Alex paused and tapped a finger beside her head in feigned mental debate. It had been a long time since they last made love. So much had happened since then, and they were different women now. But some things hadn't changed. Their love. The laughter they shared. And the constant desire for Brit that seemed to pulse through her like the blood in her veins.

Suddenly filled with desire, Alex pulled Brit close and kissed her. It was all heat and passion from the moment their lips met until they pulled apart, breathless, a moment later. "Do you want your present early?" Alex asked.

Brit pulled herself free of Alex's arms and flew across the bedroom, her smile dazzling as she reached down and locked the door.

About the Author

Jaime Maddox is a recovering ER doctor who gave up the adrenaline rush of critical care to open her very own walk-in clinic. It was a good move. Not only does she now have time for her partner and their eleven-year-old twin boys, she can squeeze in time to write for Bold Strokes Books, too.

Her debut novel, *Agnes*, was a Rainbow Award finalist and winner of the Alice B. Lavender Certificate.

Jaime lives in Northeastern Pennsylvania, not far from where she spent her childhood playing on the water and in the mountains. These days she plays golf, too, and when she has the chance she floats on the river in a kayak. Because she's a really nice person, she allows her partner and her sons to beat her at basketball.

You can contact her at jaimemaddoxbsb@gmail.com.

Books Available From Bold Strokes Books

The 45th Parallel by Lisa Girolami. Burying her mother isn't the worst thing that can happen to Val Montague when she returns to the woodsy but peculiar town of Hemlock, Oregon. (978-1-62639-342-4)

A Royal Romance by Jenny Frame. In a country where class still divides, can love topple the last social taboo and allow Queen Georgina and Beatrice Elliot, a working-class girl, their happy ever after? (978-1-62639-360-8)

Bouncing by Jaime Maddox. Basketball coach Alex Dalton has been bouncing from woman to woman because no one ever held her interest, until she meets her new assistant, Britain Dodge. (978-1-62639-344-8)

Same Time Next Week by Emily Smith. A chance encounter between Alex Harris and the beautiful Michelle Masters leads to a whirlwind friendship and causes Alex to question everything she's ever known—including her own marriage. (978-1-62639-345-5)

All Things Rise by Missouri Vaun. Cole rescues a striking pilot who crash-lands near her family's farm, setting in motion a chain of events that will forever alter the course of her life. (978-1-62639-346-2)

Riding Passion by D. Jackson Leigh. Mount up for the ride through a sizzling anthology of chance encounters, buried desires, romantic surprises, and blazing passion. (978-1-62639-349-3)

Love's Bounty by Yolanda Wallace. Lobster boat captain Jake Myers stopped living the day she cheated death, but meeting greenhorn Shy Silva stirs her back to life. (978-1-62639334-9)

Just Three Words by Melissa Brayden. Sometimes the one you want is the one you least suspect…Accountant Samantha Ennis has her ordered life disrupted when heartbreaker Hunter Blair moves into her trendy Soho loft. (978-1-62639-335-6)

Lay Down the Law by Carsen Taite. Attorney Peyton Davis returns to her Texas roots to take on big oil and the Mexican Mafia, but will her investigation thwart her chance at true love? (978-1-62639-336-3)

Playing in Shadow by Lesley Davis. Survivor's guilt threatens to keep Bryce trapped in her nightmare world unless Scarlet's love can pull her out of the darkness back into the light. (978-1-62639-337-0)

Soul Selecta by Gill McKnight. Soul mates are hell to work with. (978-1-62639-338-7)

The Revelation of Beatrice Darby by Jean Copeland. Adolescence is complicated, but Beatrice Darby is about to discover how impossible it can seem to a lesbian coming of age in conservative 1950s New England. (978-1-62639-339-4)

Twice Lucky by Mardi Alexander. For firefighter Mackenzie James and Dr. Sarah Mackenzie, there's suddenly a whole lot more in life to understand, to consider, to risk…someone will need to fight for her life. (978-1-62639-325-7)

Shadow Hunt by L.L. Raand. With young to raise and her Pack under attack, Sylvan, Alpha of the wolf Weres, takes on her greatest challenge when she determines to uncover the faceless enemies known as the Shadow Lords. A Midnight Hunters novel. (978-1-62639-326-4)

Heart of the Game by Rachel Spangler. A baseball writer falls for a single mom, but can she ever love anything as much as she loves the game? (978-1-62639-327-1)

Getting Lost by Michelle Grubb. Twenty-eight days, thirteen European countries, a tour manager fighting attraction, and an accused murderer: Stella and Phoebe's journey of a lifetime begins here. (978-1-62639-328-8)

Prayer of the Handmaiden by Merry Shannon. Celibate priestess Kadrian must defend the kingdom of Ithyria from a dangerous enemy and ultimately choose between her duty to the Goddess and the love of her childhood sweetheart, Erinda. (978-1-62639-329-5)

The Witch of Stalingrad by Justine Saracen. A Soviet "night witch" pilot and American journalist meet on the Eastern Front in WWII and struggle through carnage, conflicting politics, and the deadly Russian winter. (978-1-62639-330-1)

Night Mare by Franci McMahon. On an innocent horse-buying trip, Jane Scott uncovers a horrifying element of the horse show world, thrusting her into a whirlwind of poisoned money. (978-1-62639-333-2E).

Pedal to the Metal by Jesse J. Thoma. When unreformed thief Dubs Williams is released from prison to help Max Winters bust a car theft ring, Max learns that if you want to catch a thief, you have to get in bed with one. (978-1-62639-239-7)

Dragon Horse War by D. Jackson Leigh. A priestess of peace and a fiery warrior must defeat a vicious uprising that entwines their destinies and ultimately their hearts. (978-1-62639-240-3)

For the Love of Cake by Erin Dutton. When everything is on the line and one taste can break a heart, will pastry chefs Maya and Shannon take a chance on reality? (978-1-62639-241-0)

Betting on Love by Alyssa Linn Palmer. A quiet country girl at heart and a live-life-to-the-fullest biker take a risk at offering each other their hearts. (978-1-62639-242-7)

The Deadening by Yvonne Heidt. The lines between good and evil, right and wrong, have always been blurry for Shade. When Raven's actions force her to choose, which side will she come out on? (978-1-62639-243-4)

One Last Thing by Kim Baldwin & Xenia Alexiou. Blood is thicker than pride. The final book in the Elite Operative Series brings together foes, family, and friends to start a new order. (978-1-62639-230-4)

Songs Unfinished by Holly Stratimore. Two aspiring rock stars learn that falling in love while pursuing their dreams can be harmonious—if they can only keep their pasts from throwing them out of tune. (978-1-62639-231-1)

Beyond the Ridge by L.T. Marie. Will a contractor and a horse rancher overcome their family differences and find common ground to build a life together? (978-1-62639-232-8)

Swordfish by Andrea Bramhall. Four women battle the demons from their pasts. Will they learn to let go, or will happiness be forever beyond their grasp? (978-1-62639-233-5)

The Fiend Queen by Barbara Ann Wright. Princess Katya and her consort Starbride must turn evil against evil in order to banish Fiendish power from their kingdom, and only love will pull them back from the brink. (978-1-62639-234-2)

Up the Ante by PJ Trebelhorn. When Jordan Stryker and Ashley Noble meet again fifteen years after a short-lived affair, is either of them prepared to gamble on a chance at love? (978-1-62639-237-3)

Speakeasy by MJ Williamz. When mob leader Helen Byrne sets her sights on the girlfriend of Al Capone's right-hand man, passion and tempers flare on the streets of Chicago. (978-1-62639-238-0)

Myth and Magic: Queer Fairy Tales, edited by Radclyffe and Stacia Seaman. Myth, magic, and monsters—the stuff of childhood dreams (or nightmares) and adult fantasies. (978-1-62639-225-0)

A Spark of Heavenly Fire by Kathleen Knowles. Kerry and Beth are building their life together, but unexpected circumstances could destroy their happiness. (978-1-62639-212-0)

Venus in Love by Tina Michele. Morgan Blake can't afford any distractions and Ainsley Dencourt can't afford to lose control—but the beauty of life and art usually lies in the unpredictable strokes of the artist's brush. (978-1-62639-220-5)

Rules of Revenge by AJ Quinn. When a lethal operative on a collision course with her past agrees to help a CIA analyst on a critical assignment, the encounter proves explosive in ways neither woman anticipated. (978-1-62639-221-2)

The Romance Vote by Ali Vali. Chili Alexander is a sought-after campaign consultant who isn't prepared when her boss's daughter, Samantha Pellegrin, comes to work at the firm and shakes up Chili's life from the first day. (978-1-62639-222-9)